On The Brink

JAMES BOYD

ON THE BRINK

Copyright © 2022 James Boyd

All rights reserved.

ISBN: 9798403517973

Viper Doc Press

DEDICATION

To the thousands of nameless medical personnel of all services working diligently in the clinics, hospitals, trenches, tents, and aboard ships around the globe striving daily to keep our troops fit and healthy and, when needed, to care for their injuries and wounds.

CONTENTS

	Acknowledgments	i
	Prologue	ii
1	Medical Emergency	1
2	Medical Updates	11
3	Conference Reception	23
4	Deployment Alert	29
5	Admiral's Brief	34
6	Departure Preparation	39
7	Another Day at Sea	45
8	Flight Home	54
9	RED HORSE Deployed	61
10	Spies	69
11	Shaken Confidence	72
12	Tirade	81
13	Official Business	87
14	Dropping Anchor	92
15	Clarity	96
16	Dinner and a Show	101
17	USS Carl Vinson Reception	110
18	Going Ashore	118
19	Knocking on Forbidden Doors	125
20	Save the Puppies	131
21	Situation Report	135
22	Stanley Market	141
23	Recall	147

24	Getting Out of Dodge	156
25	Accelerated Timeline	160
26	Admiral's Update	166
27	Flight Plan	170
28	Little Dog Bites Back	174
29	Tanker Flight	178
30	Price of Another Steak Dinner	190
31	Go Time	194
32	Point of Know Return	201
33	Hero Busted	209
34	Work Progressing	215
35	Inspection Orders	219
36	Response Plans	227
37	Friendly Competition	230
38	Off to Scarborough	234
39	Hero Rejected	238
40	Firefight	243
41	Medevac	254
42	Escalation Approved	263
43	On A Big Boat	270
44	Calm before the Storm	278
45	Air Strike	288
46	Mass Casualty	295
47	Direct Pressure	309
48	Blood & Guts	313
49	Defcon Two	330
50	Aftermath	336
	Epilogue	348

ACKNOWLEDGMENTS

I love to read or, these days, listen to good stories. While talking with a very special friend on a twelve-hour drive, I jokingly said that I should be able to write a book given all the things I have seen and done during my four decades of military service. She agreed and challenged me to try. This novel is my attempt to merge bits of the four different career fields I've had in the Air Force and Navy into an interesting tale with a senior physician as the central character.

Several people have supported and encouraged me to continue with this endeavor when my motivation lagged. In particular, I want to thank Kris Belland for inspiring me to finish this story when I had almost given up on it. I was also motivated by my friend Andy Huff to have it published after his enthusiastic daily comments as he read through it. What initially was a private and fun source of entertainment may hopefully be enjoyed by others.

And last but not least, I wish to thank all the people I have encountered over my lifetime for the experiences we have shared that have provided the inspiration I have drawn upon for this book. Though occasionally inspired by many colorful people I have known, all the characters in this book are fictitious and wholly created by me. Any potential resemblance to anyone is entirely coincidental.

Prologue

Thitu Island, South China Sea

The crane operator saw a speck on the horizon out over the broad expanse of the South China Sea. Surely, it must be another supply ship headed our way. He looked away to grab a tin cup hooked onto an old metal water cooler in the corner of his cab. He filled it with ice-cold water and took a long, satisfying drink. He then held the cold cup to his forehead to cool off as he surveyed his work.

He was there as part of the construction crew attempting to expand the small runway on Pag-asa Island, as the Filipino's called Thitu Island. He was steadily building up the runway with sand and coral from the seafloor. He was wondering how long the project would last this time. Now on his third trip out to extend the runway, he hoped the project wouldn't be cut short again. He looked proudly at the progress they had made over the past three months on the two-thousand-foot extension out into the sea.

Little more than a low-lying, ninety-five-acre sandbar, Thitu is still the second largest of the "naturally occurring" Spratly Islands. Historically claimed by Vietnamese, Filipino, and Chinese fishermen, the Philippines had recently bolstered its claim by building a small runway and defensive concrete bunkers. Headstrong Philippine president Norman Magdato had twice before started upgrades to the strategically important islands. But the long distance away and strong protests from the Chinese had caused him to back down both times. Despite international court rulings and agreements, China had ignored it and built up two massive artificial islands on Mischief and Fiery Cross reefs only a hundred miles away. The Chinese continued to claim that their buildup was peaceful and would never be used for military purposes.

Now with it clear that China had ambitions to claim Thitu, being more careful this time, President Magdato had begun to thwart this with another attempt to repair and extend the length of the island's runway. He hoped to permanently garrison enough troops to defend the island outright. His ultimate goal was to build a deep water port for the growing Philippine Navy to counter China's increasingly aggressive harassment of Filipino fishing vessels in the area. Publicly, the runway and island improvements were strictly for commercial purposes to support the small fishing and emerging tourist industries. With its surrounding coral reef in warm tropical waters and nearby shipwrecks in less than a hundred feet of water, it was becoming known as a great snorkeling and scuba-diving destination, if you could get there.

With a greater show of force, he had a continuous rotation of three Filipino frigates to patrol around the island. The Chinese had surprisingly only made a mild objection through their ambassador in Manila. With China under ever-increasing international pressure because of their clear military buildup on the Spratly Islands, Magdato hoped it would keep them constrained and buy the needed time to finish the runway and the deep water port beyond the reef. Things were relatively calm and looking good. In fact, totally consistent with his flamboyant braggadocio, he had jumped at a request to send a TV news crew to the island to report on the progress generating interest in the future island resort and prove their peaceful intentions while showing that he was ready and willing to defend his country's claims.

The crane operator glanced down the runway thirty minutes later and was surprised to see not a supply ship but a military frigate closing in. No big deal. Until he swung the bucket around and noticed another ship to north, and then yet another to the northeast. As he continued to scan the horizon, he saw a total of eight warships converging on the island. The three Filipino frigates and a supply ship anchored off the reef suddenly began belching heavy smoke from their stacks. Then, awestruck, he saw the western sky fill with dots that soon grew into an entire fleet of aircraft in three layers.

Flying in formations of three-to-six abreast with three layers stacked above each other, they roared in with the lowest echelon at only five hundred feet above the waves. Leading the way were China's latest fifth generation fighters, followed by rows of fighter bombers. At one thousand and fifteen hundred feet were more fighters and bombers. An impressive 114 combat aircraft in all. They were in near perfect alignment as if performing a People's Liberation Army Navy air show for China's President Hsu. In reality, it was just that, so far. It was an awe-inspiring sight—if you were Chinese. For those on the island, it was fear and anxiety provoking. And that was before the planes came back threateningly shooting off flares as they made simulated bombing and strafing runs. After fifteen minutes of terror provoking aircraft thunder and flares, the message had been delivered loud and clear: *We can destroy you at any time! Get out!*

Coincidently, just that morning, the TV crew had arrived. They were on top of the three-story control tower as the highest point of the island to get some panoramic shots as the planes came roaring over. They got it all, including close-ups of the different aircraft and the closing Chinese warships. It was all filmed with excited commentary from the reporter. Unfortunately for President Magdato, they also filmed the rapidly retreating Filipino war ships hightailing it over the horizon. Within two hours, the video was headlining every prominent cable news channel around the world.

Sitting on the flag bridge of the sixty-eight-thousand-ton People's Liberation Army Navy (PLAN) aircraft carrier *Liaoning* (CV 16) was Vice Admiral Fa Jiang, Commander of the *Liaoning* carrier battle group. He was in his bridge chair, relishing his expensive Zhonghua cigarette as the ship's J-15 fighters landed. Ignoring the jets, he was watching the satellite TV feed of CNN International. There on a beautiful repeating news loop was a close-up video of his air-and-ship demonstration at Thitu. Everything had gone as planned. The Filipinos had been taken completely by surprise because the island's only radar had been sabotaged the night before by Chinese Special Forces blinding the island to the approaching fleet of ships and aircraft. The plan called Operation WHIRLWIND had been approved two months before, and he had been in charge of its execution.

Now the world not only knew that his new aircraft carrier was operational, but also that China was more than willing to use it in hardball diplomacy. *Step aside, America. Your time on center stage is over,* he mused. *The Chinese are returning to our position as the dominant world power.*

After a brief visit from the Chinese ambassador that evening, President Magdato ordered the evacuation of Thitu Island. The cold reality of time and distance had conspired against him again. He had lost again, and it had been seen worldwide.

Meeting the next morning with his senior staff, he admitted that they were currently unable to compete with the growing might of the insurgent Chinese army and navy. He planned to remedy that situation by ordering his staff to immediately begin plans to acquire surplus fighters and ships from its old reliable friend, the United States. In addition to purchasing military hardware, he was cajoling their president to reengage more directly with the Philippines. Luckily, it was indeed being seriously considered as part of the United States' pivot back to the Pacific as China was flexing its muscles and threatening over seventy-five years of relative stability.

Next time, he thought, *Next time, we will* not *back down!*

1 MEDICAL EMERGENCY

USS *Vinson*, Western Pacific

Who knew getting to lunch on time would be such a recurring challenge? Yet the SMO was having to race through the gray tunnel of the passageway, dodging Sailors to see if there was anything left.

Luckily, Navy Commander Derek "Leopard" Lloyd did barely make it in time for pizza before they shut the serving line down. It was the favorite meal for the Senior Medical Officer of the USS *Carl Vinson*. He had been delayed this time while getting a last-minute update on a suicidal patient.

The Senior Medical Officer, or SMO, as he was known by everyone, entered wardroom three, the officers primary dining room, down on the second deck just below the hanger bay. He snagged the last slice of pepperoni, a salad, and a diet drink from the soda fountain.

"Mind if I join you?" he said to the others at an open table.

"Of course, SMO," said Lieutenant Commander Martina Alverez his department's medical administrative officer. Sitting with her was the Gun Boss, Commander Chris Aimwell, who ran the weapon's department and one of the ship's new "shooters," whom the SMO had yet to meet. The yellow flight deck jersey with bold black letters saying "SHOOTER" made it obvious what she did.

Shooters are either naval aviators or flight officers doing a nonflying assignment launching aircraft off the flight deck.

"I'm Lieutenant Belland," the shooter said, introducing herself.

"Just call me SMO," he said while giving the shooter a nod as he sat down. "You new to the ship?"

"Yes, sir," said Belland. "I got here last week."

"Well, glad to meet you. I've only been here for four months myself," replied the SMO.

"Only one slice SMO?" asked the Gun Boss.

"Yep, I got the last slice. Besides, that's all I have time for," said the SMO. "Got to brief the Captain in fifteen minutes on our most recent psych patient.

"So how is he doing?" asked Alverez. "I have to include him in my morning situation report to Seventh Fleet."

"He'll be fine," the SMO said. "The usual story. Dumped by his girlfriend, took a bottle of Tylenol and some leftover Benadryl. We pumped his stomach, and we got most of it. He's all tucked in and sleeping it off. Rest is the best thing for him now."

"I might as well get started on the report," she said. "You know what a pain in the butt they can be. I bet they will have plenty of questions about this one, in addition to correcting my punctuation." The Seventh Fleet Surgeon's staff was notorious for being more focused on the format than the actual information relayed in the message.

As the SMO started on his salad, as his Hydra radio, known as the "Brick" because of its shape and size, squawked.

"SMO, Petty Officer Trout. We just had a medical emergency called in at 4-tac-247-tac-2 tac-echo. Someone fell and is unconscious. The medical response team is grabbing their gear."

"Copy, 4-tac-247-tac-2 tac-echo." The SMO repeated back while jotting the compartment number down on a napkin. "So much for pizza day," the SMO lamented as he leaped for the door.

"Alverez, can you take care of my tray please?" he said over his shoulder.

"You bet, SMO," she said. But he didn't hear her. He was already out of earshot and exiting the wardroom's port door and headed aft. At forty-two years old, five eleven, and 175 pounds, Lloyd was still in great shape considering the abuse his body had taken. Despite a leg injury that gave him a limp if he tried to run, he could still manage a fast walking pace as he charged down the passageway.

Ding! Ding! Ding! Ding! Ding! clanged the bell over the 1MC, the ship-wide public-address system, "Medical emergency! Medical Emergency! 4-tac-247-tac-2-tac-echo," said the announcer's voice before repeating it a second time. Because of the announcement and the fact that he was wearing his preferred at sea uniform of khaki pants, brown steel-toed boots, and a white turtleneck flight deck jersey sporting a huge red cross with 'SMO' stenciled across the front and back, everyone cleared out of his way as he bolted aft down the starboard P-way.

When the announcement finished, the SMO pressed the talk button on his brick and said, "Captain, SMO enroute." The radio channel was used by the ship's senior leadership for routine communication as well as for any significant events such as a major mechanical problem or medical emergencies. The Captain monitored the chatter and had asked the SMO to always confirm that he had heard the announcement and was on his way.

"Copy, SMO," replied Captain Ollie "Wedge" Whitehall, the ship's commanding officer.

After three months at sea, this was becoming a routine occurrence. There was a medical emergency called away every few days. Most usually ended up being for minor issues, a cut finger, a panic attack, or a bumped head, but occasionally, one was more serious. The SMO on an aircraft carrier was expected to respond to all medical emergencies to assess and take over the situation if needed. The SMO occasionally arrived ahead of his corpsmen, and he would begin to assess the patient. They were delayed by having to respond first to main medical to grab their emergency medical go bags and a Reeve sleeve stretcher.

The SMO's primary function was supervision and explaining what the medical issues were to the ship's leadership, the Captain, the executive officer who was the ship's second in command, the Sailor's department head, and often the Admiral's staff, depending on the severity of the case. The ship's executive officer, who in reality ran the day-to-day functions of the whole ship, was known as the "Big XO" to differentiate him from the many flying squadron XOs.

As he headed down the P way, he had two things on his mind. And neither was the condition of the patient. No, that would be sorted out once he arrived on scene. The first and actually most important was, *Where exactly am*

I going? The ship was a twisting maze of compartments. Frame 296 was near the aft of the ship, lots of spaces there. But it is on the fourth deck, two below the one he was currently on, meaning ladders to contend with. Either the more common forty-five degree ones or the occasional vertical ladders. An unconscious patient would have to be carried out. This could be a challenge. But his well-trained corpsmen had practiced it many times.

The second thing on his mind was that maybe, just maybe, he would beat the big XO there this time!

After four months and more than forty medical responses, he had yet to arrive at the scene ahead of Commander Thomas, the big XO. It didn't matter how fast he went or how close he was to the scene; the XO was there ahead of him. It had become and undeclared contest between them, one he had yet to win. The XO would either grimace or give a haughty sneer at the SMO when he arrived. The XO often greeted him with a ribbing such as, "Glad you could join us, SMO," or, "Sorry to disturb your nap." It was uncanny how the XO could always get there so fast.

The chastisement would have been ignored except that the SMO suspected the XO was serious. They had never gotten along. From day one, the XO had gone out of his way to establish that he was the big dog on the block. A lean, almost skeletal six three, he wore a perpetual frown. Not uncommon in XOs, but he seemed to relish the hard-ass role. He was old-school Navy and a stickler for all regulations. The SMO was convinced that if they ever drew his blood, it would be a thick Navy gray. On his second day aboard, the XO had snapped at him for not wearing the proper color-command T-shirt with his flight suit. Usually senior officers were more friendly to him, given his unique background, but not the *Vinson*'s XO. He gave no special treatment to anyone for any reason.

"Be in it by tomorrow," the XO had snapped as he got close in and glared down at the new SMO.

"Aye-aye, sir," the SMO returned, looking him in the eye without flinching. "Thanks for the clarification."

A T-shirt? Seriously! Did this guy really think he was intimidating me? The SMO remembered thinking and inwardly smiling. *This prima donna has nothing on the Chiefs at BUDS. Surely, he knew that. Probably just the way he marked his territory*, he surmised.

Things hadn't improved since then. The only good news was that the XO treated other department heads much worse. And they all report directly to the XO.

After maneuvering through a maze of several spaces, the SMO found himself looking down a vertical ladder to the third deck and several Sailors congregated in the port aft steering station.

As he stepped off the ladder's last rung, the SMO saw a deeply concerned XO.

"This looks serious SMO," said the XO.

Seeing only worried Sailors standing around, the SMO asked, "Where's the patient?"

A Sailor led the SMO on a catwalk around huge hydraulic pistons that turned one of the ship's two forty-five-ton rudders. Peering down another open hatch to the fourth deck, he saw the washed khakis of an unconscious officer sprawled awkwardly and being attended by two enlisted Sailors.

"He tripped and fell in," said a distraught petty officer. "We had just finished doing maintenance on the trick wheel when he just fell in. He hit his head as he fell through the hatch."

"Okay, got it," replied the SMO. "XO, please send someone up to guide my corpsmen down here. This place is tough to find."

The XO turned and passed the request on without hesitation as the SMO started down yet another vertical ladder into an acutely noisy compartment.

"Any idea who he is?" asked the SMO loudly.

"He's Lieutenant Sandoval, one of the Hornet naval flight officers," the XO said. "He was down here studying the rudder mechanism in preparation for his Surface Warfare oral boards. Even though junior air wing guys rarely get their Surface Warfare pin, he had begged us to let him go for it. He said he didn't want his brother, a destroyer XO, to constantly berate him for not knowing anything about ships."

"I see," the SMO answered as he continued down. *I won't be listening to a heartbeat or breath sounds down here,* he thought, climbing down. He scanned the area to ensure that everyone would be safe from the huge moving hydraulic pistons. With safety ensured, he continued down focusing on the patient. There was a small pool of blood on the deck under his head, his breathing was regular, and he had no obvious deformity. He appeared to be about twenty-eight years old and 170 pounds.

Thank God he isn't too big, he thought. The Sailor's pulse was regular. There was a small, barely bleeding laceration and swelling lump on his right temple that had mostly stopped. *Good, no arterial bleeding. Just capillary.* The SMO then did a quick head-to-toe examination, careful not to move the Sailor's head or neck, and found no other injuries.

"Hey, SMO, we're here," said Hospitalman Second Class MacIntosh peering down from above. He had arrived with three others, two male and one female corpsmen.

"Come on down, but be careful," the SMO said, pointing at the massive hydraulic pistons only feet away.

"He appears stable but may have serious head or neck injuries," explained the SMO to MacIntosh. "Get a C-collar on him, his head bandaged, and then into the Reeve sleeve. Keep good traction on his neck until he's strapped in."

"We got it, SMO," MacIntosh replied. "IV?"

"No, he hasn't lost that much blood. It'll wait," the SMO concluded. "Besides, it would just make getting him out harder."

This is the exact situation the Reeve sleeve had been designed for, he thought. *It totally encloses a patient, securing them so well that they can be lifted vertically without the risk of them shifting or falling out.*

The SMO stepped out of the way to let them get to work. *All the hard training is now going to pay off,* he thought. He had ensured that each response team would be able to treat and stabilize a patient, start an IV, and if needed, extract them vertically up several decks. Now it was for real.

As he stepped clear, his mind drifted back to a pivotal injury from his past.

It had been a hot July day on Interstate 10 in north Florida. "Roll, roll me away, won't you roll me away tonight…" was blaring from his car stereo. Lieutenant Lloyd was singing along to one of his dad's favorite Bob Seger songs from the eighties. He had finished his one-year internship at Naval Hospital Jacksonville, Florida, and was headed to his next big adventure, starting the six-month Navy Flight Surgeon's course in Pensacola. Realizing his dream since junior high school, he was finally going into the world of naval aviation, albeit as a Flight Surgeon and not a pilot. He had said goodbye to his wife and their two kids as they stayed behind to finish another school year with their friends. They would move to join him next summer at his planned assignment to NAS Oceana Virginia.

Suddenly, an erratic movement had caught his eye. A quarter mile ahead, a van swerved left, and then jerked back right, then left again. Each excursion was more severe, and seconds later, the van flipped and tumbled into the median, throwing up dirt, dust, and debris. Surprisingly, it landed upright.

Lloyd had been the second car to stop, just moments later. He popped his trunk and grabbed his emergency medical kit. There was a mom and five kids, and they weren't looking good.

"Oh my God! Oh my God!" the other driver who had stopped repeated.

"Do you have a phone?" Lloyd asked. "Call an ambulance." He quickly assessed the scene. "Better make that three ambulances."

The driver's airbag had deployed, and the mom had been belted in. She was conscious but confused and asking what happened. Her talking proved her airway was clear, and she had no obvious major injuries. Lloyd next opened the van's left-side panel door. A boy of about fourteen was unconscious and, at first, glance in the worst shape. He had a bleeding deep laceration along his left cheek showing broken teeth through the gaping wound. Lloyd could clearly hear him gurgling blood as he breathed. His left lower leg was also bent at an unnatural angle.

Okay, he'd thought, *gotta clear his airway and stop that bleeding.* He considered that whatever whack caused the cut could also fracture his cervical vertebra and endanger the boy's spinal cord. The other younger kids were all crying or screaming. *Good airways and conscious.* He continued to focus on the older boy.

"What can I do to help?" a new feminine voice asked from behind him.

"Hi, thanks. Grab that med kit just over there," Lloyd asked, pointing. "You afraid of blood?"

"Nope, raised four boys on a farm," she said. "I've seen it all."

"Great. Now get in behind him and hold his head steady and keep his head and spine aligned like this." Lloyd had demonstrated. "Let him lean slightly forward to keep him from choking on his blood."

"Okay, got it," she'd said.

Lloyd had gotten his only C-collar out and carefully placed it on the boy's neck. Next he tore open a large sterile bandage and applied a pressure dressing to the gaping wound.

"Can you hold him like that a bit longer?" he'd asked.

"I think so," she'd said.

By the time he had finished with the fourteen-year-old, several others had arrived and were tending to the other kids, including an off-duty emergency medical technician.

Together, they'd done a quick assessment of the others. There were several minor lacerations and two obvious broken arms.

As they'd finished, they'd heard sirens approaching in the distance. The man who had called for help tapped him on the shoulder.

"Hey, the dispatcher wants to talk to someone, and you seem to know what you are doing," the first driver had said, handing over his cell phone.

"Hello, this is Dr. Lloyd." He'd explained the situation and that at least one patient, the boy, should be flown to a trauma center if possible. Luckily, the nearest helicopter could be there in twelve minutes.

After the first ambulance had arrived, the paramedics had taken over the situation. They soon had the boy on a back board. However, Lloyd had to intervene when they transferred the backboard onto a stretcher.

"Whoa, hold up there," he'd said. "You need to have him tilted sideways at a forty-five-degree angle so any blood will drain out his mouth. If you put him flat on his back, he could drown in his own blood!"

They'd realized that he was right and soon had the boy properly strapped down as the helicopter was landing on the interstate.

Two other ambulances had arrived, and their paramedics had been tending to the others.

After Lloyd had supervised the loading of the boy onto the helicopter, he'd gone back and closed up his med kit and headed back to his car. The state police were now on the scene and had a single lane of traffic moving slowly by on the shoulder. He nosed his way in and was soon cruising back down the interstate.

Now that was pretty cool, he'd thought. He had made a difference. He had never had problems focusing in stressful situations. Not since BUDS SEAL training, where he'd learned to just focus on making it through the next minute. Emergency Medicine. *Hmmm, maybe I should look into that*, he pondered. *Well, maybe after being a Flight Surgeon. But I'm gonna have some fun first!*

"How is he, SMO?" asked the XO, jarring him back to the present.

"XO, he may have head and neck injuries, but he is otherwise stable. The cut to his head has stopped bleeding."

"Do you need anything?" asked the XO.

"Yeah, we need a pulley attached to that overhead hook." The SMO pointed to the steel hook welded above the center of the hatch.

With a pulley in place centered over the hatch, a rope was secured to the Reeve sleeve and run through the pulley. Most of the lifting was done physically by Sailors above and below the patient. The rope and pulley primarily guided the patient and prevented him from dropping. After repeating the process from the third to the second deck, the response team was soon on their way to main medical located in the forward third of the ship on the second deck. The SMO and XO were close behind.

As the patient was carried into the treatment room, the SMO was pleased to see that most of his team were there. In addition to the doc on call, the physician assistant, general surgeon, and family practice doc were also there. Though the SMO was a board certified emergency physician, he let the surgeon take over.

The XO stepped to the clinic's check in desk phone to call the Captain with an update.

The SMO saw that all was under control and the patient would soon be headed for X-rays of his head and neck.

"Man, I'm still starving" he said to no one in particular. He went to his office, pulled out a diet cherry Pepsi from his minifridge to cool down and then fished out a bag of peanuts from his desk.

"Well?" asked Alverez sticking her head into his office.

"Well what?" he asked.

"You know. Did you beat him?"

"Oh, the XO. Nope," he said before guzzling half of the Pepsi.

"Too bad, maybe next time," she said.

"He was there staring up at me when I finally found that hidden space. At least, he didn't bug me about it this time." The SMO's thoughts returned to the patient. "This patient may be serious. Depending on what we find, he may have to be evacuated. And his flying days may be over. I'm waiting on the X-ray results before I head up to brief the Captain. At least, I'm staying in great shape out here. This will be my fourth trip up the ten stories to the bridge today. I swear, one day I'm gonna count every flipping one of those steps to get up there. Where are we anyway?" asked the SMO.

"The Pacific," Alverez said, cocking her head to the side with a wry smile.

He gave her a friendly glare.

"Okay, okay," she blurted. "We passed north of Guam yesterday. So we may still be in range of the naval hospital there if needed. And we are due in Hong Kong in four days, so hospitals in Japan and the Philippines may be possibilities as we head west."

"Check all our options," he said before downing the last of his soda and heading to check on the patient.

2 MEDICAL UPDATES

USS *Vinson*, Western Pacific

Forty-five minutes later, the SMO was heading up to brief the Captain. Captain "Wedge" Whitehall, or just the CO, as most called him, was a stocky five-seven bundle of energy. He made up with his domineering personality what he lacked in size. His flaming-red hair was still thick with only a sprinkling of gray. Other than his intense sparkling blue eyes, his most prominent feature was his thick, bushy red mustache that clearly exceeded Navy grooming regulations. However, no one dared to challenge him on it. He had been the shortest student naval aviators in his class, but he had been determined to be the best. Graduating number one, he got his choice to fly F-14 fighters and lived his own Top Gun movie dream. He was in one of the last classes to go through F-14C training before the aircraft was retired from service. He completed his first Western Pacific deployment in support of Operation Southern Watch doing regular overflight of Iraq to keep Saddam Hussein and his military in check. After that uneventful deployment, his squadron retired their powerful Tomcats and transitioned into the single-seat F/A-18E Super Hornet. The saddest part had been saying goodbye to all his Naval Flight Officer (NFO) friends who flew in the rear seat as Radar Intercept Officers. Though he teased them almost daily that NFO stood for "Non-Flying Officer" and "No Future Outside," he missed having them to talk to on the later long eight-to-ten hour missions over Afghanistan and Iraq. The same drive that earned him his golden wings and fighter assignment eventually led to squadron command and now command of one of the most powerful war machines on earth. His crew of fifty-six hundred Sailors was nearly twice the personnel strength of many Air Force Bases.

In the "Captain's chair" on the port side of the bridge, surrounded by phones, navigation screens, and other equipment sat the CO looking out at a launching F-18 going to afterburner while simultaneously chatting with the "Gator," short for Navigator. The SMO stood back a few feet behind the CO where he could look out over the flight deck and watch the planes launching, something he never tired of doing. He was near enough to overhear their conversation while waiting for his chance to get the CO's attention. The SMO often thought that because of the CO's size, it looked like he was sitting in a kid's high chair, a thought he would definitely keep to himself.

"The problem is the wind Captain," the Gator was explaining. "They have been predominantly out of the east the last three days, so we have to head east into the wind every time we launch. We've been falling farther and farther behind our planned advance west. If we don't do something, we will not get to Hong Kong as scheduled."

"I know. I know," lamented the CO. What was unsaid but on the CO's mind was that the US Navy will not be showing up late to a foreign country without good reason, period. Not on his watch.

Though still officially on friendly terms, tensions between China and the United States had been simmering recently over both trade and territorial claims. Taiwan, Vietnam, and the Philippines all have valid claims on the sovereignty of the Spratly Islands, where China had built three major man-made islands. The Chinese appear to claim the whole area just because it was named the South China Sea. The Chinese had been particularly irritated by the new joint US-and-Philippine operations over the past six months. They had become increasingly aggressive with their naval operations and expanding their capability now with two operational aircraft carriers. It was no secret that they were peeved to no end back in 2018 when they were "uninvited" to the biannual Pacific Rim exercise. They had hoped to show off their new carrier capabilities to other Pacific countries both to impress and intimidate those in their back yard.

"What do you suggest, Gator?" the CO asked.

"I recommend we cancel night ops and have all planes aboard by 1730 and head west at eighteen knots, a speed to allow the *USS Chaffee* who is running on fumes to keep up until we can refuel her tomorrow," the

Gator explained.

"I agree," the CO decided. "Run it by the CAG and tell him we need to wrap up flight ops at the end of the next cycle." CAG stands for Carrier Air Group, the historical title still used by an Air Wing Commander.

"Tell him we may need to cut the flight schedule in half tomorrow for the same reason. He will be pissed, but at least he can plan and prioritize those that need the flight time the most," the CO said.

"Aye-aye, Captain," Gator said as he headed out to notify Captain Summerville, the Commander of Carrier Air Wing Five (CVW-5).

"And don't forget to let the Admiral know," he said, turning to the Gator as the Gator was almost off the bridge. The CO noticed the SMO standing behind him.

"Ah, hey, SMO, what have you got for me?" asked the CO as he leaned back in his chair and stretched. "It's been another interesting day." He stifled a yawn with his palm.

"I have an update on our two patients," the SMO said. "The attempted suicide patient is doing okay and is asleep on the ward with the usual one on one watch over him. He'll be seeing our psychologist later this evening. He received a Dear John email from his girlfriend back in San Diego. He lost it after unanswered emails and phone calls. He downed a whole bottle of Tylenol he received yesterday in a care package. His stomach has been pumped out, and he's now stable."

"I can never understand kids these days or why they react so stupidly to a temporary situation," the CO commented, shaking his head.

"The NFO from VF-22 who fell has me worried," the SMO continued.

"How so?" the CO asked, leaning forward and frowning.

"He is awake now, but he took a hard whack to his head when he fell. His X-rays are suspicious for a hairline fracture along his right temporal bone," the SMO explained. "He has blood behind the right eardrum, has lost his sense of smell, and his neuro exam is slightly off. We are concerned that he may have an intracranial bleed that may be pressing on his brain. Possibly an epidural or subdural bleed. It's times like this that I really wish we had a CT scanner out here."

The SMO continued. "We have him in the ICU and are watching him closely. We need to get him to a CT as soon as possible. Ideally, within twenty-four hours if he is to have a chance to continue flying. With a hit to the head like this, he will need a flying waiver, and it will be almost impossible to get without that CT. And only then if it is normal. Until then we won't know what is going on in his head."

"Why, what's the big deal as long as he recovers?" asked the CO.

"Sir, with bleeding in the brain, there is a significant risk of seizures for the next ten years," the SOM explained.

"*Ten years!* Damn SMO, you flight docs are harsh."

"It's not us sir. That is just the medical facts," the SMO answered.

The CO nodded and let out a barely perceptible groan. He hated any time he had a Sailor get sent home for any reason, illness, injury, family emergency, or being kicked out for bad behavior. None leaving for any of these unplanned reasons were going to be replaced during the deployment, and it would mean more work for those left behind.

"Well, where does he need to go?" the CO asked while repeatedly rubbing his mustache down with his thumb and forefinger. A mannerism he often did subconsciously when deep in thought.

"Ideally, depending on our location, either to the Naval Hospital at Kadena on Okinawa, or the Air Force Hospital at Yokota Air Base outside Tokyo. Both have a CT and neurosurgical capability, just in case. Kadena appears to be closest to our track," the SMO noted.

"Okinawa will be in the range of our C-2 transports tomorrow," the CO concluded. "Will that work?"

"I'm afraid not, Captain. The thing is, I can't risk letting him take a cat shot. Without knowing the extent of his head injury the sudden acceleration could increase blood pressure in his head and make any bleeding worse. Putting him either head or feet first both have advantages and disadvantages. I also considered placing him transverse on a backboard between two rows of seats. All are just too risky not knowing exactly what we are dealing with."

"Well, SMO, a helicopter won't even make it halfway," the CO explained.

"No, sir, I checked the charts. But in two days, a helo can make it to Cagayan North International airport on the north coast of Luzon," the SMO stated. "We can send him there by helo and then launch the C-2 to meet them at the airport. We can trans-load him onto the C-2, and he could have a nice, smooth, normal takeoff to Okinawa. Tokyo is too far for the C-2 to make in a single hop."

"I see you have thought this through, SMO," the CO noted, a bit surprised.

"Yes, sir. I admit I had a little help from the Assistant Navigator checking positions and distances. I already have my Admin Officer and the surgeon working the details with the hospital at Kadena. And of course, it all hinges on his remaining stable the next two days."

"SMO, you're my medical advisor, and it sounds like a solid plan. Get it going and keep me advised. It's a shame we can't get him there quicker." the CO replied.

"Thank you, sir. I will," answered the SMO.

"Ten years," the CO repeated sadly as the turned back to the flight deck ops.

As the SMO left the bridge the CO was already focused back on the final launching aircraft and checking the ship's heading and the wind speed over the deck.

Starting down, *One more task to do*, the SMO thought. *Maybe she'll still be in her office. If not, I can call her later with a quick update on the patients*. He viewed the former as decidedly more pleasant.

Each carrier battle group is commanded by a one-star Rear Admiral. In this case, it was Stephen Dale LaSalle. He was an old-school Surface Warfare Officer. Admiral LaSalle was five ten, solidly built, with a shiny bald head and just a hint of graying hair circling the crown of his head. Classic male pattern baldness. The Admiral was always upbeat and smiling. He was sharp as a tack and had a near photographic memory, so no one had to repeat anything to him.

Whenever there was a potentially high-visibility patient, the Admiral and his staff had to be notified. As most did, the SMO interacted most often through the Admiral's Chief of Staff. The SMO only occasionally saw Admiral LaSalle.

For the first month after the SMO had taken over the medical department, he would contact the Chief of Staff by phone, or the brick, to pass along updates. Occasionally, he would drop by the Chief of Staff's office for a face-to-face update if it was an important issue. In addition to overseeing the health of the carrier's crew, the SMO was actually in charge of the medical care of all the Sailors in the battle group. So, the SMO had a standing invitation to sit in on the weekly flag briefings and he went as often as he could to keep up on the big picture, but it wasn't a priority.

That dramatically changed for the SMO two months earlier. He had gotten to a meeting just before the Admiral came in. He had slipped into his usual back-row chair. It had been weeks since he had last attended a flag brief. There was a new person in the Chief of Staff chair with their back to the SMO. Sitting directly behind her, he thought she looked strangely familiar in a déjà vu sort of way. There was something about the way she carried herself and the thick, raven-black hair in a tight bun. The Admiral introduced his new Chief of Staff, Captain Jenna Tullos. As he saw her face, the SMO had a flashback to over a decade ago.

It had been a cold February day in the Mediterranean. Lieutenant Lloyd was seated facing aft in the back of a Navy C-2A Greyhound. He was leaning against the right side of the plane and had been sleeping most of the two-hour flight from Sigonella Sicily out to the USS *Harry S. Truman* (CVN 75). The Greyhound is used for Carrier Onboard Delivery transporting personnel to and from the ship, bring supplies, parts, and most importantly bags of mail out to the fleet at sea. He had learned long ago to sleep whenever he got the chance, and he had lots of experience sleeping in airplanes, usually just before he jumped out of them. But that was long in the past. As he woke and stretched to work the stiffness out of his muscles, he was grateful for the loose comfort of his green flight suit, and he was wishing that he had taken a seat by one of the two porthole windows on either side of the fuselage. The two windows were the only way to see out, and he was getting bored. He was fresh out of Flight Surgeon's school where he had earned his gold Flight Surgeon's wings. He was as proud of them as anything he had ever done. But everyone focused on the larger Navy SEAL Trident centered over those new Flight Surgeon wings on his name patch.

He had been one of ten Sailors flying out to join their ships in the deployed battle group. He may have been a Navy SEAL in a prior life, but this was his first time to land on a carrier, and the fact that he was sitting backward made it truly different.

Three days earlier, he had hugged and kissed his wife Rachel and two kids goodbye. There had been nearly constant stress in their relationship since he had started medical school. It had been a particularly rough couple of years for the Lloyd family after two moves and a family separation of seven months while he earned his Flight Surgeon wings down in Pensacola, Florida. He had been assigned as one of Carrier Air Wing Three's two flight surgeons currently embarked on the recently deployed *Truman*. He had been a last-minute substitute to replace a flight surgeon who had to leave because of a family emergency. He had originally been assigned to another air wing but that was changed, and he'd deployed almost immediately.

Needless to say, it was not a good time for the Lloyd family. There had been many late-night arguments as he was packing to head out. Before, she had been living near her parents in San Diego with what she called, humane weather. Now she was stuck in Jacksonville, and she didn't get along with her in-laws one bit. Then there was the heat, mosquitos, and daily summer thunderstorms which she hated. He was loath to admit it, but he was secretly relieved to be on deployment where he wouldn't have the stress of dealing with an unhappy wife.

He hadn't paid much attention until he'd woken up, but there were two others wearing flight suits across the aisle in the row behind his. To pass the time, he turned toward them and asked, "Why are you riding in back with the rest of us? Shouldn't you be driving?"

"We should be," said the young raven-haired flyer. "Our plane is broken, and we were diverted to Sigonella. It will be a week or more before they get it fixed, and our skipper wanted us back now."

"Oh...bad luck, I guess. I'm Lieutenant Lloyd, the new Flight Surgeon," he said, noticing that she wore Naval Flight Officer wings.

"Or good luck, depending on how you look at it. I'm Lieutenant Tullos," she said, returning a confident handshake and displaying an easy smile. "This is my pilot Lieutenant Bradford." He nodded in his direction.

"Glad to meet you both," Lloyd replied. "So what happened?"

"Well, two days ago we were practicing 2 v 2 intercepts about fifty miles southwest of Sicily when I noticed that our number two hydraulic system gauge was reading a bit low. I called the others to knock it off, and we diverted to Sigonella, which was actually closer than the boat. Anyway, we've been stuck there for two days waiting on open C-2 seats back to the ship," she said.

"What do you mean stuck?" Bradford finally chimed in. "You know that every other junior officer in the squadron is jealous of us. Real restaurants, beer and wine when we wanted in the bar, and the BOQ had HBO. Not to mention the hot chicks in town."

"Ignore him. He's a budding alcoholic," she said.

"Cool it, Tullos. Remember that he is a Flight Surgeon," Bradford chided. "He has the power of the up-or-down chit. He has the final say if we get to fly or not."

Their conversation was interrupted with an increase in pitch from the engines.

With a perplexed look on his face, Lloyd asked, "I thought we would be powering back as we came in to land?"

"It is clear weather and case-one flight operations," said Tullos. "The pilot is speeding up to come in for the break over the ship. Even the C-2 pilots want to look cool coming in to land."

A minute later, the plane rolled ninety degrees into a sharp left bank, and Lloyd felt the Gs build slightly. From there on it was just minor left-and-right adjustments and the engine power coming on and off. And then, *bang*, as the plane slammed onto the deck, and they were instantly forced back into their seat as the tailhook caught a wire.

After taxiing a few minutes, the engines whined to a halt, and the rear ramp opened up.

"Welcome to the *Truman*, Lieutenant," said Tullos.

They had hit it off that day. Before long, they were almost inseparable and were frequently seen in the wardroom or in her squadron ready room, discussing many topics and, frequently, their relationships. His main excuse for being there was her squadron had the only two seat Super Hornets he could fly in. She was engaged and looking forward to being married after the deployment. He discussed the stress in his marriage and how his wife was frustrated at the negative impact the Navy was having on her own dreams of a fulfilling career. They both soon became close and open with each other. Actually, more so than either had been with their current partners. They were almost inseparable when on shore leave, and everyone was beginning to talk.

But though they were becoming emotionally attached, he never let it become physical. Though on more than one occasion, after several glasses of wine, he was sure he could have taken it to the next level. And he definitely wanted to. Boy, did he want to. He had never been unfaithful, and he still loved his wife. He just couldn't do that to her, or himself for that matter. Still, his relationship with Jenna grew. She became the only person that he had ever been as free and trusting with. With her, he found every wall and protective barrier around his heart and soul had dropped. She was gentle, understanding, and nonjudgmental. Only with her had he been able to open up about his feelings and troubling memories from his SEAL days.

He had admitted to her that though being a SEAL was a source of pride and accomplishment, he never felt that he truly measured up. Others were far more capable that he. Outwardly, he was in total control, but he had his doubts. He had led several remarkably successful patrols. But after his team was ambushed on their last patrol, resulting in several deaths and injuries, including his own, he was convinced that it was all his fault. He had performed precisely as trained, yet he was sure he had missed something. He was never blamed for the outcome; indeed, he was given a medal for his heroics. But he was terrified at the prospect of having to risk putting his men in such a situation again, where his next mistake could be even more tragic. He was able to tell only her how he had been disappointed and yet emotionally relieved when he had been declared unfit for further active SEAL service. The burden that lifted from him at finally being able to share that with someone was life changing for him.

They eventually discussed future possibilities. They considered the implications of ending their current relationships and pressed on with what they believed was becoming *the* true love of their lives. But they had reluctantly agreed that their obligations trumped their personal feelings, and they eventually went their separate ways after the deployment. Yet her memory had haunted his dreams ever since.

That was a lifetime ago for them both. Much had happened since he had last seen her on his first deployment as a brand-new Flight Surgeon. Now they were both divorced, and he had been finding excuses to stop by her office these last few months. It had only taken a few weeks to return to the emotional closeness and intimacy they had once enjoyed. Now it was getting to the point of regular flirting when they were alone. They clearly had an interest in each other, but neither had openly broached the subject yet. But it was still complicated. His feelings were mixed again. Eight months ago, during a visit to pick up his kids for the weekend, his ex-wife had broached the idea of getting back together. She had now achieved her career goals while they were apart, and now she was thinking they should consider giving it another try. The kids missed having their dad around. They had been on a half-dozen dates before he deployed. He had even slept over one night, to the surprise and joy of his children when he walked in for breakfast. It had been a happy glimpse of how it once had been and could possibly be again. Though right for the family, and comfortable in its familiarity, at its best he still felt the old emotional walls in place, ones that had only been down once years before, with another woman.

Smiling at the memories, he made his way down from the bridge to the O-3 level, the deck just below the flight deck and then forward along the starboard side onto the lighter deck color indicating he was in "Admiral's country." He turned left into a passageway leading to the Admiral staff's offices.

Through Tullos' open office door, he admired her quietly for a moment. She was sitting partially turned away and staring at the computer screen while she slowly chewed on the end of a government pen. He knocked on the door frame.

"You got a minute, Captain?" he asked leaning in.

Looking up from her computer screen, she set her pen on the desk and locked on his smiling eyes with her own.

"Sure, SMO, and stop being so formal all the time. Not when we are alone anyway. You used to outrank me once upon a time," she said. "Have a seat. What's up?

"Yeah, but I lost two years' time in rank switching from being a line officer to medical. You have outranked me eighteen months as long as you have known me," he reminded her.

"Well, the O-6 medical promotion list should be out in a few months. With your Silver Star and Purple Heart, we should be the same rank again soon," she said.

"Those probably won't mean much to the medical promotion board. But running the Emergency Department at Great Lakes probably will, and get me that all important check in the box for Captain," he added. "Anyway, that medical emergency you probably heard called away turned out to be worrisome. We're going to have to airlift him as soon as we can to Okinawa."

"Oh, I see," she said, taking a more concerned stance. "Just how bad is he? Do I need to tell the Admiral now?"

"He's stable. We have him in the ICU and are keeping an eye on him. It can probably wait," he suggested. "I just wanted to keep you in the loop. I was up here briefing the CO. Thought I'd stop by to brief you as well," he said.

"SMO, you're always a welcome break from the constant workload," she said as she leaned back in her chair arching her back and raising her hands over her head into a long feline stretch.

He couldn't help noticing how that had accentuated her figure.

Afterward, they sat silently for several moments, just gazing at each other.

Searching for something to say, he said, "I see you seem to have an oral fetish with that pen of yours."

"Is that so?" she replied impishly. "Well, what I wrap my lips around, and when, is none of your business. Not yet."

He took a gulp and felt his mouth go dry at that comment.

"Sooooo, Jenna, we pull into Hong Kong in four days," he said, desperately trying to change the subject. "It'll be my first time there. You have any plans?"

"Maaaybe," she said with a hint of a giggle. "Well, Derek, it'll be the first time for both of us."

Suddenly feeling himself blush, he was finally able to ask her the question he had been pondering for weeks. "I mean, umm, if you don't have any plans, ummm, maybe we could have dinner one night."

With a disarming and overtly innocent grin, she replied, "Of course, that would be lovely."

"Great," he blurted like a teenager. "I'll check to see which days I'm on duty, and let you know when I can get away."

"Okay," she said, touching the back of her neck. "Let me know."

"Well, I wish I could chat longer, but I have to brief his squadron CO next," he said, standing.

The knock at the door snapped both of them out of their playful mood. Turning, they saw Captain Ball, the Admiral's Operations Officer, known by everyone by his call sign of Speedtrap. "Hi, SMO, good to see you," he said nodding toward him. "Jenna, I just stopped by to let you know that the Admiral's brief has been moved to 1630. And, SMO, come to think of it, you should attend this one. We may need your input at some point."

"Thanks, Speedy," Jenna replied as Captain Ball nodded and ducked back into the passageway. She turned back to the SMO. "He's right. You should be there. Something big is brewing in our neck of the woods. I don't know why I didn't think to invite you myself."

"I miss over half of them because of other duties, and I'm usually not required to attend. But I will definitely be there, and anytime you recommend, I'll find the time," Derek answered. "Well, I better get going. I have a couple of appointments this afternoon to power through in order to make that brief."

As he was heading out, he glanced back, their eyes meeting again. "Later, Jenna," he said. Her eyes following his every move as he exited.

Her huge smile was all the reply she gave.

What the hell was that? he wondered. He was forty-two years old and had just felt and acted like a sixteen-year-old boy asking a pretty girl out on his first date. He had dated several women over the past couple of years since his divorce, but he'd never had that reaction to any of them. He didn't even remember feeling that way at sixteen.

Suppressing the twinge of guilt he felt as he thought of his ex-wife, he had a stupid teenage grin on his face as he headed down the P-way. That warm feeling from a decade ago was back.

3 CONFERENCE RECEPTION
Shanghai, China

Vice Admiral Fa Jiang stood next to a much younger lady, enjoying the view looking west out over Shanghai.

"It's positively beautiful, don't you think?" she asked as she gazed at the amazing vista of the setting sun on the distant horizon.

He just glanced slightly her way and nodded.

"I bet it is always marvelous a sunset from this vantage point," she said, taking another sip of her expensive champagne.

"Yes indeed," he said absentmindedly as he took in the breathtaking skyline. It was a view that few got to enjoy without paying for the privilege. It was indeed an impressive expanse below of China's largest and most prosperous city. They stood on the observation deck of Shanghai Tower's 121st floor, the second tallest building in the world. The Admiral had other things on his mind just now than the beautiful young woman in the dark blue evening dress at his side.

This closing reception was for China's leading military Generals and Admirals on the last day of the semiannual leadership conference. It had included the usual intelligence briefings on other countries hardware, capabilities, and readiness, but more importantly, the latest political analysis assessing both what potential adversaries were doing and may do. They also discussed the status of their growing military bases in the South China Sea. All in all, things were going quite well. The Philippines had given up Thitu Island, and they seemed thoroughly cowed. The Philippine government was beefing up their military, but he and his superiors concluded that it was too little, too late.

The greater concern was trying to gauge the American response. They had blustered a bit as expected after the Thitu Island takeover. As expected, they had increased their right-of-navigation overflights with their ancient B-52s and had sailed destroyers within a dozen miles of the Spratly Islands every three to four months. Their government had complained loudly, but it was all part of the game. In essence, nothing had changed. America had made no moves of consequence. Things had settled into a new normal the past few years. China's neighbors were effectively helpless, and there was nothing the rest of the world was willing to do.

The United States had resumed regular port visits to Hong Kong with their Navy ships after they had been suspended for eighteen months. The new American president had talked tough on China while running for office, but his rhetoric had been focused primarily on China's economic policy and trade imbalance over the United States. His only military move so far had been more frequent exercises in the Philippines. But soon, his administration had become totally distracted and focused on China's ally, North Korea.

China's secret plan to distract the United States focus using the bantam tyrant had worked beyond their wildest dreams. Compared to the nuclear intercontinental ballistic missile capable madman, China's recent actions seemed positively reasonable.

The conference was the official reason they were there. But, more important were the sidebar meetings and connections that were made during the breaks between briefs. These private side discussions were the real reason everyone looked forward to attending. This was where the key connections were made. It was where you could learn the political climate, who was moving up in the communist party, who was out of favor, and most important of all, career opportunities. In China more so than anywhere else in the world, it was who you knew that was key to one's advancement. Vice Admiral Jiang was very adept at maneuvering within this system.

Tonight, however, was not about his future. His career was well on track with established political and military connections to the very top. Having planned and executed the operation to bloodlessly take Thitu Island, it was only a matter of time till he pinned on his third star, the rank of full Admiral. He intended to be the Navy Chief of Staff one day. But he aimed even higher, to become the first to attain the rank of Fleet Admiral and a fourth star. The rank had once existed on the books from 1988 to 1994, but never been held. The Chinese Navy had been too small then. That was over twenty years ago. Now it had almost twice as many ships, including the two of three planned *Liaoning*-class aircraft carriers with more on the way.

No, the primary goal for tonight's reception was not about him.

Ignoring his female companion, he nodded at a man who was chatting with a nearby group of men and women. It was clear that the man had remained where he could keep an eye toward the Admiral. He'd been waiting to catch the Admiral's attention.

Lieutenant Commander Liang Yao excused himself from the group and confidently strode over. He was the Admiral's thirty-three-year-old nephew, the son of his older sister. He was an experienced J-15 fighter pilot with the call sign "Hawk," a moniker that he was proud of and insisted be used by his fellow pilots when addressing him. He had also participated in the surprise air-and-ship demonstration at Thitu Island. He was attending the conference at the request of the Admiral. He had even arranged for him to fly there in one of his squadron's fighters to a base outside Shanghai.

The real reason Yao was there was to fulfill the promise he had made to his sister to look after her son. Yao had been a shy but otherwise normal, inquisitive fourteen-year-old when his father had been killed in a cargo plane he was piloting. Yao had been devastated by the loss and became withdrawn. That was before the rumors and whisperings began that the crash had been his father's fault. Older boys in the neighborhood began to tease him and pick fights. Many days, he came home with a black eye or bloody nose. The shy, introspective youth became an angry vengeful young man out to get even with the world. Admiral Jiang had promised his late sister to support and guide the young man in hopes of putting his angry outbursts behind him. Though Yao outwardly appeared to have his anger and inferiority issues behind him, Jiang worried that they were still the main driving forces in his life.

"How's the party going?" asked Jiang.

"Most excellent, Admiral," he replied deferentially. "I have met several important officers. And of course, the view is excellent." He smiled and looked at a group of ladies by the windows.

"I take it you are not talking about the view of Shanghai," Jiang deduced. "I agree, but that is not why you are here."

"Yes, Admiral," Yao said.

"I introduced you to the PLAN Air Force Chief of Staff earlier today," the Admiral stated. "You seem to only be talking to your peers. Stick by me, and I will show you how to work a room. Pay attention."

Over the next hour and a half, Yao stayed glued to his uncle's side. At times, they moved casually around the room meeting and greeting various officers senior to Admiral Jiang. But most of the time, they held court and let the junior officers come to them. The Admiral always introduced Yao to everyone they met, and always described what an excellent officer he was.

As the evening was winding down, the Admiral noticed the PLAN Navy Chief of Staff, Admiral Kao, standing alone. He was surveying the sprawling nighttime city and the colorfully illuminated Yu Gardens as they reflected off a looping bend of the Huangpu River over fourteen-hundred feet below.

Now was the chance to catch the Admiral alone that Jiang had been waiting for. He had an urgent issue on his mind. Just before he reached the Admiral he turned to Yao.

"Stay here," said Jiang, directing Yao to stand back fifteen feet for what he assumed was out of earshot. "I have business to discuss with the Admiral."

Yao nodded and did as he was told, noting that this was the first time he was not allowed to stay by the Admiral's side. But he had not gotten where he was now without keeping his ear to the ground, even though he did have a Vice Admiral for an uncle. So he pretended to pay no attention while straining to hear all he could. He heard nothing at first because they were speaking so low. After a few minutes, their voices started to rise.

"But now is the perfect time to act!" spat Jiang. "Everything could be in place within weeks. There is nothing they could do but posture."

"This I know," said Admiral Kao.

"Did he give a reason?" asked Jiang.

"No, he is the chairman. He doesn't have to," replied Kao.

"What about the latest reports from Manila?" asked Jiang. "Did he not take them into account?"

"He did, and he believes that it is not related in any way to our objective. He concluded they're bolstering their southern forces who are busy fighting Islamic separatists," said Kao.

"Possibly," mused Jiang. "But if it isn't, the possibility they are going for Minzhu is concerning."

Yao visibly stiffened at hearing the name. Minzhu Jiao! Otherwise known as Scarborough Shoal to the rest of the world. His mind was now racing. He knew that there were plans for an operation to take Scarborough. And now they were being put on hold or worse, canceled altogether. *Damn*, he thought, feeling his gut tighten. In fact, he had played a small but key part in the planning they were talking about. He knew enough to know that the operation was in the final stages before execution. *Now what?* He thought grinding his teeth. *We have no reason to stop. The chairman is becoming too timid.* He felt his rising anger as he continued to eavesdrop.

"You worry too much, Jiang. Our Coast Guard remains in control and have only allowed our fishing boats into the lagoon for years," said Kao. "There has been increasing activity from their old frigates, but they have avoided any direct confrontation. So do not worry. We have control of the situation and plenty of time to convince the chairman to change his mind if the situation changes."

"Hm," Jiang murmured.

"Now get back to the party and enjoy yourself," Kao said as he nodded toward the young woman Jiang had been with earlier. "Enjoy the pleasures your rank brings. We can discuss this tomorrow."

"Yes, Admiral," he replied, flashing a brief but insincere smile as he gave a slight bow and turned to leave.

Jiang walked back across the room lost in thought.

Yao moved to stride alongside him. "All well, Uncle?" he asked.

"Huh?" he replied, suddenly noticing Yao again.

"Is everything well?" Yao again asked.

"I don't know," he answered. "I really don't know."

"So, Lieutenant Commander," Jiang started, changing the subject, "have you found the conference useful? You must always take advantage of these events to strengthen your connections. Also, you must constantly be respectful to your peers and those you command. You never know who may have the ear of an important uncle." Jiang smiled.

"Yes, sir, I have found it to be quite informative. And I have already made some useful contacts," Yao added.

"So, back to work at your squadron next week and the regular grind of a midgrade officer," Jiang noted. "At least, you get to fly. You can still have some fun."

"Yes, Admiral. But actually I have arranged to attend a reception Monday on an American aircraft carrier that will be in Hong Kong. It will be my first chance to see those I have been training to defeat in person."

"Good. Good!" Jiang said just as the young lady from earlier came up from behind and slipped her arm into his.

"I will see you tomorrow," he said, no longer paying attention to Yao.

Yao nodded and turned away, his own mind now racing. *China is rising to its rightful place in the world*, he thought. *The Americans are clearly in decline. Was that not what he had heard at every intelligence briefing he had attended over the past twelve years? It's clear that we have been dominating them in technology, trade, and now militarily. We have no reason not to take what is clearly ours!*

He left the reception, inwardly seething while outwardly projecting the vision of calmness. His anger issues had never gone away, but he was better at concealing them. He knew how to play the game.

4 DEPLOYMENT ALERT
Hurlburt Field, Florida

"**G**et ready," shouted the jumpmaster. It was the six-minute warning and the signal for everyone to stand up facing the open troop doors near the rear of the MC-130J Commando II.

Staff Sergeant Ronald Anglin was sixth in a stick of thirty-four lining up to jump. Sixteen on either side of the plane. It was the first of two planned proficiency jumps for the day.

"Stand up," yelled the jumpmaster.

Of the thirty-four jumpers, twelve were from his unit. He was a member of the elite 823rd RED HORSE Squadron based at Hurlburt Field in the panhandle of Florida. The RED HORSE acronym stood for Rapid Engineer Deployable Heavy Operational Repair Squadron Engineer. They were one of the Air Force's heavy-construction units. Their capabilities were quite similar to those of the more famous Navy Seabees. They were self-contained units with vehicles, heavy equipment, vehicle maintainers, equipment operators, carpenters, electricians, plumbers, cooks, medics, administrative staff, and small arms weapons. The Air Force advertised them as being a highly mobile, rapidly deployable, self-sufficient, civil engineering response force ready to build an air base from the ground up, including runways, hangars, barracks, and offices. All they needed were the building materials and supplies. RED HORSE added an airborne capability in 2003. With this capability, RED HORSE could rapidly deliver small, specialized teams and equipment packages by airdrop or air insertion to conduct expedient airfield repairs.

Parachuting was the part of his job SSgt Anglin particularly loved. It had been a pleasant surprise when he had learned that the Air Force needed airborne carpenters.

"Hook up," came the next command.

Anglin hooked the end of the parachute's static line onto the half-inch steel cable running the length of the plane just above his head.

"Check static lines."

He gave it a tug to make sure it was securely fastened.

"Check equipment."

He leaned first left, then right checking that the parachute and harness of the jumper in front of him was properly fastened and everything stowed away. Then he caught it.

"Your chest strap is twisted," he yelled into the ear of the jumper in front of him.

Anglin quickly unhooked, straightened, and refastened it, giving him the thumbs-up. Anglin was pleased to see that the jumpmaster had noticed the catch as he was coming down the line doing his own quick double-check of every jumper before heading back to an open door.

"Sound off for equipment check," shouted the jumpmaster.

The amber lights were now on next to the doors on either side of the rear fuselage.

"One minute," the jumpmaster shouted, holding up his right index finger as he saw the drop zone coming into view fifteen hundred feet below them.

As always, Anglin at this point could feel his pulse quicken and his breaths get just a bit faster and shallower. He was excited and anxious to get going.

"Stand by," the ten-second warning was shouted.

Moments later, Anglin saw the jumpmaster slap the first jumper on the back of his leg as he shouted, "*Go!*"

In a blur, he was moving forward and then was engulfed by the roar of the turboprop engines and the sudden blast of wind. He only had a sensation of falling for a few seconds before he felt the sudden crunching pressure of his leg straps with the opening shock of the parachute. He immediately looked up to check that he had a full canopy. It was reassuringly full and round.

The roar of the MC-130J rapidly faded into the distance, and he had about ninety seconds to enjoy a beautiful view of the Florida panhandle. He was coming down over a two-mile-long and quarter-mile-wide auxiliary airfield that they were using as a drop zone. Though it was early November, the view below was almost as green as summer with all the surrounding pine trees. Just five miles away, he could see the clear blue turquoise water of the Gulf of Mexico. He could hear the ruffling of his canopy and saw the other jumpers in a line all floating and swaying gently back and forth. SSgt Anglin always cherished these moments as a special quiet time. But it wasn't quiet for long.

"Woo Hoo!" shouted one of the other jumpers. "Oooooh, Yeah!" yelled another.

Anglin smiled as he heard them yelling and shouting with joy like little kids.

All too quickly, he was approaching the ground, and he assumed the proper position for his parachute landing fall. He hit the ground falling to his right side letting his leg, hip, and torso absorb the energy. He was immediately up and collapsing his parachute and bundling it up in his arms.

Within ten minutes, they were all lined up at a dark blue Air Force bus to get handed a second parachute for their next jump. The MC-130 had landed on the runway after they had all cleared the landing zone and was now waiting with its engines idling on the tarmac two hundred yards away.

Just before getting his chute Anglin noticed an Air Force van pull up near the front of the bus. Out stepped Master Sergeant Riley from his unit. *This is odd*, he thought. They were all supposed to ride back to the RED HORSE compound on Hurlburt in the bus after the second jump.

"RED HORSE," Riley shouted. "Over here."

All twelve complied.

"What's up, Master Sergeant?" asked Technical Sergeant Deshotel, the senior noncommissioned officer of the group.

"We've just received a deployment Warning Order," he stated matter-of-factly, as if it happened every day. "Everyone is being rounded up. You guys are the last we had to track down. We've got a brief at 0930 at the base theater, so hop in. Don't worry, I've already made arrangements for someone to put your jump gear away."

"Play time is over," Anglin heard someone mumble as they loaded into the van.

"So much for getting off early on a Friday afternoon," he heard another grumble.

"Damn!" he heard a third say behind him. "I've got tickets to the Saint's game in the Superdome this Sunday."

After five years in the Air Force, this wasn't Anglin's first big briefing or deployment. He had previously deployed to Afghanistan and the United Arab Emirates. He had also been to Honduras twice for training exercises. But each of those had been planned months in advance. This would be his first short-notice deployment.

As they pulled into the theater parking lot Anglin could see other Airmen wearing the distinctive RED HORSE red baseball caps heading for the entrance.

As they entered the foyer, they were met by administrative Airmen insisting that everyone, deposit any cellphones or any other electronic devices with them before entering.

"Classified briefing," one of them kept repeating.

"Any idea what's going on?" asked Anglin's friend and fellow carpenter, Senior Airman Harold Stringer.

"Nope, not a clue," he said honestly while settling into his seat.

Just after 0930, the auditorium was called to attention and in from the rear strode Colonel Terry Perry, RED HORSE Commander.

"Take your seats," he said before he got to the podium. "Ladies and gentlemen, this briefing is classified secret. Nothing you hear here is to be discussed with anyone outside this unit. Understood?" he said sternly. "Not your wives, husbands, girlfriends, boyfriends, cats, or dogs! All you can say is that you are deploying for an unknown period of time."

After pausing an uncomfortably long moment to let it sink in he continued.

"We have been alerted by Air Combat Command that we will be deploying in less than twenty-four hours," he continued. He paused another moment to let the news sink in and for the expected murmuring to subside.

"We're being called upon to do exactly what we have been created and trained for. To build an operational base and airfield. But we will not be working alone on this one. We will be combining our capability with the Seabees, Naval Construction Battalions 3 and 14, from over in Gulfport Mississippi, and the 554th RED HORSE out of Guam. They all arrived at the staging location two days ago. We will be going without our heavy equipment and be sharing theirs which is already staged and ready to go. They decided just yesterday that they need extra manpower to augment the 554th because this will be a 24-7 operation once we arrive. This mission has high visibility and been personally approved by POTUS. I know that this will be tough on your families because of the holidays, but this is what we trained for, and we go when called. We don't know how long we'll be gone, so don't make any summer plans. Not all will be going. About twenty five percent will be staying behind for various reasons, pending transfers, medical issues, or other admin reasons. This afternoon, those few staying behind will get started packing and palletizing the gear we are taking, while the rest of you head home to pack. We need you all back here by 1830. We expect to be loaded and airborne on two C-17s by midnight tonight if all goes as planned," Col Perry explained. "Now listen up as Lieutenant Henry, our intel officer, fills in some of the details."

"Scarborough Shoal," began Henry as he stepped to the podium and clicked a remote control to show a picture of a triangular-shaped island on the screen behind him. This island is part of the Scarborough Shoal archipelago. This is the island where we will be building the runway and supporting infrastructure." Indicating a portion of the shoal with a green laser pointer.

"That's hardly an island," whispered Anglin to Stringer.

"If that were a pie, looks like only the outer crust is left and not much of that," Stringer replied.

"The Philippine government has long claimed ownership of this shoal, which is well within their territorial waters and only 125 nautical miles west of Luzon," Henry continued. "Their claim has been upheld in international court. The islands are also asserted by China to be within their territorial waters even though they are over four hundred miles away. As you know from the news, China has built three artificial islands further south in the South China Sea that are now essentially forward military bases that they are using to intimidate and dominate the area. There is strong suspicion that China has similar plans for Scarborough Shoal, ignoring the ruling from the court. Given their strong legal standing, the Philippine government has requested our help to block such a move by the Chinese. Though they have the capability to eventually build up the island, they can't do it quickly enough. They worry that the Chinese could and would interfere with their operations before they could establish a defensible position. This is why President DeSiard has agreed to send in the Seabees and RED HORSE," said Lt. Henry.

"Holy crap," Stringer whispered as Henry continued on with more details. "Where are they going to put all of us?"

"I suppose they have a plan," Anglin said absentmindedly. But he wasn't processing much else just now. He was trying to figure out how he was going to tell his wife, Kara, the news.

5 ADMIRAL'S BRIEF

USS *Vinson*, Western Pacific

The SMO arrived five minutes early to the brief. He took his usual seat on the second row behind the Chief of Staff. He was making small talk with the other staffers sitting with him when the Admiral's command chief stepped into the room.

"Attention on deck!" the command chief barked as Rear Admiral LaSalle stepped into the small conference room.

"At ease," he said while sitting down. "Take your seats."

Seated around the table was the core of the Admiral's staff.

"Okay, let's get right to it," LaSalle began. "Earlier today, we received a Top Secret message on an operation about to kick off. It doesn't involve our battle group directly, but is in our neighborhood, and could affect us depending on how things go."

The whole room was silent and attentive.

"Commander Monroe, please begin," the Admiral said to his Intelligence Officer.

The lights in the room dimmed, and a PowerPoint map of the South China Sea lit up the screened end of the room.

"It's called Operation SEAHORSE," Monroe began with his overview. "The Chinese have been actively claiming the larger portions of the South China Sea for the past decade as we are all well aware. They have pretty much locked down control of the Spratly Islands to the south." He identified the islands with his red laser pointer.

"As we know, they built artificial islands on three of the reefs there, all the while claiming that they would never be used for military purposes. And of course, all three are now heavily fortified and garrisoned with troops while continuing to ignore the ruling in international court against their claims," he explained. "There are squadrons of J-11 Flankers at both Fiery Cross Reef and Mischief Reef as well as surface to surface and surface to air batteries at all three."

"To the north," he continued, getting to the heart of the Operation. "Scarborough Shoal is claimed by both the Philippines and China. Over the past five years, the Chinese have been patrolling the area with their Navy and Coast Guard cutters. They frequently intimidate or directly drive off non-Chinese fishermen." The officially sanctioned harassment has resulted in several Filipino Sailors being seriously injured. There have been no official deaths, but two small Filipino fishing boats have gone missing along with their crews in the past two years."

"In 2016, the international court in The Hague officially dismissed China's blanket claim to the entire South China Sea and upheld the Philippine claims in the West Philippine Sea, including Scarborough Shoal. Our president has made it known publicly and in private conversations with China's president that we will support our Pacific allies, including the Philippines, and that he expects them to accept the ruling from The Hague.

"Philippine President Magdato intends to take control of the shoal and has asked for our help. President DeSiard has agreed to our assistance. We will be providing four heavy-construction units to assist, two Navy Seabee detachments and two Air Force RED HORSE squadrons. In four days, at noon of the Ninth the Filipino's plan to take possession of the shoal and drive away any Chinese vessels including the Coast Guard cutter that is currently patrolling the area," Monroe said pausing for effect. "After they have control, our units will arrive shortly thereafter and begin to assist with construction efforts. The plan is to build up the island similarly to what the Chinese have done in the Spratleys. The Filipinos have the capability, but not the ability to do it quickly. At least not before the Chinese could take action to thwart their efforts as they have done in the past."

"*SEAHORSE!*" the Admiral interrupted. "*SEAHORSE.* Who thinks these things up? Were they running out of names or what?" he asked to no one in particular.

"Well, it is primarily an operation composed of Seabees and RED HORSE construction units." Captain Tullos, the Chief of Staff, noted. "They might as well get some of the billing. It's actually a bit better than the self-righteous-sounding Operation JUST CAUSE."

"Sorry about that," the Admiral apologized. "Please continue."

Monroe switched to an overhead view of the shoal. "The Filipinos will be bringing in barges for dredging to build up the islands. Because there is already enough space for a five-thousand-foot runway, construction on that will begin almost immediately. At the same time, barracks, hangars, and support buildings will be started," he said pointing to the north end of the island. "Once they are able to have regular flights, the pace of the buildup will be able to speed up. Tentatively, we expect to be helping them with the construction for six to nine months."

"That's the big picture. This whole thing was put together rather quickly, and we just found out about it this morning," said the Admiral. "Questions?"

"Yes, what is the projected response from China?" asked Speedtrap. "They're sure to be royally pissed."

"Yes, they probably will be. Everyone expects that they will be upset but take no overt action. Publicly, they are expected to give the usual bluster and may increase their military readiness and activity but will not make any moves of consequence to retake the island," answered the Admiral.

"They have had success backing up their claims down south. Their confidence and belief in their cause and new capabilities may make them feel justified to retake the shoal." Monroe countered.

"That is why we are taking our additional precautions. And we don't plan to be overconfident in our capabilities. The Chinese army and navy are real threats, and we need to be prepared to support our allies and be ready to respond if necessary," said the Admiral.

"Admiral," said Captain Tullos. "How will this affect our plans to pull into Hong Kong? Are we canceling the Hong Kong port visit? If the Chinese get wind of this and suspect our involvement, our ships would be totally at their mercy bottled up in their harbor. And they could arrest anyone ashore. We have almost seven thousand Sailors getting ready to hit the streets after six weeks at sea."

"I've already asked," the Admiral replied. "The Pentagon believes that canceling the port call could also alert the Chinese. Their suspicions would be aroused, and they may start looking for a reason and stumble on what is going on. So, we are to proceed as planned. Luckily, it is only a quick three-day port call instead of the usual four to five days."

"So, Admiral, we need to be ready in case this whole thing goes south," added Captain Deville, the planning officer. "We will have to have a contingency plan."

"You're reading my mind, Mike," the Admiral responded with a smile. "Sorry, but several of you will not get much, if any time ashore. I need options ready to execute based on the possible Chinese responses—from diplomatic objections to an all-out shooting war. Let's not get caught with our pants down on this one. So, Mike, I need you in plans to come up with some workable options. Speedtrap, I need you in operations to assist him. Commander Monroe, I need you to stay on top of this and keep abreast of how this thing plays out. And lastly, Commander Grayson, I need your communications team to stay on top of the latest message traffic."

"Shouldn't I stay back as well, Admiral?" Tullos asked.

"No, Jenna," he answered. "You and I have some scheduled social events we are expected to attend. We have to keep up appearances. Everyone will be back aboard by 2330 on the eighth, and we will be underway the next morning and back at sea at least eighty miles from there by the time SEAHORSE kicks off on the ninth."

Tullos nodded, going through the Admiral's schedule in her mind. The Admiral was scheduled for a tour of the Hong Kong naval station on the morning of the seventh followed by lunch with their senior leadership including two of Admiral rank. Lt Lucas, the Admiral's Flag Lieutenant, would be accompanying him along with Master Chief Goodpine. Then there was the reception at the American Club of Hong Kong that she and the Admiral would attend that evening along with about forty other senior officers from the various ships, she recalled.

"Sir, when should we brief the ship CO and the CAG on this?" she asked.

"The CAG and his staff are already up to speed on this. Jenna, I want you personally briefing the ship's CO and XO right after this. But impress on them to keep the number briefed to a minimum for now. I don't want to risk the rumor mill getting out of control before we pull in." Plans, Ops, Intel, bring your ship and Air Wing staff counterparts in on the planning," he said.

"Aye-aye, sir," they all replied smartly.

"Anything else," Admiral LaSalle asked, looking around the room until his eyes landed on the SMO.

"SMO, glad to see you here. As you heard, we are not expected to have any play in this one. Still, we could get drawn into it quickly if it gets ugly. As my Battle Group Surgeon, you need to make sure you and your department are prepared and ready to handle casualties," the Admiral stated.

"Yes, sir, Admiral," the SMO began. "We did a mass-casualty drill just ten days ago that I am pleased to say went very well. We have all our new corpsmen trained and up to speed and ready to respond at a moment's notice. And we are fully topped off on all our required medical supplies plus some extra I was able to scrounge before we left."

"Excellent, SMO," responded the Admiral. "But remember, this is still top secret so don't be discussing it with anyone not cleared."

"Yes, sir," answered the SMO.

"Anyone else?" the Admiral asked. He saw nothing but heads shaking no. "All right, ladies and gentlemen. Let's stay on top of this as it unfolds and hope for the best and plan for the worst. That's all. Carry on."

6 DEPARTURE PREPARATION
Hurlburt Field, Florida

"He's at it again!" SRA Stringer exclaimed shaking his head as they were walking across the RED HORSE compound loaded down with their personal gear bags.

"What?" SSgt Anglin asked. "Who's doing what?"

"Technical Sergeant (TSgt) John Larto." He started. "He's chatting up that new Airman working the Admin office reception desk. AMN Sandra Eden. She transferred here last month."

"Oh, the pretty blond with the, umm, impressive figure?" Anglin said.

"Yeah. That's her," Stringer said with a grin.

"Well, it's not the first time. I saw him lingering at her station as we processed through the deployment line earlier," Anglin added. "Wasn't she issuing helmets and web gear? Anyway, I saw him talking and joking with her well after he had signed for all his gear."

"I sure hope someone warned her," Stringer lamented.

"Probably not. Either way, she seemed to be enjoying the attention," Anglin noted.

"How does he get away with it?" Stringer asked.

"He's careful. He gets away with it because he never actually follows through on making a move on any active duty women, at least not anymore. He does all his fooling around with ladies he meets at the beach or night clubs," Anglin explained. "I think he is just flirting with her and working on his game."

"It's still wrong. If he gets caught, can't he be court martialed for adultery?" Stringer asked.

"I think so. But if they started going after folks hard on this issue, they would be court martialing half the service. I think they charge someone with it if it comes up as part of some other offenses, or it was really egregious," Anglin speculated. "Plus, leadership loves him. He is our best heavy equipment operator and a solid shop supervisor. As long as he doesn't officially cross the line, they try to ignore what he does on his own time. With our constant training on sexual harassment he has learned to be careful. He just flirts with them and back's off if they aren't interested. But that's not the worst part of it. His poor wife is stuck at home taking care of a son with cerebral palsy plus two other normal kids. He is out partying and rarely spends much time at home. My wife says she has no life outside her family and is miserable most of the time."

"How is he on deployment?" Stringer asked.

"Well, there have been rumors that he once had a thing going with one of our married SSgt medics several years ago. It was a seven month deployment where we worked on two huge hangers. Anyway, we were deployed to upgrade a base in the UAE. We had a clinic but no dental care. Larto broke a tooth, so he was taken downtown where they had an American expatriate who had a clinic in Abu Dhabi. It seems that his tooth issue required multiple trips into town to be fixed. They tried to repair it but ended up doing a crown or something, at least that's the story we were told by the medics who had to drive folks to all off-base appointments. These two had been seen flirting and spending a lot of time together for quite a while before this. And though we had two medics she always ended up being the one taking him to his appointments. No one could prove anything, but the base was about 15 miles out in the desert and there were lots of sand dunes and lonely side roads going nowhere out there. And coincidently there was never anyone else that needed to go with them for other appointments and his appointment was always the last of the day so the usually got back after dark. Nothing was ever proven but those that knew him better were quite sure they were taking some side trips, to ahh, do more thorough physical exams."

"So, nothing was really known for sure then," Stringer concluded.

"Nope. But that medic transferred to another base six weeks after we got back. She had been in the unit for three years and it was her normal assignment rotation," Anglin said. "A year later when I was having lunch one day, I happened to be next to the other medic, SSgt Bushnell. We ended up talking about the rumors from the last deployment. He smiled and refused to confirm anything. But just before he transferred out he said he heard that she had a normal full term baby girl seven months after we got back. And she is now divorced."

"Damn, guys like that just leave chaos in their wake. It's all about them. The hell with how it affects anyone else," Stringer added.

"Well, the good news is that I hear AMN Eden isn't deploying on this one," Anglin said. "She's too new to the unit and we are taking only those with actual construction skills. I heard we will be using the admin staff from the 554th."

They soon arrived at the back of the warehouse where they were building up the pallets with their deployment gear and duffle bags.

"Hey, Anglin, get over here," said Master Sergeant David Winnfield. "You too, Stringer. I've got a job for you two. Get over to the armory. They need some help loading our weapons for the deployment."

"Yes, sir," they both said in unison as the dropped their duffel bags down next to the Airman carefully stacking them onto the last pallet being packed and netted.

They arrived at the unit's armory minutes later. It was in the rear third of one of their equipment maintenance buildings. Usually the only way in was through the front door that led to a caged foyer. The entrance had a large window on the left where they were issued their individual weapons whenever they had one of their recurring trips to the shooting range to keep up their marksmanship skills. Today the window was closed, and they had to knock on the inner door to get someone's attention.

After a minute, the door opened. "What do you want?" said a gruff voice from Staff Sergeant Urania. "We are busy here."

"We were told to report here to help," replied Anglin.

"Oh, okay. We could use some help," Urania said. "We are finishing up verifying the serial numbers of the M4s and packing them away in the shipping containers." The M4 is a shorter and lighter weight version of the venerable M16. "The pistols are complete. We could use you guys to help finish palletizing the ammo," Urania said, pointing to two other Airmen moving cases of 5.56 and 9mm ammunition.

They both were soon lugging the heavy ammo cases over to the large aluminum pallet that already had cases carefully stacked two rows high.

"Did you take weapons on your last deployment?" Stringer asked.

"No," Anglin said. "We did take them on my first to Afghanistan. We kept them with us everywhere we went, but we never needed to use them. We were constructing some buildings in the relatively friendly area in the north part of the country."

"Are you any better shooting it?" asked Stringer. "I just barely qualified last time. They say I need to work on my breathing. But to be honest, I think I fired the last ten rounds at the guy's target next to mine."

"A little better. I was three points short of scoring expert last time," Anglin answered. "I do love this weapon though. One day I hope to get one. There is this sweet Bushmaster AR15 over at the Eglin BX that I check out every time we are shopping over there. I really want to get it, but it costs almost a thousand dollars. And that was on sale! No way I can afford something like that on what a Staff Sergeant makes. Especially the way my wife, Kara, spends money. She loves to shop and can find the most fantastic deals. She finds beautiful clothes at seventy to eighty percent off sometimes. But no matter how good the deal, some months she spends way more than we bring in. Then it's peanut-butter-and-jelly sandwiches for a few months until we catch up on the credit card payments. I don't know how we will afford all the expenses related to a baby. We have been trying to have one the past six months. It has already sparked her baby-shopping nerve. Baby clothes, baby diapers, baby furniture, baby toys. I have successfully limited the actual spending, but she is constantly looking for deals and ideas. I'm really worried what she may do while I'm away this time. When I got back from the last deployment, she had a closet full of new clothes and shoes, many still with the labels on them and over $3,000 in various credit card bills. She raved about the great savings she got, and all I could see were the bills rolling in. We have only gotten it down to $1,500 or so. So, no toys for me for quite a while."

"I guess I am a lucky man," Stringer began. "Carla is pretty frugal, and she made up a budget and keeps us pretty close to it. The downside is that she has me on a pretty small allowance. We can only afford a movie once a month or so as a special treat. We have no big credit card bills we can't pay off and only have the car payment as our biggest expense since we live on base. Our one extravagance is our Netflix subscription. And she has a part-time job that she can work from home that brings in a little extra money. It's enough to keep us out of debt and able to take care of our kids."

"If only Kara could cut back for a while," Anglin mused aloud.

"Well, she may be expensive to keep, but you have to admit that you have the prettiest wife in the squadron, if not the whole base," Stringer added, trying to turn the topic to something more positive. "Everyone was staring at you two at the squadron picnic this past August. And trust me: they were not looking at you, dude."

Anglin surprisingly was only able to grimace a bit at that painful memory with his wife.

"You ever think we will have to use these weapons?" Stringer asked.

"Not likely. We will be on an isolated island relatively near a friendly country. And the Filipino's are supposed to be bringing a security force. So, we will just be focused on building that base," Anglin said. "Though, one RED HORSE unit did come under fire in southern Afghanistan. Their base was shelled, and there was small arms fire into the compound. Several were injured, but none were RED HORSE, and they never fired back. They just hunkered down in their shelters until the Army drove them off."

"I hope your right. I'm far better with a nail gun than a real gun," Stringer said as he set down the last ammo box on the pallet.

"Thanks for the help, guys. We'll take it from here," said Urania as they started to put on the pallet netting to hold the ammo boxes securely in place. "You guys have about ninety minutes before we all have to be back for the bus ride over to the PAX Terminal. Most folks are headed over to the BX and Commissary before they close to grab last-minute supplies and snacks for the trip. Thanks again."

"Let's go," said Stringer. "I need to stock up on some teriyaki beef jerky. I love that stuff."

Just before getting to Stringer's car Anglin again heard his name called. Turning to the sound, he saw his shop supervisor Technical Sergeant Darrel Nickel waving him over to the entrance to the structures shop. Standing next to him was Staff Sergeant Burnham, the unit's senior medic.

"Hey, I'll have to catch you later," Anglin said to Stringer as he headed toward his boss.

As he joined the two, Nickel said, "Sergeant Burnham heard that you may have some medical training. Is that true?"

"Yes, sir, some. As a senior in high school, they offered the chance to take the Emergency Medical Technician course," Anglin began. "I even took the test and was nationally certified. But I never did anything much with it. I joined the Air Force and wanted to build things. I mostly took it because I was pushed to by my dad. He said medical first aid skills are invaluable. He once came upon a car wreck years ago, and no one there had a clue what to do. He went on for years about how helpless he had felt and that I should take every chance I had to get some first aid training so it wouldn't happen to me. When he was going over the course options for my senior year, my fate was sealed. I was going to get EMT training. But my certification has lapsed, and all I have had recently is the first aid training we have all had to complete."

"Good, good. That's okay," said Burnham. "You have more medical training than most of the others around here. I want to have you as sort of a backup medic if things get busy. We don't expect anything more than the usual minor complaints and some cuts and scrapes. Still I want you to be available to assist if needed. Can we count on you?"

"Sure, I guess so. Just let me know if and when you need help," Anglin answered.

"Thanks. and if we need you it may be pretty obvious," Burnham said.

7   ANOTHER DAY AT SEA
USS *Vinson*, Philippine Sea

As he climbed up to his favorite gym on the O-2 level, the SMO was glad he could get a workout in today. It had been another remarkably busy day at sea, he reflected as he recalled the day's events. Up at 0600, a quick breakfast, then off to the morning medical department muster and announcements at 0700, followed by a brief department officer meeting in his office. Then he had to hot-foot it up to the Captain's morning meeting by 0730. Captain Whitehall got the latest update on an ongoing electrical problem in the reactor spaces. Then he emphasized his expectations and what he wanted passed on to the crew for the upcoming port visit. He wasn't going to accept any poor behavior by his Sailors. Going around the room, each HOD gave updates, and the SMO had discussed the head-injury-patient evacuation plans.

By 0830 he was back in his office for the first of three Radiation Health physicals. As he later stepped out to leave his office, he found himself *again* blocked by someone in front of Lieutenant Commander Alverez's open office door. He smiled as he realized that it was the Assistant First Lieutenant (AFL) standing in the passageway and likely again making a move on Alverez. The AFL found an excuse two to three times a day to stop by to "chat" with Alverez. It was obvious to everyone that he was sweet on her. And he was pressing hard as the Hong Kong visit was getting closer. He was never subtle in his approach.

"Think of the money we can both save," he was saying.

"Yeah, right, saving money," he heard Alverez chuckle.

"Excuse me, AFL, the SMO interrupted.

"Oh, hey, SMO," said AFL. "Think about it, Marty." He turned to leave. "I'll check back with you later."

"Is the evacuation paperwork ready to sign?" the SMO asked Alverez.

"Almost. Just waiting on some final details from Kadena," she replied. "I have to make sure we are using the proper message format for the Seventh Fleet Surgeon. This is our first medevac with them."

"Okay, get it right. Call me as soon as it's ready to sign," he said as he waved the brick in his left hand. "Hey, saving money sounds good to me. So, what's so funny?"

"By sharing a hotel room, with AFL. No, thanks!" she said incredulously. "He's nice, but I'm not that hard up. Not yet anyway. Besides, he's just looking for a 'Boat Boo,' nothing serious. He wants to get laid like about ninety percent of the Sailors on this ship and hopes to avoid paying for it."

The SMO smiled and shook his head incredulously. "He never gives up. Gotta give him points for persistence."

"Hey, SMO," Alverez said, changing the subject, "while you were in with your physicals, the XO dropped by and asked the strangest question. He wanted to know how many body bags we had in storage and where they were located. I checked and told him we had 250, and he asked if that was enough. What the hell is going on? Is he expecting World War III or something? Are the Iranians really going to attack a carrier going into the Persian Gulf this time? They've been threatening to for decades now."

"No I haven't heard anything about the Iranians we haven't heard before," he answered honestly.

Still, it got him thinking. He had already doubled the planned medical scenarios for the next GQ drill in order to keep the ship's crew and his corpsmen sharp just in case. Was the XO seriously worried we could really be drawn into an actual shooting war? Body bags? God forbid.

After lunch, he went into student mode. He was working on earning his Surface Warfare Medical Department Officer badge. He was determined to get a third warfare badge, after his SEAL Trident and Flight Surgeon's wings. He wanted to have one for under the water, above the water, and now, on the water. Today he was learning about replenishment-at-sea procedures. But today was unique for two reasons. The first was the unusually heavy seas the *Vinson* was plowing through. Even this mighty ship was noticeably rolling to port and starboard.

Second, this was going to be the first time the SMO had seen his ship giving fuel rather than taking it. He headed up to station number twenty-one, where the *Vinson* can pump fuel to other ships. What should have taken an hour took much longer. It was quite a show watching the smaller ships bounce around and crash into the huge waves. Their bows often buried and disappeared into a wave. Watching those ships pitching and rolling made the SMO really appreciate being on a large relatively stable ship like a carrier. They had a variety of problems getting hooked up. Shot lines were missed; the ships had trouble staying in position alongside, and they kept losing the hose connections. The USS *Bunker Hill (CG-52)* went first and had the most trouble but was eventually successful in getting the fuel needed after multiple approaches and attempts. The USS *Spruance (DDG-111)* and USS *Chaffee (DDG-90)* were also successful.

Back in the office, the SMO had an American Red Cross message on a deck department Sailor's wife. She was staying with her family in Knoxville, Tennessee, while he is deployed. The message read:

> **Wife was involved in a motor vehicle accident. The diagnosis is subdural hematoma with altered consciousness. Prognosis is guarded. Current condition is stable following surgery, wife is immobile, confused, currently in ICU, and cannot care for children or make decisions. Life expectancy is not an issue, and husband's presence is recommended. Wife may be hospitalized for at least another two weeks, and Dr wishes wife to stay in Knoxville near hospital after discharge for her recovery, for about two weeks.**

While reading about the car wreck, he subconsciously reached into his left pants pocket and pulled out the coin. He almost always had it with him. Ever since that horrible day long ago. It had been back in Jacksonville, Florida, in April 1996.

"And you want…to be…a Navy SEAL," Derek Lloyd had teased his brother while panting.

His brother Dustin had just reached the end of the adjacent lane and collapsed onto the edge of the pool. They had just finished a five-hundred-yard swim. As always, Derek had smoked his older brother, this time by a good thirty seconds. Dustin was his older brother, but by only a few minutes. They were fraternal twins and didn't look anything alike.

"You know that a lot of what they do is in the water, don't you?" Derek asked. "At least, you're improving. You made it in eight minutes flat, ten seconds faster than last time.

"I'll get there," he said, taking in huge gulps of air. "Only been nine months…since I started really training. Better than the 12:25 I started with. And that was just under their minimum. And I can still kick your ass on the run and pull-ups. Besides, I've got the four years of college to get my times way better than the SEAL entry standards."

"Well, I won't have to meet these crazy fitness standards to fly," Derek said.

"True, I'm surprised they have any standards at all for a sit-down job," Dustin jabbed back.

The brothers had been competing from day one, at first for their mom's attention and milk. Though twins, they were quite different. Dustin had sandy-blond hair and was heavier built at 180 pounds and an inch taller than his five-eleven younger brother. Derek was lean and had chestnut-brown hair. They had participated in the usual sports as kids and had both participated in football, baseball, and track through high school. In football, Derek had been a wide receiver and gotten all the glory scoring several touchdowns. His heavier brother had played center on offense and middle linebacker on defense. In baseball, Dustin had the edge in home runs and stolen bases. Dustin was also on his school's cross-country team. He was never the fastest but always in the top five. Derek was a sprinter and ran the 440 and 880 in track and had several wins.

Though neither had time to compete in swimming, both were excellent swimmers. They had practically grown up in the water. Their dad worked full time as a civil servant at Mayport Naval Station in Jacksonville, Florida. In his younger days, he had enlisted in the Navy and been a hardhat diver. He had spent most of his time in the Navy Mark V dive suit and the lighter weight Desco full face mask. His Navy diving career ended with an accident that left him unable to walk in the three-hundred-pound Mark V gear as required to get into and out of the water.

On weekends, the elder Lloyd supplemented his family's income by running a charter boat for deep-sea fishermen and scuba-diving groups. During slow times in the course of the fishing and diving seasons, he would be out chasing the dream of discovering sunken treasure. His boys and their mother had gone with him on these treasure hunting trips since they were in grade school. Their mom would make a picnic of it, always packing a huge cooler full of sandwiches and snacks. The boys had been diving with him since age eleven. As teenagers, both Dustin and Derek became adept at operating and maintaining the thirty-two-foot boat, though not always by choice. They had frequently rebelled with anything having to do with the charter operation after hitting fourteen. But they had complied after various forms of coercion. Typically, once out on the sea they forgot their objections. On a treasure hunting dive a year earlier just off the coast of St Augustine, Dustin had found a suspicious clump. He almost tossed it aside but since he hadn't seen anything else of interest he kept it. Once cleaned, it turned out to be a Spanish piece of eight in fair condition from 1580. Dustin loved it, and more importantly, his "little" brother didn't have one. Dustin took to carrying it with him almost everywhere. He said it was his good luck charm.

"True, bro, but I will be happy flying a plane and coming back to a nice hot meal and comfortable bed," Derek said as he hopped out of the pool. "You feel free to jump out of one and crawl around in the cold muck so you can feed the ticks and mosquitos."

Dustin followed, and they headed to the nearby chaise lounge where they grabbed their towels and clothes.

Cling! they both heard.

"Bro, why do you carry that thing around?" asked Derek. "You're gonna lose it one day. Either lost or stolen."

"It's my good luck. I was lucky to find it," Dustin replied. "And so far, so good."

"Well, maybe you should swim with it next time," Derek suggested.

"Mm, you're probably right," Dustin said.

"You're gonna swim with it?" he asked. "Seriously!"

"Naww. I better keep it safe and quit showing it around," he concluded. "Besides, it hasn't gotten me any hot dates yet."

"Good idea, bro," said Derek as they headed to their dad's old 1986 Ford pickup truck.

A week later, Derek's world was turned upside down.

He got a frantic call from his mother while visiting at his girlfriend's house.

An hour later he was at the side of an ICU bed at University Medical center. His brother Dustin had been T-boned at an intersection on Beach Boulevard by a speeding driver trying to flee the police. Though he was wearing his seat belt, Dustin had a severe head injury and was in a coma. His brain was swelling, and the doctors were doing all they could to stop it. A battle they would eventually loose. Eighteen hours later, he was declared brain-dead, and his parents made the agonizing choice to stop life support and to donate his organs.

Returning home numb after the funeral, Derek had entered his brother's bedroom for the first time since the accident. There, on his small desk, in a place of honor next to his prized sports trophies was the piece of eight.

He stood there frozen. *He didn't have his lucky coin with him!* he thought, his mind screaming. *He didn't have it with him, because I told him not to.* Could it have made a difference? His logical side said no, but his emotional side wasn't so sure. Still, somehow he felt guilty. Maybe the coin would have made a difference. Maybe the amount of time it took to get the coin and slip it into his pocket would have delayed him just enough to avoid the accident. He couldn't bear to think about it.

He didn't hear his dad come in behind him. He saw Derek staring at the coin.

"He would have wanted you to have it," his dad said as he picked it up and handed it to him.

"I...I...I can't," he whispered, his dad not understanding Derek's meaning.

"Sure, you can. It was special to him," he said. "And so were you. The pain of his loss will always be with us, but this coin...this coin will always remind us of him and who he was and wanted to be."

Derek nodded with tears welling up in his eyes.

"Son, this is a rough time for us all, especially your mother. You still have a full life ahead of you, and there will be tough times to face. You two were always able to master the hardest challenges when competing against each other. So, when things get tough, let this coin remind you that Dustin is still in there competing," he said. "Let this coin and Dustin motivate you when you're having a rough time and want to quit."

Derek continued to nod taking it in.

He held the coin in his open palm staring at it. This coin will have to be for the both of them, he thought as his mind raced.

Dustin was chasing the dream of being a Navy SEAL. While Derek had once seriously thought of becoming a SEAL, his childhood dream to fly fighter jets had been his total focus for years. *Dustin will never see his dream come true*, he thought. *But maybe...I can do it for him. For the both of us.*

From that moment on, Derek abandoned his own dream and focused on getting ready for SEAL training. After getting a college degree, that was. His father's insistence and personal history had shown that you always have to have backup options. An electrical engineering degree would be his.

The SMO spent over an hour, calling back to the hospital in Knoxville, half the time trying to convince them of who he was, then getting bounced around ultimately to the floor-charge nurse. No doctors were around at that time of night. Ship time was twelve hours ahead of US Eastern time, so it was the middle of the night there. He confirmed the diagnosis and prognosis and found out that she was doing better. He then relayed the info to the Sailor and his chain of command up to the XO. The SMO recommended that the Sailor be allowed to go home.

After moving a stack of paperwork from his inbox to his outbox, he checked his watch and realized he had just enough time to get in a good workout before the XO's daily 1700 meeting.

He finished three miles on the treadmill at a fast walk, unfortunately all he could manage these days. Surprisingly, he could go forever on the stair climber. The SMO was forty minutes into his cardio workout when Captain Tullos came in. Their eyes immediately locked as she came around to stand in front of him. He was soaked and sweat was raining off his forehead.

"Hey Jenna," he said, grabbing the sweat towel and wiping his face and neck.

She watched his every move. "Can't say you're not breaking a sweat," she said with a half smile. "I thought you SEALs were supposed to be cool and not break a sweat over something as trivial as exercise."

"Well, back when I was a younger SEAL, I didn't," he delivered straight-faced. "But that was a lifetime ago." He let a smile creep in.

"You been here long?" she asked.

"Not too long. I have another ten minutes before I have to get showered," he said.

She nodded. "Well, enjoy," she said, flashing a seductive smile.

"OK," he said, stretching out the vowel sound, a bit perplexed and wondering what she'd meant by that. *You usually don't tell someone to enjoy a workout, at least not the way she said it*, he thought as he let his eyes feast on her tight-fitting shorts and sleeveless T-shirt as she turned away.

It was a surprisingly slow time in the gym, and only half of the treadmills scattered around the deck were being used. So she chose the one directly in front of him only four feet away. Glancing back at him, she took off her T-shirt, revealing a sports bra that matched her shorts, and she began to run with long regular strides.

Oh my God! he thought trying to keep his mouth closed. He was immediately mesmerized by her slim curvy contours and graceful movements. *Yep, pure poetry in motion for sure*, he thought. Mm, mm, mm! He was most definitely enjoying what he saw.

"SMO, Alverez!" the brick in the cup holder barked.

Are you kidding me? the SMO thought.

Yanked out of his fantasy daydream, he asked, "What's up, Alverez?"

"Are you near medical?" she asked.

"Nope, O-2 gym," he replied.

"Give me a call when you get a minute," she said.

"Stand by," he said, stepping down and throwing the towel around his neck.

Sneaking one last glance at Jenna's tight ass, he headed to the phone by the door.

He dialed and heard the ringing.

"What's up?" he immediately asked.

"SMO, we have a problem. The neurosurgeon in Kadena just had to take emergency leave. Our next best option is now the Medical Center at Yakota Air Base in Tokyo. The problem is that it is beyond the C-2's range. They would have to stop for gas in Kadena and the whole trip would take over seven hours. We need to know if that is okay?"

The SMO was silent a few moments. The C-2 cruises at 250–300 knots, and a jet is twice that, he calculated as he mulled his options, including International SOS. They have aircraft on standby around the world ready with critical care medical crews to provide international air ambulance services when needed. The US Navy as well as the Air Force use them to augment their own air evacuation systems.

"What's the patient's status?" he asked.

Hold on she said, handing the phone to Lieutenant Commander Sandaal, the general surgeon.

"SMO, he's bouncing between Glasgow coma scale of thirteen and fourteen, and he is still running a low-grade fever," he said. "He really hasn't improved any. I want to get him evaluated as soon as possible."

"Copy. We will fly him off as soon as we are in helo range of an airport that can accommodate small jets," he said. "Put Alverez back on."

"Yes, SMO," Alverez said, back on the line.

"Call International SOS. They may be able to get him there faster in one of their air ambulances," the SMO said.

"And tell them we want a critical care nurse on this one," he added.

"Have the surgeon keep me updated," he finished.

"I'm on it, SMO," she said.

Hanging up the phone, the SMO took a moment to update Jenna on the situation.

"Copy. I'll update the Admiral as soon as I get back to my office," she replied. "Is he going to be all right? That is what he really wants to know."

"Hopefully, but that depends on what is actually going on. We just don't have the means to rule out a brain bleed, and he isn't bad enough for us to consider a procedure to relieve any suspected pressure. We've been monitoring him closely until we can get him to a CT. So bottom line, I can't say for sure," the SMO answered.

"Well, I gotta go. I have a meeting is in twenty-five minutes. I need to update everyone else that has a need to know. Enjoy the rest of your workout. And thanks, I did indeed enjoy it!" Derek said, smiling.

She nodded and then, switching modes from official to unofficial, said, "Don't hesitate to let me know if you need anything," she added with a barely perceptible smirk.

"I was just about to, before that brick went off," he said, looking deeply into her eyes.

"Well, good for the brick. At least, it got off," she added.

"Two more days, Jenna. Two more days," he said, letting his eyes linger on her smiling face and figure. Should he or shouldn't he, he pondered as the image of his ex-wife and kids happy around the breakfast table flashed in his memory. His gut began churning with angst as he headed to his stateroom.

8 FLIGHT HOME
Eastern China

Lieutenant Commander Yao loved the thrill he felt every time he slammed his fighter's powerful engines into afterburner. He was thrust back into his seat as the J-15 Flying Shark roared down the runway. As the plane reached liftoff speed, he eased back on the control stick and almost immediately pushed it back down slightly. He had lifted off the ground only a meter and leveled off while raising the landing gear. He was doing a risky but always impressive low transition, letting the jet continue to rapidly accelerate until reaching the end of the runway only feet above the ground. He then pulled hard on the stick until he was completely vertical and shot into the sky like a rocket. Only when reaching cruising altitude did he pull back on the throttles. He reluctantly slowed down so that his less adventurous wingman could catch up.

Once rejoined, he pushed his throttle back up to near-full military power. The flight back to his home base after the conference would take just shy of an hour, and he had plenty of fuel to spare, so why not go fast, he was not paying for the fuel. He just had to keep it subsonic, to not rattle any windows below. He engaged the autopilot and let his mind drift back over what he had learned over the past few days.

The conference had been quite an eye-opening experience for him. Though this conference was primarily for the most senior leadership, Yao felt comfortable because there were plenty of other field-grade officers (O4s and O5s) around. Until it was pointed out later, he had not realized that only he and one Army Major were wearing the green ID tags signifying that they were actually allowed to attend the various intelligence and strategy sessions as full participants. All of the other O4s and O5s were only there as aids to their bosses.

Importantly, he had learned of the divide between the senior leaders. There was clearly a vocal group that was aggressive and wanting China to assert its growing dominance more forcibly. But regretfully, they were outnumbered by the cautious or outright timid officers, which Yao had been dismayed and angered by. They are too comfortable with the status quo and their cozy lifestyles. They are just too risk averse to do anything that could topple their apple carts, he reasoned.

Yao had met many influential officers. He had assumed that all the senior officers would have ignored him. That's what he would have done in their position. But no. They had actually engaged him in conversation, and a couple actually asked his opinion on issues. Once he was able to speak with firsthand knowledge on how the Spratly Island operation had unfolded. Another time, they talked on the readiness of the naval air arm from a junior officer's perspective. They appeared to actually listen and consider his answers. Yao learned why later during a break when he had a chance to talk to the only other O4 field grade officer actually participating in the strategy sessions.

"Hello commander, I'm Major Zhou," he had said on the second day of the conference, reaching to shake Yao's hand.

"I'm Yao, pleased to meet you," he replied.

"This is quite the conference don't you agree," Zhou commented.

"It is," Yao answered.

"Have you noticed that we are the most junior officers in these meetings?" Zhou asked.

"That's right, now that you mention it," Yao answered. "I have been so fascinated by it all I hadn't noticed. I have been to other conferences before, but at those, only one or two generals or admirals would be present, and the rest were primarily junior officers. Here it is mostly generals, admirals, senior colonels and navy captains."

"Yes that's true," Zhou agreed. "And you haven't seen but a handful of army lieutenant colonels or navy commanders in the meetings either."

"I guess I hadn't noticed because I have been brought into many of the discussions after the presentations. It was much like other conferences I have been to in that respect," Yao noted.

"You know why don't you?" Zhou had asked.

"No," Yao answered honestly.

"Let me guess. You were invited here by a very senior officer," Zhou had said.

"That's correct," Yao answered mildly surprised.

"I was invited by my father. Major General Zhou," Zhou said. "You see, only the junior O-4s and O-5s with connections are invited to these senior level meetings. And everyone knows this. Since they do not want to anger our benefactors, they are careful to be nice to us. We have connections many of them do not have. One negative word from me to my father and an Army colonel could find himself guarding a Uighur reeducation camp in western Mongolia. We are special my new friend. So make the best of it. Excuse me," Zhou had said as he moved off to chat with an army colonel he recognized.

"Mako 34, you have crossing traffic at two o'clock, three hundred meters below you," an air traffic controller called snapping him back to the present.

"Mako 34 looking," Yao answered. He spoke again as he spotted the commercial airliner leaving a contrail as it was heading west. "Tally." It was just crossing the coast and appeared to be coming from Taiwan. It would cross safely below them.

At this altitude, he could see the coast of Taiwan with its proudly defiant people. They had yet to be reintegrated under communist rule. Soon. Maybe soon, he considered hopefully. And they can probably put those Uighur reeducation camps to even better use once the Taiwanese fall under our control, he mused, smiling to himself.

Thoughts of Taiwan reminded him of the discussion he had overheard between Admiral Kao and his uncle, Admiral Jiang. So he wondered, what is going on with Scarborough Shoal. He had been planning part of the air support for Operation MACKEREL. It was to follow along similarly to the earlier Operation WHIRLWIND. But this one was to be more defensive in nature. There would be no Filipinos to frighten off this time. No, they were to be ready with a massive air response if either they or their American friends tried to take it back before they were firmly established there with troops and air defenses. The Chinese have had plans to develop Scarborough Shoal for years and had so far successfully bullied the Philippines into backing down. Even Philippine senior leaders had been heard in private conversations say that they saw controlling the shoal as a lost cause. So, why was President Hsu putting it on hold? It was China's for the taking. The Philippines had essentially conceded it already, just like the Spratly Islands had been. What is going on? China needed unfettered and sole access to those plentiful fishing grounds. Because this claim on Scarborough Shoal was not about pride or having a forward military base. It was about over a billion mouths to feed.

Yao was still basking in the glow of his new special status as his jet continued south along the eastern coast of China. After a forty-five-minute flight, he touched down gently and held his nose up in a high flare letting the air resistance help slow him down. The nose slowly lowered, and he gently braked before turning onto the taxiway.

As he was directed into his assigned parking ramp by the crew chief, he noticed that standing off to the side was a young female mechanic with wheel chocks. She was ready to put them around the main gear tires once the fighter was parked in place. He had noticed her before a few times. Today she was one of the few assigned to the weekend transient crew responsible to park and fuel any aircraft that were flying on the weekend. The crew chief signaled to stop, and Yao turned his attention back to the female mechanic in her work coveralls as she rushed under the wing to chock his wheels. He was smiling with an idea as he shut off the engines and opened the canopy.

A moment later, his wingman pulled into the parking spot to his right. While on his walk-around, he glimpsed the young female as she opened up a panel on the fuselage so that she could take an engine oil sample. Because of her short stature, she had to really reach up to unlatch the panel, which caused her loose-fitting overalls to pull tightly across her ample chest. Five minutes after a quick postflight check of his plane was complete, Yao and his wingman, Lieutenant Junior Grade Gan Hu, were headed to maintenance debrief in the hanger.

"Gan, it's pretty warm for a November, don't you think?" Yao asked Hu.

"Maybe, seems pretty normal to me," Hu said, not knowing where his senior officer was going with this.

"Feels more hot to me," Yao added as he stopped and turned back toward their aircraft. "See that mechanic working on your plane now, taking the oil samples? He has stripped down to his T-shirt and tied the coverall's sleeves around his waist."

"Okay," Hu answered, really wondering what this had to do with anything.

"You see that pretty little mechanic working on my jet?" Yao asked. "I think she should be as hot and uncomfortable as that guy is," he said, turning back toward the hanger.

"I suppose, if you say so sir," Hu answered.

They continued walking on a bit before Yao continued. "You know, Gan. I bet that in order to stay cool that she's not wearing a T-shirt or a bra under that coverall," he said with a grin.

"But she is required to wear both by regulation," Hu added. "Our mechanics are carefully screened, and only the best and most disciplined are allowed to work on our aircraft. They follow all the rules, or they will face severe punishment."

"You are correct about that," Yao answered.

"Besides, we will never know," Hu replied.

"Maybe, maybe not," Yao suggested. "Gan, I'll bet you a steak dinner that she is not wearing either a bra or a T-shirt."

"What, you want to have her strip here on the flight line?" Hu asked. "Then we will be the ones getting in trouble. Whether she is wearing one or not."

"There are ways, watch and learn," Yao replied.

Twenty minutes later, they had finished reporting the status of their aircraft to the maintenance debriefer, and they were back in the rear of the hanger. They both noticed that the weekend crew of six mechanics including the lone female were standing near the hanger's tool shop and chatting just twenty meters away.

"Stay here a minute," Yao said to Hu.

Yao walked into to the supervisor's office to his immediate right. After two minutes, he stepped out with a serious look on his face as the supervisor came rushing out behind him headed to the group. Yao's face then turned into a huge grin.

"Now watch," Yao said as he motioned Hu to follow him closer to the group not far behind the supervisor.

The supervisor walked straight up to the female, reached up, and tore open her coverall to the shock of everyone. She was not wearing a T-shirt as required, but she was wearing a bra. But her bra was not regulation. It was a sheer lacy one that left little to the imagination. The poor young lady was mortified and red-faced as she quickly closed her coverall. As all the other mechanics broke out into hysterical laughter, she turned and ran toward the female locker room with her supervisor hot on her heels, yelling about uniform regulations.

Both Yao and Hu exited the hanger grinning but not saying anything until after they were in the parking lot alone. Then Yao and Hu broke out into hysterical laughter.

"You owe me a steak dinner, Commander," Hu finally said with a satisfied smile. "She was wearing at least a bra, even if it wasn't regulation."

"Yep, I sure do," he said. "But it was definitely worth it. Did you not see the nice tits on that girl?"

"What did you say to the supervisor to get him to do that?" Hu had to know.

"I just told him that there was a rumor back in the squadron that the female mechanics were not adhering to uniform regulation in hot weather. And I suggested that the commanding officer may do a surprise inspection if he hears of it. The last supervisor got canned last year when the CO's plane had a tire with low air pressure. So his temper is known everywhere," Yao answered.

"That's all you said?" Hu asked. "And we only have two female mechanics in the whole Air Wing."

"That's all," Yao said with a self-satisfied smile as he opened his car door.

"You know, Commander, it was funny but a terribly mean thing to do," Hu said upon reflection. "We could get in trouble for it too. We are officers and should be better than that."

"You are probably right, Hu," Yao answered with the smile fading from his face. "My mother had always encouraged me to look for the best in everyone. It is something I strive for, but it is difficult. I have been fighting against rumors and attacks on our family name most of my life. It is so hard for me to not see everyone as a threat to be beaten back."

9 RED HORSE DEPLOYED

Subic Bay, Philippines

It was a long and tiring trip. The sun was up, and the light streaming through the few small C-17 windows stirred Staff Sergeant Anglin awake. His watch said it was breakfast time, yet his bio clock was telling him he should be eating supper. Either way, his stomach was grumbling, and he was hungry.

Even though they had left their heavy equipment behind, it had still taken two full C-17As to fly them to the Philippines. They had been traveling almost continuously for the past twenty hours. They had stopped for two and a half hours at Elmendorf AFB, Alaska, to refuel and swap out the air crew. The C-17s were flying with augmented crews. The spare pilots and copilots had spent most of the first flight asleep in the two bunk beds just behind the cockpit.

At Elmendorf, they had the chance to stretch their legs, hit the restroom, get something to eat, and for a few, to find the nearest designated smoking area.

Anglin had slept as best he could on the uncomfortable red canvas bench seats. He had traveled in relative comfort on his previous deployments on chartered air liners. This was by far the longest trip he had ever taken. He spent most of the trip grumbling and a bit pissed that no one had told him to bring his sleeping bag on the plane with him. His was packed away in a pallet he couldn't get to. It was obvious that he still had a few tricks to learn. Most of the older and more experienced Airmen had brought one, and a Master Sergeant had hooked up a net hammock. As the plane reached cruising altitude, they had popped their bags out and found nice places up on top of the pallets or back along the rear ramp.

Those guys were soon asleep and oblivious until landing at Elmendorf. The only advantage to him of them making their little cocoons was it freed up space for him to stretch out on the canvas seat. Although he could lie down, there was always some part of the metal frame poking into his back or legs.

When Technical Sergeant Deshotel passed by on his way to the toilet, Anglin had to ask. "Sarge, why didn't you guys tell us to have our sleeping bags out for the trip?" He gave a hang-dog look. "Mine's packed away and stuck in that pile of bags you've been sleeping on."

TSgt Deshotel was one of the characters of the unit. He was a gregarious, five foot six inch Cajun from Sulfur Louisiana. He was built like a fireplug. He was almost as wide as he was tall and all muscle. But the most striking feature about him was his hands. He had huge wide beefy hands. His fist was almost fifty percent larger than anyone else's in the squadron. At work he was always outgoing and helpful. He was the electrician shop supervisor but many of the younger Airman from throughout the unit sought his advice. However, he also had a darker side. He loved to party. When over indulging he became a really mean drunk. He had a long history of getting into bar fights up and down the Emerald Coast of Florida. He had been in trouble over it more than once. The fact that he had never thrown the first punch and could claim self-defense was really the only reason he still had his rank and a job in the Air Force.

Flashing a big gap-toothed grin, Deshotel responded, "Anglin, how many good sleeping places do you see in here? If you were able to get your sleeping bag right now, where would you put it?"

Anglin looked around and realized that there were no decent places left. There were in fact only about a dozen really choice locations to put one. "Well," he said searching around, "there's no place left."

"Exactly," Deshotel said, turning and continuing on his way.

So, SSgt Anglin thought, they were keeping this little tidbit of info to themselves he realized.

Well into their second flight, his friend Senior Airman Stringer sat up from another long nap, leaned over, and said, "You look worried, my friend. What's on your mind?"

"Nothing really," Anglin deflected. "I'm not sleeping well on this damn canvas seat. A problem I see you haven't had. You've been sacked out since we left Hurlburt, and on this same bloody uncomfortable seat. You take a sleeping pill or something?"

"Nope," Stringer said, glancing at his friend with a classic shit-eating grin, letting the silence play out.

Anglin cocked his head to the side with his eyebrows raised, waiting impatiently.

Stringer leaned forward taking a huge stretch with his arms out to either side.

"Come on, out with it, Harold," Anglin demanded.

Stringer just leaned back against the seat just smiling.

"Let's just say that I was really, *really* exhausted," he said, deadpan.

"Oh," said Anglin. "We did have quite a long day. After the brief, we rushed home to pack and get back by 1830. Then we sat around the air terminal until almost midnight before we boarded the plane. It was a long hectic day. And I don't know about you, but I had been up early for my quarterly proficiency parachute jumps."

"No," Stringer nodded aggressively. "Not that."

"What then?"

"It was my wife, Carla," Stringer said with a satisfied smile.

"You mean…" Anglin started.

"Yep," Harold said, cutting him off.

"Don't you two already have a couple of kids? Is she wanting more?" Anglin asked.

"No, that's not it. We only wanted two. She had her tubes tied after the last one." Harold explained. "No, she was worried the deployment would hurt our average."

"Your average?" Anglin had to ask.

Stringer leaned in close to whisper his answer. "You see, we have been holding a pretty good average since before we were engaged. We had our dating-and-honeymoon average. Then life kicked in, kids, work, school, and such. We have been holding a respectable married average these past few years. It's not like we are trying for some kind of record. It's just that as long as that is going well, the other aggravations of life are things we can tackle together. And we never stay mad at each other for very long."

Anglin just nodded.

"I came home and told her, 'Baby, we have a short-notice deployment, and we don't know how long we'll be gone.'"

"Did she get upset?" Anglin asked.

"She just stood there a minute, thinking. I could see the wheels turning in her brain," Stringer said. "Then she said, 'Harold you start getting packed. I'll be right back.' I started getting everything out of the closets and drawers. While I was doing that, she had gotten her neighbor friend to keep our two little ones. She came into the bedroom, stopped in front of me, and quietly let her dress drop to the floor and said, 'So, we can't let our average drop because of a silly deployment.' She helped me pack between, ah…'events,' and we had a pizza delivered for supper."

Staring slack-jawed, Anglin just nodded. "I have to ask. How ma—" he started.

"Four," Stringer answered before Ron could get the question out.

"Four times," Anglin repeated. "You were only home for like six hours. Okay then. That pretty well explains it." He drifted off into his own thoughts. His departure had been a bit different, and he tried to not think about it. He dozed as much as he could, but he found himself consumed with thoughts of his wife, Kara. She just didn't seem to notice how much he loved and worshiped her. But her ever-changing moods made things so unbearably difficult for them. It had not gone well after he had broken the deployment news to her. He hoped that her reaction was because she desperately wanted a baby boy. She had been obsessed with having one since they had been married two and a half years before. He wanted one too, but he had insisted on waiting until things were going better for them. Their marriage had turned rocky after only a month, and they had been close to a divorce a few times. He had relented, and they had stopped all forms of birth control. He was hoping a baby would be the missing piece to make their marriage what he had hoped it would be. Now he was deploying, and those plans were again on hold for her. So she didn't even have a baby to plan for as a diversion while he was away.

She'd lost it as soon as she'd heard the news. She hit the roof when he told her he couldn't tell her where he was going or for how long. As he feared, it only got worse from there.

"Did you volunteer to go?" she asked accusingly. "I bet you did!"

"No, Kara," he tried to say calmly. "I didn't. Almost the whole squadron is going."

"But you want to go!" she seethed. "I can see it in your eyes, Ron. You're excited about it."

"Well, maybe a little. This is what I have trained to do," he admitted. "But I am equally sad about having to leave you, especially since we're trying so hard to have a baby."

"No...no, that's not it," she spat out while shaking her head. "You're planning on going to a titty bar with your buddies and party. Aren't you, Ron!"

"*No!*" he said, his voice rising and wondering where the hell this was coming from. "I have no interest in those places. What's the point? Why go get all worked up over something you can't have? Those places are a waste of time and money. I already have the prettiest wife in Florida."

"Oh really, you expect me to believe that shit?" she said at almost a scream. "I know how they are. The dancing in front is just advertisement for what's available in back. You can get all worked up and go do something about it. And who's to know?"

"*Kara!*" he answered, his voice rising. How could she think any woman could compare to her in his eyes?

"What happens on deployment stays on deployment," she added angrily, parroting the timeworn cliché. "Isn't that right, Ron! You can't wait to get laid by some nice skinny bitch with big tits."

Ron was furious at the accusation. *Here she goes again*, he thought. This was hardly the first time she had been this way. His wife had often spun out of control over the most innocent of issues. The fights frequently ended with her screaming and cursing at him. At other times, she could be the most tender, loving, and sexy woman alive. As with most of their fights, he decided standing his ground and fighting back would only make the situation worse. So he headed outside to take a walk down the street to a nearby park, his usual escape.

"I'll be back when you have cooled off and we can talk civilly," Anglin said over his shoulder while turning toward the front door. But this time was different, as he was about to find out.

"Go ahead, run away, you *pussy!*" she screamed at the top of her lungs, having followed him out into the front yard. "Run away like you always do! Don't stay here and face me like a *real* man!"

Ron froze momentarily, his teeth clinching. He felt the heat of his own flashing anger. Not only because of what she had said, but because half of the neighborhood had heard it. Across the street, two ladies were talking to each other across a fence while their preteen kids played in the yard. They had all stopped to stare at him and Kara.

He knew that if he confronted her now, he might just lose control, so he continued walking, picking up his pace.

She stayed right beside him, screaming and cursing. Her own blind rage made her oblivious to the public spectacle she was making, or she was purposely out to humiliate him.

When she hit him with her fist from behind, he barely caught himself from hitting back. Instead he grabbed both of her upper arms pinning them to her sides.

"*Stop!*" he said through gritted teeth. "Please stop it right now! *I love you.* This fighting is insane."

She just stood there glaring at him, standing rigid, her arms straight at her sides with clenched fists, showing her teeth in a snarl and for once not saying a word.

He turned and walked away, shaking his head and mumbling under his breath.

He had ended up packing later without any further incidents or fights with her. But neither had they made up. They hadn't spoken at all. She had stayed most of the afternoon in the living room watching TV. He tried to apologize once but she just turned away and ignored him by turning up the volume of the TV. After loading his car, he went to say goodbye, but she was nowhere to be seen. Then he remembered that she had a late-afternoon medical appointment at Eglin at 1530. She had left without a word.

Hell of a way to start the most important deployment of his career, he thought as the pitch of the jet engines outside changed, bringing him back to where he was.

Soon they were on final approach to the airport at the former US Navy base at Subic Bay in the Philippines. After engine shutdown the midday sun started working its usual magic and was waking him up as he stepped out onto the C-17's open ramp.

Dressed in civilian clothes they soon formed into a semiofficial gaggle in a nearby hangar. The pallets of gear were being loaded onto flatbed trucks.

The hanger doors were closed and then there was a shrill whistle. "Listen up," said Chief Master Sergeant McKinney.

"Ladies and gentlemen," Colonel Perry began. "I hope you all got some rest on the way here. We are now only about 120 miles from our objective. Marine MV-22s will be flying us the rest of the way out to the shoal when the time arrives. The Navy will head out on the eighth along with several Philippine and US landing craft filled with the Seabee and RED HORSE heavy equipment and supplies. They are due to arrive by noon on the ninth. The housing barge should be in place by that afternoon. It also has a galley for hot meals that we will all be able to use. Weather is cooperating, and I have been assured that everything is on schedule. Today we make sure our gear is ready to go. Then we get some hot food and rest. Once we head out you can expect long hard days."

"What's the point?" his friend Stringer asked in a whisper.

"Of what?" Anglin asked.

"These civilian clothes," Stringer answered. "Anyone who sees us will know we're military with our haircuts and two C-17s outside with their yellow Charleston Air Force Base tail stripes."

"You think about the damnedest things," Anglin replied. "Now, listen. The colonel's still talking."

"The Seabees and the 554th will be living in the air-conditioned floating hotel. However, there is not enough room for us, and since we were a late addition to the mission, we'll be using the standard Alaska shelters we are used to. So, ladies and gentlemen, job one after the island is secured will be to get our tents up. And expect to be eating only MRE's (Meals Ready to Eat) for the first day or two until they get the barge's kitchen up to speed," the colonel explained.

"Now the Chinese assume they can continue to push everyone in this part of the world around. But the Philippine and US president through various channels have made it clear to the Chinese that their illegal bullying in this part of the world must end. On the ground, it will be our two countries, but official support and money will be also coming from Japan, Australia, and Malaysia."

The hangar was completely quiet. Everyone was listening and processing what they were hearing.

"We have to be aware that this may be seen by the Chinese as a poke in the eye. Everyone is confident that they will back down, but we will need to be vigilant. The Filipinos will be patrolling the shoal with frigates and smaller patrol craft 24-7. Still, on the ground we need to keep our eyes and ears open. To that end, I have instructed Chief McKinney to set up a guard-duty rotation. You are in the military, and you have all been trained to do this. Time to put that training to use," Perry finished.

The quiet was broken as the murmuring slowly began.

"You think they'll try anything?" Stringer asked.

"I doubt it," Anglin said confidently. "Only suicidal terrorists, or angry locals attack us these days. We are invited in, and we will be in a very controlled location. The Chinese are not suicidal maniacs. Let's focus on our mission and keep our eyes peeled."

10 SPIES

Manila, Philippines

Blue smoke belched from the flatbed truck's exhaust pipe as the engine cranked to life and Francisco Lucero jostled the transmission into first gear. He had just dropped off his last load of gear from the second Air Force C-17. He had been working on the flight line of the old Subic Bay Navy base for eight years. He made fairly good money compared to many others. Still it wasn't enough to satisfy his heavy spending. He supplemented his income in two ways. The first was by selling pilfered items on the black market. The second was by providing info to his old friend whom he believed was working for a large Philippine corporation. He had been told that it was valuable to keep up with activity at the airport to ensure they could compete with larger international companies. In fact, unbeknownst to him, the information was going directly to Chinese intelligence.

He parked the truck and headed in for his mid-morning break while fishing out his cell phone to call his contact.

"Hello," answered his contact, Antonio Torres.

"This is Francisco. I may have something interesting for you," said Lucero.

"In reference to what?" Torres asked.

"Two more American military cargo aircraft arrived today," Lucero explained.

Two more, thought Torres. Something was going on. He had already gathered reports of other military aircraft arriving over the past several days.

He knew that most of the activity involved the Americans. Lucero had previously reported planes unloading heavy-construction equipment. From the markings, he knew that some of it had belonged to US Navy heavy Seabee units and some from a US Air Force construction unit. He was in the process of trying to find out if there was a planned US-Filipino joint exercise in the area. But his usual contacts knew nothing about it.

"Where are you now?" Torres asked.

"Our breakroom," answered Lucero.

"When is your lunch break?" Torres asked.

"Eleven thirty," replied Lucero.

"Meet me at the usual place at eleven forty," Torres finished.

Two hours later and right on time, Lucero was picked up by a cab six blocks from the airport.

"Where to?" asked Torres the driver.

"McDonald's, I'm hungry. I haven't had a Big Mac in a long time," Lucero said from the back seat.

"What do you have?" asked Torres as he pulled out into traffic.

"We unloaded two American C-17s today. They were full of personnel and several pallets filled with gear. No big equipment this time. They were all in civilian clothes, but it was clear from their look and demeanor they are military," said Lucero.

"Did you see which unit?" asked Torres.

"I saw several boxes that were marked with the 823rd CES," Lucero answered.

"823rd CES," Torres repeated. "Hm, the last unit was the 554th CES. Before that was the Navy construction unit with the heavy road-working equipment," Torres mused aloud. "And the 554th came with heavy equipment as well. What did you do with this group's equipment?"

"They separated and opened up one pallet with personal duffel bags. The rest were placed in the back of one of the empty hangers. The word is that we will be loading them onto other aircraft in a couple of days," said Lucero.

"So, they are not unloading here or trucking them anywhere nearby. They plan to fly it somewhere further away. And they are not doing it immediately," Torres continued, thinking out loud. "And you said the earlier heavy equipment and pallets was taken to the piers and loaded onto ships and barges. But this group and their equipment is going to be flown to its location." *So, Torres thought to himself, they must be going somewhere that has an airport. And the larger equipment is going by ship. It must be going somewhere with both an airport and harbor nearby.*

They arrived at the McDonald's drive through and ordered. After getting their change and food, Torres handed Lucero his bag and the change from the cashier. As he did so, he added six thousand Philippine pesos into the change he handed Lucero. The equivalent of just over a hundred US dollars.

"Anything else you can think of?" asked Torres.

"Just that they had some sort of private meeting in the closed hangar not long after they arrived. No Filipinos were allowed anywhere near at the time," Lucero added, stuffing fries into his mouth.

After dropping off Lucero, Torres went to one of his designated locations and left a mark to notify his contact that he needed a face-to-face meeting.

11 SHAKEN CONFIDENCE
USS *Vinson*, South China Sea

What a goat rope it had turned into, he fumed as he strode into his office. His carefully laid plans had gone off the rails. This isn't combat, where you expect things to go to hell. He dropped down into his desk chair, leaned over, grabbed a diet cherry Pepsi from his minifridge and cracked it open while pondering what steps to take. His faith in the competence of his crew was shaken. If they were to get drawn into some form of conflict with Operation SEAHORSE they may not be as prepared as he'd boasted to the Admiral. First things first. Now we have to get this transport process fixed.

"Senior Chief!" he said loud enough that he could be heard by Senior Chief Owens from next door. "We've got some training to do!"

Seconds later, Owens was at his door with a concerned look on his face. "What is it SMO?" Owens asked.

"Have a seat, and I'll tell you," the SMO said pointing to the only other chair in his small office/exam room.

Before launching into the issue with Owens, the SMO thought back on the day's events.

His morning had started off with a bang, literally. Though there is never a day off while at sea, some departments are able to relax things a bit on Sundays and occasionally have some fun training. Officially, the officers have brunch on Sundays and everyone gets a break from daily cleaning stations. Each HOD is allowed to provide their personnel with time off on Sundays, as long as it meets mission demands.

For the medical department, this meant that there were no scheduled appointments, only morning and evening sick call which was handled by the duty crew. For the air department, flight operations were not going to start until 1300. Today the head injury patient was to be on the first helicopter launched.

At the HODs meeting with the XO the night before, the SMO was intrigued by an offer made by the Gun Boss. The security department was having small arms training in the morning starting at 0700 on the fantail to be followed at 0900 by M9 pistol qualifications up on the flight deck. All the HODs were invited to participate. The SMO hadn't requalified with the M9 since his initial flight surgeon days years before.

The SMO slept through reveille but still made it to the fantail by 0700. He got to shoot weapons he hadn't used since his active SEAL days. He blasted away with both the 7.62 M240 and 50 caliber machine guns. He emptied two M-16 thirty round magazines on full auto and fired two grenades from its grenade launcher that exploded 100 yards behind the ship. Next, he shot ten rounds from a 12 gage shotgun. It was 20 minutes down memory lane for him and he was pleased he could still hit the target every time! In this case, the water!

He impressed everyone with the M9 and was officially re-qualified. He scored a 239 just missing a perfect score of 240 because of one stray shot a half inch outside the center. The SMO already had the respect of the ship's officers and chiefs, but it only grew after they learned he hadn't touched a pistol in almost ten years.

After shooting, he met with the MAO, LT Alverez for their regular brunch in wardroom three and to discuss plans for the coming week. Sunday's were special because of the fresh, made to order waffles and eggs to go with the piles of bacon, sausage, and his favorite, fresh fruit.

Following Sunday brunch, he had checked the status of the head-injury patient and to make sure they were good to go with the helo. He called flight deck control to ensure either the upper-stage-four or upper-stage-two weapons elevators had no planes parked on them and would remain clear. Both were. The weapons elevators were used to transfer bombs and missiles from either the hanger bay or the second deck directly to the flight deck. Each was about ten feet by eight feet. They were the most efficient way to move a patient that is unable to walk up. He next went to the flight deck Battle Dressing Station to make sure a corpsman was ready with a safety harness so he could escort the patient up the elevator. The Battle Dressing Station is located on the starboard side of the island. After the XO's meeting the evening before, the SMO had asked the Gun Boss to use upper-stage two since it was the elevator nearest medical. Stopping by the

Air Transport Officer (ATO) shack, he informed them the patient would be ready by 1215. The ATO was to call when they were ready for the patient, and he was to be sent straight up to the flight deck and loaded directly onto the helo. The SMO had made sure everyone involved knew the plan and how to transport and load him.

He was in his office reviewing charts and occasionally glancing at the flight deck activity on the PLATT TV. Lieutenant Commander Alverez stepped in to discuss transfer orders for the patient and happened to mention that the patient was already gone. That lit his fuse, and he felt his face flushing with rising anger. He had specifically made it clear that the patient was not to move until called by the ATO.

And the patient's orders were messed up again. The Training Officer was sending him off unfunded. The Training Officer controls the funding for personnel traveling on and off the ship. He had refused to put him on "Cost" (Funded) orders and insisted on "No Cost" even after being shown a copy of the instruction that clearly stated that *any* patient sent for care over night or longer will be put on funded orders.

"Alverez, send these back and get them changed to funded," the SMO said angrily.

"I already have, and they still refused," she replied. "They essentially said not no, but hell no."

"Not the time to mess with me, Alverez," he said. "Everything needs to go right for this patient."

The SMO called the training department and got the training chief: "Chief, where's the Training Officer right now?"

"I don't know, sir," he said.

"I don't know where he is either, but in a few minutes, he'll be in my office!" The SMO snapped as he hung up the phone.

Pulling his brick off his belt, he keyed the mike. "TRAINO...SMO, it is urgent I see you in my office ASAP," he said more calmly than he felt, because the CO, XO, twenty-two Department Heads and their assistants all monitored that channel. The Training Officer arrived minutes later.

"This constant pushback on funding has to stop," the SMO launched into him.

"I read that instruction again, SMO. To me, it's too vague," the Training Officer responded.

"We'll catch hell from the Seventh Fleet Surgeon if he is sent off on no-cost orders. But more importantly, it's the right thing to do. That is why I was double-checking the orders in the first place," the SMO explained.

"SMO, we have no idea the route he will eventually take to get back to the states. Things change. We have no way of knowing how much funding to set aside for the trip, and our budget is tight. Keeping track of what is spent on him will be a nightmare," the Training Officer explained.

"So," the SMO began, "essentially, you're saying that it is too hard to predict what they may spend, and tracking what a patient actually spent afterward is equally hard. So to avoid all that work, it's just easier to just say no in the first place. Meanwhile, an injured patient may have to pay for lodging or transportation costs halfway around the world out of pocket and then beg to be reimbursed sometime afterward. Do I have that right? Do you have any idea what our junior Sailors make? You could be asking them to spend months of their pay for something the Navy is responsible for. Luckily in this case, he is a Lieutenant and may actually have some money in the bank. But we can expect to send off junior enlisted in the future."

The Training Officer was beginning to visibly squirm as the SMO rebuffed his argument.

"Fine, is there anything else, *sir*!" he finally said curtly.

"No, that's it," the SMO said. "The patient is about to leave on that helicopter. And we needed those orders modified five minutes ago." He pointed to the helo on the PLATT TV.

Alverez, who had heard it all from ten feet away in her office, stepped in, grinning, with the corrected paperwork in her hand ready to sign.

After the Training Officer signed and left, the SMO said to Alverez, "I just won a battle I shouldn't have had to fight. We will see if we win the war."

"Probably not," Alverez said. "He is sure to find a way to get even in the future. He does control all the training funds."

"If it happens again, I'll be taking it to the XO," he said. "Triple-check those orders again just in case."

As the orders were being re-checked, the SMO grabbed his flight deck gear and headed up. He quickly bounded the five flights up to the flight deck Battle Dressing Station and stormed in. There was the patient laying on the treatment table with his eyes closed. Right where the SMO had specifically told *everyone* he was *not* to go! He was supposed to go directly onto the helo. He lit into them.

"Why the hell is he here? Who called to send him up?" an obviously annoyed SMO demanded to know.

"I did," admitted Hospitalman Third Class Cockerham. "I was getting him staged early for the helo."

But the SMO lost all decorum when he found out this patient who has had balance problems since his head injury had been forced to march up five decks. He should have ridden up in a stretcher on an elevator.

The SMO uncharacteristically chewed out Cockerham and then slammed the door for effect as he stalked out. He immediately realized that he was an ass for losing his cool in front of the patient and his troops. He headed out across the flight deck to cool off and check on the helo's status. It took them another twenty minutes before it was ready. After all he had done to brief everyone and arrange every detail, one corpsman ignored what the SMO had said and moved the patient forty minutes early and in the wrong manner. This wasn't the first patient transfer that hadn't gone smoothly.

We are going to have some come to Jesus meetings and get this hammered out! He was dammed sure of that.

Finally, the helo was ready, and the SMO supervised a proper stretcher transfer of the patient and ensured that he was carefully loaded and secured. And he had funded 'cost' orders in with his other paperwork. Afterward, the SMO headed up into the island's O-10 level to watch the helo launch from Vultures' Row. More importantly, it gave him a chance to calm down. He regretted that he had lost his temper in front of his corpsmen. What would they think of him now? After the helicopter was airborne, he headed back to his office to resume powering through the two large stacks of medical records that he had planned to finish this afternoon.

After discussing what happened with Senior Chief Owens, they decided on a plan to address and prevent the problems from recurring in the future. *Well, at least the transport part,* he mused. Not so sure on the orders part.

"Senior, this evening I want to inspect all five of our storerooms around the ship. I also want a current status report on all of our prepositioned emergency response lockers. I need to know of any discrepancies. Tomorrow we'll inspect all of our Battle Dressing Stations and I want the crews that man them there at the time. Come up with a workable schedule. We have all gotten a little too complacent, and we need to get refocused on our mission." He couldn't tell him why, but the XO's surprise question and today's blunder had shaken his confidence. They need to up their game in case China didn't sit back and let the Philippines take Scarborough Shoal back.

After Chief Owens left, the SMO turned around and grabbed a stack of charts from his exam table. As the senior Flight Surgeon, he was required to validate and sign off all the flight physicals.

Unable to stay focused on the details of the exam he was reviewing, he realized he was still too keyed up and needed to calm down a bit more. So, he put the first chart aside and went exploring the ship as he liked to do. He always enjoyed talking with the Sailors he met along the way. He found it enlightening to learn where they were from, what their jobs were, and what their dreams were after the military.

Five minutes later, he found himself on the ship's fantail, one of his favorite places to relax. He was taking in the cloudless sky and the deep blue water that was being churned frothing and white by the *Vinson*'s four massive propellers. He could hear the whine of jet engines up on the flight deck above as they prepared to launch.

What a beautiful view, he thought. *It would be even better if I had someone to share it with.* He allowed his mind to drift to Jenna. He really did like her a lot. Well, far more than a lot, being honest with himself. But he still had mixed feelings about it.

He let his mind drift back over his and ex-wife Rachel's years together. He recalled his college days when he first laid eyes on her at a ROTC drill competition when they were both sophomores. He was an engineering major in Naval ROTC at the University of California San Diego, and she was pre-Law at the University of Southern California. He was on UCSD's drill team and she was there with a girlfriend who was competing on the USC Air Force drill team. They had met in line at the concession stand and had hit it off immediately. After a 19 month romance up and down interstate 5 they had secretly married in July on a trip to Las Vegas. Both were committed to finishing school, so the miles continued to rack up on the interstate. They each had their lives planned out. Derek was aiming to be a Navy SEAL after graduation if he could make it through BUDS. But he planned to put in his time with the teams and be out in six to eight years. Rachel had her law career mapped out.

They both had dreamed of cashing in on the good life one day and being able to live in a seaside home in La Jolla or maybe even in the beautiful town of Coronado, across the bay from San Diego. But as she was applying to law school the projected costs became overwhelming. Reality was slapping the young married couple in the face. With the Navy ROTC Scholarship, Derek's school was paid for. His parents were lower middle class and still lived in Jacksonville, Florida. The Navy had been his ticket to pay for college. After he paid back the time for his ROTC and SEAL commitments he could walk away proud and do whatever he chose. Her parents had been upper middle class and had planned to pay for her college and graduate school. Even after they were married. But during her senior year, her father's company had been downsized and her dad was out of a job and her parents were just barely getting by. They were unable to help with law school. Still she had applied to California graduate schools hoping to be accepted to a San Diego or Los Angles school and maybe pay for it with a scholarship or student loans. Then while preparing the applications they found out that Rachel was pregnant. With the prospect of three mouths to feed, a full-time graduate student living on a scholarship stipend and loans was impossible. Even with his potential military officer pay.

Rachel had never been happy about being a future "Navy Wife," and was actually not much of a fan of the military in general. But she was in love with Derek and figured she could put up with the military for a few years then eventually get back to her law school plans. Sadly, that first pregnancy had ended in a second term miscarriage. But not before it had disrupted her chance to start law school.

A few years later Derek had been wounded, ending his SEAL career. His long recovery in the hospital led to his interest in medicine and desire to apply for medical school. He could have paid for it using his GI Bill, but he had discovered the Uniformed Services University of the Health Sciences (USUHS) in Bethesda Maryland. It was a military medical school where he was paid full active duty pay with all the usual active duty benefits such as medical care for the family, and housing allowances. All medical school expenses were covered, but it came with an eight year commitment added to the two he still owed for ROTC. It was a lot longer in the military than Rachel had wanted but she reluctantly agreed it was the more financially sound plan.

He interviewed in his crisp Navy blue uniform with its shiny SEAL trident, and he had fit right in. With a 3.7 GPA and strong MCAT scores he was accepted. What had been a six year military plan had grown to ten or possibly thirteen if he did a medical specialty residency. This was clearly not what she had wanted, and they still planned on her going to law school. Rachel got the bittersweet news that she was accepted to the California Western School of Law in San Diego, just days after realizing she was pregnant again. She reluctantly declined and moved to the Washington DC suburbs.

Their daughter Brenda was born kicking and screaming at the Bethesda Naval Medical Center. Fourteen months later she was joined by her 'loving' brother and nemesis Austin. Rachel had her hands full with the kids and could only occasionally dream of law school. Derek was consumed with his med school studies and she was alone in a world where she knew no one but her husband. Her family was on the other side of the country and financially unable to visit. With the small children she couldn't participate in much of the med school spouse events because they couldn't afford a babysitter. Derek had his nose buried in books until late at night or was away with a study group. Rachel had been overwhelmed, lonely, and depressed, while Derek was excited by all that he was learning. They rarely had time for any of the one on one personal time they had enjoyed before the kids and medical school.

Following graduation Derek was off to a busy transitional internship at the Naval Hospital at NAS Jacksonville Florida. He had hoped that being near his parents would be good for them all, and they could help Rachel with the kids. Unfortunately she had never gotten along with them. She complained regularly that he hadn't tried hard enough to be assigned to the Naval Hospital at Balboa in San Diego close to 'Her' parents. After the fast-paced internship, he had the option of becoming either a general medical officer somewhere or a flight surgeon. Having always dreamed of flying he jumped at the flight surgeon option. Contrary to what the title implies, a flight surgeon is a physician who learns the unique physiological challenges of operating in various military aircraft, from modern fighters, to cargo planes, and helicopters. When at their home station the flight docs also take care of the aircrews' spouses and children. After his three year tour and two deployments as a flight surgeon he had applied for a military Emergency Medicine Residency. To Rachel it was becoming clear that she may never get to live any of her dreams. She frequently lamented that she was just a modern day "camp follower." He completed his ER training and was again back on a regular deployment rotation to the middle east.

He was too busy to notice that they had slowly drifted apart. The joy of their relationship had been gone for years even though they had maintained a comfortable routine. Their marriage had become more of a burden to her than pleasure. He was frequently off on deployment "having fun traveling around the world." At least, that was how she had described it when explaining why she wanted a divorce after a deployment. She had been left at home, sad and lonely, taking care of the kids, and watching the world pass her by as her own aspirations faded away. He had been stunned at the time. But looking back he could see that she had been heading that way for a while.

The marriage had ended, and luckily, it hadn't been an ugly divorce. For the first couple of years after the divorce, he had hoped that his recurring deployment pace would slow down, and they could get back together. He really missed her and his kids. But the demand for emergency docs overseas had remained high to support ongoing combat operations even though the wars seemed to be winding down. So part of him still wanted to get his old life and family back. His ex was seriously acting as if she wanted to get back together. And he had been cautiously exploring that option.

When the divorce had been final, his first urge was to find Jenna. But he was sure she had moved on and was living a happy married life of her own and he had refused to interfere. Then Jenna had walked back into his life. Now that he had reconnected with her again, he was feeling the conflict inside. His responsible self said to go with the family it would be best to have a stable home for them all again. Yet the kids were almost grown and would soon be off living their own lives. What then? Could he ever be as close to his ex as with Jenna. Not in a million years was that possible. So, would he do what was best for him or for his kids? The choice should have been easy. His whole life had been focused on serving others. What he wanted came secondary. Or had it? He could have waited on med school and let his wife pursue getting into law school.

Now here he was again deployed on an aircraft carrier enjoying his time at sea. After the divorce, Rachel had gotten her law degree. Now that she had achieved her own goals, he had occasionally wondered if maybe they could be a family again. Now he was aching to be with Jenna, but he was feeling guilty at the thought. Why? He wasn't married, and the dates with Rachel were trial runs. They had been nice but not great. As he thought of Jenna again on the treadmill, a broad smile lit up his face as he turned and headed back into the ship. He was now only thinking of the future possibilities with Jenna.

12 TIRADE

Hong Kong, China

Lieutenant Commander Yao parked his silver Nissan 370Z sports car in the hotel's covered parking lot. He had arrived a day early to avoid the frequently occurring traffic delays. He did not want to chance an unforeseen auto accident that could cause him to miss the *Vinson* reception.

Before checking into the hotel he headed to the American consulate to pick up his ticket to the reception. Lieutenant Suyong, the squadron's Intelligence Officer, had made the arrangements at Yao's request. Suyong had informed him that his ticket would be available for pickup at the consulate's reception desk starting four days before the reception. He just had to show some form of identification. Yao took the subway from near his hotel to midtown where the consulate was located.

After clearing security at the entrance, he stepped over to the reception desk where he was greeted by a smiling Chinese American woman.

"Good afternoon, how may I help you?" she said in accented but otherwise flawless Chinese.

"Good afternoon," Yao responded in English. He wanted a chance to use his rough English skills before the reception tomorrow.

"Yes, I am here to get my pass for the reception on the American aircraft carrier," he explained.

"Ah, yes," she answered, switching to English. "I can help you with that. I'll need your name and a photo ID please."

"Yao, Liang Yao," he replied simply as he handed her his driver's license.

The receptionist checked his ID and double-checked that the photo matched the person in front of her. She then began flipping through the accordion folder that had the reception tickets on a table behind her. After several minutes of careful searching, she returned empty-handed.

"I'm sorry, I can't seem to find a ticket for you, Mr. Yao. Possibly you are part of some larger group that has already had someone pick them up," she suggested.

"No," he began as he felt the first hint of anger rising. "I was specifically told to pick it up here."

"We have very few individuals requesting tickets directly. Usually they make the request through some other organization. Were you part of some larger request?" she asked.

"Yes, my request was part of the People's Liberation Navy," Yao replied with irritation.

"Okay, just a minute," she said as she tapped on her computer screen. "I see that the People's Liberation Navy was allotted twenty tickets, but that we received only nineteen names. And there is no one named Yao on the list."

"There must be some mistake," he said with a mask of politeness that hid his antagonism toward the ineptness of these Americans.

A moment later, after the whir of a printer, she handed him the list. He quickly scanned it, noting a few names that he knew. Most were unknown to him. He saw that his name was not there as his face flushed with anger.

"You could be the missing twentieth name," she suggested. "Perhaps you were mistakenly left off or not properly processed. I suggest that you check with your military contact responsible for giving us this list. Possibly you could be added on."

"Thank you," was all he could manage to say through his clenched teeth as he turned away. He could taste the bile from his gut as his mind raced to figure out what had gone wrong. This could not be happening to him. He was special. He had connections. Somebody does not know who they are messing with. *This will get fixed, or there will be hell to pay!* he thought as he headed to the exit.

"Mr. Yao," called the receptionist.

Yao halted and turned back to her. "Yes."

"You will have to hurry to get your name on the list. We have a skeleton staff working this weekend preparing for the reception, and they leave for the day at 1700. Tomorrow morning at 0800, any unassigned tickets will automatically be given to those on a waiting list. If you can get your name on the list today, you can pick up your ticket tomorrow," she told him.

"Thank you, I'll get right on it," Yao said. Damn, it was worse than he first thought as he checked his watch. It was 1410 in the afternoon. He had less than three hours to get this resolved.

As soon as he stepped outside the consulate, he pulled out his cell phone and called his squadron's duty officer. As soon as the Lieutenant on duty answered, Yao barked, "This is Lieutenant Commander Yao. Get me Lieutenant Suyong's phone number! *Now!*"

As soon as he had the number, he hung up, not bothering to thank the harassed young junior officer. Moments later, he heard the line ringing.

"Suyong," he said as he answered his cell phone.

"Lieutenant, this is Commander Yao! Why is my name *not* on the list to attend the American carrier's reception?" Yao spat through his phone as he continued down the block and stepped into a side alley and behind a trash dumpster for privacy. "You did request a ticket for me, didn't you?"

"I…," Suyong trailed off as he thought back to that day almost two weeks ago. Yao had insisted that he be added to the list. He had checked with the organizer to see if there was still a ticket available and had told him that Yao was wishing to attend. He just had to follow it up with a formal request letter. He had the letter drafted and signed and was about to scan and email it when he had been called to the commanding officer's office. Then he had been busy rushing to research what the boss had wanted an answer to. That had taken him three full days to complete the final presentation. He did not recall actually sending in the formal request.

After the prolonged silence, Yao asked, "Well, did you, or didn't you?" he yelled through the phone.

"I…I am not sure," Suyong confessed, terrified at having angered the mercurial Yao. "I thought I did. I had the signed letter in my hand, then the commanding officer had—"

"Did you get my name on the list!" He shouted this time as he held the phone out in front of his mouth.

"I may not have," Suyong said sheepishly. "I'm sorry, Commander. I'll work on it first thing in the morning if it isn't too late."

Yao hyperventilated for a moment trying to regain his composure but failed. "No, no, no, no, no! Hell *no!* You are going to get my name on that list right now! You have two hours before they give my position away."

"But, Commander, I am at the beach with my girlfriend an hour's drive from the base," Suyong weakly protested. "And I'm sure the organizer is not working today even if I were to get it to him in time. He won't see it until tomorrow."

"I don't give a damn where you are or what you are doing. My name had better be on that list before 1700 today, or I'll kick your ass from here to Mongolia!" Yao screamed as he was pacing back and forth in the alley.

"But—," Suyong started to reply.

"Do you understand?" Yao roared, red-faced and spitting into the phone.

"I will be back to the consulate first thing in the morning for my pass. If I do not get it, I will be coming straight back to the base, and you and I are going to have a private little discussion," Yao threatened.

"Yes, Commander," Suyong answered, already on his feet pulling his girlfriend up off her beach towel.

Yao ended the call, but his fury was unabated. He saw no practical way that Suyong was going to be able to get this done in just over two hours. His plans of getting onto the carrier to see the enemy aircraft up close and talk with their pilots was vanishing before his eyes. Maybe he could call his uncle he thought, as he continued pacing and his anger continued to build. But if he did that, it would make him look inept. No, he couldn't ask Uncle Jiang. He wanted to punch the wall with his fist. But he had done that once before when he was a junior officer resulting in a boxers fracture and a cast that kept him out of the cockpit for three months. He couldn't do that. With all his pent up energy and rage it had to find an outlet. He drew back his right hand and threw his smart phone against the concrete building wall with all the force he could muster. The phone's shattered screen and bent case landed relatively quietly in the alley. As he slowly calmed down, he knew he would have to retrieve the phone's SIM card to transfer all his data to a replacement phone. Why did he constantly lose his temper like this? he wondered for the thousandth time. He needed to get himself under control. His poor mother would have been mortified by his actions. He took a deep breath to calm down and told himself he wanted to get a new phone anyway. As he reached down to pick up the mangled phone, he froze a foot away. It was lying in a fresh pile of dog crap. His day was not getting any better.

Two hours later, Yao had checked into his hotel, but he could not relax. He did not want to watch TV. And he was starting to get hungry. He was looking over the hotel restaurant's menu when his new smart phone rang.

"Hello," Yao answered.

"Commander, this is Lieutenant Hu," he said. "I knew you were going to be in Hong Kong tonight. I'm in town seeing my girlfriend, but she is at work right now until 2130. Anyway, I was wondering if I could claim that steak dinner."

"Sure, I was getting hungry," Yao answered. "You have any place in mind?"

"You did say the steak dinner of my choice," Hu clarified.

"Yes, your choice," Yao confirmed.

"Great, the address is 89 Queensway, a few blocks from Fenwick Pier," Hu told him.

"Okay, 89 Queensway," Yao answered checking his watch. "I'll see you in forty-five minutes. What's the name of the restaurant?"

"It's Ruth's Chris Steak House," said his wingman.

"I should have known you would have picked the most expensive place in town," Yao said, shaking his head. This was really going to cost him.

"It isn't the most expensive steak house in Hong Kong. It's the best steakhouse in Hong Kong," Hu replied, knowing all along that he intended to get the most expensive steak they had. He would never be able to afford eating there on his salary.

Yao was momentarily pissed, but he would go through with it anyway. His surge of anger melted away as he smiled to himself recalling the reason for the steak dinner. He took pleasure again at the memory of the barely covered female and her shock and terror, all the while knowing he should feel ashamed for what he did. He needed the companionship, and it would be good to have a friend to spend the evening with and hopefully keep him out of trouble.

He glanced at his watch and noted that the time was 1648. Unable to wait till morning, he searched for the number and called the United States consulate. He was soon talking to the same receptionist again.

"This is Mr. Yao," he said. "Could you check to see if my name is now on the list?"

"Yes, Mr. Yao, I remember you. People's Liberation Navy list. Correct?" she inquired. "Let me check."

"Yes, that's correct," Yao said, almost holding his breath as he listened to her tapping on the computer keyboard.

"Yes, Mr. Yao, you are now on the list. You can stop by and pick up your ticket any time after 0800 tomorrow. We are about to close for the day," she replied brightly.

"Thank you," he said as he let out a sigh of relief. But Suyong was still going to pay dearly for putting him through this, he thought as he began to plan his revenge on the junior officer. No matter how he tried, his true vengeful nature kept dominating him.

13 OFFICIAL BUSINESS

USS *Vinson*, South China Sea

Later that evening, the SMO headed up again to brief the CO and CAG with the latest news on the injured pilot. It was also a legitimate reason to stop by Jenna's office again. She had just finished a short strategy session with the other members of the Admiral's staff and was about to sit down at her desk when the SMO popped in.

"SMO, always glad to see you," Jenna said, smiling. "Not that you need much of a reason to hang around these days, I suppose."

"Official business, Jenna. Honest," he replied. "Well, mostly."

"Come on in and have a seat," she said, gesturing him in with a nod.

The SMO stepped past her and sat in one of the chairs facing her desk. She quietly closed the door and sat down across from him.

"I've had no time for the gym today, but all the trips up and down these ladders are a surprisingly good workout," he commented. "I wanted to give you an update on the head injury patient. I just briefed the CO and CAG."

"So how is he, Derek?" she asked with concern in her voice.

"First off, he's going to be fine. But it was as we feared. His head CT showed several minor skull fractures of his temporal bone. There was some subdural bleeding under it, and another small bleed deeper in the brain. He also has nose fractures which caused him to have a loss of smell. The good news is, there is no evidence of active bleeding and no need for surgery. He is stable and doing well," the SMO finished.

"Hm. Okay, if you say so. Bleeding in the brain never sounds good to me."

"True enough, but it was minor and has stopped. The body will absorb it over time," the SMO added.

"Then about as good as we could have expected I guess," she replied. "What's next for him?"

"He's at the appropriate level of care now. Eventually, he will be transferred back to Balboa in San Diego. He should recover from most of the injuries. He will be at increased risk of developing seizures, and he may or may not get his sense of smell back," he added.

She nodded. "I'll pass the word to the Admiral. He has been asking for status updates daily," she said.

"Well, you look like you're busy. I'll get going," the SMO said as he started to rise from his chair.

"I am, but I need a mental break for a few minutes. Please stay, Derek," Jenna replied.

"Sure," Derek said with a smile as he eased back down into the hard aluminum chair. "You know that I do love these chats we have been having since you arrived."

"Oh, you've been mixing business with pleasure, have you?" she teased. "But me too," Jenna added. "Actually, I have begun to look forward to them." After a brief pause, she seemingly changed the subject. "So how are your kids?"

"They're fine. Brenda, the oldest, is focused on college, and her little brother is focused on girls, which is pretty normal for a junior in high school."

"Yeah, all part of growing up," said Jenna. "They are probably still pushing that old adage that they are in their sexual prime as teenagers, and it will all be downhill after their mid-twenties."

"Little do they know," Derek replied, getting both excited and uncomfortable about the direction the conversation was going. "Like a fine wine, it only gets better with age."

"So how's their mom doing?" Jenna asked.

"She's doing fine. She seems happy with her job at a small Los Angeles law firm," Derek explained.

"Are you two getting along okay?" she asked. What she really wanted to ask was if it was really over for them. She knew that they had been divorced mostly because of her unfulfilled dreams of being a lawyer, not because she'd grown to dislike Derek. Now that she had her career on track, Derek was only a few hours away if she wanted to renew the relationship. Who knew? Kids are known to put pressure on their parents to get back together. And Derek had yet to mention her.

"Yeah," he replied. "When I stop by to get the kids, she is as friendly as ever. We never did fight all that much, and she has never limited my spending time with them. On the contrary. On one weekend, she graciously brought them down to me and picked them up two days later."

Jenna was secretly hoping that she had brought them down because she had a hot weekend planned with some other guy. But she said, "That was nice of her."

"It really was," Derek said as his thought back.

"Or she already had other plans," she said, fishing.

"Who knows?" Derek said. "It doesn't really matter. She has made it clear on more than one occasion that she is happy now and still has no love for the military." He left out that they had been dating. He didn't want anything to spoil his possibilities with Jenna. "I have to admit that our breakup did hit me hard. We had a good life, at least from my perspective, and I do miss having someone on the other side of the bed in the morning. I had the best of both worlds—an exciting and rewarding career with lots of travel and a beautiful family waiting for me at home. They just got tired of the waiting, I suppose."

"So, are you over it?" Jenna asked.

Derek sat their thinking for a moment. "I think so. I have secretly wanted us to get back together, especially since I figured you were happily married with six kids somewhere. And we have talked about it." He again left out that it had gotten to the dating stage. "But then you popped into my life, and, well, I think any thoughts of resuming a life with her are definitely on hold."

"So, she still has a chance with you, but you're fair game, so to speak," Jenna cut in.

"Besides, as I was about to say, I really haven't thought all that much about *her* these past few months," he finished truthfully with a grin and catching her attentive eye.

"Oh really now, do tell," she said with a broadening grin showing gleaming white teeth.

"Look, Jenna. We have been good friends since we met back on the Truman. Okay, a lot more than friends. Then we went our separate ways until you arrived here. Seeing you again, well, we just sort of continued from where we left off. And you are one of the few that I can relate to out here."

"But there is one major difference this time, Derek," she said.

"Yeah, you're a newly pinned on Captain, and I'm a Commander. We were both Lieutenants back then," Derek said, trying to be funny.

"No," she replied, ignoring his attempt at humor. "This time we're both single. Back then, we both played the what-if game. What if you weren't married and I weren't engaged. What if we had both been single then. Should we have let it become more than friendship? I'll be honest: I now wish we had. Look, I was in love with my fiancé, but I kept seeing qualities in you that I wished that he had."

Derek just sat there listening excitedly and remembering back to his own memories from before. He had wished that his wife could have been more like Jenna—in the Navy, with them sharing the adventure together. He also recalled other occasional, more intimate thoughts that he would never admit to.

"Yep, me too," he was only able to say with a dry throat. "So"—he swallowed hard—"I guess it is time to admit that we both want to see where this goes. I have to admit that you have been on my mind a lot lately."

"I agree," she said. "We are not kids anymore. We are adult enough to see something we want, evaluate the pros and cons, and to go for it. We have been doing it our whole careers."

"That's easy for you to say, Jenna. I'm feeling like my teenage son on this one," said Derek. "So"—he stretched out the vowel—"would you like to have dinner in Hong Kong?"

She sat there letting him squirm for a few moments, then said. "Derek, I would love to. I thought you would never ask," she answered, watching him let out the breath he'd been holding.

"Great!" he blurted out. "Tomorrow night? Wait, I'm expected at the reception, so it will have to be after that, if it's not too late. I expect to head ashore after the ship's reception is finished just after 2100."

"That will be fine. I'm attending the reception as well, and I need to check on a few things afterward that may take a half hour or so," she said, thinking that she will need to get the latest on Operation SEAHORSE before leaving the ship. "Where shall we meet?"

"I have a room booked at the Connor Hilton," he said.

"Excellent, me too. It seems to be the recommended hotel among the ship's leadership. How about meeting in the hotel lounge," she suggested.

"Okay then. I'll see you around 2230 or so," he said with a smile. "A bit late to start a first date, but I'm game if you are."

"The life of a Sailor," she replied with a big genuine smile. "I'm really looking forward to it Derek. Now get outta here. I've got a lot of work to get back to."

"Aye-aye, Captain," he said failing to suppress a grin.

14 DROPPING ANCHOR

USS *Vinson*, Hong Kong Harbor

Commander Lloyd was feeling great even though he had been up early to watch the Sunday night football game as his team the Jacksonville Jaguars pounded the Pittsburgh Steelers forty-five to sixteen.

To top it off, his Admin Officer, LCDR Marty Alverez, had made a bet on the game. She was a diehard Steelers fan. Her office was decorated in Steelers paraphernalia. She had banners, posters, a Steelers mug, watch, and a footstool with a Steelers cover. She even had replicas of each of their five Super Bowl rings. The winner of the bet would get the soda of their choice brought to them once a day for a week. The SMO had never intended for this to cost her a dime if she lost, so his bet was for diet cherry Pepsi. And the only place on the ship it could be found was in his personal office fridge just eight feet from his desk. This morning he didn't say anything to her as he passed her office on the way into his. After the Steelers poor showing, he didn't want to gloat. At least not yet. Soon after he got to his office, she came in and made a big production about getting one out, wiping it down with a napkin, opening, and then formally presenting it as if it was a fine wine, and she was a professional waiter.

"SMO, please enjoy this properly chilled beverage," she said before quietly about facing and going back to her office.

Ah, the sweet taste of victory, he thought as he sipped it down.

By 1030, he was up on the O-10 level of the ship's island as they were pulling into Hong Kong. He was looking down at the flight deck and admiring the aircraft handler's handiwork. On the aft third of the ship, the F/A-18s were arranged into the shape of a large arrowhead. The base was the width of the flight deck, and the point almost even with the island. Those parked on the bow were lining the edges in the shape of chevrons. All the planes were carefully placed, and he found the whole effect was quite pleasing to the eye. Their F-35s were sequestered in hanger bay one out of sight.

While he was looking at the flight deck, he was wondering if pulling into Hong Kong was a good idea after all. He was looking forward to it personally, but he was having increasing reservations about the wisdom of continuing with the port visit with Operation SEAHORSE about to kick off. At least, he was feeling better about his medical department. After his recent inspections, he noticed a more focused attitude in his corpsmen and providers. And he had found that everything actually was in fighting shape and ready to go. He was at least reassured on that count.

A moment later, he heard the hatch behind him swing open. Out stepped Alverez. She had a bad habit of staying too focused on her work and had gone weeks without seeing sunshine. He had called her on his brick after he had arrived on Vultures' Row and insisted that she come up and enjoy the fresh air.

"Thanks, SMO," Marty said. "What a magnificent view."

"It is indeed," he replied, looking at the deeply forested, deep-dark-green mountainous island they were passing to their right. Up ahead, they could see several smaller ones to the left of the ship's course. The *Vinson* was moving ahead at a slow, careful speed. The shipping traffic into and out of Hong Kong was quite heavy.

"Who knew?" he asked.

"What's that, SMO?" she responded.

"Who knew that there would be so many islands just covered in trees? I guess I had expected something more like New York. A big island just covered with skyscrapers. But this…it's so…so green! There's not a building in sight anywhere. This is Hong Kong's main island. I checked the chart in the bridge on the way up," he said.

"It is absolutely beautiful," she agreed.

"Yep."

"It sure is nice of the Chinese to give us and escort," she said, referring to the four Hong Kong police patrol boats that surrounded the *Vinson*.

"A protective escort? Or do they have other reasons?" he asked.

"Probably both," she said.

"Are you attending the reception tonight?" he asked, changing the subject. In addition to the senior leadership from the ship, Air Wing, and Admiral's staff, thirty other officers had volunteered to attend the event in their dress uniforms to meet and mingle with the guests. The SMO was one of them.

"I heard from the SUPPO at this morning's department head meeting that our S-2 Division is going all out to put out a great spread for our guests," the SMO continued. "They have spent the past twenty-four hours chopping, cooking, frying, and baking over eight hundred pounds of food. And they have a dedicated team assigned to transform hangar bay two into a proper reception area."

"It sounds like quite the production. But, no, I'm not going," she said. "I have other plans. I'll be on the first liberty boat into port after anchoring. I'm not going to spend one of my two liberty days-off here waiting around for a silly reception. I'm out of here. I've been on this boat long enough."

"Do these plans involve the AFL?" he teased.

"*Hell no!*" she exclaimed.

"I had to ask. He sure seems to have plans for you."

"In his dreams," she said, making a disgusted face and visibly shuddering at the thought.

"What about you, SMO?" she countered, thinking of the ever-increasing times the Admiral's Chief of Staff had found a pretext to stop by over the past several months. Often, it was for the most trivial of reasons. Marty was secretly hoping that there was something there for them both. Though he was always smiling and appearing in good spirits most of the time, she sensed that there was a loneliness just under the surface.

"Well, I've never been to China, so this will be a new adventure for me. And I didn't have to pay to get here," he added. "I'll see the sights, do some shopping for my kids, and eat at some nice restaurants. Maybe sample some real Chinese food."

"Me too, SMO. Me too," she agreed.

"There it is," he said, pointing to the tops of several tall buildings that were appearing as the ship rounded a point of land. Within minutes, the vast skyline of Hong Kong appeared.

"Wow!" Marty said, referring to the impressive variety of the buildings' architecture. Though many were the standard square and rectangle shapes familiar in most US cities, there were many that were curved while others looked to be built out of a larger version of a kid's stacked irregular building blocks.

"We're not in Kansas anymore, Marty," he said. "That is impressive."

Over the next 45 minutes they enjoyed the view as the ship glided to its anchorage point. They soon heard the rapid clanging of the Vinson's port anchor chain followed by a distant splash as the thirty ton anchor hit the water.

Alverez checked her Steelers' watch. "I have to run, SMO. I have some paperwork to check on and must finish packing. The first liberty boat is due at the stern dock in two hours."

He took one last look around, admiring again the symmetrical pattern the aircraft made down on the flight deck. *It should indeed impress our guests*, he thought as he turned to open the hatch into the island. He had already finished packing. He headed back to his office with a smile as he thought of Jenna and the possibilities during his time ashore.

15 CLARITY
Malacañang Park, Manila, Philippines

Torres was at the park looking out over the lake. He had a bag of fish food that he was casually tossing out into the water. He watched the battle between the colorful Koi fish and the seagulls to get to the pellets first. Occasionally, a gull would catch a piece in the air. After ten minutes, he noticed that someone had joined him in tossing food to the fish.

"Good morning. A lovely day for a vacation," Torres said.

"Who has time for a vacation these days?" his contact, Hai Jun, said with the proper reply.

"I have an update," Torres said. "Yesterday morning, two more American C-17s with military troops in civilian clothes arrived. They are from a different heavy-construction unit but without any heavy equipment. At least, none has arrived yet that we know of. They are expected to fly to their next location within a couple of days. No one knows the destination."

Jun nodded. "Go on," he said.

"So over the last few days, we have had several US heavy-construction units arriving with equipment," Torres continued. "I did some checking online of their unit numbers and found out that two of them are Navy Seabee units, and the other two are Air Force RED HORSE squadrons. There have been no announced joint exercises involving construction. The majority of the equipment was loaded onto Filipino cargo ships. So wherever they are going it may be along the coast to somewhere with a harbor. And this last group will be flying to their location, so it must be relatively near an airport, that is, if they are all going to the same place. My contact in the Philippine State Department knows nothing about it. They are usually directly involved with coordinating any joint exercises."

"Whatever is going on it is pretty significant given the number of personnel and heavy equipment involved. And it is all very secret," Jun concluded. "And the cargo ships are all Filipino Navy. So they are definitely a part of whatever is going on."

"There is a scheduled joint US/Philippine Air Force exercise that has been scheduled for over a year. There is no idea if this is somehow connected," Torres added.

"Hmm, these units are often associated with humanitarian work around the world. But their primary military mission is to build military bases and airfields where no base had been," Jun added.

"There are plenty of humanitarian opportunities here in the Philippines," Torres stated. "Oh, this is not from one of my sources, but I have a cousin that mentioned last week that he got a great-paying job two weeks ago. He is a diesel-engine mechanic. I didn't think much of it at the time. But now…anyway, he mentioned that it is on a harbor-dredging crane and that he was one of several mechanics hired to work on the same equipment. Not a big deal in itself. They are constantly working to keep our harbors and waterways clear. But he told his mother that he may be away for several months. He may be working on one somewhere else. There are more than a dozen or so operational around the Philippines. But why are they adding extra mechanics?" he asked.

"Yes, it may not mean anything. It may or may not be related to what the Americans are up to. I want you to continue trying to find out what is going on. Try following the equipment. Keep me updated with any new developments. Get it to me directly. Use the Gmail account and be sure to use the encryption pad I gave you. I have an alert on that account, and I will get notified immediately. Things may happen quickly, and these meetings take too long to set up," Jun said. "I hope you enjoy the rest of your vacation."

An hour later, Torres was back at the Subic Bay docks. The area was moderately busy with activity, and he had several friends that worked there. He made his way to a popular snack shack where the dock workers frequently took their breaks. He ordered a sandwich, bag of chips, and a soda. After his order arrived, he sat down at one of the many picnic tables scattered around the front and sides of the building. He picked a seat that gave him a view of both the ships and the entrance to the snack bar. He slowly began to nibble at his sandwich and watched.

A half hour later, workers from all directions began to converge for their lunch break. Some formed a line at the snack bar while others had brought their lunch from home and just needed a table to sit and eat. After a few minutes of scanning faces he saw one he recognized. It was Reynaldo Juachon, a friend of his for several years, who was one of the truck drivers working the docks.

He waved and called out. "Hey, Reynaldo, over here."

"Hey, my friend. What are you doing here? The cab business slow?" Juachon asked.

"Yes, it is, unfortunately. But I just let off a fare around the corner and decided to get something to eat while I was here," Torres lied. "How are things with you?"

"So-so," Juachon began. "We were really busy last week but things are slowing back down to normal. Not much happening today. At least, I was able to get in some overtime hours. Mama and the kids are already working on their Christmas lists."

"I know what you mean, my friend," Torres answered. "So what had you so busy?" He tried to ask nonchalantly.

"We had a surge of unexpected heavy equipment that needed to be loaded onto some Filipino amphibious cargo ships. Most of it was done by their crews, but they did need some of our help since it was our docks they were working from," Juachon answered.

"What kind of equipment?" Torres asked already knowing the answer.

"Bulldozers, motor graders, large flatbed trucks, Humvees, cherry pickers, forklifts, backhoe tractors, and even a couple of bobcats. There were also two huge generators. I bet they could power a town with those monsters. Then there were crates and crates of large equipment. I'm not sure what was in them," Juachon stated.

"Sounds like they are getting ready to build a new town," Torres mused.

"Who knows?" Juachon answered. "The Sailors we talked to didn't know much when we asked."

"How many ships?" Torres inquired crunching down on a chip.

"Just three, but they were packed pretty full since they were not too large for cargo ships."

"I know that was a lot of equipment, but ships can carry huge loads," Torres noted.

"But these don't have the typical huge cargo holds because they were also designed to carry large numbers of troops," Juachon explained.

"Wait, these are not normal cargo ships?" Torres asked, perplexed.

"No. Like I said, they are amphibious cargo ships," replied Juachon. "Actually, they are old US LSTs from the 1960s, you know, Landing Ship-Tank."

"No," replied Torres, who thought a cargo ship was a cargo ship that only varied in size. In truth, he knew little of shipping, he realized.

"Yeah," Juachon continued. "These ships have a shallow draft and are designed to steam right up onto the beach, open their clamshell bows and unload the vehicles directly onto the beach.

"Really," Torres answered as his mind was racing.

Juachon changed the subject to his family and how his oldest son was doing in soccer. Torres continued the small talk until his meal was finished, said goodbye to Juachon, and headed to his car.

As he was starting his engine, he heard the whine of several aircraft fly directly overhead. At first, he thought they were helicopters by the beat of the blades, until he looked up. But he watched with growing excitement as CV-22 Marine Ospreys, one after another, passed overhead as they came into land at the airport.

He immediately picked up his cell phone and called his informant, Francisco Lucero, at the airport. After a brief discussion, they agreed to meet later in the afternoon during Lucero's break.

Later that evening at 1730, Jun felt the vibration of his phone. As he checked it, he saw the alert from one of his email accounts. He went to his secure vault within the Chinese embassy and opened the email. After using his single-use pad cipher, he read the following message from Torres: "Heavy equipment loaded onto three amphibious ships that can unload directly onto a beach. Ten US Marine Ospreys arrived today. The recently arrived cargo has been tasked to be loaded onto them the morning of seventh. Crews relaxed and going into crew rest. Anticipate departure within twenty-four to forty-eight hours."

As he had done earlier in the day, Jun immediately forwarded the information to China's intelligence service in Beijing. From there, it was shared with the separate military intelligence services.

16 DINNER AND A SHOW
Manila, Philippines

"Quiet! Listen up!" called out Chief Master Sergeant McKinney to the murmuring crowd.

"Today, your shop supervisors will go over your specific tasks for the first few days," began Colonel Perry. "Our unit will be the last to arrive and will be working the 1900 to 0700 shift. So, try to stay on the night shift. Your circadian rhythms are still set to Florida, and that's just about the same as the night shift here. That's why we let you sleep in today. Also, though the Filipinos will be providing some security around the island, most of you can expect to be on a guard-duty rotation."

Thirty minutes later, Staff Sergeant Anglin and twelve others were listening to Technical Sergeant Nickel going over the initial goals for the first week. "So, we will all be delivered to the location on the initial wave of MV-22 Ospreys. The bulk of our equipment will arrive on the second and third waves," he continued. "On day one, we will be setting up our Alaska shelters near our primary work location. Understand that space will be tight. And contrary to popular lore, we will *not* be building the golf course first. That's goes in after the chow hall is complete."

There was a hearty chuckle all around the room. "Good, glad to see you are all listening," Nickel continued.

"We better," someone interrupted from the back of the room. "I heard that Colonel Perry brought his golf clubs like he did on the last deployment."

"Take note that the runway will be located here," he said, pointing to a location on the map. "About a third of its length will be created by dredging to extend it out along here." He pointed to a point of land. "The RED HORSE heavy-equipment operators will be clearing the area for the remainder of the runway. With just the initial two-thirds length it will be able to accommodate C-130s and C-17s, which both have short field takeoff and landing capability. The longer runway will be needed for regular airline transport aircraft and the fighters they plan to base here. Then we will have a more robust air-bridge supply line. The Seabees will be working to build up the harbor area and docks capable of accepting medium-size cargo ships. This will require dredging the proposed harbor area and entrance to the lagoon. The dredged material will be used to help extend the runway. Until then, they'll be using Philippine Navy LSTs to transport the heavy equipment and supplies to our location."

"What is the timeline on this project, Sergeant Nickel?" asked one of the new Airmen.

"If our supply chain keeps bringing everything we need when we need it, we're estimating seven-to-nine months until our part is finished. We have to leave this place with enough infrastructure to support an operating fighter squadron, its maintenance support personnel, and a military garrison robust enough to fend off an attack. This includes housing, hangars, office buildings, desalination water system, fuel storage, et cetera. So, step one is the runway, Step two is a tarmac for the fighters to park. Step three, permanent water source. Step four, fuel depot. Step five, aircraft maintenance hangar for rainy weather work. Then more permanent locations for the initial five to six hundred troops to live, eat, and work. After that, we can go home, and the Filipinos can then continue the ongoing buildup of the base. Of course, some of these events will overlap and be done concurrently because of the different capabilities we bring to the fight. Our initial project will be setting up our unit's shelters. Everyone else will be living the high life on the barge that has bunk rooms, showers, a chow hall, and even a small store. Water will be at a premium, though. It will be shipped out there daily. We need it not only for food and personal use but vast amounts for the concrete we will be pouring as footings for the buildings and eventually the runway. All of it has to be shipped here for use until a large desalination plant is set up, but that is months away."

"What if our Filipino friends are slow at delivering?" an Airman asked.

"Then don't make plans for next Christmas either," Nickel answered.

"What about the Chinese? What will they do?" Senior Airman Stringer asked the big question on everyone's mind.

"We don't know. It's well above our CO's pay grade," said Nickel. "Worst case, we may end up being in an international game of chicken. But hope isn't a plan, so let's all do our job and be ready for anything. Now along those lines, behind you on the wall I have posted the guard-duty rotation. Take a look to see when you will be assigned to security patrols. As you can see a Technical Sergeant or above will be leading each shift of the five-man security teams. On those days, you will report to the First Sergeant's tent to be briefed on your assigned patrol locations and schedule, and then be issued your weapons. You will be carrying live ammo so remember your training and be safe."

Anglin turned around like everyone else and began searching for his name until he found it. He was assigned to guard duty on November eleventh, his older brother David's birthday.

Three hours later, he was in a cab with four others from his squadron. They were tasked to stay awake most of the night, which easily matched their current wake-sleep cycle. They were now headed out on the town to eat, for what meal did they call it? Breakfast, which matched the time they would be working on? Lupper? Who cared? They were hungry, and a nice steak sounded like just the thing for guys staring at lots of MREs in their future.

As it turned out, Anglin ended up in a cab with Technical Sergeants Larto, Nickel, and Deshotel as well as Staff Sergeant McCartney. They had all been chatting in the hanger and deciding on what to go eat. Anglin had heard this group decide on steak and he immediately joined in. They had told the cab driver that they wanted to go to a steak house.

The driver dropped them off in a part of town with lots of bright flashing lights. The driver, with broken English, said, "Makati. You find what you want here." He pointed down the street. There were indeed plenty of restaurants, but there also seemed to be quite a few strip clubs as well. This seemingly suited Larto just fine. They spotted an establishment that had "Steak" in the name and headed off down the street.

The early evening crowd was just starting to arrive. Loitering near the cab stand where they were dropped off were a group of six young women. Some in skin-tight mini-skirts or shorts and half shirts. They seemed to swarm in their direction.

As expected, TSgt Larto was the first to engage in conversation with them.

"Hello ladies," Larto said with a big grin.

"Ahhh. You American?" One said flashing a big toothy smile. "You want massage? Me give good massage."

They were all surprised at the aggressiveness of the girl who looked to be only sixteen. But a mature sixteen Anglin had to admit.

Anglin was particularly shocked. He had heard of street walkers but with his previous deployments to Muslim countries he had never seen anything like this. He was thinking, where would she give a massage or anything else she may offer?

It was clear that Larto was interested. "How much?" he asked.

"2,000 Pesos," she replied quickly.

"Nahhh, too expensive," Larto said as he turned to head on down the street.

She quickly grabbed his elbow as they all turned away. "1,500!" She said earnestly. "You like. I give good massage."

Larto winked at the others in the group before he turned and said, "Sorry, too much for me." And he again, turned away.

Pleadingly she asked, "How much you pay?" Never letting go of his arm.

He appeared to think it over a long moment before answering; "Maybe, um, 1,000 Pesos," he answered.

With a bit of pique and a frown she said, "Ok Joe, just this one time."

"Forget it John," TSgt Nickel cut in. "We're here to eat. You're not going off with some underage vixen."

"Ahhh, you should let us have some fun," said TSgt Deshotel who was equally enamored with a young lady who was aggressively bargaining and leaning on him.

"Ok, let's go eat," Larto relented and waving goodbye to the young lady. "But, dude, I was about to get laid for twenty bucks! And she was one hot chick."

"They all were," chimed in Deshotel.

"Maybe, but you have no idea what kind of big brother she has around the corner waiting for you," Nickel said. "It might have cost you a lot more than twenty dollars. Now let's eat. We're all starving."

Minutes later, they were being seated in a nice upscale restaurant. They all ordered their preferred steaks and sat back to relax as the drinks arrived. They engaged in small talk and avoided any conversations related to their mission or the military. It was mostly making fun of TSgt Larto and his unquenchable libido.

As their steaks arrived, music began to ramp up from an open doorway at the back of the restaurant behind Anglin. As the volume grew and a heavy bass beat began, Anglin turned to look in the direction of the music. He could see flashing lights reflecting off the walls. He assumed it was a dance club with its disco ball going.

Their easy banter continued all through their meal. Several had wine with dinner.

"Now that's what I call a breakfast!" commented McCartney as he leaned back and stretched, rubbing his full belly.

"Yep, and I think I see where we can find dessert," said Larto, staring at the doorway with the music now blaring in.

"Sure, let's check it out," said Deshotel.

As they entered the room, the light and music hit them in waves. The room was dark, with tables packed tightly around a well-lit stage. Up on the stage were four Filipino women dancing to the music and calling out to the men seated at the tables. They were dressed but only in skimpy underwear.

"Now that's what I call dessert," said Larto.

"I hear you, brother," said Deshotel.

But Anglin wasn't too sure. This looked really close to a strip club to him. And it may have been only a period of time before those ladies started taking off what little they were wearing. He had promised his wife that he wouldn't be going to a strip club. He still hadn't heard from her since he had left. Their internet connectivity was limited given their transient situation. He had a smart phone, but he didn't activate the international option because of the expense and that their ultimate location would have no cell phone service. So far, he had been unable to access his personal email account.

After entering the room, they were taking in the layout of the place when a small, middle-aged woman greeted them with a smile.

"This way, gentlemen. I have good table for you," she said as she led them to a table across the room but close to the stage. After they were seated, she spoke again. "I send you company. You not sit alone."

"What did she mean by that?" Anglin asked. "We're not alone."

"You'll see," said Larto, who shared a knowing smile with Deshotel and Nickel.

Within moments, five young ladies, dressed like their counterparts on stage, pulled up chairs to each of them. And along with them was a waiter asking what they wished to drink.

Anglin immediately felt uncomfortable. This was becoming something he was definitely not interested in, but he was clearly in the minority.

All but Anglin ordered beer. He got a soda. He didn't want to get drunk in a strange city. At first, the others teased him about it. But he insisted that this wasn't a place he could relax in. The others relented and decided that he would be the designated driver, so to speak.

"You be sure and get us home, Anglin," said his supervisor, Nickel.

Soon some of the customers started putting money on the stage, and the clothes started coming off.

The others were enjoying drinks with their new companions, but Anglin was ignoring the lady at his side. After a while, she gave up trying to engage him in conversation. She just quietly sipped her drink.

Anglin couldn't focus on the dancers. He truly did see them as a distracting waste of time. None compared to his hot, beautiful wife Kara. He sat there becoming increasingly uncomfortable. He could only recall the fight and accusations that Kara had made. He had earnestly denied them and now here he was, stuck in a strange part of town in a strip club. He felt horribly guilty and ashamed. Twice, he tried to get one of the others to leave with him, but they all refused, calling him a party pooper. He didn't dare leave alone.

As time dragged on, his guilt grew. How could he tell Kara? How could he face her and deny that what she predicted had actually happened? Even though he had no intention of being here and was in no way enjoying it. He just hunched down in his chair watching the others have a fun time while he felt miserable for the next four hours until they finally left.

During that time nature took its course. All the others had drunk more than Anglin and had to go to the toilet. Larto was the first to feel the need to go. After standing up and looking around he could see no obvious restroom markings on any of the several doors in the room. He leaned over and asked his companion where the toilet was. She stood up and took his arm in hers and led him to the rear of the room. They went around the back of the stage and out of sight. Thirty minutes or so later they were back, and he ordered another round of drinks.

One by one the same thing happened with each of the others. They and their companions all seemed to be gone twenty five to thirty minutes. But no one was really watching a clock.

Eventually, Anglin was the last needing to take a leak. When his lady stood up to go with him, he gently pushed her arm away. "No thanks, I have an idea where the bathroom is," he said gently. He went around behind the stage and entered a long hallway. The bathroom was clearly marked at the far end of the hall. On his way to it he passed numerous doors on both sides. Some were open and others closed. The open rooms were dimly lit and unoccupied, but he could see that there were beds in each of them. I'll be dammed, he thought. Kara was right again. For a fleeting moment he wondered how Kara knew so much about such places. Was there something in her past she hadn't told him? He dismissed the thought and shook his head in disgust and headed on to the restroom. Well, now I know why they were gone so long.

Back at their converted barracks hotel, most of the others drifted off to bed. Anglin was still awake and headed to the dayroom that functioned as a lounge. It had a TV on, tuned to a mixed martial arts fight. Others were reading, and several were surfing the internet with their smart phones. One of those on his phone was Staff Sergeant Urania. Anglin sat down near him and started watching the TV.

"Hey, Anglin. Thanks for the help the other day with the ammo. We really needed the assistance. You can only go so fast carrying that heavy crap before you're exhausted," Urania said.

"No problem," Anglin graciously accepted, even though he had been ordered to help them.

"So, what's the latest news?" he asked, assuming Urania had read some news on the phone.

"No idea. I've been chatting with my girlfriend back home. She was just on her lunch break, and we were able to have a live chat."

"Sounds great. I couldn't afford to activate my phone over here. So I haven't been able to check my email yet," Anglin explained.

"I can't afford it either, but my parents have plenty of money and insisted on paying it for me. On the agreement, of course, that I call them occasionally and email them regularly. I told them cell service could be questionable, but my mom insisted. Anyway, most of my time is spent staying in contact with my girlfriend."

"If you want, you can borrow my phone to check your email. It's the least I can do after your help. My back really thanks you," he said, handing the phone out to Anglin. "We were just finished. She had to get back to work."

"Sure, thanks," Anglin replied, taking the phone.

It took a few minutes until he was able to get to his personal email account. He was really hoping to have something from his wife, Kara. He was praying she had calmed down and was no longer upset. But nothing yet.

He did however have an email from one of his friends who worked at the Eglin AFB Medical Group on the other side of town from Hurlburt Field. He and Staff Sergeant Jacob Esler had been friends since they met in basic training at Lackland AFB, Texas. This was a bit of a surprise since he hadn't talked with him for months.

In the subject line, he said—"You Need to Know, My Friend"—was a bit ominous. It only got worse when he opened it up.

The email began: "Ron, I'm sorry but I think you need to know. I was out with friends last night."

Anglin checked the date and saw that it was sent on the fifth. He continued reading.

"We had decided to drive the hour over to a downtown club in Pensacola. We had been there a while when I saw someone I recognized out on the dance floor. I'm afraid it was Kara. And she wasn't alone. At first, I thought she was just out with you, or maybe girlfriends and some guy had asked her to dance. You had mentioned that she likes to dance, and you don't. So I knew it wasn't uncommon for her to occasionally dance with someone else in a friendly way while you were on the side talking with friends. No big deal, right? I thought that you had to be there somewhere, but I couldn't find you. It wasn't until today that I found out that you were deployed. I'm pretty sure that she never saw me. Mostly because of what I saw later. I'm sure she thought she was anonymous that far away from home. I'm not sure who the guy was. But he had a military haircut and looked somewhat familiar. But I have no idea when or where I may have seen him. Anyway, I was able to take a few pictures. They say it better than I can describe. I debated long and hard about telling you. I almost decided not to and just stay out of it. You are my good friend, and I don't want to see you hurt. But I know that your relationship has been rough, and I don't want you to be taken advantage of. I'm sorry, my friend. Jacob."

Anglin sat their shaking. "What the hell?" he said aloud to no one in particular.

He continued staring at the screen. The email had three unopened attachments. It was almost a minute before he dared open one.

The first picture showed a dimly lit dance floor with about ten couples out on the dance floor. It appeared to be a rock tune based on the movements the dancers were making. The photo caught Kara almost facing the camera and her partner facing away. She was wearing what she called her favorite drop-dead-sexy dress. It was a black, low-cut, tight-fitting short dress. He loved it because it showed off her long legs, slim figure, and ample breasts. It was the one she said she wore for him when she wanted to keep his attention. She had her usual dancing intense half smile, but her eyes were locked on the guy's face that was about two feet away from hers.

The second picture showed them slow dancing cheek to cheek. Kara had her back to the camera and her partners face was partially obscured by her hair. But they were clearly in a close embrace.

The third picture was the worst. They were still in an embrace as if slow dancing. Two things leaped out of the photo. The most obvious was that they were in a passionate kiss, and she was holding him tightly. The second was that she wasn't wearing her wedding ring. She had rarely taken it off before. Usually only to have the diamonds polished up.

Anglin was devastated. He just sat there staring at the photos, not saying a word.

"You all right?" asked Urania. "You look white as a ghost."

Anglin could only nod slowly. He closed out the screen and handed the phone back.

17 USS *CARL VINSON* RECEPTION
USS *Vinson*, Hong Kong Harbor

Lieutenant Commander Yao was on the top deck of the ferry to get a good look at the USS *Vinson* as they approached. He was excited to personally get a look at what he clearly saw as his undeclared enemy. More than most, he wanted to prove his metal in the air against an adversary. The acknowledged top dog when it came to air superiority was the United States. Though China and Russia had comparable capabilities and aircraft, they had only been used in relatively minor direct combat actions. Russia in Syria and China during the show of force against the Filipinos. The United States on the other hand had been on a war footing flying combat patrols in the Middle East since the first Gulf War in 1991. Yao was considered one of his squadron's best at dogfighting, but in reality, they spent most of their time practicing formation flying. They perfected large precise formations for the big military air demonstrations. These were designed to impress their own people and hopefully send a message to the rest of the world. So though he was good, the only way he felt he could prove it was by shooting down another jet in a dogfight, preferably an American.

He was on the first of two ferries out to the carrier, each carrying about 250 passengers. The visitors were a mix of Chinese, US ex-patriots, and the staff from embassies in Hong Kong representing many countries. There were actually quite a few officers from the People's Liberation Navy in their dress uniforms going out to meet their counterparts on the US ship. Yao was in civilian clothes. He was hoping to move around more freely to see what he could of the ship and to avoid being engaged in a discussion he may not want. He planned to get a good look at the F/A-18s and newer F-35s. He knew almost everything about each version of the two aircraft and had studied photographs of them. Still it was no substitute for standing next to one for a personal perspective. He also hoped to engage a pilot in conversation, hopefully without giving away that he was one too.

As they approached from over a mile away it seemed roughly the same size as his carrier the PLN *Liaoning* (*CV-16*). The biggest difference was that there was no jump jet ramp on the bow. The Americans use catapults to launch their jets into the air. The Chinese get a running start and hit the ramp that vectors them up into the sky. But as they closed the distance, it soon became clear that the American ship was bigger. Not just bigger, it was massive. Though the *Liaoning* and *Vinson* were roughly the same length at three hundred meters, the *Vinson* was wider and taller. The *Vinson* was almost twice the gross tonnage of the *Liaoning*. He could also see the crowded flight deck filled with aircraft, most of them F/A-18 fighters. The *Vinson* could carry twice the aircraft of the *Liaoning* as well, he recalled regrettably.

In spite of his animosity to the United States, he found himself momentarily overwhelmed with the firepower and capability the ship represented. But this quickly turned to irritated resentment. A bigger ship is just a bigger target, he decided.

Yao watched as the ferry tied up to the stern dock of the *Vinson*. Lashed to the stern was a large flat barge that was the width of the ship. The ferry was soon tied up to the barge and they were allowed to disembark. The VIPs including several ambassadors were escorted off first followed by everyone else. Yao was purposely near the back of the line to be able to linger a bit longer if he saw something interesting to avoid being pushed along by the crowd. Everyone was impressed with its size. Many were looking up above at the protruding flight deck eight meters above them. As Yao turned with the others to the left, he noticed to the right a line of American Sailors in civilian clothes waiting to board the ferry into town.

He walked through large open doors into the engine shop and on through a passageway with shops on either side for about twenty meters before entering the first of the *Vinson*'s three hanger bays.

The hanger bay which he learned was officially called hanger bay three, had supplies, and several types of maintenance gear and carts stacked in pallets in the aft section and no aircraft. Once past the pallets, they stepped onto a long red carpet leading to hanger bay two, the middle hanger bay. On either side of the carpet, spaced equally apart were the fifty state flags of the United States. The huge sliding hanger bay doors they were approaching were closed except for a ten-foot opening gap for them to pass through. He noticed huge murals decorating the hangar doors.

Entering the second hangar bay, he could see that it was impressively decorated. The entire hangar bay deck was covered in a green outdoor-turf-type carpet, and there were several tables set up all around the hanger perimeter with some in the middle elaborately laid out. Some had hors d'oeuvres and others served wine, beer, and sodas. In the center of the hanger, he was astonished to see a large ice sculpture. Hanging horizontally along the left wall, opposite the aircraft elevator, were massive American and Chinese flags side by side, from floor to ceiling. A platform with a microphone was centered just in front of the flags. Hanging from the ceiling were row after row of the colorful international maritime nautical signal code flags, each representing a number or letter of the alphabet. Hanger bay one's doors further forward were closed, and whatever it contained was hidden from view. Scattered about the hanger in small groups were American Sailors in their formal-dress blue uniforms. Many were engaged in lively small talk with their guests.

As he entered the hanger two F-18s immediately caught his eye. This was what he had come to investigate, and here they were, to his left, with one in each corner. Both had colorful decorations painted on them. One just had its vertical fins painted in what he assumed were the squadron's colors. The other had quite a menacing appearance with its fins and upper spine to the cockpit in black. On the nose were painted the eyes and teeth of a shark with a blood-red tongue. Both planes were roped off, and strategically placed in front of each was a table with various drinks where Sailors wearing white long-sleeved shirts with black bow ties served the guests.

He immediately headed to the nearest one and got in line. As he waited for a soda, he focused on the pilot in a flight suit standing by the nose of the closest plane. Here was his chance. After getting his drink, he moved to look at the plane. He could see that one of his fellow uniformed PLN pilots was already talking with the pilot. He eased over to listen in.

"How long you fly Hornet?" asked the Chinese pilot. "You fly combat?"

"About four years," answered Lieutenant Prichard. "Yes, I have flown combat missions."

"Where you fly? Afghanistan? Iraq? Syria? You drop bombs?" The Chinese pilot asked in rapid fire succession.

"I can't talk about that," responded Prichard, having been warned to keep his responses very general.

"Hornet good in dogfight?" he continued asking. "It better than F-16 Falcon?"

"It does okay," said Prichard, thinking, *Man, this guy is not being subtle, is he?*

"Hornet rate fight or angle fight," he continued to press.

"We just go around and around till I can get a shot," Prichard said. There was no way he was going to discuss dogfighting tactics with this foreign national. This guy clearly knows his stuff he thought. Though all fighter planes dog fight similarly, each has its unique advantages and disadvantages. Generally the tighter circle you can make in the air the faster you can get around behind the other guy. If doing a rate fight, the fighter is counting on his plane getting around the circle faster and will eventually get into a firing position. Air Force F-16 'Vipers', as they are affectionately called by the pilots that fly them, instead of the tamer official 'Fighting Falcon' name, are great rate fighters. Angle fighters such as the F-18 have the advantage of being able to cash in their energy to get their nose pointed at the other guy for a shot if needed. With modern missiles you can shoot your opponent in the face. In a fight against different aircraft, how you fight against them will vary. Going against F-16s, an F-18 Hornet pilot may find that a skilled and patient Viper pilot will eventually get around behind his Hornet and into shooting position. To counter this, the Hornet pilot can shift to an angle fight by pulling hard to put his nose on the Viper in a threatening way, taking full advantage of the F-18's large elevators that can point the nose of his plane at his opponent from the opposite side of the fight circle. He may or may not get a shot off. The Viper pilot will have to honor the threat of the Hornet's nose coming at him and pull all he has to neutralize the Hornet's sudden advantage taking him out of his rate fight. They would then merge back to a neutral head to head pass and the fight resumes into another of the round and round circular fights commonly called a fur ball. Ultimately, it is the skill of the pilot that determines the victor in such a contest. A great Hornet pilot can defeat an above average Viper pilot and vice versa. But in reality with modern weapons and radars, a face to face dog fight situation is unlikely to occur. It is far more likely that a missile from afar would reach out and ruin their opponent's day far beyond visual range without ever actually seeing them. Still, every fighter pilot in the world trains strenuously for a face to face dog fight.

Yao was looking at the details of the plane as he was intently listening to the conversation. Fool, he thought. His fellow fighter pilot, whom he did not actually know, was clearly pressing too hard. The American was obviously alerted and would now only be giving generic answers to any questions. He moved over to the other aircraft and the pilot assigned to it. After ten minutes, it was clear he would gain no new information about the aircraft from listening to them talk about their F-18s. They were pretty much saying the same things over and over as different people came up to ask all the same questions.

Aside from wanting a close-up look at the American hardware, he wanted to gauge the metal of the pilots that flew them. The two assigned in front of their aircraft were too busy repeating useless basic data. It was clear that they were intelligent and careful about what they said. He hoped that several of the other American officers he saw were pilots. He decided to head to the nearest officer that was wearing two badges. One clearly appeared to be wings. He had no idea what the other one was. Some sort of eagle holding a three-pronged spear. The officer's sleeve-rank insignia indicated that he was a Commander. He was already engaged in conversation with an Aussie and two Chinese, all in civilian clothing.

"I don't get to fly as often as I like, I'll tell you that," the SMO said to the late-twenty-something, pretty blond Aussie female.

"Do you fly all of them?" she asked, clearly flashing her eyes at him.

"Well," he said thinking, "actually I do, or at least, a version of each of them."

Hearing this, Yao was definitely interested. A pilot of skill that can fly them all, he relished talking to.

"Which do you like most?" she asked.

"Oh, that's easy. The Super Hornet," he replied, noticing the new addition to their little group. "There is nothing like the kick in the pants you get with a fully loaded Hornet cat shot."

"You ever get used to it?" asked one of the Chinese.

"If you do it often enough. But each cat shot is different," the SMO said.

"How so?" asked the newcomer to the group, Yao.

"Well, some are pretty benign shots as catapult shots go. But others are a real kick in the pants, almost as if your spine was going to rip out of your back and merge with the seat," said the SMO. "Those are the ones you never forget."

"Why shot so hard?" Yao asked.

"It's all based on the total weight of the aircraft. The heavier the plane, the faster you have to be flying at the end of the cat shot. The distance we have to get airborne is always the same, so the heavier we are, the harder the catapult has to be to push us up to the faster flying speed," the SMO explained.

"You hold stick while launching?" Yao asked.

"No, the pilot is hands-off during the cat shot to avoid inadvertently moving the stick due to the catapult forces. But for me, I never get my hands on the controls," the SMO lamented.

"Why, you fly automatic?" Yao was suddenly desperate to know.

"Not that. I always fly in the back seat, and there are no flight controls in back," the SMO explained.

"You not pilot?" Yao asked incredulously.

"No. I'm a Flight Surgeon, not a pilot. I fly routinely to help me understand the physical and mental stresses of the aircrew I care for," said the SMO.

"I see," said Yao with a smile. But inwardly, he was pissed. He had wasted time on a useless staff officer who does not really know anything. *Not a real warrior*, he thought as he politely moved on.

As Yao was walking away in disgust the *Vinson*'s CO began his greeting to the guests. "Hello. I'm Captain Whitehall, the commanding officer of the USS *Vinson*. On behalf of the United States and Rear Admiral LaSalle, I wish to welcome each and every one of you to the finest ship and crew in the United States Navy. I would like to thank the Chinese government and the city of Hong Kong for this opportunity to visit your wonderful city. We hope you enjoy your time aboard and take the opportunity to enjoy some refreshments and meet with our crew. As a special treat, we will be taking the aircraft elevator behind you up to the flight deck every fifteen minutes. Feel free to go up and take in the view of your beautiful city and get a closer look at our aircraft."

Captain Whitehall continued talking a few minutes before introducing Admiral LaSalle. But LCDR Yao was no longer listening. He was slowly making his way toward the huge aircraft elevator. He wanted to be on the first trip up. He went to the table nearest the elevator and got a small plate of boiled shrimp, chicken wings, and broccoli to nibble on while waiting.

Once the Admiral had finished speaking, he went out onto the elevator as others were starting to congregate there. Within minutes, several Sailors came out to stop further boarding. They were corralled into the center of the elevator and away from the edges. Stanchions rose up out of the deck around the elevator entrance. A loud bell started ringing and then the elevator rose smoothly and quickly up to the flight deck.

Yao saw that they were just forward of the ship's island superstructure. And everywhere he looked were aircraft. The arrangement was both impressive and pleasing to the eye. Though the planes were still roped off so that you could not touch them, he could get within five feet of most. He took note of the various types of aircraft on the deck.

He completed a careful but quick stroll so that he could view most of the flight deck to see the distinct types of aircraft there were aboard. It was mostly as he had been briefed, F/A-18 fighters, SH-60 helicopters, and E-2C early warning turboprops. He saw all but the F-35s and C-2A Greyhounds.

Yao stayed focused on the fighters. There were the single-seat, older legacy F/A-18C Hornets and the larger single-seat F/A-18Es Super Hornets, which were about twenty five percent bigger than their older cousins. He also identified over a dozen of the two seat F/A-18F and newer F/A-18G Super Hornets. He spent most of his time carefully looking at the details of each version of the F-18s, taking note of their similarities and differences. He paid particular attention to the engine exhaust nozzles. Most were wide open, and a few were closed down and smaller. This could be valuable knowledge in a potential dog fight against one. If you can see an opponent's exhaust nozzles from across the fight circle you can know roughly what his power settings are. If they are flared wide open then he has gone to afterburner to increase his speed and/or energy level for maneuvers needing extra power. Knowing this before his opponent actually executed the move can give him an edge to anticipate what may be coming and prepare to counter it. He also wondered if the smaller F-18s were able to turn better than the newer larger ones. Increasing size may translate into more weapons-stations but comes with an increased weight cost requiring larger and thirstier engines needing even more fuel. He assumed the smaller ones were more nimble and had the advantage in a dog fight. He noted that the wing strakes were further forward to the front of the windshield on the older legacy Hornets and that the engine air intakes and horizontal elevators were rounded. The Super Hornets had shorter wider wing strakes and sharper angles with rectangular engine intakes and squared off horizontal elevators.

He spent ninety minutes studying their every detail up close. By the time he heard the call for the last elevator trip back down, he was confident he would be able to identify which version aircraft he was up against should that day ever come. He hoped that day would be sooner rather than later. It could even be against one of these very aircraft. As he rode the elevator down, he could not suppress the grin on his face as he imagined one of those American aircraft in a huge fireball as it was blown from the sky by one of his missiles.

18 GOING ASHORE
Hong Kong, China

When the reception officially ended at 2100, the SMO quickly headed to his stateroom to change into civilian clothes and grab his packed overnight bag along with the cell phone he had been issued for use while ashore. He double checked to make sure he had two copies of the phone numbers of all the other key ships officers. One for his wallet and one for another pocket just in case his wallet was snatched. He had already removed from his wallet all but the actual items he would need ashore, cash, two credit cards, and his military ID. Two days earlier he had exchanged US $500 for $3,800 in Hong Kong dollars at the disbursing office.

Stepping out of his stateroom on the second deck, he headed aft toward the stern. Once there, he headed directly down to the stern dock. The CO had invited him and several other senior officers to go ashore with him on his personal boat, the Captain's gig. It was due to cast off at 2115 sharp, so he had hustled. On the port side of the stern dock was a large double-deck ferry with a long line of Sailors loading. On the starboard side was the smaller twenty-five-foot Captain's gig. He quickly climbed aboard and was greeted by a dozen of his fellow department heads. The CO wasn't yet aboard.

"I see that I made it in time," the SMO said.

"Just barely," replied the Gun Boss, nodding toward the entrance where the CO was entering.

The SMO sat down and turned to see an enormous bag of golf clubs filling the cabin entrance. Behind it was Captain Whitehall maneuvering the monster into a corner of the cabin. It was apparent that the Captain was a huge golfer and took his game seriously.

Within moments of the CO settling in, the boat's lines were cast off, the engine rumbled to life, and they were soon heading to Hong Kong. The SMO was fascinated by the colorfully illuminated buildings they were approaching. As he noted before, the architecture here was as much about beauty as function. He had expected a large metropolitan city, but not a beautiful one.

They soon pulled into the recently renovated Fenwick Pier. Once ashore, most of the others scattered, going their separate ways. Some headed to hotels, while others were eager to check out the local night life. The SMO headed to the street hoping to catch a cab to his hotel. He knew roughly where it was but preferred a taxi tonight until he learned his way around. On his way out, he noticed the CO loading the enormous bag of golf clubs and luggage into his rental car. *It must be great being the boss*, he thought. *Your own personal boat and car when in port.*

"Hey, SMO, where you headed?" the CO asked as he passed by.

"I'm headed to the Conrad Hilton, sir."

"So am I. Throw your bag in and ride with me," the CO offered.

"Thanks, sir, that will be great," he accepted happily.

As they pulled into traffic, the Captain asked. "Your first time to Hong Kong, SMO?"

"Yes, sir. My last ship deployment was to Europe and the Middle East through the Suez Canal."

"It's my third time here. They have some fantastic golf courses. Are you a golfer?" queried the CO.

"No, not really. I have played with friends off and on over the years, but I never really had the time or motivation to get into it.

After a short trip, they arrived at the Hilton, parked, and checked into the hotel.

As they parted, the SMO said, "Thank you, sir, for the ride. Have a good evening."

"Don't mention it. Always glad to share," the Captain replied.

The SMO was soon in his room enjoying a long, hot, steaming shower. Something that wasn't allowed on a ship where water use was carefully regulated. After showering, he headed down to the lounge to wait for Jenna.

As he punched the elevator call button, he was imagining a late romantic dinner with her in a corner table. He was headed down now to scout out the possibilities in the hotel restaurant and possibly others nearby. Who knew how this evening would turn out, he thought with a growing smile on his face as the elevator doors opened.

At the hotel restaurant, he was disappointed to see that it was in the process of closing and the last guests were leaving. The maître d' said that all the other restaurants were closed by this time. *Well, maybe tomorrow night*, he thought as he headed to the bar lounge disappointed.

"Hey, SMO," he heard as he entered. Off to the right was Captain Whitehall sitting alone and waving him over. "Won't you join me?" asked the CO.

"I'll be happy to, Captain," he replied. "I'm waiting for a friend to join me in a bit."

As he sat down, the CO said, "SMO, we are both semi-off-duty, and this is an informal setting. How about you call me Wedge for the evening. I've been called Wedge most of my career and only been exclusively called Captain since I went from flying jets to driving boats. And honestly, I miss just being Wedge.

"Yes, sir, Wedge, it is. For this evening," the SMO replied.

After the SMO ordered a soda, the Captain asked. "What's your call sign, SMO? You're bound to have one. You have been a Flight Surgeon for a while now."

"It's Leopard, "the SMO informed him.

"Leopard," the Captain repeated. "Must be a great story behind that. Did you get into a fight with one? Or did you get scratched by your pet cat?"

"Neither. At a squadron naming party, they were offering up various doctor-related names. All typically related to various exams that you pilots dread. The top contenders were Fingers, Juggler, Knuckles, and worst of all, BOSCO. BOSCO was for 'Bend Over and Spread Cheeks Open.' I was dreading them all. I already knew of a Flight Surgeon with the call sign of

TACAN, alluding to the backup navigation stations we use. However, it was spelled T-A-C-N but was pronounced the same. It stood for 'Turn and Cough Now,' like we say when doing a hernia check. I wasn't allowed to vote or offer any better names. They made a great show of debating the merits of Fingers versus Juggler for me. They even had me hold up my hands for all to see. At the last minute, just before the final vote, someone from the drunken peanut gallery suggested Leopard. He said that I had been an active Navy SEAL wounded in combat and was deserving of a more honorable call sign. He went on to explain that a leopard seal is the most aggressive and deadly of all the seals and would be fitting for me. They all cheered and immediately voted to name me Leopard. I later learned that leopard had already been picked weeks before and they were just yanking my chain with the other options. But at the time I was greatly relieved and proud to be called Leopard."

"How about you? What does Wedge refer to?" the SMO asked. "It's obvious that you are a big golfer. Do you spend a lot of time getting out of sand traps with a sand wedge? Or is it for the simplest tool ever invented? I once knew another Wedge, and he earned his by being the dumbest pilot in the squadron and always failing his surprise NATOPS boldface emergency procedures tests."

The CO gave a wry smile. "Well, neither. Let's just say that either would be what I would like most folks to think. But it is for another reason altogether. Back when I was a single, young fighter pilot, we would occasionally get to take cross-country trips. We would almost always end up in a bar or club hoping to meet and impress pretty young ladies. I, of course, would want the hottest babe, as did the other pilots. Even though I may have not been the first to meet a pretty lady, I would find a way to chat with her. Often she would forget the other guy and end up leaving with me. After this had occurred on several trips with different pilots, the word was getting around to watch out for me stealing the hot chicks away from them. And one guy was explaining how I always found a way to wedge my way between them and the hot babe. Pretty soon, I was officially known as Wedge. There are only a few still around these days that know that story. Most have left the Navy to fly for the airlines or retired. Not even my wife knows that story, and those skirt-chasing days are well behind me. And I don't want her having anything extra to worry about. Now I spend my spare time chasing a little white ball around a golf course. Something I find relaxing and I'm fairly good at.

"So Leopard, how does a Navy SEAL end up as a Flight Surgeon?" the CO asked.

"It's a bit of a convoluted story but here goes," said the SMO. "I have always dreamed of flying. For years, I planned on being a Navy fighter pilot. My dad had been in the Navy for six years and then worked at NAS Mayport in Jacksonville as a civil servant until he recently retired. So I've been around Navy ships and airplanes while growing up. My twin brother was dreaming of being a Navy SEAL since he was sixteen. We both grew up on the water and have been scuba-diving most of our lives. My dad had a boat that he chartered out on weekends for either fishing or scuba-diving. So that is how we were interested in Navy stuff."

"So why did you switch from wanting to be a pilot to being a SEAL?" the Captain asked.

"Because of my brother. We had both been accepted to college and were planning on Navy ROTC to help pay the way. I was headed for an engineering degree. But just before graduating high school my brother was killed in a car wreck. It was hard on all of us. I thought more and more of how he would never get to live his dream of being a Navy SEAL. So over time I decided to do it for him. It was my way of honoring the memory of my brother. Besides, it was my second choice anyway. After graduation, I was accepted for BUDS and made it, but it wasn't easy. I actually loved being a SEAL. It was both physically and mentally challenging, and there was a huge personal satisfaction being in such an elite organization. Plus, we did a lot of cool things."

The CO nodded as the SMO continued.

"But as you know, since 9/11, things have been deadly serious. After almost two years of training I was assigned to a team and soon on my way to eastern Afghanistan. Within days of arriving, we were running covert missions tracking down the remnants of Al-Qaeda. On one of these, we ended up in a heavy firefight. Two of my team were killed, and all but one was wounded. I took a round in my right hip that shattered my upper femur and did some muscle damage. An Air Force Combat Controller on patrol with us called in an Air Force AFSOC gunship. It orbited overhead raining down 40 mm and 105 mm rounds on the Taliban forces until we could be extracted. He saved our bacon that day, and he probably saved my life. Our team medic was one of those killed. After getting the gunship engaged with the enemy, he personally bandaged me up and controlled the bleeding.

I was patched up and evacuated to Germany where they pieced my femur back together as best they could. Weeks later, I was sent back to Balboa for three more surgeries and physical therapy. I was in the hospital for about four months before they would let me go home as an out-patient. I got bored stuck in the hospital and started listening to the doctors as they made their rounds to all the patients twice a day. Before long, I was allowed to follow them on these rounds. First in my wheelchair and later on crutches. I became fascinated by the whole medical process.

It eventually became clear that I would be able to walk okay. But I had lost some of my hip range of motion, which limited my ability to run. In short, I would be a liability on a SEAL mission. My operational SEAL days were over. I was pretty depressed about it for a while but continued on the medical rounds with the docs. Before long, I decided that I really liked all that medical stuff and decided to try for medical school. I was lucky enough to get into the Uniformed Services University of the Health Sciences in Bethesda, Maryland. It's an exceptional school. The camaraderie there among everyone was great. Almost as good as in the SEAL teams. After internship, I had an exciting time as a Flight Surgeon for a couple of years, finally getting to fly in those jets. After that tour, I continued my medical training as an Emergency Medicine doc. First at Portsmouth Naval Hospital in Virginia for almost five years where I deployed every twelve months or so. That was the breaking point of my marriage. My wife and I had drifted apart, and she was fed up with the military life, and I still loved it. She was tired of the deployments, moves, and giving up on her dream of law school. When I got orders to Great Lakes while I was on my last deployment, she had had enough and flat out refused to move to Illinois and asked for a divorce. We're still on good terms. She is now a lawyer in Los Angles, and I will be near her and the kids again after this deployment. After the divorce, I was looking for a change of pace and applied for the Residency in Aerospace Medicine. I still love flying, and this is my first assignment after finishing that program. It all worked out, and I have had a great career. The only downside was the divorce, and I lost two years' time in rank going from a line officer to a medical officer," the SMO finished.

"You're right. That is a heck of a story," said the Captain. "So that is how you became a doc. Leopard, tomorrow at 0800, I have a tee time at this wonderful golf course. You may not be that good, but you are welcome to join us. There are only three of us and have room for a fourth player. We promise not to make fun of you."

Just then, Jenna Tullos stepped into the lounge, looking around. Her long hair was down framing her face, and she was wearing a fashionable, knee-length red dress. It was not tight fitting but was still quite suggestive of the curves below. She had transformed from the professional, all-business naval officer into a beautiful, elegant woman out for the evening. And she was now looking straight at Derek with a glowing smile.

"Thanks, Wedge," he said, looking only at Jenna. "But I may have other plans. Please excuse me. My friend has arrived. Thank you for a nice evening."

"Your friend is more than welcome to join us," the CO said with a toothy smile.

"Not a chance, Wedge," the SMO said emphatically. "I don't believe for a minute that your wedging days are over."

"Ah, you never know," the CO replied. "Have a great evening." The CO raised his glass to the SMO in a toast as the SMO rose and headed toward Jenna.

19 KNOCKING ON FORBIDDEN DOORS
Hong Kong, China

The SMO met Jenna at the lounge entrance.

"You look amazing, Jenna! Absolutely amazing," said Derek.

"You are looking pretty sharp yourself, Derek," Jenna replied.

"I'm afraid all the restaurants are closed this time of night. Our choices for dining are pretty slim unless you want something from the McDonald's by the pier," he said, looking into her eyes.

"I'm not all that hungry. I had a late lunch," she said, returning the deep look.

"Neither am I,", he said.

"But I am thirsty though," she added.

"Okay, there are plenty of quiet tables here," he said, gesturing to a window booth with a wonderful view of the city.

After their drinks arrived, they both sat there a moment in silence as they gazed at each other.

"Do you remember when we first met?" Jenna asked.

"Yeah, how could I forget?" Derek began. "It was the day of my first carrier trap. Let me see. I believe it was back almost ten years now. I was trying to get used to sitting backward on that C-2 Greyhound that was flying us out to the USS *Truman*. I was fresh out of Flight Surgeon's school on my way to my first assignment with my shiny new Flight Surgeon's wings. I was as proud of them as my SEAL Trident."

"Uh-huh," Jenna answered. "And I remember noticing you in that obviously brand-new flight suit. You had slept most of that flight, as I recall. I was curious and wanted to know who this new handsome stranger was."

"Is that so?" Derek said as he felt his face flush. "Well, um, I learned long ago to sleep whenever I had the chance. I had plenty of experience sleeping in planes and helicopters, usually just before I jumped out of them. Little did I know then what life on the ship was going to be like. I had been on ships at sea before, including submarines, but those were for just short periods. I spent most of my SEAL time in the high deserts and mountains of Afghanistan."

"And you asked me why I was riding in the back of the plane with the rest of the cargo?" Jenna recalled. "You wanted to know why I wasn't in the cockpit driving, and I pointed out that I was a Naval Flight Officer who flew in the rear seat of an F-18F Super Hornet."

"You remember that? I'm impressed." Derek admitted, both surprised and pleased.

"Actually, we should have been," Jenna continued. "As you may recall, our Hornet had a hydraulic problem, and we had diverted to Sigonella, Sicily. Once our skipper learned it would take a week to fix the jet, he wanted us back on the ship ASAP."

"Yeah, I remember now," Derek chimed in. "I recall your pilot was pissed because you two had to head back to the boat. He was excited about having a private hotel room, with access to bars and women. As I recall, you told me that he was a budding alcoholic."

"Yep, he was, and terrified of your Flight Surgeon power to ground him," Jenna said.

"Yeah, quite a few of the younger aviators avoid us as much as possible. The older guys had figured out over the years that most flight surgeons were on their side and wanted to keep them in the cockpit. They knew we would always want to bum a ride with them."

"You guys have always taken good care of me," Jenna answered.

"You know, Jenna," Derek said. "I've never forgotten our first meeting either. I remember I had said something like 'Bad luck, I guess,' for the problem you were having with the Hornet. And you curiously said, 'Or good luck, depending on how you look at it.' That always stuck with me. I wonder why that is? I think it was the way you were looking at me when you said it that left such a lasting impression. I've often wondered what you meant."

"You to have a good memory," Jenna said. "I guess we both saw something in each other from the first moment. Well, if you must know, I really liked you. Probably the reason we were such good friends on that first cruise. But you were married, and I was engaged, so neither of us was looking for more than friendship. You were really cool and easy to talk to."

"Me too, Jenna. You had made it an easy transition into the aviation world. Besides, we kept bumping into each other in the ready room. Your squadron was the only one that gave me a chance to fly in an F-18. The EA-6B was pretty cool but just not the same. And I already had plenty of time in helos."

"I still recall how we talked about our relationships over meals up in wardroom one," Jenna said. "Your wife was frustrated with the impact on her own career plans, and I was worried how married life would affect mine."

"We did become very good friends," said Derek scratching the surface of what they had yet to openly discuss over the past two months. Partly because he was afraid it would never be what it had been and equally afraid that it would be. His ex-wife was expecting them to continue exploring the possibility of making it work again. Guilt kept bubbling up at the most unwanted times.

"Yeah, but we became much more that casual friends, Derek. We haven't talked about that, have we?

"No, we haven't," Derek answered, swallowing a dry lump.

"We developed a closeness I have never had with anyone else," Jenna continued. "You know that as well as I do. I loved my fiancé, but our relationship had become so much more intimate, and we had almost kissed that one time. Your sense of honor to your wife held you back. I was ready to give it all up for a chance with you. And I know you wanted the same."

"Yeah, I remember. All too well. You were the only one I have ever been able to open up to." Oh, how he missed being able to bare his soul to someone without any fear. "You have no idea how liberating that was for me," he continued. "You were never judgmental."

"I could see where your marriage was headed, even if you couldn't. But you were devoted to her and your kids. And honestly, I respected you even more for that," she confessed.

Jenna reached over and gently took his hand in hers and said, "I tried so very hard to recreate what we had during my marriage. But it was, he was, just different. He was loving but in some ways distant and focused only on his own concerns. We loved each other, but I felt more like a beloved pet and not a partner. He could never match what we had, and it just finally fell apart."

"I'm sorry it didn't work out for you, Jenna. You deserved the best."

Deciding to shift the topic a bit before it became too uncomfortable, Derek said, "I guess we'll have to wait till tomorrow for our dinner date, I suppose. Wait, shoot, I have a reception to attend tomorrow night here in Hong Kong at 2000."

"That's all right. I'm going to that one too with the Admiral," Jenna said. "Maybe we can just have an early dinner."

"True, but I was kind of hoping for it to be the start of a nice, long, relaxing evening together. That reception kind of throws a monkey wrench into things."

"Well, we still have the rest of tonight," she said with a seductive smile.

They continued the small talk for another twenty minutes as they finished their drinks. They then began drifting away from the lounge and down the corridor toward the elevators as they continued their conversation.

"So, how did you enjoy the ship's reception?" she asked.

"It was quite impressive. The SUPPO and his folks did a phenomenal job," he replied. "And I met quite a few interesting people. Who knew there would be so many different countries represented? I had a wonderful time. I met Chinese, French, Russian, and several American expats. And there was this young Australian lady that seemed to spend quite a lot of time chatting with me," he said, looking to gauge Jenna's response.

"Did she now?" said Jenna, slightly glancing in his direction. She had noticed that he had an entourage of young ladies around him during the reception. She had been busy staying near the Admiral and hadn't had a chance to chat with Derek.

"Yep, but I stepped away, and two Navy Lieutenants quickly took my spot. I'm probably too old and mature for such things these days," he said with a suppressed smile as they arrived at an elevator.

"Too bad," she said as she turned and punched the up button.

They entered the elevator closest to the lounge, each keeping a casual but respectable distance from the other on opposite sides of the cab. They were not alone on the elevator, but none of the three others appeared to be American. They each separately pushed the call buttons for their floors. Derek and Jenna both noticed that all the others would be getting off before reaching his lower room floor. He could see her eyes smiling back at him while she kept a straight face. He, on the other hand, was grinning sneakily like a kid about to open his Christmas presents two days early. After the others had exited the cab, she smiled back and reached out her hand to him invitingly. He reveled in their first intimate touch as he took her hand in his, noting its softness and warmth. They stood there, hand in hand, not saying a word, each enjoying the moment.

The heck with it, he thought. Tonight he was going to be totally selfish and do what he wanted. When the door opened to his floor, she stepped out, leading him by the hand toward his room.

He never said a word as he pulled his keycard out and opened the door. He let her enter the room first, which was beautifully furnished with a king bed in its center. The room was lit only by the soft-colored glow from outside building lights. He reflexively reached for the light switch but felt her soft palm stop his hand as he was about to flip it on. He glanced toward her as she nodded her head gently from side to side. Still holding his hand, she pulled him slowly toward her as the door closed quietly behind them. Now only inches apart, they both looked deeply into each other's inviting eyes. He smiled, leaning down to kiss her as she tilted her head up to meet him. The sensation of their warm lips touching in their first kiss was electric. Kissing was slow and deliberate at first. She soon began kissing his face and neck, then back to his lips with increasing intensity. Gently embracing, he was pleasantly surprised as her tongue slipped in and toyed with his. Her arms pulled him ever closer until their bodies were touching lightly. Their kissing intensity rose as their hands began to explore each other. She guided his right hand where she wanted it to go, and he felt her quiver at his touch.

Kissing ever more passionately, his hands began to roam, exploring other areas of her firm body.

Jenna was exploring as well, as he heard her softly say, "Mm," in appreciation at his now obvious arousal. She let go and led him toward the bed. Reaching the bedside, she turned and unbuttoned his shirt as he reached to unzip her dress. The dress dropped silently to the floor, revealing nothing underneath. Derek just stood there mesmerized.

"Are you going to stand there enjoying the view, or are you taking that shirt off?" she asked.

Derek took just a moment to pull out his personal smart phone. He quickly put on music he had discovered in the past year that he thought would be perfect for a situation like this. He slid his phone onto the night stand as the hauntingly seductive sound of Enigma's *MCMXC a.D.* began its rhythm and beat as he kept his focus on Jeanna's inviting charms.

His clothes hit the floor, and she gently guided him onto the bed where they resumed their passionate kissing and exploring. Before long, their bodies merged as one, and they were soon matching the slow rhythm of Enigma as their passion rose. Jenna was soon driven to repeated waves of ecstasy as Derek kept pace with the alluring music. The album repeated a third time before they finally collapsed satisfied into each other's arms and drifted off to sleep.

After a brief nap, Jenna gently awoke Derek as she resumed where they had left off. She was soon crying out again with spasmodic pleasure before they again collapsed breathlessly into each other's arms.

"Wow! That was amazing!" Derek said, breathing heavily, speaking for the first time since entering the elevator.

She nuzzled him softly and kissed his neck. "Um-hm," she replied.

She laid her head on his shoulder and played with the hair on his chest listening to his heavy breathing slow as he drifted back to sleep. She stayed awake caressing him, savoring the feeling of his strong, warm body next to hers until she too fell asleep.

20 SAVE THE PUPPIES
Hong Kong, China

*R*ing-ring. *Ring-ring. Ring-ring.*

"What the hell!" exclaimed the SMO as he was suddenly awakened from a deep sleep by the unfamiliar ring of his issued cell phone. He slid to the edge of the bed and groped over the nightstand in the dark for the annoying phone.

"Commander Lloyd," he said, trying to shake himself awake.

"SMO, this is Alverez. Sorry to wake you, but you needed to be notified of an incident involving one of our corpsmen," she said.

"Go ahead. I'm listening," he said, yawning. "What time is it?"

"It's almost two thirty in the morning, sir. Petty Officer Second Class Llortman appears to have had too much to drink tonight and was acting strange. We got him under control, and I escorted him back to the ship an hour ago. The doc on call is getting some lab work in case someone spiked one of his drinks. He is asleep on the ward now with an IV going. He should be fine. The local police were not involved, but he did come to the attention of the Shore Patrol. I wanted you to be aware in case the CO or XO ask you about it in the morning. They will be notified of the incident," she said.

"Okay, thanks. Anything else going on?" he asked.

"Not really. A few other drunks. We heard of some fights before we headed back to the boat, but we saw nothing," she reported. "Llortman seems to have gotten the most attention so far."

"Okay. Don't hesitate to call if anything else comes up. Now you get some sleep too," he added. "Good night."

He clicked off the phone and set it on the bedside table.

As he rolled back over, he noticed the form of Jenna lying under the sheets. She was turned toward him with her eyes open.

"Anything serious?" Jenna asked.

"Doesn't appear to be. One of my corpsmen had too much to drink. He is back on the ship sleeping it off," he said easing up next to her warm soft body. "Sorry to wake you."

"That's okay," she said. "It goes with the job. But since you're awake"—she leaned over to him—"you left something running, and you still have unfinished business, mister." She eagerly pressed her lips to his.

The next morning at 0645, after yet another passionate round of lovemaking, the SMO was standing in the shower, letting the steaming water wash over him and do its magic. Jenna had earlier headed to her room where she had fresh clothes to do the same. He needed to get ready for the day. By 0730, he was down in the hotel restaurant with Jenna for breakfast.

"Good morning," he said. "You look well rested for someone who got so little sleep. You hungry?"

"Starving," she said.

They were able to order breakfast before his phone rang again.

"SMO," he answered.

"SMO, Alverez here. I wanted to give you an update on Petty Officer Llortman," Alverez said.

"Go ahead. Is he okay?" he asked noticing that Jenna's phone was now ringing.

She continued. "It seems that he started drinking as soon as he got ashore, getting very drunk. He ended up fighting with some of his fellow corpsmen who were trying to get him back to the ship. It took five to drag him back to the pier and our medical station set up there. They eventually had to give him Ativan to calm him down. He made quite the spectacle before he quieted down. Luckily, he was a friendly and happy drunk, but he started acting strange and yelling that he had to 'Save the Puppies!' No one knew what he was talking about. Several of the corpsmen decided he'd had enough and gently tried to guide him back to the pier and the ship. But he resisted them and began pushing back saying he had to go the other way to save the puppies. It eventually required five to tackle him in a crowded Hong Kong street. I heard that it was quite difficult to get him back to the pier, and he resisted all the way. At the pier he was taken to the medical station, and they strapped him onto a stretcher, and he fought to get free. It took two shots of Ativan to finally knock him out."

"Copy," the SMO said shaking his head. "Any other problems?"

"Well, it was a pretty busy night after all. Over a dozen Sailors got into altercations with locals late last night. No major injuries. Mostly bumps and bruises. But there was a broken nose and a possible boxer's fracture," she answered.

"Is that normal? Seems like a lot to me," he asked.

"Yes, a bit more than expected," she replied. "When the USS *Nimitz* was here two years ago, they had only one reported fight over a five-day port call. And that was between two Sailors fighting over a woman. We had fourteen last night, all involving Chinese locals. The incidents all occurred in the section of town near the pier with the bars and strip clubs. No reported problems with Sailors in other parts of town. They are all likely alcohol related. I bet the CO will be pissed after the stern warning he gave about being on their best behavior in port."

"Hm. Alverez, tell any of our Corpsman going ashore that I am ordering them to avoid that part of town. Those wanting to party will not like it, but I don't care. And have them pass it along. Get the word out," he said.

"Aye-aye, SMO," she responded.

"Call if you need me," he said before hanging up.

He watched Jenna finish up her own call as he took a sip of coffee. He noticed a look of concern on her face as she put her phone away.

"That was an update on my Corpsman that got drunk last night and caused a ruckus," Derek said. "No fighting but he was belligerent, and the shore patrol logged it. Given the CO's strict policy he will likely be going to Captain's Mast for nonjudicial punishment. That should be fun." His sarcasm was evident. He paused before continuing. "It was a busy night for the pier medical station taking care of several injured Sailors involved in fights. You looked worried. Anything up?"

Jenna began. "It was a call from my duty officer. He reported the fights and also that we had two Sailors arrested by local police for fighting. This is highly unusual. We usually don't have many serious incidents ashore. There as always a few who go a bit crazy when they get off the ship. But not this many and never on the first night."

"From what I just heard, most of them involved Chinese nationals. They are usually very friendly and glad to see us from what I have heard," he added. "It makes you wonder if something else is going on."

"It sure does," she mused, thinking of the pending operation that few on the ship knew about.

"Do you have to go in?" he asked.

"No," she answered. "I have the day free until the reception this evening at the American Club. I have to be back at the hotel in time to get ready and meet the Admiral."

"Well, I'm going too. So, in the meantime, are you up for some shopping?" he asked. "I promised to get my kids something special from each port."

"Sure. That sounds like fun," she said.

"One of my Chiefs said that the Stanley Market is the place to go, wherever that is. Hong Kong is much bigger than I had suspected. I always thought it was about the size of Manhattan Island in New York, but it appears to be bigger than all of five boroughs of New York City combined," he speculated out loud.

"Transportation around here is great," Jenna said. "We have the option of taking the subway, a bus, a cab, or just walking. Since neither of us has any idea where it is, I suggest we take a cab."

"A cab it is then," he replied.

21 SITUATION REPORT

Hong Kong, China

Liang Yao, was checking out of his hotel when his new cell phone rang.

"Yao," he answered.

"Lieutenant Commander Yao, this is Lieutenant Ping, Vice Admiral Jiang's personal aide. Are you still in Hong Kong?" she asked.

"Yes," he answered simply.

"Excellent," she replied. "If you are not otherwise engaged, the Admiral would like to meet with you before you return to your team."

Yao wanted to ask how they knew he was in Hong Kong before remembering he had mentioned it to his uncle. "Of course. When and where?" he asked, wondering what his uncle Jiang wanted.

She gave him the address and told him he would be seen as soon as he arrived.

After taking down the address, he grabbed his luggage and tossed it into the trunk of his sports car in the hotel garage.

Thirty minutes later, he was being ushered into an executive office atop one of Hong Kong's many buildings overlooking the harbor.

At a receptionist's desk sat whom he assumed to be Lieutenant Ping. She was stunningly beautiful and in her mid-twenties. Yao once again saw that rank did indeed have its privileges.

"This way, Commander," she said without a formal introduction.

She led him to a corner office and opened the door after a soft knock. "Admiral, Lieutenant Commander Yao is here," she announced.

"Liang, come in, come in. Have a seat," Admiral Jiang said, gesturing to chairs across from a coffee table. "Lieutenant, please bring us some tea."

"Thank you, Admiral," Yao said as he sat down.

"So, what did you learn from your visit to the American aircraft carrier last night?" Jiang asked.

Right to the point, Yao thought. "I was impressed with the actual size of the ship. It was bigger than I had anticipated," he answered. "Their number of aircraft is more than anything we could match if it was a ship-versus-ship situation."

"True, but we are unlikely to ever have to face them in a true blue-water situation far from our shores. For the foreseeable future, we will be focusing on controlling our historical territorial waters," Jiang stated. "What of their aircraft?"

"What I know from our intelligence briefs gave me far more information that I gained looking at them. But I did get to see the size of them, and I studied details from various angles that could be useful in the future. Their Super Hornets look impressive, but you cannot gauge much of their capability from that," Yao said. "And they kept their F-35s out of sight."

"What did you think of the Americans?" Jiang asked.

"They are very talkative. But the pilots did not do more than talk in very generic terms. Nothing technical could be gained from them."

"What else? What was your impression of them overall?" Jiang pressed.

Yao though for a moment. "They were overly friendly. And...they seemed very confident in themselves. Yes, they were very self-assured and confident. They were unafraid to let us wander their flight deck and get almost close enough to touch the planes. Why even one officer was bragging about flying the planes, and he was only a staff officer. They exaggerate."

"Possibly. But do not forget that the Americans have been involved in combat missions for more than twenty years, though they rarely faced any significant challenges, at least against aircraft. Mostly, they have become good at dropping bombs on relatively defenseless ground troops."

The office door opened after a soft knock, and Lieutenant Ping brought in a tray with a pot of hot water, two cups, and an assortment of various tea bags.

"Thank you, Lieutenant," Jiang said. "That will be all. Make sure we are not disturbed."

Ping nodded and quietly left the room.

"You were involved in Operation WHIRLWIND in the South China Sea to reclaim the Spratly Islands, as I recall. Jiang said as he poured steaming water over a Hibiscus tea bag.

"Yes, Admiral, I flew as a flight lead during that operation," Yao replied, fondly remembering the glorious event. It had been a highlight of his career to be involved in an actual operation.

"Well, things are about to be heating up, and you are likely to be involved. Normally, I would not be briefing such a junior officer on this, but I have been impressed with your career so far. What I am about to tell you is Top Secret. It will not be disseminated down to the squadron level, at least not yet."

Yao sipped his own tea in anticipation as Jiang continued.

"Our military intelligence is convinced that the Filipinos and Americans are about to do to us what we did to the Filipinos in the Spratleys."

Jiang noticed that Yao stopped in mid-sip at the realization of what he had just said.

"Are you saying we are about to be at war?" Yao managed to ask with a surge of excitement and fear. "Are you certain?"

"That is unclear. It will depend on what the chairman decides to do. But we are fairly certain that something is about to happen. The Filipinos have been upset since we pushed them off the Spratleys. Now we suspect they are about to make a move on Scarborough Shoal. We have had hints that they have wanted to do this for some time. But we now know that the personnel and equipment they need to take it is in place. And it appears that the Americans will be directly involved at some point."

"Why would the American carrier and support ships be here in our harbor at our mercy if they were planning such a thing?" Yao asked.

"I suspect to keep up appearances. Like I said, all indications are that this is a fast-moving operation. The *Vinson* Battle Group has been scheduled for this port call for six weeks. If they were to cancel it at the last minute without a legitimate reason, they may have feared it would make us suspicious. As it is, we just got the confirming piece of intelligence yesterday evening after the ship was anchored."

"Can't we move our ships there to block them?" Yao asked.

"We are. Several ships at sea are being diverted there now, and others are preparing to put to sea. The problem is the time and distance. They may actually get there before we do. We only have one small ship there now. They have been put on heightened alert, but we are not telling them more than that at this time. We do not want them trigger happy and forcing us into a shooting war we are not ready for."

"But we are ready, Admiral," Yao insisted. "For years we have been preparing for such an opportunity."

"They have the jump on us this time. We do not want to engage until we are ready. There are larger implications to this," Jiang explained. "The international court has ruled that the Scarborough Shoal belongs to the Philippines. A ruling we, of course, do not recognize. We plan on eventually developing it ourselves once we have completed the buildup of our bases in the Spratleys. Who has actual physical possession on the ground will ultimately be the deciding factor in who ultimately wins. Also, we still have a huge dependence on trade for many of our critical minerals, our food, and our petroleum. If our trading partners decide to boycott the products we sell and impose sanctions on us, our economy could be crippled. So we have to move carefully. We have to have some semblance of being in the right on this one."

"Admiral, it sounds like we may just let them get away with it," Yao said frustrated. "If they push us off, then we should push right back before they can get established."

"I like your thinking, Liang. We need more in senior leadership with your bold approach. But, alas, our chairman and senior officers are more cautious. And like you said, the Americans may be overconfident. Also, some of our leaders doubt the intelligence. Others of us want more action now. So officially, we are in a wait-and-see mode and will not take any action other than increase our ships in the area."

"Can we surround and bottle up their ships while they are here in port?" Yao asked.

"Based on what? That would clearly be seen as a belligerent act on our part. One without official provocation. Nothing has occurred yet, and even when it does, we are not sure exactly what part the Americans will play, or when they may get involved. If the Americans take the shoal, then they are the belligerent aggressor. If only the Filipinos drive us away, then we have no basis to move against the Americans," Jiang explained. "The rest of the world acknowledges that the shoal is theirs. If they take possession of it and invite the Americans in to help develop it, then we will be on shaky legal ground as far as world opinion goes. You see, Yao, much of what we have accomplished was based on bluster and obfuscation as to our true intentions. Once we were established, then there was no one strong or motivated enough to kick us out."

"So our best chance is to get more troops on the shoal to keep any landing from occurring," Yao observed.

"Yes. And the window to accomplish that may have passed," Jiang said sadly.

"Surely, Admiral, there is something we can do?" Yao pleaded.

"Nothing officially. In fact, I am to attend a reception this evening with much of the senior officers from the American Battle Group at the American Club," the Admiral added. "Unofficially, the Triads that run the Hong Kong underworld have been contacted by some that had demanded immediate action. Last night, they were allowed to harass and steal from the American Sailors. This morning, they will be cleared, and shall we say, 'encouraged' to become even more aggressive. We hope to instigate incidents to cause many of them to be arrested or moderately injured and unable to perform their duties. Also, it is to generate negative headlines for the Americans. Our government can easily deny any involvement. Hong Kong is still officially semiautonomous. It will be a police matter. All we can really do is harass and distract them at this point and try to decrease their military effectiveness a bit."

"Respectfully, Admiral, I think we should be far more aggressive," Yao pushed.

"Neither you nor I are in charge of this, Liang," Jiang said. "I will push for an aggressive response, yet I expect to be ignored. I fear our senior leaders are far too comfortable in their positions and do not want to do anything that upsets their comfortable lives. Even at the risk of losing a strategically important shoal."

"Yes, Admiral," Yao said. "What do you wish me to do?"

"Go back to your unit as soon as possible. I anticipate that our military forces will be put on alert very soon. At the least, I expect there will be some significant bluster on our part. You may get to see those F-18s again sooner than you expected," Jiang said as he stood up.

"Yes, Admiral," Yao said taking his exit que as he rose and headed for the door. "Thank you, Uncle, for sharing this information with me."

The Admiral nodded and added. "Remember: do not share this with anyone. This was just background information."

"Yes, sir." Yao answered. As he departed, he was too focused on what he had just learned to even notice the smile of Lieutenant Ping as he headed for the elevator. He felt a growing anger in the pit of his stomach. How dare anyone take what is rightfully ours! An upstart world court has no right to tell China, which has existed for millennia, what our borders are, he fumed. By the time he reached the ground floor, he was seething and red-faced with barely controlled rage.

22 STANLEY MARKET
Hong Kong, China

After a forty-five-minute cab ride, Derek and Jenna were dropped off at Stanley's Main Street on the south end of the island. They spent most of the ride taking in the sights and having occasional small talk. Derek's thoughts of his ex, Rachel, kept intruding. What was he going to do? His night with Jenna had been amazing. The sex was phenomenal, but the physical intimacy was only a part of it. His walls were down and again, and his soul felt free. Yet the tug of responsibility to his family was causing the familiar and unwanted pangs of guilt to creep back in. He shook his head trying to physically keep the unwanted thoughts at bay.

"Great call on getting a cab," Derek said. "We would have never found this place."

"Wow," he said as they entered the shopping market. They found themselves wandering through a meandering maze of covered alleyways from shop to shop. They spent the next several hours looking and purchasing several items. For lunch they found an outdoor table at a bistro overlooking a relaxing view of the harbor and ordered sandwiches.

"We spent three hours in there and saw maybe half of it," she said.

"Yeah, you can really get lost in there," he noted. "Still, as far away as we are, I saw at least two dozen Sailors I recognized from the ship. The good news is that I only need one more thing for my daughter. Maybe something unique to wear."

"Your teenage daughter, right? How old is she? What size does she wear?" she asked.

"Wow, slow down. Yes, she's seventeen. And I have no idea what size she is. She is a couple of inches shorter than you and about 115 pounds."

"Okay, that's a start. We will find her something nice," she said.

***

Neither of them were aware that they were now being followed. There were four young Chinese men a block away watching them as they ate and chatted. They were in their late teens or early twenties, and they all sported tattoos. These young punks had been cleared to specifically target the Americans.

Chirp-chirp. Chirp-chirp, sounded their leader's phone.

"Hello," he answered. "Yes, we do. Yes. Are you sure? Yes. All right," he said, hanging up.

"Well?" one asked.

"Things have changed," he started. "We are no longer to harass and pick fights. We are to seriously injure the Sailors. And we can keep any cash we may steal."

"All right!" a skinny one said. "That older couple we noticed earlier look like they have plenty of cash."

"There they go. You know the plan," the leader said.

***

"What about this?" Derek asked, holding up a decorated red silk blouse. "I'm not sure if it is a shirt or pajama top."

"It can probably be either," Jenna said. "What about this black one?" She held it up in front of her.

"Definitely not!" he answered quickly.

"Why? It's nice," she asked.

"Because it's too damned sexy. She's only seventeen!" Derek said, letting his paternal instincts show.

Jenna just gave him a quizzical look and said, "She's going to grow up, Derek, whether or not you're ready."

"Well, not yet," he said stubbornly.

Derek noticed a young Chinese man in a black T-shirt and jeans looking directly at him as he turned to hang the shirt back on the rack. The young man averted his gaze as their eyes momentarily locked. Derek's senses went on full alert. There was something too intent about that man's gaze. And they were in an unfamiliar maze of shops surrounded by other shoppers.

"I'm not sure what she would like," Derek answered.

He casually looked around, pretending to look at other shirts and noticed two other young men to his right on either side of the alley in different shops. He caught them furtively glancing their way.

"You know, Jenna. I think I saw just the thing back at that shop on Fenwick Pier. I think we should look there." He gently but firmly reached to hold her hand and pull her in a direction past the first man he had seen.

"But—" she started to say. She was cut short by the surprise that he was holding her hand in public.

"Now!" he added, cutting off further discussion.

Moving past the first man he had noticed, Derek saw a fourth openly staring at them. He was not quite sure where he was in relation to the streets after all the turns they had made wandering around the past half hour. He took his best guess and was hoping to get to the open streets and catch a cab.

"We have company, Jenna," he said quietly. "And they don't look too friendly. Don't look back. I counted at least four that were watching us. They may be a pickpocket gang or something. We should get back."

"Okay," was all she managed to say. She had been a cool customer when in the cockpit of her plane, surrounded with her familiar screens, switches, and sounds. Here, while shopping, with a possible physical threat, she felt less prepared. Still she was very fit and had taken several self-defense courses. She knew some basic moves but had never had to put her skills to the test.

Derek turned them right onto what looked like a main thoroughfare, hoping it would lead them out. It quickly turned out to be the opposite as it curved around into a dead-end wall. This back part of the flea market had far fewer customers. They turned around to back track and immediately saw that the four Chinese men were still following only twenty feet behind. A smile came across the skinny one's face as he pulled out a knife.

"Stay at least five feet behind me, Jenna," he said, glancing quickly to his left and right for some sort of weapon. To his left was a vendor selling toys. Nothing there. To his right was one selling cookware. He thought they might have cutlery, but no such luck. He saw only pots and pans. The alley was only eight feet wide at this point, so it was only a few feet to the nearest big steel pot on a display table. He grabbed its lid in his left hand and the pot itself in his right. Luckily, the lid didn't have the knob-type handle on top but one he could get two of his fingers looped into.

As he stepped back to the center of the alley, the first two were almost upon him. They didn't make any demands; they just went for him. As the first two closed, he could see that the other two planned to slip past him and go for Jenna.

His sudden moves had caused them all to hesitate for a moment. He almost started to try and reason with them, but his long-ago SEAL training was kicking in. SEALs are among the absolute best at sneaking into and out of places to gather intelligence or perform more overt acts. The perfect mission is one where no one ever knew they had been there. But when they did come into contact with the enemy, they were trained to bring overwhelming force to bear. They would take out the enemy or at least make them fall back long enough for them to disengage and get away. So he was now engaged, and it was time for sudden overwhelming force.

None of the four were too impressed with the threat of a pot from a fortyish-year-old man. They expected him to throw the pot at them and then have no real defense. Not against the two now wielding knives coming for him.

Both were right handed, he noted, and he was certain from their demeanor that they wouldn't hesitate to severely injure or kill. This was no simple robbery. Something else was going on. But he didn't have time to ponder what. Instead, Derek tossed the pot almost straight up in the air, raising his head as if he was watching it. But he kept his eyes on the two advancing rapidly on him now only four feet away. The two knifemen couldn't help momentarily glancing up to make sure it wasn't going to hit them.

As soon as he saw their eyes look up, he sprang into action. He knocked away the knife arm of the assailant on his right with his improvised shield while delivering a crushing knuckle punch to his throat. The assailant dropped the knife and crumpled to the floor, grabbing his throat while gasping for air through his smashed larynx.

The left attacker had quickly recovered and was swinging his knife around. Derek had anticipated the reaction and was already ducking below the arcing arm. As it passed an inch over his head, Derek grabbed the now off-balance attacker's knife wrist with his right hand. Before the attacker could bring his left arm into the fight, he was hit squarely on the right side of his head with the pot lid, stunning him. Derek forcefully extended the knifeman's arm and delivered a solid blow to the back of his elbow. Derek heard a satisfying snap as the attacker's elbow was broken and bent outside in, into what his physician's brain registered as a decidedly unnatural anatomic position. Derek grabbed the attacker's knife before letting go of his wrist. The second attacker was now screaming and down out of the fight.

Now he had a knife and a shield, such as it was. The suddenness of his attack caused the other two to pause and step back. But only long enough for them to pull their own knives. These two would not be so easy to handle, but now he was no longer unarmed. They started to move to either side of him planning to attack simultaneously. He couldn't watch both of them at the same time that way. He thought of retreating to have the wall at his back, but he had to stay between them and Jenna. He had lost track of her for the moment. Derek decided to make a quick spinning feint to his left, toward the one now moving close to the toy racks. As he did so the attacker backed up into the now vacated room. As expected, the one to his right had lunged for him but far quicker than he had anticipated. Had he not planned on continuing his spin to the left and into a crouch, he would have been stabbed in the back. As it was, he caught a glancing knife cut on his left forearm as he raised the pot lid to block the wicked thrust. But the attacker's momentum carried him forward. Derek surged up, driving his knife into the attacker's solar plexus and into his heart. It took only a moment, but it was enough for the last assailant to close on him from behind. Derek caught a blur out of his right eye as an object went flying past his head. The last attacker raised his hands and ducked to fend off the missile Jenna had thrown that was heading squarely for his face. That moment was just enough for Derek to move in with an uppercut to the jaw rather than the blade of the knife. He didn't want to kill if he didn't have to. The last attacker was down but only dazed. Derek picked up the pot and laid the attacker's right forearm across its wide open mouth. He then stomped down with his heel hearing a satisfying snap followed by a scream.

Derek quickly did the same to his left arm. He turned to Jenna who held a small frying pan in her hand ready to swing.

"You okay?" he asked.

"Yeah, I think so," she said, dropping the pan she was holding.

"We gotta get out of here. Now! They may have friends. We can wait for the police in a safer place," he said, folding the pocket knife and slipping it into his back pocket.

23 RECALL

Hong Kong. China

After several wrong turns, Derek and Jenna eventually found their way out of the market's turning alleyways. They found themselves away from the beach and at the taxi and bus drop-off loop. Here all was quiet with normal foot-and-street traffic.

"Jenna, keep an eye out for a policeman to flag down. We have to report this," Derek explained. "And we need to check in and tell our bosses what just happened."

"You got it," she said with a bit of a quiver in her voice. "I don't know why I'm shaking all of a sudden."

"It's perfectly normal," he said, leaning over to give her a quick kiss on the lips. "It's the excess epinephrine dumped into your system back there during the attack. Your body is still primed to fight or run. Not a bad thing. We may not be in the clear yet." He reached for his cell phone.

Derek noted that he had several missed calls in the past five minutes that he hadn't noticed in all the excitement. He initially started to call the duty officer. He decided to call the CO instead.

The CO answered on the first ring. "Captain," he answered sharply.

"Captain, SMO here. The Chief of Staff and I—" was all he got in before the Captain cut him off.

"SMO, are you on your way back to the ship? If not, get there now. Something is going on. A lot of our Sailors have been involved in fights and altercations. Others have been arrested on the least pretext. I have issued an immediate recall. Avoid anything that could get you involved with the police. We have several injured, and I need you to get me an update ASAP."

"Aye-aye, Captain, but there's more." Derek was just able to squeeze in before the CO cut him off again. "Captain, we were just attacked in Stanley Market. We disabled them, but it appeared they were seriously out to injure us. It looked to be more than a simple robbery. We got away and are looking for a policeman to report it to."

There was a brief pause. "Are you two okay?" the CO asked.

"Yes," the SMO exaggerated.

"Then don't engage the police for now. Get back to the ship. You can report it once back aboard. Given what has been happening, they are likely to arrest you instead of your attackers," the CO explained.

"Copy, we're on our way," the SMO said, flipping his phone closed.

Jenna was on the phone as well and still looking around for a policeman. While still listening, she mouthed the words, "Talking to the police."

Derek immediately gave her the cut sign, waving his hand back and forth across his neck.

She gave him a bewildered look but nodded that she understood. She then said, "Yes, I believe I see a policeman arriving here now. Thank you," she finished before switching off the phone. "What's going on?"

"No police! I'll explain on the way. We gotta get moving," he said as they heard the shrill sound of nearby police whistles rapidly heading in their direction.

There were no empty cabs available at that moment, so taking Jenna by the arm, he guided her onto a double-decker bus headed to downtown Hong Kong. They had just settled into their seats on the upper deck as the bus pulled away. On the sidewalk where they had just stood were six policemen. Derek noticed that back near the market entrance, standing calmly next to another policeman was one of the attackers holding an injured right arm. Several policemen looked into the bus, but luckily none looked up to the second level.

"What the hell is going on, Derek?" she demanded. "Why did we run from the police? This could get us in big trouble."

"Jenna, that attack was not an isolated incident," he started. "We aren't the only ones being attacked. It's happening all over Hong Kong. Our Sailors are the ones being arrested. And there have been lots of injuries. The CO has issued a ship-wide recall. He said to avoid the police, and we'll report it after we're safely back on the *Vinson*. Didn't you see that guy holding his arm chatting easily with that cop? He was the thug attacker and yet was not running from the police. He was doing the opposite. So—"

"So, they are in on it together. Damn," she said, cutting in to finish his thought. "And to think I was on the phone telling them right where to find us."

"Probably good that you did," Derek said. "They were expecting us to be standing around looking for them, not running away. If they thought we were running, they would have stopped all cabs and buses to be searched. As it was, we got away. We probably have about ten minutes before they start backtracking. They will check bus routes and call cab companies to see who picked up an American couple from the market, that is, if they are really out to track us down. There is a lot going on in the city right now. Still we would be a big prize to catch, and we were being followed. So they may know who we are."

"Then we better not stay on this bus too long," Jenna concluded. "I need to check in too." She started dialing her phone.

Derek did the same redialing his last missed call.

"SMO, there you are. It's crazy here." Lieutenant Commander Alverez said breathlessly.

"Slow down, Alverez. First, where is 'here'?" the SMO asked.

"Here at Fenwick Pier. Our first aid station is overrun with various types of injuries. And that's not all. We seem to be in a bit of a standoff with some local police. The big XO is in talks with a police officer who is wanting to come in and arrest some of our Sailors. The shore patrol is maintaining an effective barricade for now. Someone from the State Department is on the way here. That is probably why they haven't stormed the place so far. In the meantime, we are loading the ferries as fast as we can and getting our Sailors out of here. Most of the injuries are mild. The kind we see from any bar fights, but some had pretty severe beatings. Forty-five minutes ago, a couple came in with minor knife wounds. Surprisingly, the attacks seem to involve the senior enlisted and officers. Not many of the younger Sailors that usually get in trouble," she said.

"And, SMO, I just got a report that we have six in the local hospitals and one dead," she added somberly.

"Copy, do we have enough corpsmen there?" the SMO asked.

"I think so. We have the two on duty. Plus, four more have arrived that were off duty and jumped in to help," she added.

"You do know about the recall, don't you?" he asked.

"Yes, sir, the word was passed here fifteen minutes ago. Several onshore patrol and Chiefs from various departments were sent out to pass the word," Alverez added.

"Okay, here's what I want you to do. Use Sailors that are sober to accompany those with minor injuries back to the ship and main medical. We have pushed hard to get them trained up using the GITMO 8 first aid procedures. Any with more serious injuries send in with a Corpsman," the SMO instructed. "Also, grab anyone you need for additional manpower to help move any stretcher patients. Call the department and have everyone on the ship report to medical to take in the wounded. We may have more injured yet to arrive."

"SMO, you do know that almost two-thirds of the ship's crew are ashore right now. That's almost four thousand Sailors scattered all over Hong Kong. There aren't many from the medical department aboard the ship now," Alverez advised.

"I know. That's why we need the few we have there on duty and providing care. Alverez, which providers do we have on duty today?" he asked.

Our surgeon Dr. Sandaal, the physician assistant Lieutenant Junior Grade Belah, and Hospitalman First Class Nebo our Independent Duty Corpsman," she replied.

"Excellent. As our medics report in there at the pier, get them to the ship, preferably escorting a patient if needed. I'm on my way back now, and I'll be there as soon as I can," he said. "Marty, you're doing a great job! See you in a few." He flipped the phone off.

"Jenna, it's getting crazy at the pier. Police are trying to arrest our Sailors, and many are showing up injured. This is no accident. This seems organized," he concluded.

Jenna just nodded absentmindedly, appearing to be deep in thought and not really looking at him.

After several long moments, she turned to look him in the eyes with a serious and concerned expression, "Derek, do you think you may have killed one of those guys back there? Not that he didn't deserve it," she questioned.

He knew he had to tell her the truth. No sugar-coating it, he decided. He started nodding and said, "Yes, almost certainly the third guy. And possibly the first one, I probably crushed his larynx. He may or may not make it. Does that bother you?"

"No, I suppose not. It just happened so fast, and I have never been in anything like that up close before. I've been in this business my whole career, training to find and kill an enemy using a plane and bombs. The concept doesn't bother me. It was just so sudden and unexpected. Really, I just wanted to say thanks for all that back there," she said, regaining her usual confident composure.

"You're welcome, but we aren't in the clear just yet. Not until we are on the ship. They likely have expanded their hunt for us. They may have started checking buses by now, so we need to get off soon," he said.

At the second bus stop after entering back into the city, they quietly exited the bus and strolled along for a few blocks pretending to be window shopping. They even spent five minutes outside an expensive oriental carpet shop, pointing out the colorful rugs they liked. Three blocks away on a different road than the bus route they caught a cab back to Fenwick Pier.

"What about our bags at the hotel?" she asked Derek.

"I only had a change of clothes and a shaving kit. I say ditch 'em and get to the pier. Besides, they surely know where we stayed and may have police there already," he surmised.

Jenna nodded in agreement.

Fifteen minutes later, they arrived at Fenwick Pier. Derek noted that the police were talking with a Caucasian in a suit that he assumed was from the US embassy. Surprisingly, the police were letting a steady flow of Sailors through to the pier unimpeded. He and Jenna entered separately with a group of young Sailors. They went straight to the medic station.

"Hey SMO, thank God you're here," Alverez said, stepping up to him. We just had a serious knife wound arrive. It happened about twenty minutes ago as a couple of Sailors were on their way back. One was cut on the arm, and the other was stabbed in the belly. The one with the belly wound actually used his GITMO 8 training to bandage up his buddy's arm. He then walked here on his own. He has a small puncture wound from what I was told. He said that he thinks the knife barely punctured his skin. He was doing fine when he arrived, but he's started acting a bit more worried."

The SMO turned to Jenna. "You get on the next ferry out of here. I'll see you back on the boat later."

Jenna nodded and headed to the rapidly filling ferry.

"Alverez, do we have a surgery tech on the ship?" he asked as they headed to a corner office where the patient could be seen sitting on a stretcher.

"No, but one of the surgery techs is here on duty." She pointed out Hospitalman Second Class Otwell across the room.

"Excellent, get her to the boat now! Call the surgeon and tell him that we may have a surgical case headed his way. I want him and the operating room prepared just in case. And there may be other injuries," he said as he continued to the patient.

"SMO!" he heard Alverez call out in surprise.

"What?" he said, turning back.

"Is that your blood?" she asked, gesturing to his left arm with a concerned look on her face.

He had forgotten his wound as they were on the run back to the ship. He looked down and saw the four-inch diagonal laceration across the back of his forearm. Not too deep and only an inch of it would require Steri-Strips, he analyzed. The dried blood made it look worse that it was. "Yeah, nothing serious, I'll tell you about it later." He turned back to the patient.

The SMO entered a corner office that had been converted for use as an examination room while they were in port. Speaking to the Corpsman in charge of the patient, he asked, "What have we got here?" The SMO shifted into being an ER doc again.

"SMO, this is seaman Walker, he arrived here in mild pain and holding his stomach. He has a half inch laceration to his abdomen about three inches above the umbilicus and there is no obvious bleeding. His pulse ten minutes ago was 120, blood pressure of 105 over 75, and respirations of 22. But he has been getting more anxious. I have just started an 18 gage IV of normal saline just in case. I had him lying down, but he now insists on sitting up," reported HM2 Benson.

"Seaman Walker, I'm Dr. Lloyd. How are you doing now?" The SMO inquired. As he did so he noted that Walker was leaning forward and taking deep rapid breaths.

"I'll be fine. I think it's just the shakes you get after being in a fight. He barely scratched me, and we fought him off. Though I am now feeling a little bit dizzy," Walker answered.

"Well, you just lay back for a bit and let us check you out." As seaman Walker was laying back down the SMO noted that the veins of his neck seemed noticeable and slightly enlarged.

"Benson get another set of vitals and find me a stethoscope," the SMO ordered quickly.

The SMO closed the door to the room for privacy and had Walker undressed so he could do a proper examination. While his corpsman worked on getting a new set of vital signs, he did a quick but thorough head to toe examination, noting the two centimeter laceration in his upper abdomen. His stomach was soft but tender to the touch. He had clear deep rapid breath sounds. But his heart sounded distant and muffled for a healthy young Sailor.

"SMO, here's the new vitals," said HM2 Benson. "Pulse is 115, blood pressure of 88 over 70, and respirations 28."

The SMO thought for a second. He hadn't seen a case like this since his days working in the ER. But this was presenting as a classic case of cardiac tamponade. A situation where fluid, or as is likely in this case, blood, was filling the protective sack around the heart restricting its ability to pump effectively. And if not drained off it could rapidly prove fatal. It was apparent now that the stab wound went further than just breaking the skin. This was a true medical emergency that needed treatment immediately. The increasing lack of blood getting to the heart would soon lead to shock and cardiac arrest. Normally he would have confirmed that there was a large amount of fluid around the heart with a bedside ultrasound. But he didn't have one and it would take too long to get the patient to the ship. His options were to send him to the local ER by ambulance along with the unknown delays in their evaluating him. Or he could take measures himself.

"Benson get me your longest needle and IV tubing. Quickly!" The SMO barked. "And get me towels, iodine swabs, and sterile gloves, size seven and a half, if you have any."

Heading out of the room with Benson he asked, "Where can I wash my hands?"

Benson pointed to the bathroom and asked, "What's up SMO?"

"It looks like his pericardium, the fibrous sack surrounding his heart is filling with blood and compressing it, restricting its ability to pump." The SMO answered. "This Sailor has the three classic signs called Beck's triad. They are a low blood pressure, with a narrowing of the difference between the systolic and diastolic pressures, muffled heart sounds, and swollen or bulging neck veins. He is also increasingly anxious, with a high pulse rate and is more comfortable sitting up leaning forward. Sitting forward is a common way patients unconsciously try to relieve the pressure on the heart.

After washing his hands and forearms, the SMO returned to the patient and said, "Walker, you have fluid building up around your heart. I'm going to have to remove it using a needle."

Walker looked at him anxiously and nodded. "Do what you have to doc, I feel pretty bad and it's getting worse."

The SMO nodded to him reassuringly noting that everything he had requested was there.

"Sorry SMO, we only have large clean examination gloves. We didn't plan for any sterile procedures other that wound management and giving IV fluids," HM2 Benson apologized. "We do have plenty of betadine preps, IV fluid and a variety of needles."

"That'll have to do," said the SMO. He took a towel and wiped away the sweat and blood around the stomach wound. After cleaning a ten inch area around the wound with three separate iodine packs, he used a fourth to thoroughly coat a fresh pair of gloves.

"Hey Benson, cut open the tubing of a bag of saline and rinse off my gloves," the SMO directed. "Otherwise they'll be too sticky."

HM2 Benson did as she was asked.

"Well, that is as sterile as we can get I suppose given the circumstances," the SMO stated. Carefully grasping a two inch long 18-gauge needle and catheter, he said, "Walker, you might feel a little pinch, but you will soon feel much better," he told his patient who again nodded. Using his knowledge of anatomy, he carefully inserted the needle just below the lower part of his sternum called the xiphoid process, and into the pericardial sac. He immediately got a gush of blood indicating he was into the sac. He then removed the needle and secured the catheter in place before attaching IV tubing. In all, he removed roughly 300 milliliters of blood.

Within minutes Walker rapidly improved. His blood pressure normalized, and his breathing slowed to a normal rate. His pulse was still 105 but to be expected given the situation.

"Thanks doc! I'm feeling much better," Seaman Walker thanked him.

"You bet. Any time. That's what we're here for. Now we are going to get you back to the ship and patched up," the SMO replied as he stood up.

Turning to HM2 Benson the SMO said, "Ok, now let's get him packaged up and on the ferry to the boat. And send word to Dr. Sandaal we have a case for him.

24 GETTING OUT OF DODGE
USS *Vinson*, Hong Kong Harbor

"This is Boatswain's Mate Third Class Pollock, age twenty, who is two hours post-op for multiple stab wounds to his arms and abdomen with perforation of the small intestine," began general surgeon Lieutenant Commander Kris Sandaal as he was finishing evening rounds on the second of his two ICU patients. With him was the SMO, Lieutenant Searcy—the family practice doc, Lieutenant Junior Grade Belah—the Physician's Assistant, and the ICU nurse, Lieutenant Commander Renee Stooksbury.

"His vital signs are stable, no fever, and an O2 saturation 98 to 100 percent on room air. He has had three liters of ringer's lactate with a urine output of 1800 cc's in the past two hours. He has two eighteen-gage IVs one in each arm and his urinary catheter is still in place. His metabolic panel labs are normal. His CBC shows a mild anemia at 3.9 that we are keeping an eye on, but it isn't surprising with his mild blood loss. The white blood cell count is normal showing no sign of infection so far. We also have him on IV ampicillin, ciprofloxacin and flagyl for prophylaxis. His pain is under control with a morphine drip. On exam he is currently sleeping but arousable. His sutures are clean dry and intact. We plan to—"

"SMO!" interrupted Lieutenant Commander Alverez as she stood in the doorway to the three-bed ICU ward. "You wanted me to remind you of the COs meeting. You have four minutes to get up there."

"Oh, right. Thanks for the reminder, Marty. Excuse me, guys," the SMO said.

Damn, I better hustle, thought Derek as he glanced at his watch, thinking of the four decks to the Captain's in-port cabin. *Well, given this crazy day, he will understand if I'm a tad late.*

He arrived a minute late but noticed that he wasn't the only one just showing up. Glancing at the head table, he saw that the CO and XO had not arrived either. He took his seat along the far wall just under one of the port hole windows. He was sitting next to his good friend and fellow department head Commander Archie Beauregard, the ship's Intelligence Officer.

"Hey, SMO. What a flipping crazy day," Beauregard said as he noticed the bandage on the SMO's left forearm. "I heard you and the Admiral's Chief of Staff were attacked as well. Glad you two are okay. I didn't hear that you were injured."

"Thanks, Archie. We were lucky. I was cut, but it took only five stitches to close it. I really didn't notice it until someone pointed it out to me later. It's nothing that'll slow me down," the SMO answered. "Any idea what the hell is going on?"

"Actually, I do. I was just in a meeting with the Admiral's staff along with the CO, XO, CAG, and DCAG. But it is up to them to pass it on, as I'm sure they will in a few minutes. They're all in a meeting with the Admiral now," Beauregard replied.

"Attention on deck!" someone called out as the CO and XO entered.

"As you were," Captain Whitehall said as he took his seat. It was clear from the serious looks on all their faces that whatever was going on was not over.

"Okay, ladies and gentlemen, this will be a focused meeting. First of all, we have orders to get underway as soon as possible rather than at our scheduled noon departure tomorrow. So we have to get our sea and anchor detail ready to go. We will have our departure brief at 1945. I expect to be underway by 2100. And, yes, I know it is dark, and we do not typically get underway at night. But this is an unprecedented situation," the CO said. "To that end, I need some key information from each of you."

"RO, how soon can you get the reactors up and producing steam?" the Captain asked the Reactor Officer.

"Sir, I set the watch as soon as I got back aboard. We will have full steam and power up and ready by 2000."

"Excellent, RO. Strong work," said the Captain. The Captain turned to the administrative officer. "ADMIN, how many personnel do we still have ashore?"

"Captain, we have twenty-two ship's company unaccounted for, mostly junior to mid-rank enlisted. The Air Wing has fifteen unaccounted for, including three junior Hornet pilots from VFA-94. We have reports from the Hong Kong police department that eight are under arrest. We have a senior chief ashore with three Master at Arms Sailors at the pier to round up the stragglers as they arrive. There is also an embassy representative there assisting and will take in any that show up after we depart. Also, we have an additional three getting treatment and observation at one of the local hospitals. The embassy is also overseeing their care as well."

"Thanks, ADMIN. SMO, give us a medical update," the CO requested.

"Yes, sir," the SMO started. "There is the one that was DOA from the deck department. Of the three in the hospital, two underwent surgery for injuries they received. The third is under observation following a head injury. All are currently stable and expected to recover at this point. However, I recommend that we have them transferred home via International SOS as soon as they are able to travel. They will likely need weeks or months of recovery."

"Yes, SMO, set it up," the CO concurred immediately.

Continuing, the SMO said, "We have six patients on the ward following injuries ashore. Two had surgery and are recovering in the ICU and doing well so far. The others are in primarily for observation. We had a total of fifty-three that required treatment for various minor injuries and were returned to duty."

"Do we need to send those in the ICU home as well?" the CO asked.

"Yes, sir. But it is not critical that we do so immediately. We can airlift them off later in the week, so there's no rush, and I prefer not to do it from here given the situation," the SMO finished.

After getting updates from the other department heads, the CO continued. "Okay, you have all been wondering why these attacks have happened. We've had a brief from the Admiral's Intelligence Officer and been cleared to share this with you. There is about to be a US-supported operation by the Philippines to establish an airstrip and military base on Scarborough Shoal the day after tomorrow on the ninth. We suspect that the Chinese, who have also been claiming the shoal, have gotten wind of it, and these attacks are their way of unofficially voicing their displeasure. They have said nothing officially and claim that these attacks are from the Hong Kong Triads. They claim to be vigorously tracking them down. We know this is a bald-faced lie based on the debrief the SMO and Chief of Staff gave. Still, we have officially accepted their explanation. But we are leaving tonight and not telling them until we weigh anchor. We don't want to get bottled up in here. We are also going to resume normal flight operations starting at 0900 tomorrow. We are going to show that we are fully operational and engaged in our normal routine, while doing fight ops in the general vicinity of the shoal to provide air cover if needed. This is a Filipino operation to take control of the shoal. Afterward, our construction units will be involved in the base development and building of the runway. We will have our usual meeting tomorrow morning. Okay, then, I will see you all in wardroom three for the predeparture brief in fifteen minutes."

25 ACCELERATED TIMELINE
Manila, Philippines

Staff Sergeant Anglin couldn't focus on the ongoing brief from one of the Master Sergeants who was giving updates on the supplies and equipment delivery plans. All he could think about was his wife, Kara, and it had only gotten worse. He had been in a mental loop since opening that first email and was replaying the events of the past eighteen hours over and over in his mind.

Upon getting out of bed, he had been having wide mood swings. From rage to just raw emotional pain. He went from wanting to lash out and punish her in some way, to trying to find some way to win back the beautiful woman he adored. What he had already known was bad enough. Where his imagination was taking him was far worse. He got almost no sleep when he finally went to bed. After lying awake for four hours, he got up and went looking for some way to access his email. It was late morning local time, and he found his way to the hotel front desk. He had been relieved to see that they had a business office with two computers for use by the guests. He was soon online and checking his email again. There was still nothing from his wife. And nothing new from his friend Staff Sergeant Esler.

He took a deep breath and started an email to Kara. He hoped that there was a reasonable innocent explanation for what he had seen. Maybe she was just out with friends. Maybe that guy had just made a move on her that she didn't really want. Maybe she was regretful for the guy getting the wrong message.

"Dear Kara. I am so sorry for how we parted. I miss you more than you can know. I hope you are no longer angry with me and doing well. I know that these deployments are rough on you and our relationship. This one really was a surprise for everyone. We have an important job to do, then we will all be heading home. Please let me know how you feel. I love you! X X X O O O X X X"

He had to try. There just had to be a reasonable explanation, he thought. Yet his mind replied, *You're a fool. She knew just what she was doing and is done with you. That hot beautiful babe is ready to get it on with someone else.* But he refused to accept the worst case. No! Not yet!

He was about to log off the screen when he got a surprise reply. It was from Kara.

Not only did she get his email, but she had responded immediately. His heart leaped with joy. This had to be a good sign.

But her response was neutral. No emotion at all. 'I am fine. No longer angry. K.'

That was it. Nothing else. No I-love-you. No I-miss-you. No I'm-sorry-about-the-fight-too. No asking how he was doing. No do-your-job-and-hurry-home.

He clicked on the instant-chat option.

Anglin: "How are you doing really? Keeping busy?"

Kara: "I'm okay. Just cleaning the house all afternoon. You know I can't stand anything being out of place."

He found that surprising. She did indeed keep a perfect showplace house. But he had been gone for over three days and she would have had the place just as she liked it in hours. And she wouldn't let it get messy. So, her needing to clean the house seemed like a red herring. He decided to let it slide.

Anglin: "Have you been out with Jamie and the others?" He wanted to cut to the chase. Jamie was her best friend from the neighborhood. She was Kara's running buddy most of the time. Jamie was married to an Air Force enlisted man as well, and both didn't have any children. Some others from their small group often had a ladies' night out most weeks. A couple times a year, they would go to a local club to dance for a few hours. They never stayed out very late.

Kara: "No, been home moping most of the time. We may go out in a few days."

He keyed on "most of the time."

Anglin: "So nothing fun? Same here for me." He said it with a partially clear conscience.

Kara: "Nope."

Anglin: "Surely, you got out of the house some."

Kara: "Just here watching Netflix every day. I only went to my medical appointment at Eglin the day you left, and then the commissary after. It's been boring."

I told you, dude! She is lying her ass off to you now. You know it. Anglin's mind was screaming at him. He could feel his face flushing. His hope was gone. His seething anger again jumping to a boil.

He sat there clenching and unclenching his fists. He had deep rapid breathing and felt the muscles in his neck, jaw and head tightening as he clenched his teeth. After almost a minute he typed.

Anglin: "Really?"

Kara: "Boooorrrrrriiiiiinnnnngggg!"

That was it for him. His rage was back at floodtide. She was lying and pretending nothing had happened. Maybe she was guilty and didn't want to admit it, his reasonable mind tried to argue. But he ignored the fleeting sentiment.

Anglin's response wasn't angry or carefully crafted. He just sent the picture of her kissing that guy. After a moment, he chased it with another text.

Anglin: "You look really bored!"

He waited for a response. But after a few seconds, the chat box closed, and she was gone.

After sitting there for a few minutes, he emailed his buddy Sergeant Esler.

Anglin sent his first reply after the initial devastating email from the day before.

"Jacob, my friend, I wish I could say thank you for the email. But I can say thank you for being a friend. I know that was tough on you too. As you can guess, I am royally pissed about now. I want to pound the walls with my fists. Maybe if I do, I can break a hand and get sent home where I can deal with this shit. We ended up chatting a few minutes ago, and she said that she had been home since I left and never gone out except to a doctor's appointment and the commissary. Said she was only bored and cleaning the house. So when she denied going out, I of course sent her the kissing photo. No response after that, she just logged off. Thanks for being in my corner. At least, I have one good friend back there I can count on. Ron."

Anglin tried going back to sleep but it was impossible. He eventually gave up and went walking the streets now teaming with mid-day traffic. He found his way to a local pharmacy where he hoped to get some 'Over the Counter' sleeping pills. He expected that he was likely to have trouble sleeping for the foreseeable future. He was surprised to see that a generic form of Ambien was available without a prescription. He bought 30 and headed back to his room. It was too late in the day to take a pill now, so he just stayed awake and tried to think of anything else. But of course, he couldn't.

He was snapped back to the present when Chief Master Sergeant McKinney yelled out, "Stand by!" He along with everyone else jumped up from their seats in preparation of coming to attention.

Colonel Perry was waving them back down as he made his way forward from the back of the room.

"As you were. RED HORSE, we have an update," Perry began. "We just received word that the operation has been moved up. We will be going in tomorrow a day early. No word on why, but we will have a short day today. We all must be back here and ready to depart by 1300 tomorrow. So, given our night shift, you are getting up early, and it will be an exceptionally long day for all of us. Finish up what you need to today and go and get as much rest as you can."

Two hours later, Anglin was back at the hotel's business office to check his email again. His emotions were still swinging back and forth. Maybe she would have something to say. There was nothing from her. But there was a reply from his friend, Jacob Esler.

It began. "Sit down and take a deep breath. I'm afraid I have more bad news. I now know who that guy was and why I recognized him. It turns out that he is an HPSP military scholarship med student from LSU in New Orleans. He is here doing a six-week rotation, and I found out that he's working in Family Practice where Kara was seen. She probably met him there. Those guys come and go, so I don't pay much attention to them. I spotted him in the hospital cafeteria and decided to sit at the table near his. He was eating with two other med students, and they were laughing as I sat down. And I'm sorry, but I just have to tell it like I heard it. He was bragging about what a fun time he was having on this rotation. This is what I heard."

"'You learning a lot?' one of them asked.

"'Nope, not that,' he said. 'I'm getting laid a lot. I met her Friday afternoon, and we went out Saturday night. She can't keep her hands off me. She screws like there is no tomorrow. And, boy, is she hot. She took me to her house that first night, and we tore the place up. We did it on the couch, in the bed, and in the shower. There were clothes, couch cushions, pillows, and bedding all over the place. We even broke a few things that fell off the end tables in the living room. I'd fall asleep and wake up with her on top of me. I've spent the past two nights over at her place. I asked if she wanted to go out to dinner or something, but she just wanted to stay in and get it on. Though we did order takeout both nights. I mean, I've had girlfriends before but, none as aggressive and insatiable as Kara. Tonight I'll be bringing Chinese. And she texted me an hour ago to bring some whipped cream and cherries. Man, who can think about patients with that waiting for him at the end of the day," he concluded.

"Is she single?" one asked.

"Forget that," the other said. "Does she have a friend or sister?" The third asked laughing.

"No. No sister and she is sort of single. She said she is separated and that her future ex-husband works out of state. Man, I guess that guy just didn't know how to take care of business."

"I heard a little more, but it was his friends being jealous of him," said Staff Sergeant Esler. "Again, I am sorry, but this confirms that it wasn't just a kiss. I know it's tough, but you will need to move on, my friend. Hang in there the best you can."

Anglin's only reply was, "Got it."

Well, now I know why she needed to tidy up the house, he thought numbly.

He eventually found his way back to his room. In robot fashion, he packed up and laid out the uniform he would wear the next day. Outside his room in the hallway was a vending machine that carried beer. He got two cans and drank them quietly in his room. With his last sip, he took two Ambien he had gotten from a local pharmacy. He needed his mind to shut down to end the raging emotions and hopefully be able to function the next day.

26 ADMIRAL'S UPDATE

USS *Vinson*, South China Sea

After twenty minutes quietly observing the underway operations up on the bridge, the SMO headed down to the Admiral's spaces. He hoped to get a minute or two with Jenna. He was a bit worried about her, but he knew she was tuff.

"Knock, knock," he said after a few seconds' studying Jenna through her open door. She looked up and immediately flashed him a tired smile.

"Hey, Derek," she said waving him in.

"I just wanted to see how you were doing. I haven't seen you since we got back to the pier," he said, giving her space to answer.

"To tell you the truth, I haven't had any time to process what we went through," she said. "I've been going nonstop since I got back to the ship. Oh crap! We didn't get that blouse for your daughter. I'm so sorry."

"Don't worry," Derek said with a chuckle. "That wasn't a priority at the time. Really now, how are you doing?" he asked again. "Those guys were out to hurt us,".

"I am totally fine. Seriously. I am. It happened so fast, and those guys got what was coming to them. I want to thank you for protecting me, Derek," she said reaching across the table toward him.

He reached back, taking her hand in his for just a moment of intimate contact. "Anytime Jenna." Breaking the contact, he shifted topics. "So, we were all briefed on the Filipino operation on the ninth. At least, we know why we were all targeted."

"Hey, Derek, you're just in time," Jenna said, checking her watch. "We have a meeting in a couple of minutes to update the Admiral, and you have an open invitation to our regular staff meetings. You've been briefed on the operation, so why don't you stay? Besides, the Admiral may want a medical update."

"Sure," he replied as he followed her into the conference room.

Rear Admiral LaSalle and the rest of his staff were already seated, and he was in a conversation with Commander Monroe, his Intelligence Officer. He nodded to Jenna as she took her seat.

"Welcome, SMO. Good to have you here. Jenna briefed us on your little scuffle. Thanks for taking care of business and getting you both back safe," the Admiral said. "I guess you haven't forgotten some of your SEAL combat skills."

"Hardly," the SMO replied, holding up his bandaged left arm. "If I had been in better shape, this wouldn't have happened.

"SMO, this is a semiformal meeting, so why don't you go first and give us a medical update on our Sailors," the Admiral requested.

The SMO gave him a repeat of his brief to the CO earlier. Nothing of significance had occurred since then.

"So, one death, and none critical at this time," the Admiral summarized.

"Yes, sir," he answered.

"SMO, we have been getting police reports and information from other intel assets," began Monroe. "There have been no reports of any attack or injuries from the Stanley Market area. Your attack was the only one we are aware of that occurred in that part of Hong Kong. Jenna said that three were down and seriously injured, yet there have been no police or medical reports. Did you just stun them, and they later scrambled away?" asked Monroe.

"No," the SMO answered grimly. "One was almost certainly a fatality. The second had his larynx crushed and may or may not survive. The third, I disabled by breaking both of his forearms. And the fourth had a broken arm, and I later saw him chatting easily with a Hong Kong policeman. Not something you would expect to see from a local gangster unless they were on the same team or at least shared a common goal."

"Damn, SMO!" the Admiral interjected. "Jenna downplayed it a bit. She reported that you took on four armed guys, disabled them all, and led you both to safety. You described a more serious encounter than we had initially suspected. Thanks for saving my Chief of Staff."

"I had help. She wacked one on the head with a pot that was about to take me out . It was a joint effort. We may not be here if it hadn't been for her timely intervention," the SMO finished.

"Thanks for the update, SMO. Okay, let's get back on track," the Admiral redirected. "Commander Monroe, please start with your brief."

"Yes, sir. The latest traffic from Fort Meade assesses that Chinese intel has deduced the overall plan and intent of Operation SEAHORSE. Either the plan was compromised within the Filipino military, or their assets reported the personnel and equipment movements. Or a combination of the two. As a result, they have concluded that the attacks on our personnel was a harassment activity, possibly with the goal of reducing our military effectiveness. But if so, we have no reduced operational capability. The speed and efficiency of our recall probably surprised them. They expected to have had more time to injure and arrest more of our troops. The consensus is that they are trying for a delaying action to allow them time to move assets into place to block the operation," Monroe said. "There are reports of Chinese frigates far to the south heading north fast. So the window of opportunity to pull this off is rapidly closing. After consulting with Philippine President Magdato and their Chief of Staff, they have concluded that they are ready and able to accelerate the operation's timeline twenty-four hours. So they will take the shoal tomorrow morning instead of on the ninth as originally planned," he concluded.

"Speedtrap, what is our status. Will we be ready to support?" the Admiral asked, turning to Captain Ball, his Operations Officer.

"Admiral, all ships are underway and will be out of the channel within the next hour. We will be in international waters by midnight. We are already scheduled for normal flight operations starting at 0900. So, everything is in place to support the operation. We will brief the aircrews on the operation and Rules of Engagement. We can't directly provide support until the Filipinos have full control and our troops are in place," Ball replied.

"Excellent," the Admiral replied. "Make sure they are up and ready to go and the aircraft are properly armed."

"Yes, sir," he answered.

"Jenna, what updates do you have?" The Admiral asked his Chief of Staff.

"Sir, we were just informed that a contingent from SEAL Team 1 will be arriving on a special flight from Okinawa on the tenth. They will then be transferred to Scarborough Shoal after our troops arrive to support initial security operations there," she said.

"Hmm, guess that isn't a surprise," the Admiral said. He turned to the SMO. "Wasn't that your old unit? Maybe you can see some old friends."

"Maybe, sir," the SMO replied. "But it is unlikely that I know anyone after all this time. Special Ops is a young man's game and takes its toll on the body."

"Mike, what is our role after the island is secure and construction operations are underway?" the Admiral asked his Planner, Captain Deville.

"Admiral, the latest is that we will remain in the vicinity for the next two weeks until the USS *Ronald Reagan* gets underway from its home port in Japan. They are due for their regular Southeast Asia patrol. We will then proceed to the Arabian Gulf as originally planned with only a two-week delay to our original schedule. I have already coordinated with our supply ships to keep us topped off on aviation fuel, food, parts, and mail."

"Anyone else have anything to add on this?" the Admiral asked. "If not, let's all be on our game and prepared for anything."

27 FLIGHT PLAN

PLAN Air Base, China

Lieutenant Commander Yao awoke keyed up and imagined the day ahead while still lying in bed and staring up at the ceiling. Today was going to be a fly day for him. Any fly day was one he looked forward to, but today he planned for it to be a special flight. With the information he gained from his uncle yesterday, he hoped to overfly the American carrier as it headed out to sea in the early afternoon while it was still in Chinese waters.

As he sat up in bed, he noticed the form curled up facing away from him. For a moment, he mulled having another go with her. Normally, he would have indulged himself, but he was already too focused on the flight. So he had no further use for her. He ripped her cover off and slapped her extremely hard on the buttocks and said to the woman he had picked up in a local bar the night before. "*Out!* I am done with you. Be gone!" he shouted at her tersely.

He ate a quiet breakfast out on the balcony of his small apartment that had a distant view of the South China Sea. Today he was out of sorts, and he was not sure why. He sipped his tea and inhaled the pungent but enticing aroma as he let his mind replay the events of the past few days. His experiences with his uncle the Admiral at the conference. His time on the American aircraft carrier and the news about the possible taking of the Scarborough Shoal by the Filipinos. Was all the planning he had helped with on Operation MACKEREL now to be wasted? Were the Americans to be allowed to check their moves in their own backyard? How can this be allowed? What is President Hsu worried about? He could feel is irritation rise and disrupt his usual relaxed morning. At least, his career prospects had taken an unexpected boost from his uncle Jiang.

The more he pondered it, the more he kept coming back to his interactions with the Americans. What was it? They were not hostile. No, not really. They had actually been pleasant and open with everyone. Was it an arrogant attitude he had heard about that many Americans exhibited? No, that didn't seem to be it either. What was it that had his gut churning? They had been friendly to everyone but careful not to discuss any confidential information. They pulled into the harbor and threw a big party that was the talk of the town. That in itself was not unusual. An American carrier comes into port every year or so and thousands of American Sailors stream ashore. They were all care free and happy to be there. They walked the streets like any Chinese citizen. Hm. That was it! That was what was bothering him. These Americans walked around as if entitled to go anywhere they want here in China and the world. It was their carefree confidence that was shaking him. They acted as it the world was their playground and were not showing any real deferential respect for his country and people. No matter what they said, they walked around like China was theirs. And now he knew that they were even likely to act on their beliefs to support the taking of part of his country's historic territory. They were acting as if the recent reclamation of the South China Sea islands was of no consequence. Well, he hoped that his leaders would not allow this disrespectful attitude to go unchallenged for long. And he was determined to be at the forefront of any future action if it came to that. They need to understand that their day in the sun is fading fast and that there is a new economic and military power in the world. His irritation continued to chew at him as he showered and dressed for work.

Two hours later, he was in the squadron planning his afternoon flight. As a flight leader, he was planning the route that his flight of two J-15 Flying Sharks would take. At the moment he was studying a large chart of the South China Sea that included the area near Hong Kong. He was trying to estimate the approximate location of the *Vinson* as it headed to sea in the early afternoon. He wanted to be able to fly close enough to observe it as it was steaming out. But he needed to wait until it was out of Hong Kong's airspace where he would have the freedom to maneuver as he wished.

"Good morning, Commander Yao," said Lieutenant Suyong, the squadron's Intelligence Officer with a slight bow. He was trying to continue past the notorious Yao without further incident. He needed to get to his small office, and he had no option but to walk past Yao, the one man he wished to avoid for, for the rest of his life, he thought.

Unless he needed something from them, Yao usually ignored him or any junior officer or enlisted. Not this officer, not today. Yao froze Suyong in place with a malevolent glare, saying nothing. "You cost me a cell phone and caused me to waste most of my afternoon," Yao finally said after an unbearably long silence.

"I am indeed sorry, Commander. How may I make it up to you?" Suyong pleaded.

"You can start with a new cell phone. I had the latest Samsung smart phone. I had a nice red one. The store did not have the proper color replacement. You can take care of that for me," Yao said smugly.

"Yes, Commander, is there anything else?" Suyong asked deferentially.

"No, now get out of my sight," Yao barked.

Before he could get two steps Suyong heard, "Wait! Get me the exact time that the American carrier *Vinson* is due to depart Hong Kong," Yao demanded brusquely.

Suyong had a puzzled look on his face. "Commander, I thought you would have been informed," Suyong said hesitantly.

"Of what? Don't play games with me, Lieutenant!" Yao replied impatiently. "What has happened?"

"They're gone, Commander," he said cautiously. "They notified the harbor master they were departing last night only ten minutes before they were actually underway at 2050. The carrier and its escort ships weighed anchor and slipped out in the dark."

Yao sat there momentarily stunned. They were gone. Any chance of bottling them up was now clearly gone. The irritation that had been simmering in his gut now blossomed into full-blown anger. Even the cold pleasure of humiliating Suyong did not help.

"Where are they now?" Yao shouted at Suyong as if it was his fault. "Show me on the chart."

Suyong quickly pointed to an area on the chart 115 miles east/northeast of Hong Kong. "About here, from one of our asset's last reports an hour ago. They have begun flight operations."

"Any activity around Scarborough Shoal?" Yao asked carefully. He didn't know how much this junior intelligence officer may actually know. And he surely wasn't going to give away anything to this incompetent idiot.

"No, nothing special has been noted there or anywhere else," Suyong replied quickly. "Our radar indicates that the bulk of the Air Wing is flying sorties southeast of Taiwan. We have detected nothing unusual in their operations. The only thing unusual was their sudden departure. And that was clearly in response to the many incidents that had occurred in Hong Kong."

Yao just nodded.

His mind was racing. He was bouncing from anger to excitement. They had made it into international waters, but that also provided an opportunity. Maybe just maybe he could fly in the vicinity of the carrier if his squadron Commander would approve.

He waved and called over to Lieutenant Junior Grade Gan Hu, the pilot who was his usual wingman. "Hu, plan a mission to patrol this area," Yao said, tapping the chart at the *Vinson*'s last-known position. "I will brief you when I get back. First I have to talk to the squadron Commander. Then I will make sure the maintenance officer provides us with two jets with drop tanks. We may need the extra fuel."

28 Little Dog Bites Back
Scarborough Shoal, South China Sea

It was a bright, sunny day with the usual scattered white puffy clouds building up. The Captain of the Chinese Coast Guard cutter handed the finished breakfast tray to the waiting galley steward. He leaned over to check the radar screen. Nothing unusual he thought. It showed about a dozen fishing boats around the shoal. One medium-size Filipino fishing boat was to the north side, casting nets. To the south side were six smaller Filipino fishing boats scattered around. There was also one large Chinese fishing boat near them. Two other Chinese fishing boats had left earlier this morning with full loads heading back to their home port. Three more were due any day.

In general, since the Chinese had started posting a Coast Guard cutter at the entrance to the Shoal's large central lagoon, the Chinese fishing boats had outnumbered the Filipino boats. The Filipino boats had been tolerated and allowed to fish under close and aggressive supervision. And they were not allowed into the coveted lagoon. Occasionally, when a Filipino boat found a particularly good spot, the cutter would assist a Chinese fishing boat in running off the Filipinos and take over the area. There were always complaints, but what could they do? Occasionally, the Chinese Navy would send frigates or destroyers to patrol past the shoal just to remind everyone who really was in control of the area.

Still, the American's had passed by within ten miles every few months. The Filipinos' newly refurbished frigates had also been patrolling in the vicinity more frequently but had kept their distance, and no overt actions had been taken.

The cutter had been on station for six weeks and was due to rotate back to home port in two weeks. Mostly, it was boring duty. Even today, in spite of the cryptic message they had received instructing them to be more vigilant. Finishing his tea, Captain went below for an unscheduled tour of the engine room and was just starting to inspect the maintenance logs when the overhead speaker went off.

"Captain to the bridge! Captain to the bridge!" said an urgent metallic sounding voice over the intercom.

"What is it?" he demanded as he stepped onto the bridge.

"Captain, we just received a call for assistance from the *Mǎ lín yú*."

"The fishing boat. Do they have mechanical problems? A fire?" the Captain asked as he strode to the starboard side of the bridge to look in the direction of the fishing boat. He could just make out part of the upper deck of the 135-foot fishing boat across the island that was just visible through the palm trees. Even with binoculars, he saw no unusual smoke, and the ship appeared motionless.

What he could not see were the smaller Filipino fishing boats surrounding it, blocking any movement without fouling its nets or damaging its hull. It would be more destructive on any of the smaller boats if they collided, but the Captain of the *Mǎ lín yú* clearly did not want to risk it. Not with an armed Chinese Coast Guard cutter just minutes away to deal with these irritating Filipinos.

"No," replied the Officer of the Deck. "He reports being surrounded by the Filipino fishing boats who are now blocking his path."

"He's far bigger than any of them. Tell him to just run them over," he said. "They'll get the message."

"He already said that he could lose half his nets doing that, and he doesn't want to damage his ship," the Officer of the Deck replied.

"Fine," he said with an inward smile. "Raise the anchor. Once it is clear of the waterline, ahead full." *Finally, a little action after three weeks mostly at anchor*, he thought.

"Yes, Captain," replied the Officer of the Deck, who then repeated the orders to the bridge crew.

Within five minutes, they had left their position guarding the entrance to the lagoon and were charging forward at thirty knots.

The Captain checked the radar again. The lone Filipino fishing boat to the north was still slowly dragging its nets away from them to the northwest. Ahead and to the southeast was just one big blob, representing the tight cluster of boats that he could easily see after moving out into open water. There was nothing else on the radar horizon.

"Have the twenty-five-millimeter gun crew ready," the Captain ordered. "Hail them on the radio."

"Filipino fish vessels, Filipino fish vessels," he said in broken English, the international language he assumed both could understand. "This Chinese Coast Guard ship *Fáng yù zhě*. You violate safety of Chinese fish vessel *Mǎ lín yú*. You stop now."

He waited for a response on the radio or a hint that they were backing away. Seeing none, he repeated his call two more times. Still no response.

The small boats continued holding their positions around the larger boat, blocking its movement.

As they rapidly closed the distance to the ships, they detected no movement.

"Filipino fish vessels, if no stop, we force you away."

As they neared, the Captain directed them to slow to quarter speed and to head toward the Filipino boat, blocking the bow of the *Mǎ lín yù*.

The Captain was not afraid to ram the small fishing boat. Besides, he knew who would win this game of chicken.

At the last minute before they would have collided, the fishing boat darted forward away from the oncoming cutter. But as soon as the cutter passed by in front of the Chinese fishing boat, the nimble little Filipino fishing boat was back where it had started, blocking the larger Chinese fishing boat before they could get moving.

This both infuriated and perplexed the cutter Captain. He had never seen the Filipinos act so boldly. "What are the up to?" he asked no one in particular.

"No more playing," the Captain growled. "Stand by to fire shots across their bow after we come around."

After the cutter had looped back around, the crack of the twenty-five-millimeter gun could be heard across the waves as the spray of the rounds rose like geysers twenty meters in front of the stationary fishing boat.

This had the immediate effect the Captain had intended. Within moments, all six of the Filipino fishing vessels were moving and departing to the east.

The *Fáng yù zhě* Officer of the Deck called the *Mǎ lín yù* to ensure that all was now okay, which it was.

What the *Fáng yù zhě'* crew had not noticed was that as soon as they had turned to the altercation, the larger Filipino fishing vessel to the north had cut its nets away and raced to the entrance to the lagoon. Once there they anchored, blocking the channel.

They were halfway back to the channel entrance before they realized what had happened.

"This is becoming annoying," the Captain said. "We start with the twenty-five-millimeter this time."

"Captain, the radar," the Officer of the Deck exclaimed. Converging from eight points of the compass were eight large returns. Their tracks soon showed that they were moving at thirty knots, straight for the mouth of Scarborough Shoal. They would be on them in less than fifteen minutes.

"Chinese cutter *Fáng yù zhě*, Chinese cutter *Fáng yù zhě*. This is the BRP *Ramon Alcaraz*," crackled the radio. "You are trespassing Philippine territory. Depart the area immediately."

Everyone on the bridge of the cutter stood in stunned silence. All were staring at their Captain.

"Chinese cutter *Fáng yù zhě*. This is the BRP *Ramon Alcaraz*," the radio repeated. "You are trespassing Philippine territory. Depart the area immediately."

"Captain, what do we do?" the Officer of the Deck pleaded.

"Chinese cutter *Fáng yù zhě*. This is the BRP *Ramon Alcaraz*," the radio crackled. "If you do not depart, you will be fired upon. I repeat, if you do not depart, you will be fired upon."

"There's nothing we can do," he said, looking down at the rapidly approaching targets on the radar screen. Dejectedly, he finally said, "Head for home port, but go at quarter speed. We will not be seen running away. Get me Coast Guard headquarters on the satellite phone," he said, heading to his cabin.

29 TANKER FLIGHT

USS *Vinson*, South China Sea

The SMO was pleased that all was going well in the medical department this morning, considering the craziness of the previous day. The two ICU patients were awake and doing well. They were expected to be moved to the regular ward tomorrow. Of those kept overnight for observation, all but two were released and given light duty for a week. Back in his office at 0830, after the CO's morning meeting, the SMO answered an unexpected call.

"Commander Lloyd, this is Lieutenant Franklin, VFA-22's flight scheduler," he said.

"Oh, hi, Sheriff," Lloyd said, remembering the call sign Franklin had earned for breaking up several bar fights involving his fellow pilots. "What can I do for you?"

"Actually, Commander, I called to see if you were available to fly this afternoon on a tanker flight. I saw a yellow sticky note on my computer from two weeks ago when you stopped by asking to get on the schedule. We had one of our NFOs get sick this morning, and we have an open back seat on a tanker mission."

Lloyd's mind was already racing to see if his schedule was clear. It was.

"Maybe, I have to clear it with my boss. I'll get you an answer in twenty minutes," Lloyd said. "And thanks."

"Any time, Commander," answered Sheriff Franklin as he hung up.

Flying in fighters was a thrill he never tired of, and he reveled in every opportunity. But competition to get one of the coveted seats was fierce. He had to compete not only with the regular NFOs, but also with the two flight surgeons in his department.

After hanging up, the SMO hustled up to the bridge to ask the CO if he could fly. Anytime one of the CO's senior department heads would be off the ship, he needed to know. Even if it was for a few hours to fly.

Waiting for a lull in the bridge chatter, the SMO finally saw his opening.

"Captain, I have a chance at a Hornet tanker flight this afternoon. Everything is quiet on the ward, and I haven't flown in three weeks, and that was in a helo. Do you mind if I go?" he asked expectantly.

The Captain spun his bridge chair around to fully face the SMO. "SMO, you had a pretty eventful day yesterday. And you got your arm sliced up in the process. So, Doctor, are you medically and emotionally fit to fly?" he asked with a serious look.

"Yes, sir. Absolutely!" the SMO quickly replied with a grin. "It was just a scratch."

The CO let the silence hang as he fixed him with a penetrating glare before answering.

"Uh-huh, I bet you are," he finally replied. "Go ahead and have some fun. Chase a few clouds for me while you're up there." He gave the slightest of smiles. "Now get out of here. We have planes to launch."

At noon, he was up in VFA-22's para-loft to get fitted out in borrowed flight gear. He was in the ready room well before the brief's 1245 start time where he met his pilot, Lieutenant Commander Ash Tioga.

"Hello Commander Lloyd, I'm Commander 'Two-Dogs' Tioga, your pilot today." He introduced himself to the SMO with a huge blinding smile. "You ready to go have some fun?"

"I'm glad to meet you. And, boy, am I ready. This is just the ticket to get my head in the clouds and forget the past few days for a little while. And just call me SMO. Everyone else does," the SMO answered. "Tioga, that's an unusual name. Where is it from?"

"Sure thing, SMO. I'm three-quarters Choctaw, and I grew up in central Louisiana," Tioga answered as they sat down in two adjacent ready-room chairs to begin the brief.

Tioga went over the weather brief, which was forecast to be clear to the moon. Then he went through the standard brief of what the mission was to include.

"SMO, this will be a standard recovery-tanker mission," Tioga said. "Our call sign is Beef Eater 206. We will launch first, do a package check with the off-going tanker, then sponge any excess fuel he has before he lands. There are no long-range missions today, so we have no scheduled fuel offloads. We are only there in case one of the planes from the earlier cycle has trouble landing and gets low on fuel. After the last plane lands, we will be cleared off to do whatever we want until we have to be back for our recovery and check out the next oncoming tanker. Any questions?"

"No, sounds like the other flights I've had," the SMO answered.

"Well, I need to do some practice strafing runs today," said Tioga. "And we may have to do some surface surveillance and photograph any ships we spot.

Tioga continued to ensure that the SMO was familiar with getting strapped in and configuring the cockpit displays. At the end of the brief, Tioga gave the SMO the computer hard drive to install in the rear cockpit that contained the pre-programed flight plan. Next they went to get suited up in life support. Whoever's gear the SMO borrowed, it was a good fit.

Back in the ready room after getting their flight gear on Tioga checked to see if their assigned plane was ready and where it was spotted on the flight deck before they headed up. They came up on the flight deck's starboard side just aft of the island. It was a beautiful clear day with just a few white puffy clouds off in the distance at about 5,000 feet. They headed towards the bow and to their assigned plane located just forward of the island in an area called the Six Pack. It had four drop tanks plus the buddy store, which meant that it was going to weigh about sixty-six thousand pounds. The SMO calculated that this was by far one of the heaviest he would launch in. *It's going to be one hell of a catapult stroke,* the SMO thought.

They were met at the plane by the brown shirted plane captain who had completed the preflight inspection. He showed them all the safety pins that he had pulled and told them the jet was ready to go. The SMO climbed up the ladder and over to the rear seat while the pilot did a preflight walk-around inspection. After inspecting the ejection seat, the SMO inserted the computer hard drive and latched the cover closed before then easing down into the seat. It took a minute, but he finally got his leg restraints attached before next connecting first the lower and then upper Koch fittings that joined him to the ejection seat and parachute. He then turned to his left to plug in his G suit hose to the side console, followed by his oxygen hose, and finally the communications cord. Nine connections in all, and he was ready to go.

Lieutenant Commander Tioga finished his preflight and climbed up and strapped himself into the front cockpit. After sitting for ten minutes and checking out the intercom they got the signal from the plane captain to start their engines. The pilot first started up the auxiliary power unit which in turn provided the power to start the engines. Next, he started the number two engine on the right side. As the engine spooled up the generator came online, and the cockpit came alive. The SMO turned on his four displays and set them as he wanted. The upper one was set to mirror the pilot's Heads Up Display. The SMO soon noticed the smell and felt his eyes burning from the engine exhaust of the other planes starting up in such a confined area. He snapped on his O2 mask for fresh air now that the oxygen generator was operating with an engine running. Tioga then lowered the canopy after first making sure the SMO's hands were clear. After the number one engine was started, the pilot went through his flight control and avionics checks. Once complete, they waited for the signal from the plane captain to be 'Broken Down.' This was done by disconnecting the tie down chains that held them firmly to the deck. Just before the chains were removed, they armed their ejection seats. Until they were safely chained down again after the flight, they would need the option of ejecting.

"You ready, SMO? Here we go," Tioga said over the intercom.

"All set. Let's get this beast into the air!" the SMO replied.

They were directed to taxi forward about 15 feet which gave them enough room to spread and lock their wings for flight. It also allowed a red shirt ordinance woman the chance to pull the safety pins and arm the sidewinder missiles on each wingtip. Once armed, the yellow shirt directors had them taxi aft of the number four arresting gear cable, then turned toward the port side of the ship. At one point, the SMO was convinced that they were being driven over the side of the ship. In fact the plane's nose and the pilot were actually briefly hanging out over the port side catwalk as they turned.

They inched forward along the very edge of the flight deck's port side to catapult four along the angled deck. To his left, the SMO was seeing mostly water. As they neared the catapult, one of the blue shirts came and held up the weight board for the pilot to verify. This is the final verification that they have the correct weight for their plane dialed in, so the proper amount of steam is directed to the catapult as they are launched.

Taxing the last few feet, the SMO could feel the just attached hold back stop their forward movement. After a minute, the shuttle came back, and it hooked into the lowered nose bar. The nose bar is the part of the plane that is actually pulled forward along with the rest of the plane. The SMO felt the plane squat down a bit as the plane was put into tension. It wouldn't be long now, the SMO thought as he sat up high to see forward.

The shooter just fifteen feet to the left signaled for full military power. The SMO recognized the yellow-shirted shooter as Lieutenant Belland. Holding onto the cockpit dash handholds, he leaned a little forward in anticipation of the surge to come. The SMO could feel the roar and vibrations as the plane tried to jump forward. Tioga did a final check of his flight controls by moving the control stick all the way around in a circle while stepping fully on first the left then right rudder pedals. After the 'wipe out' control check Lieutenant Belland gave the signal to go to afterburner by pushing up her hand over her head several times. The roar increased to a screaming level, then Tioga called out to the SMO, "Here we go!"

Tioga saluted Belland. Then she bent over and touched the deck, the signal to activate the catapult. The SMO subconsciously took in a deep breath just as he felt the crushing force of the catapult slamming him back into the seat. The constant intense acceleration seemed to take forever. But it was only seconds.

Man, what a ride, the SMO thought. *Zero to 160 knots in 2.5 seconds. People would pay good money to do this just once.*

Immediately following the launch, they did a thirty degree clearing turn to the left to deconflict with any planes launching simultaneously off the bow catapults. They stayed down low at around five hundred feet for about ten miles before popping up to seven thousand feet and returning back overhead the ship.

Entering into a circular orbit above the ship they were joined by the off-going tanker to do a package check to ensure that they could give fuel if needed. Tioga deployed their refueling hose and attached drogue basket.

The off-going tanker moved back and connected to test that their refueling system was working properly. After the package check, Tioga retracted the drogue and dropped back behind the off-going tanker and began taking their excess fuel. They took onboard 1,800 pounds, which was roughly 300 gallons of fuel, only 10 minutes after they launched.

"Glad I don't have to pay our gas bill!" The SMO said.

They then orbited over head for the next twenty-five minutes, watching the final launches and then all the planes land successfully. None needed any extra gas today. The Air Wing was conducting an exercise one hundred miles east of the carrier, so they headed west to stay out of their way and to have some fun. After checking out the several container ships, Tioga pulled back up to five thousand feet to set up for the first of several simulated strafing runs at imaginary targets on the ocean surface.

"Beef Eater 206," crackled a voice over the radio, "this is Overwatch 603," clarifying that it was from the current E-2C Hawkeye Airborne-Early-Warning aircraft.

Tioga responded. "Overwatch, this is Beef 206, go."

"206, you have two bandits at Bull's-eye-three-one-zero at one-fifteen, Angels two-three, speed 550 knots, headed toward mother," Overwatch relayed.

"Copy, two bandits, Bull's-eye-three-one-zero at one-fifteen, Angels two-three, speed 550. Toward mother," Tioga repeated.

This simple statement told Tioga and the SMO a world of information. Bandits were known bad guys and were bearing 310 degrees from Bull's-eye, at 115 nautical miles. Bull's-eye is a designated reference position that changes daily. In reality they were only thirty-five miles west of them and closing fast at an altitude of twenty-three thousand feet.

"Roger, 206. We have been monitoring them since they took off, and they have been patrolling west of your position. But it appears they have mother on their radar and are headed in that direction. We recommend that you buster to mother," Overwatch recommended.

"Copy, we are return to base," Tioga answered. "So much for the rest of our fun flight, SMO. We will head back overhead the boat. Those guys are just probably out sightseeing and want to do a flyby of the ship. I will head a bit north to stay out of their path to the ship."

"Well, I don't know about you, but I have already had a great time. I grew up wanting to be a fighter pilot, and though I got pulled in other directions, I have never lost the love of doing this whenever I can," the SMO answered.

Tioga headed northeast in the general direction of the carrier at fifteen thousand feet and 350 knots. They still had almost twenty minutes before they were expected back overhead the ship. He estimated that the bandits would pass south of him about fifteen miles off his right wing.

"Hey, SMO, keep an eye out the right side for those bandits," Tioga requested. "They should be passing us in the next couple of minutes. But given their higher altitude and the time of day, they may be in the general direction of the sun about now."

"Looking," the SMO answered. The SMO squinted through his tinted visor, but he couldn't see anything against the glare of the sun.

"Beef 206, bandits now at your four o'clock, fourteen miles. They should be passing by you in the next minute," Overwatch advised.

"Copy, looking," Tioga replied. "You see anything, SMO?"

"Nothing yet. Wait…tally two at three o'clock high," the SMO answered a bit excitedly.

"206, they are turning hot your direction. I repeat, they are turning hot in your direction!" Overwatch said emphatically over the radio.

"SMO, keep your eyes glued on them. They may just be curious and want to check us out," Tioga said in a surprisingly calm voice. "We're only ten minutes from the boat. But we are out here all alone."

Tioga held his course and speed and kept his eyes mostly on the rapidly closing bandits with quick glances back to his Heads-Up Display, or HUD, that gave him a snapshot of his flight instruments, radar, and weapons status.

The SMO heard a buzzing sound a second before he heard Tioga suddenly say, "Oh shit!" and he felt the sudden onset of G forces slamming him down into his seat.

"Hang on, SMO," Tioga called over the intercom as his training kicked in. Over the radio, he called out, "Beef 206, spiked!" This was to tell Overwatch that they had just gotten an indication of a missile threat on their radar-warning receiver. At least, one of the approaching fighters had his radar missiles on and tracking them. He slammed his throttle to the firewall for full military power and turned to point his nose at the threat now only four miles away. This move reduced their target profile and somewhat neutralized their challenger's advantage. Now at a closure rate of almost nine hundred miles per hour, they were seconds from a head-to-head pass with the lead fighter.

"What the hell is this guy doing?" Tioga said out loud as they were about to pass less than a thousand feet apart. "Is he just trying to yank our chain on a quick flyby? We'll know in a second if he turns on us."

Just as they were abeam the lead fighter, Tioga and the SMO saw him roll ninety degrees in their direction and the sudden appearance of a vaper condensation cloud over his wings, indicating that he was pulling hard into them in an effort the get behind them.

Tioga immediately bumped his throttle into afterburner and rolled up and left toward the slightly higher and now clearly recognizable J-15 turning on him. "206 engaged!" he called over the radio, telling all that he was now in a dogfight. "SMO, check the wingman."

The SMO heard a bang and felt the aircraft buck slightly as Tioga jettisoned the four empty drop tanks and the buddy store refueling package. The drop tanks were now empty, but they still caused significant weight and drag, severely limiting the Hornet's ability to maneuver. As soon as they were away, the SMO felt the Gs increase pulling him down into his seat, with the near simultaneous crushing squeeze of the G-suit on his legs and abdomen. He took in a breath and tensed all his leg and abdominal muscles in an anti-G-straining maneuver to counteract the blood pooling toward his feet and away from his brain. Properly done, the maneuver will keep enough blood pushed up to his brain and eyes to keep him functioning for just over nine Gs.

As it was, his vision begin to grey-out before he got a good strain going.

"Copy," the SMO said through clenched teeth as he continued taking in short sharp breaths of his G-straining maneuver while doing his best to keep the second plane in sight as it turned toward them from almost a mile away.

The goal now was to get behind the other plane or at least keep him from pointing his nose at them. With the new modern missiles, they could shoot you in the face. All they needed was to be pointed enough in your direction for their missile to get a lock. Tioga ensured in a glance at his HUD that his Sidewinder missiles were activated but not actively seeking yet.

They were pulling hard in a classic near-horizontal dogfight.

After one and a half turns, it was clear that they were evenly matched, and neither was gaining an advantage. They were still across the circle from each other and pulling hard. Though not in a position to threaten the J-15, he had clearly neutralized him for the moment. Tioga knew that he had time on his side as long as he could keep his adversary from being able to get a lock on them. The *Vinson* was close, and this guy was over 140 miles from his nearest base.

The Chinese pilot also understood the time constraints. Tioga saw the J-15's engine nozzles flare, indicating he had gone into afterburner, and the vapor appear on his wings again.

So much for a rate fight, Tioga thought. The J-15 pilot was now clearly cashing in his energy to pull hard and point his nose at them. *Damn,* thought Tioga, *that looks too easy.* The J-15s canards effortlessly pointed the nose of the fighter at them. And to make it even worse, Tioga saw that the J-15 still had its drop tanks. He was maneuvering that well with all that extra drag.

He had no choice but to cash in his air speed and energy to do the same to neutralize him again. But this is the realm that the Hornet was designed for, high-angle-of-attack dogfighting. It meant that the Hornet could get pretty slow and still be able to point its nose up in any direction in order to get off a missile shot at an adversary.

The SMO increased his straining maneuver as the extra Gs piled on. He could feel the Hornet shaking significantly as its nose came around toward the J-15.

Thankfully, neither Tioga nor the SMO heard any indications of a missile lock. So Tioga did not activate his Sidewinders. The last thing they needed was an inadvertent weapons release.

Both jets were now again racing toward each other for another head-to-head pass, though both were significantly slower. To gain speed, both nosed down about twenty degrees to unload and get a gravity assist. It was also to not let the other gain separation and therefore potential angles that the other could exploit to get behind the other. They were at only one-half G as they approached for another nose to nose merge on his left side.

"SMO, where's number two? I've lost sight," Tioga asked in the moments he could relax his G-straining maneuver.

"He's two o'clock high. He appears to just be orbiting overhead," the SMO replied.

After a quick glance up, Tioga replied, "Got him." Then over the radio he called out, "206, still engaged."

For the first time, Overwatch replied. "Copy, Beef 206, help is on the way."

This time, Tioga was going to dictate the terms of the fight and not just react to the other guy. Turning first, he did a snap aileron roll to his left and pulled his nose down into a forty-five-degree, hard seven-G slicing turn. The J-15 responded immediately and countered this move by pulling into a tight forty-five-degree climb resulting in another circular fight. After a half turn of the circle, Tioga had gained enough energy to pull even harder and point his nose at the J-15 across the circle. The Chinese pilot didn't anticipate this and delayed his response a couple of heartbeats before again pulling toward the Hornet. Because he had gone up, he was at a lower energy state than the Hornet and a bit slower in turning.

Tioga lined up with his opponent and knew that if needed he could have taken a shot. But they again headed into another pass. As they zoomed by each other in another merge, the SMO could clearly see the helmet of the Chinese pilot looking at them. As they passed, both planes pulled up into a climb this time, pulling toward each other.

"Bandit two at five o'clock high is just orbiting overhead. Not threat yet," the SMO called out.

With a quick glance back over his right shoulder, he called, "Tally."

After three barrel rolls, Bandit one suddenly disengaged and dove down, performing a split-S. This move clearly left him vulnerable to the Hornet. Tioga was soon lining up for a firing solution.

Scanning the sky in search of Bandit two, the SMO finally spotted him. "Bandit two at two thirty high," he called out.

The two Bandits had timed it perfectly. Bandit one's move had set them up to move right in front of the now diving bandit two. They were clearly in his sights as Tioga pulled his nose hard toward the diving bandit.

"He's got company," the SMO got out through clenched teeth. "The cavalry has arrived."

They continued their turn hard into bandit two. Tioga glanced to see that two F-35Cs were rapidly closing on bandit one. As they continued toward bandit two, the SMO glanced back to see the F-35s maneuver into position only feet from either side of bandit one's wing tips. The one off his right wing elevated slightly and opened his weapons bay doors, revealing his missiles inside. The message was clear and universal, "Back off!"

The bandit pulled up and turned west and was soon joined by his wingman.

"Thanks, guys," Tioga called to the F-35s over the radio.

"Anytime," the F-35 lead pilot replied as they continued to trail the J-15s west.

The two F-35s followed them at about a thousand yards for the next thirty miles, ensuring they were safely headed home and no longer posing a threat.

"You okay, SMO?" Tioga asked.

"I'm fine, but I'm drenched in sweat," he replied.

"Me too, SMO. Me too. That was insane. Those guys were serious. I really thought that they were going to light us up. I had a couple of good shot opportunities, but I didn't dare arm up. But they had more chances to shoot us down. And thanks for the extra set of eyes, SMO. I totally lost track of number two during that fur ball. Otherwise, we would have been squished like grapes," Tioga said as they headed back overhead the *Vinson*.

The SMO checked his watch and noted that from the time they had been called about the bandits until the F-35s had ran them off, had been only seven minutes. And he was exhausted. He was clearly not used to pulling that many Gs for an extended period of time.

"SMO, any idea what the hell that was all about?" Tioga questioned.

"Your guess is as good as mine," the SMO lied. He actually had a rather good idea what had the Chinese pissed off, but he wasn't sure Tioga was briefed in on it. At least, not yet.

Back overhead the ship they established an orbit at seven thousand feet. They watched as the planes on deck taxied to the catapults and began to launch off. They followed the first one which was the tanker for the next cycle and joined up with him as he climbed up to their altitude. The crew of the oncoming tanker looked incredulously at their clean jet with no drop tanks or buddy store. The pilot gave a 'what's up 'shrug. Tioga maneuvered behind them to check out their refueling equipment. After the check they began to circle down as the other planes from their launch cycle began to land only a minute after the last plane launched. As their turn came, they were down at five hundred feet and came zipping by the starboard side of the ship. A mile in front of the ship they did an easy break to the left and entered the downwind pattern, dropping their landing gear and tail hook. Rolling into the groove behind the ship, Tioga called, "Rhino Ball, two point three to let the ship know that he had sight of the Fresnel lens giving the ideal landing glidepath, and that they had two thousand three hundred pounds of fuel left.

Before the break, the SMO had made sure that his shoulder straps were aligned properly, and that the inertia reel was locked. They were about to stop abruptly, and he didn't want to fly forward and crack his noggin on the dash. A most undignified prospect. He leaned to the left as much as he dared to watch as they approached. He gripped the cockpit handholds again and was pushing himself back into the seat. He noticed a blur of the ship passing by on his left and right and he braced himself. He felt the hard touchdown as the pilot went to full power just as the sudden deceleration started and he was thrown forward against his harness. In moments, they were at a complete stop and the pilot retarded the throttles as the arresting cable pulled them backwards slightly. A yellow shirt signaled Tioga to raise the tail hook and directed them to taxi out of the landing zone. They were stopped and the missile safety pins inserted before they folded their wings. Another yellow shirt directed them to taxi to the stern where they were parked at a forty five degree angle to the ship. As Tioga shut down the engines the canopy was raised. The SMO disconnected from everything, got out of the seat, retrieved the hard drive, and climbed down the plane's ladder.

"WOW! What a ride!" Exclaimed the SMO.

"It sure the hell was," Tioga said. "You did a great job, SMO! I don't think my regular Naval Flight Officer could have done much better."

'Thanks for the compliment. I really appreciate it," he replied. But the SMO knew full well that a trained NFO would have been much more capable, in not only keeping track of the other bandit, but would have been operating the radar and weapons while backing up the pilot.

"Oh, and, SMO. No ditching your equipment and heading straight back to sick bay this time. We are about to start the debrief from hell, and you're not bailing out of this one," Tioga added.

30 PRICE OF ANOTHER STEAK DINNER
South China Sea

Lieutenant Commander Yao reached up to wipe the sweat from his brow. He was drenched in sweat from the intense physical exertion of the past few minutes. He looked over to his right to check on his wingman, Lieutenant Junior Grade Hu, a kilometer away in a modified combat spread formation. Clearly trailing Hu was an American F-35 a hundred meters behind him. Just like the one he could see in his rearview mirror. They had been dogging them the past ten minutes. Ever since they had forced them to disengage from the dogfight.

Yao was agitated and upset as he began to replay the dogfight in his mind against the Super Hornet, and it was a Super Hornet, he thought, recalling its configuration. He had detected the aircraft on his radar as he was headed to the *Vinson*. As soon as he was close enough to see that it was a lone fighter, his plans of doing a flyby of the American carrier were dumped. It was his chance of a lifetime to prove himself, but it had not gone as he had expected. He was just getting a firing solution when the American had reacted faster than he had anticipated. The Hornet had turned into him immediately, throwing off his initial lock. Yao could have relocked the Hornet, but they were closing rapidly at that point, and he had hesitated on what to do next. He had delayed in acting too long, he angrily critiqued himself. The Hornet pilot was good and had neutralized Yao's every move. Even being in a position to shoot at him more than once. He was not just good; he was exceptionally good. The Hornet pilot had gone against the two of them and held his own. Still, Yao had the advantage and probably would have gained a solid firing solution that could have taken the Hornet out. Except that those damned F-35s showed up. He shuddered again at the memory of them surprising him like they did. One second he was focused on turning to get back on the Hornet and the next he had an F-35 on either wingtip in the turn with him. He could not bear to admit it, but he had been afraid. Not just afraid, it had been momentary panic. The memory of his weakness and how the Americans made him feel was humiliating, he recalled with self-loathing.

After he was forced to level off, one F-35 had moved slightly ahead of him and open his weapons bay to show his missiles. More chillingly, the other one had dropped back behind him with his weapons bay open and within gun range. All he could do was head for home at that point. Heading home with an unwanted escort, that was.

Five minutes later, the Chinese mainland was rapidly approaching as he checked his moving map, where he saw they were a kilometer from internationally recognized Chinese borders. He turned to see if the Americans would be foolish enough to violate their airspace. Yao was impressed to see that they waited until the very last second to turn away and head back out to sea.

His thoughts of bragging about his superior dogfighting skills were choking in his throat as he recalled what had really happened. He was still going to brag, but he would always know that Hu knew the truth. The two of them had been unable to successfully take on a single Hornet. At least, he had the satisfaction of causing the Hornet pilot to jettison all his drop tanks. He secretly hoped he would be forced to pay for them. Then he was pissed again at the thought that the rich American pilot could probably easily afford to. "The Damn Rich Arrogant Americans," he yelled into his oxygen mask to no one. Yao was in reality, more angry with himself. His own opinion of his flying skills and self-importance was revealed to be flawed. "This will never happen again!" He again yelled as he pounded his fist against the canopy repeatedly.

After a couple of minutes to calm down, he began to consider how he was going to report this event. He certainly had every right to maneuver close to a foreign military aircraft. He now realized that he was too aggressive, having overstepped his authority when he locked up the Hornet with the tracking mode of his weapon's radar. It must not be seen as a provocation by the Chinese. That could have extremely negative implications for him and his career. He doubted that even his powerful uncle Jiang could rescue him if this turned ugly. It must be spun properly to his advantage. He could get in trouble if this came out the wrong way he thought, as he went into self-preservation mode. He needed to cover his ass by making sure that both he and Hu had their story straight.

Yao rocked his wings signaling his wingman to move into a closer wingtip formation. As Hu closed the distance between them, Yao checked his communications card searching for a radio frequency that was not being used by air traffic control or a tower within three hundred kilometers. After Hu was on his wingtip, Yao used hand signals to indicate to Hu the frequency to switch to. He needed a clear channel so he could talk freely with his wingman. Yao listened to the radio for a full minute to ensure that there was no one on that frequency before he called, "Forge 24, are you up?"

"Forge 24, standing by," Hu replied.

"We must have a consistent story about how the American fighter came at us first," Yao began. "Remember: we were innocently flying to see the carrier, and we responded to his actions."

"Copy. I understand. He turned on you," Hu said. "As I recall, I was focused on the carrier when I heard you call he was turning to engage."

Yao could not believe his luck. Hu was actually going to play along. If they could keep the blame on the Americans, he could avoid the possibility of having provoked a potential international incident.

Then Yao said, "He apparently had been directed to intercept any aircraft approaching the carrier."

"I'm sure he was," Hu agreed. "Other than that, do we tell how the engagement went after that?"

Yao thought for a moment and then asked, "And how did you see it?"

"Well, the American was very good," Hu began. "After you engaged him, I mean, after he engaged you, it was a pretty neutral fight. He got his nose on you a couple of times and just as I was rolling in, he successfully switched from you to me. I never had a clear shot on him. It looked like you got your nose on him once after you first rolled on him. You probably would have soon had a clear shot at him if the F-35s hadn't intercepted you."

"Yes, his skills were impressive, but remember to leave out that part about me rolling in on him first," Yao clarified. "The big picture is that we were attacked. I neutralized his initial advantage and soon had a firing solution on him. We had him where we wanted until we had to disengage due to fuel considerations. And let us say the F-35s showed up and followed us after we were already heading home."

"Copy," Hu said. "And I think you now owe me another steak dinner for this one."

Yao looked over to his wingman only ten meters away and nodded in the affirmative. "Switch to channel five," Yao said getting them up on the approach control frequency.

At a small town airport 325 kilometers inland, two air traffic controllers in the tower were staring at each other slack-jawed.

"Did you hear that?" the senior controller said to his junior.

The junior controller nodded yes and said, "I sure did. And we have it recorded."

"Good, this must be reported to our superiors," the senior controller said.

31 GO TIME

Scarborough Shoal, South China Sea

"Okay, RED HORSE, now that we are all here, it's time to get our game face on," Colonel Perry began. "You all have been briefed on the objective for the next forty-eight hours. All our gear has been loaded onto the MV-22s, all except what you brought with you today. The Osprey crew Chiefs will take us to our aircraft to load our gear and give us all a flight safety brief

Thirty-five minutes later, Staff Sergeant Anglin was headed down the flight line with his duffel bag slung over his shoulder looking for tail number 5845. He was quite impressed with the Ospreys as he got closer to them. Back at his home base of Hurlburt Field, he saw the Air Force CV-22 version flying overhead almost daily, but he had never actually been up close to one before. He found himself fascinated with the huge vertical engine nacelles with their massive three-bladed props at the end of each wing. After locating his plane, the crew chief gathered them around for the safety brief. The brief was similar to many he had heard before, so Anglin was only half listening. But he perked up when the crew chief mentioned that, though unlikely, the Osprey could flip upside down during a water landing. Something that he hadn't heard of or considered before. They were told to stay strapped in until the plane stopped moving and rolling until it stabilized, even if it was filling with water. Then he was to hang on to a reference point, with either his left or right hand as he unbuckled, so that he would know which direction to go from there to the nearest exit. After hearing that, he made sure he was in the rear seat right next to the open ramp. He was determined to know exactly where his exit was. The big open hole just six feet away!

Soon they were all strapped in and ready to go when Anglin heard the engines start their whine to life. As the engine began to crank, it belched a huge white cloud of smoke that engulfed the rear half of the aircraft. Anglin began to unbuckle his seat belt for an emergency exit as they had been instructed, thinking the engine was on fire. Luckily, the gunner was standing near the rear ramp and reassured him that it was actually normal.

Halfway into their hour-long flight out to the shoal, they were flying at two thousand feet over the beautiful blue waters of the South China Sea. Anglin had a splendid view out the open ramp while sitting in the right rear seat of the Marine CV-22 Osprey. From his vantage point, he could see three other Ospreys trailing behind them. He was one of fifteen aboard this Osprey that could carry up to twenty four. The rest of the space was taken up by their gear and weapons strapped to the deck.

Though he had a beautiful view, his thoughts kept drifting back to his wife, Kara. Most of the day he had been angry and wanting to get even somehow. But now? Now he was just sad, disappointed, and honestly relieved. The more he thought about it, the more he wanted it to just be over. He had halfway expected them to break up any of a half-dozen times over the last eighteen months. He had even found himself wishing for it the year before. But he wasn't one to walk away from his commitment to himself or her. His agreeing to try for a baby had been his last ditch hope to bring them together. But now, as he reflected on the situation, he felt more than a little relieved she wasn't pregnant. He recalled that her period had ended just a few days before he had deployed, and they hadn't had sex after that. So this marriage was about to end, and he was thankful there wouldn't be any kids dragged into the mess. Well, at least not his.

He was brought back from his thoughts when the Osprey started a steep sweeping turn over the tropical island of Scarborough Shoal with a huge jade green central lagoon. Well, I guess that's home for the next few months he reflected. The Osprey continued its turn and descended. Anglin could feel the deceleration as the MV-22's props transitioned from facing forward, like a regular airplane, to vertical like a helicopter. As they maneuvered to land, Anglin could see four Filipino LST cargo ships driven up near the surf line and unloading the heavy-construction equipment. Five minutes later they landed in a sandstorm created by the two hundred mph winds from the props that lasted until the engines slowed to idle. They then all stepped out onto a soft sandy beach.

After the Osprey's departed three things hit him: the stifling heat, the humidity, and just how quiet it was with only the faint rumble of diesel engines off in the distance and the lapping of the waves on the shore. They had been deposited on the wider outer beach. They would have to transport their gear across the island to be next to the lagoon where they were to set up camp.

As they faced inland, Anglin saw only a tangle of green. Most of it was between knee to shoulder height, with frequent palm trees jutting up above it all. Up on a near rise, they could see the huge white rectangle shape of the housing barge as it was slowly being maneuvered into is mooring position along the lagoon's near shore. It was where everyone would live. Everyone but them.

They hacked their way across from the outer beach to the inner lagoon beach. Though it was only a distance of four hundred yards, it took them over an hour. After establishing a workable trail, they brought their gear to an area near the barge.

"Finally!" said Senior Airman Stringer as he heard diesel engines rumbling closer.

"You got that right," agreed Anglin as they both looked down the beach. Both were covered in sweat and had long ago removed their outer uniform shirts. Though it had been just over two hours since landing, their T-shirts were soaked, and their red caps were already showing white rings of salt from all the sweat.

They were both excited to see a Seabee bulldozer headed their way along with everyone else. Thirty minutes later, there was a wide clear path from one side of the island to the other. They began loading up their gear onto a heavy duty truck. They finished getting it all unloaded at their bivouac location as the sun began to touch the water on the horizon to the west.

They had just unloaded the last truckload when Chief Master Sergeant McKinney, the oldest member of the unit at age fifty-four, drove up in a Humvee to check on their bivouac area. Technical Sergeant Larto was not far behind, as he came rumbling up on one of the RED HORSE bulldozers, followed by Staff Sergeant McCartney on a road grader.

"Anglin," called McKinney.

"Yes, sir," he answered, striding over.

"Anglin, you and Stringer head back down the beach and get us a couple of light carts. It will be getting dark soon, and we have a lot to get done tonight. Take my Hummer," McKinney directed to Anglin.

"We're on it, Chief," Anglin replied.

They both headed to the Humvee, but Stringer was surprised to hear Anglin call out, "Shotgun," as he handed him the keys. Anglin loved driving the Hummers and never passed up a chance. But so did Stringer. The last time Anglin drove one was two months ago back in the back pine forests of Eglin Air Force Base. He had enjoyed testing its off road capability and seeing just how large of a pine tree he could knock over with one. Traveling ten to fifteen mph, he found that about three inches was the limit without leaving a mark on the vehicle. At least in the sandy soil of Florida.

Anglin sat quietly looking out at the ocean as they headed across the island and down the beach to the growing accumulation of heavy equipment and supplies.

Stringer spotted two light carts and backed the Humvee up to the nearest. Together they pulled the first up to the Humvee's rear hitch, and then hooked the second one up to the rear of the first.

As they started back, Stringer looked at Anglin and finally asked, "What's up? Why are you so quiet? You've hardly said a word all afternoon. And why the blank stare?"

"It's nothing. I'm just tired," Anglin replied.

"I don't think so," Stringer added, shaking his head. "I've seen you tired plenty of times, and you always had a cheerful attitude.

"Seriously, I haven't been sleeping well. I think I'm jetlagged or something," Anglin deflected.

"Don't give me that crap, Ron. Something's eating at you. And come to think of it, you have been keeping to yourself the last few days," Stringer added. "Come on. I'm your friend. Maybe I can help."

Anglin just sat there staring ahead and letting the long silence build. "You wouldn't understand," Anglin finally said.

"Maybe, but for sure, I can't if you don't talk," Stringer said.

After another long silence, Anglin finally said, "It's Kara."

"Is she sick?" Stringer asked hurriedly. "Is she pregnant?" Stringer saw Anglin wince at the last question and realized he had hit a nerve. He knew that Kara had wanted to get pregnant for years. Not knowing where this was headed, he wisely just said nothing to give his friend Ron a moment to sort out his response.

"No, that's not it, thank God," Anglin began as the story came tumbling out. "I just found out that she is screwing around. It probably started the day after we left." He told him about the fight they had the day they left and what his friend from basic training, Staff Sergeant Esler had seen and later confirmed. About how he had confronted her and her denials.

Stringer listened quietly not interrupting, as his friend told the story. He even slowed to a crawl along the beach as they returned, to give him time to vent.

"It probably wasn't the first time either. I have suspected that it happened on my other deployments as well," Anglin added.

"Really, how so?" Stringer asked finally breaking his silence.

"I had no proof. It was just a feeling," Anglin admitted. "Our fighting was almost constant after our first year of marriage. It was her history," Anglin explained. "I don't think I have ever told you this, but Kara was married once before. It had lasted less than a year. She was open and honest about her past while we were dating. I probably should have listened to that little voice inside, now that I think back. But she was the most beautiful woman I have ever seen, and I was head over heels for her. Anyway," he continued, "she told me about this serious boyfriend she had in high school. After graduation he went off to another state for college. He came home to see her as often as he could, usually once or twice a month. And they were talking about marriage before he had gone away. Though outwardly bold and in control, Kara is very insecure and lonely. She needs constant feedback and reassurance that she is loved. And I do mean constant. Her loneliness drove her to dating others while her almost fiancé was away. Soon she was dating two at the same time, neither knowing about the other. She kept up dating both, and decided to go with the new boyfriend, probably because he was around all the time I suspect. They soon got married, but it quickly became constant fighting she said. Much as our marriage has been. But then I had believed her when she said it had always been instigated by her ex. He eventually asked for a divorce. Before they had decided to split up, she admitted that she saw the marriage as failing, and was soon secretly dating someone else. They had a steady relationship going until after the divorce was final. She had a female roommate by then, to keep expenses down, but she spent several nights and weekends at her new boyfriend's home. That is how it was going when I came into the picture. I soon asked her out and after a few weeks she agreed to take a weekend trip with me to a bed and breakfast. We had an amazing time. She was soon sleeping over with me a few times a week. But on several weekends, when I asked her to do something special, she said that she was busy or had to work or something. It wasn't until after we were married that she inadvertently let it slip about the other guy. She had still been having sex and spending just as much time as before with him. Neither of us knew about the other. She didn't stop seeing him until after I proposed to her. So, the bottom line is, and what I consciously ignored, was that since high school, she has consistently never ended a relationship until the new one was well established. She has always ended up sleeping with two guys at the same time, and then going with the one she deemed the most promising. Before me, she had one and often two lovers at a time. Her beauty and sex are her primary assets, the things she knows she always has to attract companionship, so she has never had to be alone for long. Now I appear to be on the other end of the Kara cycle. She is trying to lock in the next guy before officially dumping me. That is why I suspect that this current guy isn't the first. I suspect she has, "interviewed," several during my last two deployments. She has always been emotionally distant while I was away. She didn't want to talk or email much. If there were any, I suppose that none of them met her standards and were dropped when I got back."

"Man, I'm so sorry. But you are wrong. I do understand. My parents fought constantly when I was a kid before they finally split up. So I have seen it from the kid's view," Stringer said. "I think that is why Carla and I are so close. We are both determined to make our marriage work because we have seen how bad it can be."

Anglin just nodded then said, "And you know, the worst part is that it was a medical student." Anglin continued. "Since I was little, I've always respected doctors more than anything. It was magical how they could look at you when you are sick and tell you what was wrong, then give you something to make you better. During my EMT training, I worked closely with a couple of medical students in the hospital emergency rooms. I looked up to them like real doctors too, even though they were still in training. Now I see them all for what they are. A bunch of entitled, privileged, rich ass holes. They think that they can do what they want, with anyone they want, just because they are *doctors*. Well, to hell with them all. Honestly, Harold, the way I feel now, I wouldn't piss on one if he was on fire."

"I understand, Ron. You hang in there and don't do anything stupid. You can come to me anytime, okay." Stringer said as they pulled up to the bivouac area. "Now let's get these carts set up."

Anglin slipped back into his quiet mode as they unhooked the light carts and went back to setting up their camp.

By sunrise, they had made considerable progress. A two-acre area had been cleared and twelve Alaska shelters were erected for sleeping and office use. A large generator was up and running to provide each of the shelters power and air conditioning. To the north an area had been cleared to park the RED HORSE vehicles with two huge fuel bladders nearby capable of holding thousands of gallons. Two fuel trucks had been transporting loads of fuel from the LSTs and had the bladder two-thirds full by morning. A similar bladder dedicated for fresh water was erected on the south side of the compound, but no water had been available to fill it.

At 0720, an exhausted Anglin stumbled into his assigned air-conditioned shelter. He set up his cot and ate a MRE while letting the cool, refreshing air wash over him. Unfortunately, none of them were able to take a shower. Luckily, he had packed several tubs of moist wipes, allowing him to freshen up a bit before collapsing onto his sleeping bag. His last thoughts were looking back and wondering what he could have done differently to make his life with Kara better, and how could he win her back. Or should he even try.

32 POINT OF KNOW RETURN
USS *Vinson*, South China Sea

"This is a drill. This is a drill," came the announcement over the ship-wide 1MC. *Ding, ding, ding, ding, ding, ding.* "Man overboard! Man overboard! Man overboard port side. Man the starboard lifeboat. This is a non-mustering drill only. Boat recovery only. This is a drill. This is a drill." *Ding, ding, ding, ding, ding, ding.*

So began Commander Derek Lloyd's busy day. The announcement confirmed to the SMO that it was indeed Thursday. Since deploying, they had a weekly man overboard drill to practice rescuing the floating manikin called Oscar. At least I don't have to worry about getting the muster list in on time, he thought. The last weekly mustering man overboard drill hadn't gone so well. One of his night shift corpsmen had slept through the announcement. After the muster check, it was assumed that she had been taken as a hostage as often happens. This is to ensure the departments are turning in honest reports and that everyone was actually accounted for. After the runner sent to double check her rack had reported it empty, her name had been sent in as missing. Then he had gotten the call on his brick to report to the quarter deck. There he was met by a worried and agitated XO who said that they didn't have his Sailor held hostage, and that he had better find her. "NOW SMO!" The XO had barked for all to hear.

She was found dreaming away in her rack. It turned out that she didn't hear the alarm, but the noise did wake her. She had apparently gotten up to use the head at the time her rack was checked. Then he and the sleepy Sailor, along with her ID card, had to report to the irritated XO quarter deck to prove that she had been found. They then both received an ear full of the XO's invective. At least this time he wouldn't have to confront an angry XO. Well, not for that anyway. The XO usually found something to yell about.

He responded directly to the starboard Rigid Hull Inflatable Boat (RHIB) davit after swinging by his office to grab his hard hat and float coat. The RHIB boat crews and the Sailors to launch them report immediately to the boats as well as a corpsman with a medical bag. They lower the boat into the water as soon as the ship has slowed down enough. Since he had reported aboard the ship the SMO had required that a robust medical scenario be a part of the overboard drills. He had Lieutenant Commander Stooksbury, his ICU nurse, and leader of the medical training team, to come up with a series of injuries and illnesses for Oscar, the floating manikin, to have when he fell overboard. In addition to the medical response corpsmen standing ready at the boat davit, there were Stooksbury and Hospitalman First Class Nebo in their white medical training team ball caps to observe, grade, and instruct. As usual, the SMO was there on hand along with the XO and Safety Officer observing the evolution. The first lieutenant, the head of the deck department, was in charge of the event and was calling out orders as the RHIB was slowly lowered to the water with each of the five boat crewmembers holding onto the knotted safety monkey lines as it descended.

Once the boat was launched it raced out bouncing over the swells to the smoke signal about five hundred yards away that had been thrown to mark Oscar's general location. As the RHIB was heading back, the CO called over the radio that the simulated patient had a broken leg and hip. Once the RHIB had been winched back aboard, Oscar was carefully unloaded onto the deck, and the medical team took over. The wet Oscar was swapped out for a medical training manikin that was loaded onto the stretcher. Stooksbury supervised and taught the corpsmen what to do and consider. The patient was packaged up, then was carried down a ladder, out into the hangar bay, and over to the upper-stage-two weapons elevator for transport down to the second deck. Upon arrival to the medical treatment room, the surgeon took over and continued to conduct more detailed trauma training.

The SMO was glad for the man overboard drill, even though he had to face some quizzical glares from the XO who was also there observing. After the crazy events of the past few days, he was pleased to be settling back into this regular routine. As he headed to his office, he smiled as his thoughts returned to the wonderful time he'd had with Jenna.

Back in his office, he took a few moments to quietly review some of his SWMDO training materials. A scheduled Replenishment at Sea, was scheduled to start in less than two hours. Since he didn't have any patients scheduled, he wanted to take the opportunity to observe and learn all he could as the *Vinson* maneuvered alongside the USNS *Timothy Murphy*.

Up on the bridge two hours later, the SMO watched the *Vinson* maneuver alongside the *Murphy*. The CO was sitting in his starboard bridge wing chair monitoring the relative position of the two ships. It provided an excellent view of the *Murphy* just seventy feet away as cables and fuel lines were connected being between the two ships. Once the transfer was well underway, the SMO headed down to observe the activity in the hanger bays.

On hanger bay three, there was movement everywhere. Most of the aircraft were parked back out of the way. The deck was covered with pallets and Sailors unpacking them. He had to be particularly careful that he didn't get run over by one of the many forklifts moving back and forth.

This Replenishment at Sea was typical and was taking on fuel, food, aircraft parts, various other supplies, and most importantly, mail. This was turning out to be a great learning opportunity for him to observe the ship handling and signaling. All, important knowledge he would need to pass his oral board exam to earn his Surface Warfare badge. In addition to the lines and hoses pumping fuel, there were two sets of cables connecting the *Vinson* to the USNS *Murphy* with one each in hanger bays two and three. Sling loads of pallets came across two at a time on electrically powered pulleys. Sailors with dollies were lined up to get the pallets and move them to the center of the bays. In the deck of each bay, panels had been opened for access to small transport elevators where the refrigerated food was loaded and sent directly down to the storage coolers and freezers. In hanger bay three, the SMO had to be careful with a dozen forklifts zipping by all over the place working from both port and starboard elevators.

Near one of the food elevators, he spotted Hospitalman Second Class Vesel one of his public health corpsmen. He was there inspecting the food. He paid particular attention to the fresh vegetables, frozen food, and precooked meals before they were taken down for storage in the coolers and freezers.

"How's it looking today?" the SMO asked Vesel.

"No real problems so far, sir. I did have to reject one case of lettuce. But the rest were fine," he answered. "We're almost finished up with the frozen foods. I have some samples to take back to the medical ward for testing. We work closely with the supply chief to make sure we don't have any spoiled food. We have each other's back."

As he was talking, a Sailor walked up with a box in his hand for Vesel.

"The Chief told me to bring you this," he said before setting it down at Vesel's feet.

"Thanks," he said to the departing Sailor.

"What's that?" the SMO asked, looking down at the brown box.

"Samples, sir,' he replied matter-of-factly.

"Samples?" the SMO repeated.

"Yes, sir, we have to have samples to test the adequacy of the refrigeration while enroute," Vesel answered.

"But that's a case of ice cream sandwiches," the SMO noted.

"Yes, sir, it's the best thing to test to ensure the *Murphy*'s freezers didn't allow anything to thaw out. It's my story, and I'm sticking to it. Sometimes they give us three-gallon 'samples' of hard-packed ice cream," he explained. "And, from time to time, we overlook the extra cases of steaks and lobster headed to the Chiefs' mess that aren't on the supply manifest. The Chiefs always eat better than the officers at sea as I'm sure you are aware."

"I'm about to take them down to medical now to conduct the inspection. I always have lots of volunteers to help in these inspections. You are welcome to join us," Vesel said.

The SMO just shook his head and grinned. "No, you go ahead. Maybe next time. But let me know if you discover any problems."

"Aye-aye, sir," Vesel said as he picked up his gear and the ice cream and headed to the nearest hatch leading down to the second deck.

The SMO watched as the transfers concluded and he observed how the lines and cables were disconnected. He was there until the break-away music started playing to signal that the Replenishment-at-Sea evolution was complete. Captain Whitehall always played the same song over the 1MC after these events. The SMO headed back to his office listening to "Point of Know Return" by Kansas.

Over the next two hours, the SMO started working on his Christmas letters in earnest. He had offered to write a Christmas letter to be sent to whomever they wished, spouse, parents, or grandparents. Twenty-three had taken him up on the offer so far. Luckily, most of the letter was the same. But he took his time to personalize the second paragraph that described the Sailor's day-to-day job. He was reviewing the one he had just finished for one of his officers.

Mr. & Mrs. Robert Stooksbury
3354 Longwood Way
Mount Karla, MO, 63469

Dear Mr. & Mrs. Stooksbury,

I am Commander Derek Lloyd, the Senior Medical Officer of the Medical Department on the USS Carl Vinson (CVN 70). In this capacity, I have the privilege of working directly with your daughter, Critical Care Nurse, Lieutenant Commander Renee K. Stooksbury. Please allow me to express my personal appreciation for your daughter's impact on the U.S. Navy.

Renee serves as our Intensive Care Unit Nurse providing these important medical services in support of nine primary care providers caring for 5,100 Sailors throughout the ship. But more importantly, she has become one of my most trusted officers supporting the ship's global mission. She is responsible for a 3.8 million dollar supply and material program plus over $500,000 in consumable supplies, all pharmaceuticals valued at over $45,000, as well as a maintenance and repair program on medical and dental equipment worth over $2.5 million, and she oversees 13 officers and 43 corpsmen. Here are just a few of her accomplishments since I arrived in July of this year: she led our department to a Medical Readiness score of >98%; and overall Chief of Naval Air Forces grade of C-1, and we were rated # 1 of 5 aircraft carrier dept's inspected this year. She aggressively acquired a surplus refrigerator dramatically increasing the lab's capability and saving the command $15,000; she planned and implemented the 3rd fleet & BUMED flu vaccine campaign; immunizing 3,550 Sailors in 2 days. Renee has proven to be a very innovative planner and motivator by renovating our triage program and patient processing plans which were tested & perfected during 3 mass casualty drills. Renee has and continues to be ready to respond at a moment's notice to support any event, from a medical emergency called away anywhere aboard the ship, to an aircraft crash, fire, or attack with mass casualties... and more importantly assuring that these functions can operate underway at sea in a war setting.

Lieutenant Commander Stooksbury does all this on one of the busiest front-line aircraft carriers in the Navy. The Air Wing's aircraft have flown over 1,200 sorties totaling more than 11,323 flight hours in support of the Global War on Terrorism. She performs her duties superbly with an air of professionalism and respect for everyone she works with. As a Naval Officer, she has impressed me with her compassion for our patients and crew, and she goes above and beyond by putting in long hours of dedicated work to make sure that this department not only succeeds but excels to stand out as one of the best in the Navy! Bottom-line, Renee has a direct and important impact in the overall mission accomplishment, and she provides an example for us all.

Mr. & Mrs. Stooksbury, this letter could spread several pages explaining Renee's many contributions. Suffice it to say, your daughter is a special woman. She makes our Navy better, our American flag fly prouder, and the world freer. Thank you for raising such a terrific daughter and Sailor. And though we will be deployed, may you have a wonderful Holiday season.

Sincerely,

DEREK P. LLOYD, CDR, USN, MC, FS
Senior Medical Officer, USS Carl Vinson

The SMO had just finished signing the letter when his phone rang.

"Derek, this is Jenna. You busy?"

"Just doing some paperwork. Why?" he asked.

"The Admiral wanted me to invite you up for his weekly cigar social up on the smoking brow just outside the Admiral's bridge at 1600," she explained.

"Sure, but I'll have to leave in time for the XO's meeting at 1700," he said.

After swinging by his stateroom to get a cigar from his personal stash, he climbed up to the Admiral's bridge on the O-8 level. He rarely smoked, but he liked to puff on one for special occasions. And this clearly was one. He selected a Montecristo, one of his favorites. When he opened the hatch out onto the outdoor brow, he was surprised to be greeted by the sound of a guitar. It turned out that Yeoman Third Class Keen on the Admiral's staff was a budding musician. He was playing great tunes with a pipe clamped firmly in his teeth and smiling.

The Admiral, who, as it turned out, was an avid cigar smoker, was already there chatting with his Admin Officer, Captain Colfax.

The Admiral spotted him and waved him over. "Welcome, SMO. Glad you could join us. It is a fine day to catch a sunset at sea."

"Thank you, sir. Thanks for inviting me," the SMO answered.

Captain Colfax was clearly taken aback when the SMO pulled out his cigar and lit it.

"Damn, SMO, I thought you would be up here hiding in the corner from the smoke. Aren't you supposed to be preaching for us to stop all forms of smoking?" Colfax asked.

"I'm the first to admit that smoking regularly is bad for you. In addition to heart disease and cancer, it has a huge negative impact on any smoker's overall health," the SMO explained. "But almost anything, if done in moderation, will not have a huge negative impact. A fine cigar is a special treat I allow myself from time to time."

"Good to know," Colfax said as he took a big puff of his cigar.

The SMO was relaxing and enjoying the fantastic view of the ocean as the sun slowly sank toward the distant horizon. He was watching the flying fish leap out of the water as the ship passed by when Jenna stepped up beside him.

"Hello, Sailor. You come here often?" she asked.

"Hey Jenna, ahhh, I mean Captain," he quickly corrected himself.

She let out a soft giggle. "Either is fine out here, Derek. We are sort of off duty now," she responded.

"Whew," he said.

"It is a relaxing view. I don't get up here often enough to enjoy the sunshine and fresh air," she complained. "I'm buried in email all day. Then there is the exercise planning and ensuring everything is coordinated for when we continue on over to the Arabian Sea. Iran has been threatening action against our ships for years. And we must take those threats serious. One day, some rogue Revolutionary Guard idiot may decide to take a shot at us. So, what's going on with you?" she asked.

He was thinking about their growing relationship and his feelings for her when he realized that this wasn't the place or time where they could have a personal conversation.

"You mean besides meeting up with a beautiful lady, being in a knife fight, and then a dogfight? Not a thing," he said with a chuckle. "Today was just another day at sea." They enjoyed small talk until he had to leave for his afternoon meeting.

As he said his goodbyes she said, "Derek, if you have the time, stop by my office later this evening so we can talk. We've had an interesting couple of days. Wouldn't you agree?"

"Sure, Jenna," he replied stealing a look into her smiling eyes.

"I'd love to," he whispered back, thrilled at any excuse to stop by and see her.

Unfortunately, it never happened. They were both too involved with other issues that kept them busy until taps.

33 HERO BUSTED
PLAN Air Base, China

Lieutenant Commander Yao was basking in the adoration of his fellow officers. Things could not have gone better for him. He and his wingman Lieutenant Junior Grade Hu were the only ones in modern times to have gone head-to-head with a foreign fighter aircraft. There had been none since the Korean War. In the debrief the day before, Yao had decidedly downplayed any role Hu had played and left out the fact that he had been unable to get a good firing solution after the Hornet had responded. Everywhere he went in the squadron, groups of his fellow wanted him to retell the story over and over again. After the fourth time, it was decided by his commanding officer that he would give a formal brief to the whole Air Wing the next day on his firsthand details of the capability of the Super Hornet.

This left him in somewhat of a quandary. In his version of events, he had dominated the fight throughout and the American could only helplessly respond to his moves. He could not tell that everything he had done had been successfully countered. Yet, he needed to give his fellow pilots some useful information on the F-18F's capabilities in case they ever had to fight one.

The answer to his problem came earlier this morning when discussing the fight with his executive officer. That was when he learned that the carrier often would have a single tanker aircraft airborne for contingencies. That explained the plane being alone and the five drop tanks he had seen jettisoned. He could sell his version of events by inferring that the pilot flying a tanker mission was clearly much less capable and had been relegated to such menial flights. He decided to tell accurately the maneuvering capability of the aircraft, but just that the pilot was not up to the task of capitalizing on the Hornet's capabilities. He knew that this was a two-edged sword. He would get out the actual potential threat the F-18F was while at the same time they would see that he had controlled the fight against a mediocre pilot. Many would see this, but he still had been in a fight they could only dream about. Only his wingman Hu knew the truth, and he was firmly in Yao's back pocket, and he intended for him to stay that way.

His anger and frustration from the day before had been eclipsed by his new hero status. He was not surprised in the least when he was summoned again to his commanding officer's office.

He was asked by the commanding officer's secretary to take a seat. She assured him that it would only be for a moment. He was there less than a minute when Lieutenant Suyong, the squadron's Intelligence Officer, exited the office. He had a serious demeanor as he passed by Yao without any form of greeting. Yao thought that he detected the slightest hint of a smile cross Suyong's face as his eyes noticed him sitting there.

"You may go in now," the secretary said.

He entered the room where he saw the commanding officer, executive officer, and a Commander he did not recognize seated at a small conference table.

Yao felt some foreboding as he entered. But this was quickly allayed by the warm welcome given him by Commander Chen, his commanding officer, who was seated at the head of the table.

"Come in. Come in," Commander Chen said in a pleasantly welcoming tone of voice. "Please have a seat. I do not know if you have met Commander Xu. He is our Air Wing's senior Intelligence Officer.

"Pleased to make your acquaintance," Yao said as he greeted Commander Xu before sitting down across from him and his executive officer.

"Lieutenant Hu will be joining us in a moment," Commander Chen continued. "Commander Xu is of course interested in your adventure from yesterday. Needless to say, it has gained attention at the highest levels. You are becoming quite the celebrity."

Yao just bowed his head slightly, but inwardly feeling puffed up and proud of his status.

"Indeed, it has," said Commander Xu. "The United States has lodged a formal complaint with our Ministry of Foreign Affairs. They assert that you engaged them for no valid reason in international airspace, which is contrary to your report. But that is typical. They frequently complain when we intercept their spy planes, claiming we were acting in an unsafe manor. As you can attest yourself, our pilots are professional and highly skilled. Their every move was safe and controlled."

Yao sat quietly and nodded. He had expected that the Americans would be complaining as they usually did in other air-to-air encounters, so he was not too concerned.

"In fact, the encounter was reported on CNN International this morning. There was a brief account of it," Xu continued.

There was a knock at the door, and Hu was escorted to the table by the secretary where he sat down quietly as the conversation continued.

"Commander Xu, this is Lieutenant Hu, Yao's wingman from yesterday," said Commander Chen, interrupting momentarily to make introductions. "Lieutenant Hu, this is Commander Xu from wing intel."

They both nodded slightly to the other, and Xu continued. "But since they had no video or pictures, it only lasted three news cycles and was dropped.

Yao was pleased to hear that it did not appear that this was going to escalate into a larger event. It was definitely something he wanted to avoid at all costs.

Xu could see Yao visibly relax at the news. Hu on the other hand sat there stiffly, with a drop of sweat rolling down his right temple. He appeared to be extremely nervous, Xu noted.

"We have your two debrief statements of the events of yesterday," Xu said. "It was a lot to recount. Since you have had a good night's sleep, do you recall anything else to add that you may have missed yesterday?"

Xu noted how Hu's eyes quickly glanced fearfully over to Yao and back.

Yao felt a momentary surge of trepidation but was outwardly as calm as a stone. Was he not the hero fighter pilot of the entire PLAN? Was he not on the fast track up the chain of command now with his connections? Yes, he was, thought Yao. Before long he would surpass everyone at this table. Then they would be answering to him.

With a newfound surge of confidence, Yao said, "No, my statement was thorough and complete."

Hu only managed to shake his head no as he noticed a hardening of the three Commander's faces. Hu was in near panic at the sight as he watched Commander Xu reach down for something in his briefcase at his side. He again glanced over to Yao for guidance.

"You are sure that the American turned to engage you? You are certain he wasn't making some innocent maneuver that you interpreted as a turn to engage?" asked Xu.

Hu hoped that Yao would jump at the plausible proffered explanation. If Yao would just take it. Such a thing could explain the entire event as an unfortunate misunderstanding. He glanced at Yao with pleading eyes. But it was no use. He could see that Yao was full of himself, as he usually was, and going to stick to his story.

"No, he clearly engaged me as I was flying past him on the way toward their carrier," Yao said definitively.

"Well, then, we have a problem," Xu said as he brought a small digital recorder onto the table. "This morning we were provided this by the Ministry of State Security." Xu noted that Yao's brow furrowed slightly and that Hu's eyes were as wide as saucers as he pressed the play button.

"Forge two four, standing by. We must have a consistent story about how the American fighter came at us first," began the recording.

Xu noted the frank terror in Hu's eyes, and Yao's slight scowl.

There was a long silence after the recording of their complete conversation finished playing. No one spoke for almost a minute until the executive officer could contain himself no longer.

"What the hell were you two thinking?" Xu yelled as Yao and Hu sat there with nothing to say. "You are both idiots."

Yao finally found his voice and said, "Sir, I spotted the lone American fighter and, well, after seeing their arrogance firsthand, I wanted to put them in their place. So I turned on him and locked him up almost without thinking. Then he turned on me, and, well, it just quickly went into a full-up dogfight from there.

"Not that, you shit for brains," jumped in Commander Chen. "With this recording, you may have given them proof of what happened, putting us at a distinct disadvantage in world opinion. Something we can't afford to have happen just now."

Yao had a surprised and puzzled look on his face but wisely said nothing.

Chen continued, "We don't care that you engaged the American. Half the PLAN air forces would have done the same given the chance. But we cannot appear to be the aggressor. Your mistake was using the radio to get your stories straight."

Yao's mouth formed into an inaudible O as he thought back.

"If we could pick it up and record it, don't you think they can as well?" chimed in the executive officer.

"And they may very well have done so," added Commander Xu. "We were tracking a US Air Force spy plane just north of Taiwan at the time. If they do have it, we are unsure why they have not released it yet. Regardless, we have to assume they have the same evidence and plan accordingly."

"Why the hell didn't you just use your cell phones?" the executive officer asked. "You could have connected by Bluetooth. The range would have been limited. Not much more than thirty yards or so from inside your aircraft. No one would have picked it up unless they were in formation with you. No, instead, you had to broadcast it to the Americans and the world. You had better pray to your ancestors that they didn't get it."

"Yao, you may have put our country at a distinct disadvantage," said Chen. "I'm not sure what to do with you. If I had my way, your flying days would be over. And if this comes out, they probably will be. But right now, you are seen as a hero, one who has gone up successfully against the feared Americans. You have proven that they are not ten feet tall after all."

Yao said nothing, his mind racing, trying to take in the sudden swing in his status. Walking into this room, he had been on top of the world, with his career flying to the top. Now he was in the doghouse with his command. Even if this blew over, it would still be out there, lurking and waiting to pop up and unexpectedly spoil his plans. His anger flared as he realized that his future was now dependent on the whims of the Americans. Do they have it? Will they release it? *Damn*, he thought.

"So I have a problem. The intelligence you two brought back on the actual performance of the F-18 against our aircraft is invaluable," Chen continued.

"If the truth were to come out, it would be very embarrassing and demoralizing for our squadron. I have no choice but to let you get away with it."

"Yes, sir, I understand," Yao finally said meekly.

"Understand that we are in no way forgiving or forgetting this incident," the executive officer said. "You had better hope the Americans never release that conversation. Lieutenant Hu, you have been a solid pilot and officer until this incident. You were forced by a senior officer to go along with this. Still, you could have told the truth. You will be assigned to another squadron next month. The official reason is to share your experience against the Americans with others. But the real purpose is to hopefully salvage your career."

"If it does come out, we will of course deny it and claim that it is American propaganda, in their parlance, 'fake news,'" said Xu. "But we can't hide the voices. If this is heard by those in your squadron, they will know the truth."

"If it does"—the Commander took over speaking directly to Yao—"your flying days are over. And your call sign, Hawk, know that from now on, every time me or the XO hear it, we will not be thinking of a proud aggressive bird of prey. No, we will be thinking of a chicken hawk instead."

34 WORK PROGRESSING

Scarborough Shoal, South China Sea

Staff Sergeant Anglin awoke at 1700 in the late afternoon. He was groggy from the fitful night's sleep he managed to have. He was feeling sticky all over and felt like he had cotton in his mouth. He wiped down again with the moist towelettes he had. He couldn't wait until he had a chance again for a real shower, but not today. He dressed and brushed his teeth outside with water from a half-liter bottle . After using the newly built latrine, he joined the gathering crowd by one of the trucks next to Colonel Perry's command tent.

As he arrived, he was tossed one of the hated breakfast MREs from Staff Sergeant Urania. "Sorry, Ron, it's the last one in the box, and I'm not allowed to open another case until our midnight meal."

Anglin looked down and saw that it was one of the breakfast MREs. Uggggh, he thought grimacing. Each case has a variety of meals to choose from and contain one or two of the breakfast type. The thing was, almost no one liked them. Even though you could now heat them up in a warming sleeve, they just never tasted right. This one had scrambled eggs, hash browns, a slab of ham, and a pack of M&Ms. Well he thought, at least I can eat the ham and chocolate. Too bad we don't have a dog around here to feed this to, if the dog was starving. He had learned long ago to be one of the first to pick through a new case of MREs to find the best ones. But he had been exhausted mentally and physically and was the last to arrive.

He found a spot in the sand looking out over the lagoon as twilight slowly faded into darkness. Out beyond the lagoon, he could see two Filipino frigates slowly circling the island.

"Can you believe how much they have done so far?" Senior Airman Stringer asked as he sat down by his friend.

"I hadn't really noticed. I just got up and grabbed breakfast," Anglin said.

"Well, I was up earlier and have been wandering around. The day crew has already cleared over a thousand feet of the runway. The structures crew has surveyed and staked out the airplane ramp and the first hangar. Technical Sergeant Nickel says that we will be starting on the footings tonight," Stringer said. "At least, you will."

"Look over there," Anglin pointed down the lagoon to his right beyond the housing barge.

Stringer looked and could see a flat barge with a large clamshell crane on it. The big crane's boom was slowly swinging to the right as they watched it dump a load of sand along the beach. It was the dredging barge already in place and working to deepen and widen the entrance into the lagoon for larger ships.

"Hey, what did you mean, at least, I will?" Anglin asked.

"Oh, just that I will be on guard duty tonight and not out there digging in the sand with you. So have fun," Stringer replied.

"Well, you better do a good job of protecting us from the crabs and sea gulls," Anglin retorted. "And if they give you any trouble, toss them these scrambled eggs. That will keep them away." He snickered.

"I'm glad to see your sense of humor returning," said Stringer. "I was getting worried about you."

"Yeah, well, not much I can do about it out here, and I have a date with a shovel, it seems," Anglin continued. "I realize that there isn't anything I can do to change Kara. I'm beginning to realize, now that I'm about over the shock and anger, that I almost feel relieved. I see that it's probably finally over between us. I've been miserable most of the time this past year. I kept hearing from many saying that they envied me sleeping with such a beautiful woman. I just smiled and let them think what they wanted. But the truth was that it almost never happened that way. Even when I came home horny and wanting to jump her bones. All too often, within minutes of stepping into the house, we were in a fight over nothing. She was a true passion killer most days. When we did get it on, I just hurried to be done as quick as I could. I rarely got into it like I wanted, and I sensed she felt the same way. Neither of us made much effort to make sure the other enjoyed it too. We both missed out. Three to five minutes max and we were done. Then we each rolled over to our side of the bed. I usually fell asleep, and she started reading a magazine or watching TV. No cuddling.

And the sad thing was, that I really did know how great it could be. With my former girlfriend Chris, we routinely went at it for forty five minutes to an hour almost every time. And frequently more than once a day for the two years we dated. Alot Harold like you and Carla seem to have it now. It was rough when Chris had ultimately decided we were just too incompatible in other ways. A year later I met Kara, and I assumed I could have with her what I had with Chris and even more. It didn't turn out that way. Well enough of this self-pity. I'll be all right eventually. Tonight I just need to stay focused on my shovel. Well, that and getting a decent MRE next time."

Off in the distance, they heard a whistle blowing.

"Well, that's our call to report for duty," Stringer said.

Over the next ten hours, Anglin and the others from the structures crew were working alongside a backhoe as it dug out a trench for the footings. The trench was five-to-six-feet deep, depending on the irregular level of the ground. Because it was sand, there were frequent cave-ins requiring a team with shovels to clear it back out. It was exhausting and backbreaking work. By morning, the perimeter trench was ready for the concrete forms to go in. These would be built by the carpenters out of plywood sheets and two-by-fours.

As they headed back toward their compound, they heard the familiar refrain,

"RED HORSE, over here."

This time it was Colonel Perry. After everyone had gathered around, he said, "You have done an excellent job overnight. We are a bit ahead of our projected schedule. You have all earned a good night's rest. But first I have good news. The dining facility on the barge is now up and running at full capacity and you are having your supper over there. They will have two chow lines going. One serving a normal breakfast and the other serving a dinner meal. But not only that. They have enough fresh water for you to each take a quick shower. However—"

Loud cheers erupted from everyone before he could finish.

"However, it will have to be a 'Navy shower.' Run just enough water to get wet, then soap down. Then just enough to rinse off. No long, hot, steaming showers like you'd take at home. No…what was it they called them, Sergeant?" Perry asked Chief Master Sergeant McKinney.

"Hollywood showers," McKinney answered.

"Right, no Hollywood showers. Short and sweet, in and out. So, everyone, grab a change of uniform and head down to the barge. Some should shower first while others eat and then swap. That way you can minimize the lines. Again, you are all doing a fantastic job. Keep it up," Perry concluded.

35 INSPECTION ORDERS
USS *Vinson*, South China Sea

At 0450 the SMO was startled awake by his stateroom phone, in the middle of a very nice dream about him and Jenna. Hell of a way to wake up, thought the SMO. The duty corpsman called to tell him of a medical emergency. This one was up forward on the O2 level, in a fighter squadron's eight man officer stateroom.

It turned out to be a pilot that had developed diarrhea and vomiting the evening before. He awoke in the night with his gut rumbling and the immediate urge to go again. His nearest head was seventy five feet away down the P-way. In his rush to the toilet, he jumped up quickly to grab his robe and shower shoes and passed flat out. The combination of his dehydration and sudden rise combined to cut the blood flow to his noggin and, lights out. Luckily, he didn't hit his head or otherwise injure himself in the fall. But that wasn't the worse of it. What control he had exerted on his anal sphincters was completely lost before he hit the floor.

This was obvious as soon as the SMO neared the open doorway. The foul smell was reeking. All but one of his roommates were standing well clear of the space. One brave sole was in there calming the confused unfortunate pilot. He was crouched down holding his mouth and nose in the crook of his elbow in a vain attempt to hold back the stench from the pool of brown liquid diarrhea the patient was lying in.

After checking that the patient was stable and starting to come around, the SMO stepped back and let his response team take over. He was as proud of them as ever. They were totally professional. They used spare sheets to give him a quick wipe down and got him on the stretcher and off to medical. The one funny part to the story occurred after the patient had been washed down and taken care of in medical. The patient's roommates called to medical and actually demanded the duty corpsman send someone up to clean their room for them. They claimed that it was infectious waste, not to mention the horrible smell.

The SMO grabbed the phone and in no uncertain terms said, "We are not a cleaning service! Find a mop and bucket and get to work. When you're finished wash your hands thoroughly. That sort of cleanup is not the medical department's problem," he reiterated stifling a laugh as he hung up the phone.

After the CO's morning meeting at 0900 the SMO was up at the bow of the flight deck to participate in the morning pre-launch FOD walk as it is known. FOD stands for 'Foreign Object Damage'. Modern jet engines act like huge vacuum cleaners as they are powered up. The smallest bit of metal or debris can cause extensive damage to an engine. So, the flight deck is searched twice a day. A line of personnel forms up shoulder to shoulder across the width of the deck, and slowly walks aft looking for any small bits of debris. They typically find dropped screws, washers, or bits of safety wire. These innocuous appearing items were just waiting to be sucked up at full power and seriously damage a jet engine. Because there had been three FODed engines in the past month costing several million dollars, the XO had pushed for HOD support to get more bodies up to participate. It was also a great chance to get some fresh air and sunshine for those usually stuck working below decks. The SMO followed just behind the main group's first wave. He still found a few things that they missed lurking in the pad-eyes used to chain down the aircraft.

As he was about to head down into the ship from a flight deck cat-walk, his brick squawked.

"SMO, this is the OOD. You have a call here on the bridge."

"On my way," he replied to the Officer of the Deck. This was unusual thought the SMO as he headed into the island. What kind of call? If it was from one of the other ship's in the battle group, they would usually call him directly using a normal phone. The communication satellite links were amazing these days. He had called to talk to his kids a couple of times and there had been no delays on the line, even though they were on opposite sides of the world.

When he reached the bridge, the OOD waved him over. "SMO, we are in contact with a Malaysian frigate twenty-five miles southeast of here. They are on their way back to home port following modification work in Japan. They say they have a medical emergency and need to speak to our doc," said the OOD handing him a phone from its cradle on the bulkhead. "We are limited to the ship to ship radio phone."

After a brief but difficult conversation with their ship's doctor who barely spoke English, he learned that they had a thirty five year old male patient with worsening chest pain. After discussing the situation with Captain Whitehall, it was agreed that the patient could be brought to the Vinson for treatment. What was interesting was that their helicopter pilot would not take off until they had the Vinson in sight. It seemed that their pilots wouldn't fly out of sight of either their ship or land. The SMO made the necessary arrangements so that the patient could be transported to medical quickly. Their helicopter landed with the patient and the Malaysian ship's physician about forty minutes later. The SMO was out on the flight deck and ready to go. He had with him his corpsmen, nurse, and purple shirt stretcher bearers standing by. The weapons department had the upper stage two weapons elevator open and ready to go directly to the second deck. He was transported down to the waiting team led by the family practice doc who had been told to expect a possible heart attack.

After an extensive evaluation, including ECG, bloodwork, and X-rays it was determined that the patient had a relatively simple, but painful case of pericarditis, an inflammation of the sack surrounding the heart. It was easily treated with the non-steroidal medicine ibuprofen. To be on the safe side, Doctor Searcy decided to keep him overnight to repeat a set of cardiac enzymes. The SMO was kept busy for a while keeping the CO, flag watch, and the Admiral's staff informed of the status of the patient. Later Admiral LaSalle accompanied by Jenna even came down to meet with the patient and the Malaysian doctor. He gave both one of his personal coins. The admiral had even written a letter for the captain of their ship. He was taking the opportunity to have some positive international relations following the events in Hong Kong. The Malaysian "doctor" thanked them profusely before he had to return to his ship.

After the admiral had left, Jenna lingered behind a few minutes to chat with the SMO in his office on the pretext of getting more info on the patient.

"Well, Derek, how are you?" she asked once the door was closed behind them. "Are you okay?" "You have definitely had an eventful couple of days."

"I am perfectly fine. Don't you start worrying about me," he replied, noticing the concern in her voice. It was heartwarming to have someone care about him this way. But he suspected that what was really on her mind was how he felt about her. They hadn't had any time alone since returning to the ship to discuss what had happened between them. Suspecting this, he cut right to the chase. "Jenna, I want you to know that the night I had with you was amazing, and the most wonderful time of my life. But it was even more than the sex, which was phenomenal. I really felt comfortable and relaxed with you in a way that I have honestly never experienced before with anyone else but you. Believe it or not, I have always been a little reserved around women. Even in my marriage, I always felt I had to keep my guard up. I don't feel emotionally at risk with you."

Jenna stood there with a widening smile as he spoke. When he had finished, she came close and gave him a long, lingering kiss. "Me too. I know what you mean. We made a real connection. I—" She was about to say more when her brick went off.

"Tullos, Speedy," he said.

"Go ahead," she answered.

"Tullos, the Admiral wants a brief at 1600 this afternoon. We need to go over some details," said Speedy Ball the Admiral's Operations Officer.

"Sorry, I've got to go," Jenna lamented.

She started to step away, but he gently reached for her hand.

"Just at sec," he said as he went for a deeper long kiss. As they finally came up for air, he said, "I just wanted to have another one of those. Now get back to work, I'll see you later," he added as she stepped out the door.

Since he had already missed lunch, the SMO grabbed his favorite cookies from a stash he kept in a filing cabinet and washed them down with a diet soda as he checked his email. Finding nothing urgent, he headed to the ward to check on the other patients there.

Standing in the now-open door was Lieutenant Commander Alverez with a huge, satisfied grin on her face.

"What?" he finally had to ask after an unbearably long silence.

She let him twist there a moment longer before answering.

Finally, she said, "I think the SMO has himself a Boat Boo!"

He just stood there with is mouth half open, not sure how to respond. His hand went subconsciously to his lips to wipe away any telltale lipstick before remembering Jenna didn't wear any on duty and clearly proving Alverez's suspicions. He couldn't honestly deny it. Still, he didn't want to openly admit it either. He was only just now realizing that Jenna was clearly more than a simple fling.

"What? How did…I mean, what tipped you off?" he finally was able to ask.

"Don't worry, SMO. Your secret is safe with me," she began reassuringly. "I have noticed over the last two months that you and she have found reasons to bump into each other. You have briefed her on far more things than you ever did the previous Chief of Staff. But I really knew when you kept wandering around here the past couple of days smiling more than ever. And you have been humming your favorite songs when you are in here working. It was obvious that something was making you happy," she said. "And I was pretty sure it wasn't getting attacked in Hong Kong."

"Okay, you got me. Please don't spread this around," he asked. "I don't want to make things complicated for her."

"I don't see how. You are both single consenting adults, and you are not under her command," she answered.

"Well, we are all under the command of the Admiral, and she is his Chief of Staff," he countered.

"The Admiral likes you, and I'm sure it won't be an issue. But either way, my lips are sealed," she replied. "And good on you, SMO. I'm happy for you."

In the afternoon, the SMO saw his routine scheduled patients. The SMO was typing his last note when the phone rang.

"SMO," he answered.

"Derek, this is Jenna," she said. "You busy?"

"Yep, but I always can find time for you," he replied. "Just saw my last patient, and I'm finishing up the note."

"Good. The Admiral has requested that you be here for our meeting at 1600. Can you make it?" she asked.

He glanced at the clock on the bulkhead and saw that the time was 1543. "Yep. I do have a meeting at 1700, but I guess I can get Alverez to cover that one for me, just in case," he decided aloud.

"Excellent! See you there," she said before he heard the phone hang up.

He stood and stretched as he realized he had just enough time to hit the head before heading up.

At 1600, everyone was in place in the Admiral's conference room, including the SMO, who was seated on the back row behind the Chief of Staff as usual.

"Okay, let's get to it," Admiral LaSalle stated. "What's the latest on Operation SEAHORSE?"

Taking his cue, the Intelligence Officer, Commander Monroe started. "Sir, the Filipinos as well as the Seabee and RED HORSE units have set up their positions. The Seabees and one of the RED HORSE units are living on a barge with barracks and a galley. It is similar to the ones we have back home for use when a ship is undergoing extensive repairs and is temporarily uninhabitable. The barge was towed into place and is anchored in position inside the shoal's lagoon. The second RED HORSE unit is living ashore in Alaska shelters. They all will be getting some meals from the barge's galley that has a Filipino staff and will be operating 24-7. They have been unloading their heavy equipment from Filipino Amphibs, including the bulldozers, motor graders, tractors, trucks, generators, and some older Humvees needed for the operation. Today they will set up more infrastructure to support long-term operations. They have begun clearing spaces for their equipment depot, to include huge bladders to store both water and fuel. The plan was that basic clearing for a runway will start soon and for the Seabees to survey and begin dredging the lagoon to convert it into a functioning deep water port."

"Any response from the Chinese yet?" asked Captain Jordan.

"Officially, no. Nothing yet." Monroe answered. "Not unless you count the hijinks when those two fighters jumped our tanker yesterday. But that was probably just an isolated incident. We believe that they are working on a careful response because technically the Filipinos are only occupying their own territory."

"Any hint on whether their response will be made militarily or diplomatically?" asked Commander Grant.

"Given their history, they have typically backed down when checked," Monroe answered. "They won't hesitate to bully their weaker neighbor's but have never seriously challenged the United States. They are not expected to do so now either. The Philippine government has the international courts on their side, they are much closer to the shoal, and US military units are now ashore. In the short term, we expect lots of back channel grumbling and some possible trade tariffs or embargos on American goods. But that hurts them as much or more than it would us."

"That brings us to the request we received this morning," started the Operations Officer, Captain Ball. "The Seabee Commander has requested that we send one of our doctors there in a week to check on their medical set up. They have an Independent Duty Corpsman there in charge, but unlike the controlled environment of a ship, they want the doc to oversee that their public health plans are adequate. And they would like their food preparation areas inspected since it is provided by a Filipino vender. He doesn't want any foodborne illness outbreaks threatening to hamper their operations. Also, while operating in the area for the next few weeks, we may be their nearest higher level of medical care if needed."

"So, SMO, you're our Battle Group Surgeon. What do you recommend?" asked Admiral LaSalle.

"Sir, I would recommend sending one of the Air Wing's flight surgeons. They have received training in public health issues, food and water inspections, and vector control. I would also recommend sending one of our public health corpsmen to back them up and assist with the inspections. The corpsmen do it every day and are probably better at some of the technical aspects of what they are asking for anyway," the SMO answered.

"What about you going?" the Admiral questioned.

"That would be overkill, sir. This can easily be handled by a junior Flight Surgeon," he answered.

"Maybe, but I still think you are a better choice," the Admiral replied.

"But, sir, with all due respect, as you said, I am the Battle Group Surgeon. I have a fairly busy schedule and responsibilities here. And the Flight Surgeon's schedules are much more flexible," the SMO countered.

"SMO, this is an important operation for our country and the Philippines. You bring a unique background that a shiny new Flight Surgeon just doesn't have. I want you to get a good feel for how things are going there and brief me when you return. I trust your judgement, and I want your perspective of things on the ground there. Our part of this operation is peripheral at best. This is my chance to get a reliable firsthand report from there. So, you're going tomorrow, not in a week. Keep your eyes open. I want you to give me a full report when you get back. And besides, you'll be back the next day. Also, you will be going in with the SEAL Team we will be ferrying over there tomorrow. A chance for you to hang out with your old buddies."

"Aye-aye, sir," the SMO answered, having lost the argument.

"SMO, that was a hell of a flight you had yesterday. I hear that you were quite helpful during that dogfight. Good job," Admiral LaSalle added.

"Thank you, sir. It was definitely not your routine tanker mission. I hope I proved to be a bit more than self-loading baggage," the SMO answered, referring to how many pilots viewed flight surgeons as dead weight. Quite a few would gladly trade a Flight Surgeon in back for extra fuel.

Now, Commander Hill, what's the latest status update on *Bunker Hill*? Have they gotten their number three turbine back online yet?" the Admiral asked his Resources Officer.

The SMO was distracted and didn't hear much more as the meeting moved on to other topics. *Well, that was unexpected*, he thought. It was clear that the Admiral had already made up his mind on this before he arrived. Why hadn't Jenna warned me ahead of time? She was probably too busy or didn't know. No matter. He started going through what he would need to pack for the overnight trip. Not much.

36 RESPONSE PLANS

PLAN Air Base, China

Lieutenant Commander Yao entered the squadron at 0700. He was tired and agitated after a fitful night trying to sleep. His paranoia was getting the better of him. He had convinced himself that at any moment the truth would get out, making him the laughingstock of the base. His future was in the hands of those who knew what had happened. Them and the damned Americans. Mostly, the Americans. He was confident that his leadership would keep things quiet. It was in their best interest as well that it remain so. The influence of his uncle was well known, and they all had ambitions for higher rank and status. This getting out would taint them all. The one wild card was the incompetent lieutenant Suyong. Did he know anything or not? Yao just didn't know. He may know nothing at all, or everything. The worry was maddening. Suyong was junior enough to not care if this got out. In fact, Yao concluded at 0300 in the morning that it might even be to Suyong's benefit if the story came out. Indeed, it could enhance his status in the secretive world of intelligence. So, will he or won't he? After the way Yao had berated him earlier, he may be just motivated and reckless enough to do it. Yao now both loathed and feared the intel officer. The more it ate at him the more Yao's disdain became pure hate of the junior officer. How dare he cause him to feel this way?

Yao despised intelligence officers in general and Suyong in particular. Now his fate was out of his hands. Yao was furious at the thought that he may have to go out of his way to get on Suyong's good side. Or, maybe, just maybe he could get something on Suyong. Yes that is it. He has to have some vulnerabilities. No way he was going to grovel to that little worm. He decided that he would have to quietly check into that. Yes, that would be much better he thought. Get him back under his thumb. Yao was not going to be at the mercy of that little incompetent wimp.

He dropped his briefcase at his desk and was in the breakroom getting a cup of tea when the announcement came from the overhead speakers. The fact that the squadron public-address system was even being used hinted to the importance of what was being said.

"All officers, report to the auditorium for a 0730 meeting. That is all," said the announcer.

Yao felt immediate apprehension. Was this about him? Was he about to be embarrassed in front of the whole squadron? His brief to the Air Wing pilots on his dogfight experience was to be later in the afternoon at the base auditorium. So what was this?

"Any idea what is going on, Commander?" Lieutenant Junior Grade Hu asked as he stepped over to Yao.

"Not a clue," said Yao honestly. "But it must be big because I have never heard them use the squadron PA before."

"Something's going on. I just hope it isn't about us," Hu said speaking what was on both their minds.

Ten minutes later they were all seated in the auditorium murmuring to their neighbors, trying to find out what was going on when the room was called to attention.

Squadron Commander Chen entered the room and strode confidently up to the podium. He left them all at attention as he began to speak.

"We were informed of major developments involving the Americans and Filipinos early this morning. It appears that they have used our own tactics to seize Scarborough Shoal. This happened two days ago. Many of you have been in on the planning for us to make a similar move. In fact, our plans to establish a base there was in the final planning stages. But they have beaten us to it. They have moved construction crews in and are rapidly developing a permanent base there. Our senior leadership has tasked us to devise response plans. The first option will include full-up operations to destroy the fledgling base and drive them off. So we have to be ready to take on the American fleet and any Philippine based Filipino or American fighters that may oppose us. The second is to have a massive show of force to intimidate them into retreating. If they know that they are well within our sphere of air dominance, they may see their base there as untenable. We must have these plans finalized by noon tomorrow. They will then be presented to President Hsu to decide on. Lt Suyong has additional details you may need for your planning. The good news is that these will not be too different from the plans we have already devised. Commander Yao, your brief to the Air Wing is, understandably, canceled for now. Now get to work. I want updates at noon. Dismissed."

Yao was both relieved and angry. The damned Americans! The intel his uncle had confided in him had proven to be correct. And President Hsu had let it happen. That, or he was just an idiot for not listening to his intelligence officers. Yao did not see the irony, given his own poor view if intel officers. Yao could not envision President Hsu standing up to this outrage. Still, hopefully, his uncle and others like him would convince him otherwise.

As Yao and Hu headed out of the auditorium Yao noticed that Lieutenant Suyong was watching him intently with a wry smile on his face. At least, until he saw Yao notice him. Then the smile dropped and switched to a bland respectful expression as he looked away.

Yao felt a chill of fear run down his spine. He was now certain that Suyong knew the truth about his dogfight and was just waiting for the proper timing to discredit him. Yao was immediately back to scheming on ways to discredit Suyong before he struck.

"Wow," said Hu. "We may not be the only ones with experience fighting the Americans if this gets out of hand."

"What? What did you say?" Yao asked after a long hesitation.

"I said. We may not be the only ones with a chance to fight the Americans if this gets out of hand," Hu repeated.

"I hope you are right, Hu. I hope your right. Now let us get those plans dusted off. I want to make sure that we are at the forefront of whatever happens. And we need to make sure this sends a message the Americans and the entire world will tremble at seeing."

37 FRIENDLY COMPETITION
Scarborough Shoal, South China Sea

Staff Sergeant Anglin and Senior Airman Stringer had just finished maneuvering a heavy four-by-eight-foot section of the plywood forms into place down in the trench when their supervisor Technical Sergeant Nickel told them to take a break. They had been working hard for three hours, and they had been steadily building and setting the concrete forms in place. The day crew from the 554th had completed over a third of the forms for the footings. The leader of the carpenter day crew happened to be an old friend of Nickel's from a previous assignment, Technical Sergeant Kelly Grayson. Grayson had shown what they had completed so far and what still needed to be done. It was during the turnover brief that the real competition began.

"These footings are scheduled to be poured in two days," Grayson said. "The portable cement plant should be set up and functional by then. All during the day, ships have been delivering more construction materials and hardware. We have completed the first third of the forms. We expect that you will do a third tonight, and we will finish up tomorrow. After that, we will start on the footings for the second hanger. We will have a team start pouring the cement into the forms once the plant is up and running. Then after a couple of weeks for the cement to cure, we will be back to start erecting the hangers."

Following the brief and after the day shift had left, Nickel called them together again.

"Ladies and gentlemen, I don't know about you, but I take it as an insult that they think we can only do a third of the job," Nickel challenged. "I know Grayson and how he does things. He divides up his team and assigns them a section to build. So it gets built piecemeal. Well, I come from Detroit, and we are going to follow in the steps of Henry Ford and create us an assembly line. I bet we can get far more done than they did and not have to work any harder, just smarter."

He set up the critical points in the construction. He had some bringing the plywood and two-by-four lumber stock. Others measured and cut the boards to the proper length. Another couple laid it out, and another nailed it all together. Once a completed section was finished, it was moved into place. As the night progressed, their speed and efficiency steadily increased, and they almost finished their assigned third of the work by midnight.

After getting a decent MRE to eat, Anglin heard his name called.

"Anglin, over here," Nickel called.

"Yes, Sarge," Anglin said as he came over.

"You guys are doing great. We are really kicking butt tonight. Do you think we can be done with all of it by morning?" Nickel asked.

"Well, maybe. We can probably get all these forms set in place, but I don't know if we could get in all the outside supports to brace them for the concrete pour. As I see it, we have two options. We can brace them with two-by-fours from the sides of the trenches as we usually do. Then we can knock the braces away once the concrete is set and then reuse them for the next building, saving time and material for the next hangar. We can't get the bracing done tonight. The day crew would have to take over that. The other option would be to backfill the sides of the forms with the sand we dug out of the trench. That could be done quickly with a couple of front-end loaders. But so they won't collapse under the weight of the sand we will have to internally brace the forms with rebar now instead of putting it in later. But that would require a lot less bracing and material and could be done rather quickly. Then once the concrete is poured, we just leave the forms in place. It is a semipermanent building after all. The plan is for permanent structures to be built later after the base is up and running."

"Hmm, well, money and materials don't seem to be an issue right now. Time seems to be their biggest concern which is why we have double crews out here working 24-7," Nickel mused. "Let's go with option two. Once all the forms are built and in place, we can have everyone working to install the internal bracing. It should go pretty fast. After we eat, I'll run it by the boss for approval, and then I will go arrange for the front-end loaders for the backfill. Oh, I almost forgot the reason I called you over. Staff Sergeant Burnham wants you to stop by their makeshift clinic in the morning before going to bed. He said it would only take a few minutes.

As dawn was breaking, a front-end loader was filling in the last twenty feet of the trench. They had done it. They had finished the rest of the footings for the first hanger. When Grayson and his day crew arrived, they were stunned.

"Change of plans, Kelly," Nickel said with obvious pride as they arrived. "You need to get started on hanger two's footings. This one's done. I'm going to head over and see if I can get the concrete-mixing crew hurried up."

On his way to breakfast and a shower, Anglin went into the Alaska shelter used as their medical clinic.

"Thanks for stopping by," Burnham said as Anglin entered. It was situated on the beach near where the housing barge was moored. It was shared by the Navy and Air Force medics.

"On each twelve hour shift there are two Air Force Independent Duty Medical Technicians and a Navy Independent Duty Corpsman and a basic corpsman, something they call a quad zero. Whatever that means," Burnham explained. "We are pretty well manned to handle the routine stuff we are seeing," Burnham continued. "I asked you before we left if you would be able to assist if we needed help. It's unlikely, but I wanted to show you around and introduce you to everyone while they are all here at shift change."

"Sure, whatever I can do to help if you need it. Just let me know," Anglin answered.

Turning to the others, Burnham said, "This is Staff Sergeant Anglin, the one with the EMT training I told you about." After introductions and shaking hands all around, Burnham showed him how the clinic was set up and where their emergency gear was stowed.

"In case of an emergency this A-bag with medical supplies will be stored just inside the CO's office door where it will be safe. If an accident or something were to happen, you may actually know about it before we do and can respond quicker. We wanted you to know what is in it and if you have any questions. They showed him the bag and emptied it out. It was filled with bandages and dressings of various sizes. Some with a hemostatic agent that would rapidly stop significant bleeding. There were tourniquets, IV fluids and tubing, oral airways, wire splints, Kerlix and even eye patches.

"Well, I can use most of this, but I hope you don't think I'm going to start an IV," Anglin said. "I've never done that."

"Oh no, one of us will use that if needed. We just want you to do the basics, splint broken bones, help stop bleeding, and make sure airways are clear. All the basic stuff you learned. We will likely be there within minutes to take over," Burnham explained.

They checked out everything in the emergency bag and made sure that he was comfortable with what was there. He then headed for a shower and supper. Later, feeling refreshed and with a full stomach, he was walking back to his tent when he heard the sound of an approaching helicopter. A Navy gray SH-60 flew directly over him as it turned on its approach to land near the Seabee compound. He stopped to watch a moment as men hopped out of it before he turned into his air-conditioned tent and the bed that was calling his name.

38 OFF TO SCARBOROUGH
Scarborough Shoal, South China Sea

The SMO's day had begun an hour earlier than normal at 0500 to get ready for his 0700 brief with the HS-19 crew for his flight to Scarborough Shoal. He planned for an early breakfast, clear up some last-minute paperwork and to ensure that Hospitalman Second Class Vesel, one of his public health corpsmen, had everything he needed to accompany him on the trip.

After meeting with Vesel and going over their plans, he went to his stateroom for his overnight bag. He headed up early for the flight brief so he would have time to see Jenna before he left.

"Hey, Jenna," he said as he knocked on her open office door. "You got a minute?"

"For you, always. Official or unofficial," she asked?

"Unofficial," he replied.

"Aren't you about to leave on your tropical vacation?" she asked sarcastically.

"Hardly a vacation, as you well know. But it should be less hectic than the past couple of days. I still think we should send one of the junior flight surgeons. But, hey, I lost that battle, and the brief is in ten minutes. And, Jenna, ah, I just wanted you to know that I'll be thinking of you. You probably knew that already, but I wanted to tell you anyway," the SMO said.

"I do, and I'm glad you did, Derek," said Jenna. "You keep your head down out there, and when you get back, we will find some time to talk. I think we both like how this is going. Now you better get to that brief."

In HS-19's ready room, he met up with the SEAL Team members for the first time. They had a quick introduction, and the SMO couldn't help but notice how young they all appeared. Had he ever been that young? It seemed like a lifetime ago since he had been a young, bold, self-confident SEAL, just as these looked. He didn't have time to mention that he had once been a SEAL. But he didn't have to. They had noticed his flight suit name tag that had Flight Surgeon wings under the SEAL Trident. He and the SEAL Team stood around and chatted for a few minutes. That was when he realized that he recognized one of the names.

"Rhinehart. Are you related to Culinary Specialist Master Chief Alan 'Buckeye' Rhinehart?" the SMO asked.

"Yes, sir, that's my dad," Bosun's Mate Second Class Rhinehart answered. "Do you know him?"

"Oh yeah, you can say that," the SMO answered. "Your dad was the Master Chief of our team when I showed up as an arrogant young ensign. Master Chief Rhinehart, thinking of him takes me back. He recognized right away that I didn't know crap and that I still had a lot to learn. But after establishing that he would win any pissing contest, he took me under his wing and taught me a lot about tactics and how to be an effective leader. I owe your dad a lot. Where is he now?" the SMO asked.

"He retired twelve years ago," Rhinehart answered. "He never got cooking out of his blood, and he opened a restaurant back in his hometown of Shreveport, Louisiana. It's, of course, called Buckeye's."

"That sounds just like him. He always was in charge of the grill when the team had a cookout. Well, if we have time later, I would love to tell you some stories about your old man. I bet you can really appreciate them now that you are a SEAL too. But I have to grab my flight gear before we head up in a few."

"Yes, sir, that would be great," Rhinehart answered.

As an aircrew member logging flight time, the SMO was issued a loaner set of flight gear whenever he flew with them. He would be able to hear and talk with the crew while they flew rather than sitting in the back with only hearing muffs and an inflatable life vest. While checking out his gear, he noticed that his HEEDS bottle was a little low and they topped it off for him. It is essentially a mini scuba tank to use for emergency escapes if the helicopter was to crash and flip upside down in the water.

Up on the flight deck the weather and temp were perfect as they headed to their SH-60F. As the senior officer aboard, the SMO got his pick of seats and he chose the right rear seat. He would be right in the open door catching the wind blast, but he loved the exhilaration of it along with a great view.

Soon the engines began their whine into life, and the helicopter's blades began to slowly turn and were soon just a blur as they began to beat the air into submission. As scheduled, they lifted off the deck and headed on their way toward Scarborough Shoal. Enroute they were vectored to the location of a suspected Chinese fishing boat eight miles from the carrier that had been suspiciously near the ship for the past two days. It appeared to be a typical fishing boat that had the usual fishing gear out on the decks. However, this particular fishing boat was staying near and paralleling the carrier matching its course changes and the carrier's speed, which meant that it was going extremely fast for a boat supposed to be out fishing. As they flew closer one of the pilots saw someone briefly out on deck wearing a camouflage uniform before he quickly ducked below out of sight. The crew chief took several photos for the intel bubbas back in the Vinson's intelligence shop to go over later.

After they checked out the pretend fishing boat, they continued on to Scarborough. As the shoal came into view, they could all see the horseshoe shaped atoll with its huge emerald green lagoon. It reminded the SMO of an undeveloped miniature version of Diego Garcia out in the middle of the Indian Ocean. As they got closer, they could see the large, white housing barge and the flat one with the crane dredging at the lagoon's entrance. He could also make out white patches that had recently been cleared of vegetation and were dotted with tents and heavy equipment.

After a forty-five-minute flight from the *Vinson*, they touched down, and the SMO unbuckled, stepped off onto the sand, removed his borrowed flight gear, and handed it to the crew chief. After grabbing his bag, he moved clear of the helo's spinning blades along with the six SEAL Team members. Now that they had finally arrived, the SMO was looking forward to a relatively calm and relaxing day after its early start.

As he watched the helicopter liftoff, he was going over his plans for the day. It should only be the arrangement of some meetings and inspecting how the medical teams are set up. He knew that Vesel would be busiest, doing public health inspections of the food storage and preparation areas. Then he would do testing of their water supply to ensure that it is properly chlorinated. He would also bring samples back to the ship for further testing. The SMO planned to accompany Vesel on the galley and the clinic inspections. First up, he needed to check in with a courtesy visit to the command leadership, which he and the SEAL Team leader would do together.

39 HERO REJECTED
PLAN Air Base; China

Because of his new celebrity status, Lieutenant Commander Yao was just one of a dozen midgrade officers allowed to be at the brief to the wing Commander, Admiral Luo. He was sitting in a chair along the side wall of the Admiral's conference room. At the table with the Admiral were the wing's squadron Commanders. The senior squadron Commander was briefing the wing's part of the planned air demonstration as it was being called. It would involve tactical aircraft from seven bases along the east coast of China. The plan was for a major show of force for those on Scarborough Shoal. It would include both air and surface assets. It was step one in what could lead to a temporary blockade of the shoal. Their leadership had made it clear that they must not get in a shooting war with the Americans. But they were willing to go just short of war. They wanted to make it clear to everyone that protecting and maintaining a base on the distant shoal would be untenable in the long run. If China could make it clear early on that they would ultimately win, then hopefully the Filipinos and Americans would abandon their efforts before they were further financially and emotionally invested in the endeavor.

Yao, of course, disagreed with the timid approach as he saw it. He had done his part as one of the primary planners. His major success was in convincing his leadership to insist upon being armed with weapons for the event. He had used his own official version of being attacked by the American fighter to justify such a stance. He had pointed out the aggressive and unpredictable nature the Americans had recently shown when they had engaged him. If the Americans were to respond aggressively, their air armada would be at the mercy of the power-crazed Americans. Yao beamed with great satisfaction as he heard the Admiral agree with the recommendation. Each of the aircraft were to be fully armed. Just in case, of course.

The main thrust of the operation would be directly at the shoal with the bulk of the air forces. The naval air forces were to make a similar demonstration at the American battle group still currently operating in the South China Sea. Yao had made sure that his squadron would be targeting, so to speak, the USS *Vinson*. This time, he intended to see the ship from his cockpit. He was relishing the chance to humble them all and send them the message loud and clear that their influence in the Western Pacific and particularly in the South China Sea was coming to an end.

In the end, the Admiral insisted on some minor changes to the plan, but they were mostly cosmetic, happy-to-glad type of clarifications. It was really just his way of showing that he was still in charge. Now they only thing remaining was waiting for President Hsu to green-light the demonstration and set the date. Yao hoped it would be soon.

By early afternoon, Yao was headed to Hong Kong for some fun during what was left of his weekend. He was mulling the events of the past week. It had indeed been momentous. He was on the fast track now with the support of his uncle. He had been on the USS *Vinson* and met American pilots face-to-face. He had been in a dogfight, though it pained him to admit that it had been a draw after the advantage was all his at the start. And now China was about to finally show them that there was a new and bigger dog on the block. Overall, things were looking rather good for him personally and China. He enjoyed the upbeat spirit for the first hour of his trip. Then his naturally pessimistic and insecure personality kicked in. He began ruminating on the dogfight again and how it had not been as easy as he had hoped. That led to his being reminded of the inept intel officer, Lieutenant Suyong and the possibility that he likely knew the truth. This played heavily on his growing dread of being exposed as a fraud and a liar.

He was in a foul mood when his cell phone rang.

"Yao," he answered gruffly.

"Lieutenant Commander Yao, this is Lieutenant Ping, Vice Admiral Jiang's personal aide, as you may recall. The Admiral would like you to join him for a private lunch tomorrow. That should give you plenty of time to relax after you arrive in Hong Kong," she said.

"Yes, that will be fine," he answered. "I should arrive at my hotel within the hour."

"As we expected. I will let the Admiral know you will be joining him. It will be in the same location where you last met," she said. "Do you need me to give you the address again?"

"No, I still have it," Yao answered.

"Very well, we will see you then," she said before abruptly hanging up.

Yao was left staring blankly at the road ahead as he pondered her last statement. How had they known he would be in Hong Kong tonight? He had told no one of his plans. His trips into the city were frequent but irregular. He sometimes went several weekends in a row and then go four to five weeks without a visit. He often did not know himself what he planned to do until the weekend arrived. Today he had told no one of his last-minute plans. He had only decided to get away from the local area while day-dreaming during the Admiral's brief. He had gone by his house and grabbed some overnight clothes. He called to make a hotel reservation while on the road.

Was his phone being monitored? Well, the answer to that was yes. Everyone is subject to being monitored. Still, with such a huge population, the fact was that only so many calls were actually listened to at any given time. The chances that his exact call was monitored and relayed to the Admiral were small. Unless he had been singled out for monitoring and tracking. Though everyone knew of the constant surveillance by the state, he had felt relatively immune from it by being in the military. Given his already sour mood, this thought that he was being spied on further irked him. Wasn't he special now? Wasn't he now one of the chosen few that did not have to be bothered by such rules that should apply only to the lower classes or troublesome civilians? Like the students and professional's in Hong Kong that had taken every opportunity to protest the eventual total control of their government by Beijing. At least, China's leadership had finally clamped down on the insurgence and taken over security in Hong Kong soon after the protests of 2020, he thought with a satisfied smile.

Two hours later, Yao was having dinner alone in the hotel restaurant. Two tables away were three Chinese women in their mid-twenties having dinner. They were laughing and having a fun time. Yao could not keep from glancing over their way. As he watched them, he began debating on when to approach them. With three, he was confident that his chances were better than even that one would surely want to spend some quality time with him. This was usually the case when he played his trump card of being a fighter pilot. It worked well in mainland China. But not so much in Hong Kong where the people were spoiled with Western ideals. Still, on most trips to the city he rarely went to bed alone. He often would go to a bar to meet young ladies. It occasionally took a while, but his track record was fairly good.

He could feel his sexual desire rise as he finished his dinner and decided to make his move. He took a sip of water to clear his throat and headed over to the table.

"Hello, ladies, would you like to join me for dessert?"

Two of them looked at each other and giggled while the third let her eye contact linger a moment with him. She glanced at her companions before answering him. "I'm sorry. This is our girls' night out. We really are not looking for anything else tonight. Maybe another time," she said with a genuine smile, hoping to let him down gently.

"Come on, it's only dessert. We can have a few laughs for a little while, and you can be on your way," Yao persisted. "Help a lonely man out."

"I'm sorry. We really are just having a girls-only night. Thank you for the offer," she said, turning to her friends and her back to him.

Yao frowned at the dismissal. He usually was not cut off so abruptly. He headed back to his table. He cringed when he heard the ladies whispering and then break out into a stifled laugh. He was convinced that they were laughing at him.

He was suppressing his anger as he sat back down at his table to have a cup of after dinner coffee.

He was finishing his coffee and calling for his check when he noticed a lone white man approach the ladies table and address them in English. He could not hear much of what was said. They talked for a few minutes, and Yao watched them all laughing together at something he said. He assumed that the newcomer was about to strike out as he did and was astonished when he was invited to join them at the table.

Here he was, a respected and important officer in the Chinese Navy. More than that, he was seen as a hero by his fellow pilots. They should be begging to spend time with him. How dare they reject him. He had supposedly been brushed off by these women because they were having a girls-only night. Yet a white foreigner had succeeded where he had failed. He was convinced that it was clear that the girls-only night out was a ruse to fend off unwanted advances. But to lose out to a Caucasian was just unacceptable. He had thought that he detected a British or Australian accent from what he had heard. But as their talk and laughter got louder, he realized that it was actually an American accent. By the time he charged the dinner to his room, he was seething with rage as he left the restaurant. Damned Americans!

40 FIREFIGHT

Scarborough Shoal, South China Sea

At 1850, Staff Sergeant Anglin reported straight to the armory after breakfast to get issued his M4 carbine and two clips of ammo. It was his turn on guard duty. Initially, he had dreaded boring guard duty pacing the perimeter, but they had been working hard the past few nights, and he was looking forward to some easy duty as a nice break.

As he started into the Alaska shelter that had a makeshift armory in the corner, he was met by Staff Sergeant Urania on his way out.

"Hey, Urania, I was just on my way to see you guys," Anglin said. "It's my turn on guard duty tonight."

"Didn't you hear about the brief?" Urania asked.

"Yeah, we are to meet over by the command tent for our assigned patrol areas," Anglin answered.

"No, not that one," Urania explained. "The one over in the barge's chow hall. A SEAL Team flew in today and they are briefing us on how to be better guards. They briefed day shift this afternoon between meals. You'll get issued your weapon after the brief. It starts in ten minutes."

"Oh, okay. But who'll be guarding while we're briefing?" Anglin asked. "Day shift is supposed to be relieved by 1930."

"They know about the delay and will cover during the brief until you can get there," Urania said.

"Hmmm. Real Navy SEALs?" Anglin asked. "I don't know whether to be thrilled or scared. Don't they only go where things are serious? Surely, they don't think anything will really happen here."

"Probably nothing to worry about. I heard that they were just in the area and were asked to beef up our guard skills. That's all," Urania explained as they started up the brow onto the barge.

After they were all settled into seats in the galley, they heard a Sailor call out, "Attention on deck!" They all leaped to their feet as Colonel Perry strode to the end of the galley where a projector screen was set up.

"Take your seats," Perry began. "As you know, we are involved in serious business. The assessment from intel is that China will not take any overt action. Still, our intelligence is quite sure that the Chinese sanctioned the attacks on American Sailors that were visiting Hong Kong four days ago. Several were seriously injured and hospitalized with one killed. Though we are legally in Philippine territorial waters and are patrolled by their Navy, we will be prudent to keep alert. We are great at what we do but we are not combat troops. The SEALs are here to make sure we know what we are doing while on patrol. With that, let me introduce Lieutenant Junior Grade Deville."

Deville stepped up and then introduced the other five members of his team.

"And I would also like to introduce Commander Lloyd," Deville added, pointing him out. "He's there standing in the back. He was an active SEAL and saw some serious action back in his day before he decided to go to medical school. He's now the Senior Medical Officer of the *Vinson*."

The SMO was a little surprised at being introduced. He was only there at the brief in hopes of getting some time later to talk to Bosun's Mate Second Class Rhinehart. He had finished his inspections early and had taken the opportunity to get in an afternoon nap. As he waved and smiled at the crowd of mostly a mix of inquisitive or bored faces, there was one that stood out. There was no mistaking the one that was glaring at him with open hostility. *What's up with that guy?* he wondered. Not the usual reaction SEALs or doctors usually engender. Maybe a SEAL stole his girlfriend or something, he mused, since it wasn't an uncommon occurrence for a SEAL to use his status to get his pecker wet.

Anglin's suppressed emotions came flooding back. The emotional anguish and pain was back in full force. Being focused on the demanding work and long days had kept him distracted for the most part. Until the mention of medical school. *A fricking doctor! The hell with them all*, he thought.

Over the next hour, Deville briefed them on what to be looking for when it came to sabotage, where to patrol, to make the rounds unpredictable, to light up the areas as much as possible, and that the most susceptible time for an attack or operation was from three to four a.m. That's when the human circadian rhythm is at its lowest ebb with its decreased alertness and reaction times, Deville had explained. But Anglin barely took in any of it. He was too distracted by his rage and pain that was again overwhelming him.

Six hours later, Anglin was on patrol on the north side of the compound. He was following a well-worn trail through the vegetation. His route took him near the heavy-equipment parking area in one corner and by the two full fuel bladders in the other. At the moment, over half of the equipment was out being used on the growing air strip and could be heard rumbling off in the distance. His patrol area was pretty gloomy, with just enough light for him to follow his path from the work lights over two hundred yards away.

For the most part, he was patrolling in automatic mode. His rage had dissipated, mostly thanks to the infuriating mosquitos he kept slapping away from his face, in spite of being slathered in insect repellant. But even with the buzzing, he was again ruminating on his situation with Kara and wondering what he could have done differently. He was approaching a parked motor grader only looking where he was going to step next when he heard, "Hey, over here."

He almost jumped out of his skin at the voice that was only ten feet away. He was still fumbling with the weapon slung on his shoulder when he saw a figure step out of the shadows by the huge machine's rear wheels.

"Calm down, Airman. We're friendly," Rhinehart said as he continued to step forward slowly into the light with his hands up.

"Dude, you scared the shit out of me!" Anglin said.

"Good," Rhinehart said. "We've been watching you for the past fifteen minutes. You are just walking around with your head down and staring at the ground. You are not looking around or checking anything. Didn't you listen to anything we said at the brief? You keep that up, and you'll be toast if someone was to try to sneak in here."

"Yeah, I know. But the way I feel, they would probably be doing me a favor," Anglin said as a lame excuse.

"Well, you better get your head out of your ass, mister. Right now! This isn't a game." Rhinehart chided. "It's not just about you or your personal problems. It's about your buddies over there. And the success of this mission."

Anglin just nodded, still looking down sheepishly as a second figure stepped out of the shadows.

Anglin glanced up at the new arrival, and his guilty face transformed into a seething animosity that was unmistakable even in the dim light.

"Good, get angry. Use it to help you keep focused," Rhinehart said, misinterpreting the sudden change in Anglin's attitude.

But the SMO suspected differently. *This is about me for some reason*, he realized. He hadn't become angry with Rhinehart. Something is really eating at this guy.

"Hi, I'm Commander Lloyd," he said ,trying to break the ice, reaching out with his right hand.

"I know who you are," Anglin said tersely. After a long pause with the SMO holding his hand out, he reluctantly shook it. He then shook Rhinehart's hand as well.

Taking a softer approach, the SMO said, "Look, we have been making the rounds with the two other guards, giving them pointers and answering questions. We'd like to do the same with you if that is all right. We just want to help."

After a brief hesitation Anglin said, "Sure. I know I'm a lousy guard. But I'm one hell of a carpenter," he said in his defense with a bit of pride.

"I bet you are. Now let us help you with your guard skills," the SMO said.

"First, you have to get off this same old path. You're too predictable staying on it," Rhinehart began as they headed off on a new patrol route.

They were on their second time around Anglin's patrol area and were approaching the fuel bladders.

"And you've got to use your flashlight to check things out," Rhinehart continued. "Shadows are your enemies' best friend. Get yourself a good bright LED flashlight if you can. They last forever, but still bring extra batteries just in case. Earlier, we were by that grader out in the open, and you didn't see us just standing there because of the shadows."

"Well, that's part of the reason," Anglin confessed with his rage once again depleted for the moment.

"So, you have to check those shadows regularly. If an enemy sees you checking, that can keep them at bay and limit what they may try to do."

"Now, let me show you some of the sabotage things you can keep an eye out for," Rhinehart explained. "You'll find that looking for them will help keep you focused and awake. Its far less boring if you are hunting for something. Now take this bladder full of diesel fuel for example. This can be attacked simply by cutting it open and letting it drain out. Quite simple, but pretty easy to patch and you have fuel delivered out here every couple of days. If they really wanted to make a statement, they could set a pyrotechnic grenade such as white phosphorus and have this thing go up like a Roman candle. And we would always set two charges just in case one failed to ignite."

He shone the flashlight under the shadowy lower edges of the bladder while they were walking. "Now, if I wanted it to look a bit more like a possible accident, I would just use and explosive squib. Just enough charge to blow a small hole and hot enough to get it burning. The fire would start slowly but soon grow out of control. There would be a question for a while as to what the cause was.

"If I was smart and had seen you checking the shadows, I would have to be extra sneaky," Rhinehart continued. "The darkest shadows farthest away from the lights would be the easiest place to get in unseen to plant a device. But now you know to check those kinds of places. So if I was really good, and I am, I would sneak over to the side with the most light to set it where you would least expect it. You may assume that because of the light they wouldn't dare attempt to work there. Then I could set it off when the guard was far away and looking elsewhere so he wouldn't see the small explosion. Or I could use a timer for any time I want after we are long gone."

Anglin nodded intently as he followed Rhinehart and the SMO as they showed him where to look.

"Let me show you. I'd place it right along here and then cover it up with sand. Then I would have to cover my tracks," Rhinehart said as he shone his light along the lower edge of the bladder facing the lights. Then he froze. "What the hell?" His light settled on a small mound of sand under the bladder with two barely visible wires leading up to the skin of the bladder.

"Oh, crap," the SMO said as he started scanning around them. He then grabbed Anglin by the arm and started pulling him back away from the device just as he was leaning in for a closer look. "You have a radio, Rhinehart? We need to call this in."

"Damn right," Rhinehart replied. "But we need to get away from here first. Our radio signal could trigger it."

They all moved away from the bladder being careful where they stepped. They went behind a bulldozer that was seventy-five yards away. Rhinehart figured that they were far enough from the device to likely not trigger it using his headset radio. And if not, they would probably be safe enough from the blast if it went off.

"Nemo One, this is Nemo Three," Rhinehart called.

"Nemo One, go, Three," Deville answered.

"We have a suspected explosive device on the northwestern fuel bladder. This is *not* a drill."

"Copy, device on northwestern fuel bladder," Deville answered back calmly. "Nemo Team, copy?"

"Two," "Four," "Five," and "Six," came the acknowledgment replies from each of the other team members.

"Nemo team, we may still have active intruders on site. Two and Four, you clear the west side moving north. Five and Six, you sweep the east side. Three, you are furthest north so hold your position and keep your eyes open. Only clear around your immediate area until we arrive," Deville ordered. "I'll notify leadership here."

"Okay, as you have figured out by now, we may still have active intruders on sight," Rhinehart explained in a low voice since the SMO and Anglin couldn't hear what Deville had said in his headset. "We are to clear our area here and then hold our positions. Two other teams will be clearing the east and west perimeters."

"Anglin, you know how to shoot that thing?" Rhinehart asked, referring to the M4 he was carrying at port arms.

"I'm one of the best shots in the unit," Anglin replied with some pride.

"Well, this ain't target practice. If you have to use that thing, make sure of your target and aim for center of mass as you've been trained," Rhinehart replied. "And keep it on safe until you're ready to fire. I don't want you shooting me in the ass by accident. Commander, you two stay here while I go clear the rest of these vehicles. I'll be back in a few and then we can wait for the cavalry to arrive."

"Can you spare a weapon?" the SMO asked quietly, noting the Sig Sauer P226 at Rhinehart's side in addition to the M4 he carried. "Don't leave me here naked."

Rhinehart unhesitatingly handed over the pistol and an extra clip of ammo before slipping silently away into the darkness. Anglin and the SMO set up back to back down on one knee, and each began scanning the area in front of them. The SMO scanned north in the direction that Rhinehart had gone and Anglin was looking roughly in the direction of the main compound.

All was relatively quiet for the next six minutes. There was the usual rumble of the heavy equipment off in the distance and the hum of the portable generators. Occasionally, they could hear the distant whine of a Skilsaw cutting lumber and the bang of hammers.

Nemos Five and Six were stealthily clearing their perimeter, checking the various stacks of lumber and plywood as well as the larger pieces of equipment and vehicles. Anywhere that was a place to hide or a good target for sabotage. That's when they stumbled on a man dressed in black under a Humvee doing something under the engine. It was parked only thirty yards from where a carpenter crew was working. Though it was parked in dark shadows, the intruder was clearly visible with their night vision goggles.

The intruder was busy at his task and didn't hear the quietly approaching SEALs. They split and approached on either side of the Hummer while staying behind the intruder and out of his view.

Nemo Six eased his rifle against the head of the intruder and said, "Don't move." The intruder froze, leaving his hands up where they had been. Nemo Five went down and removed a knife from his hand and a machine pistol that was strapped to his chest.

Once he was disarmed, Nemo six flipped the intruder face down and began zip-tying his hands behind him as Nemo five called in while scanning the area around them for others.

"Nemo One, Nemo Five, we have captured an intruder thirty yards east of the hanger two worksite."

"Copy. Hold him there," Deville answered. "We'll have extra armed guards to you in five mikes or less."

"Copy, holding for—" was all Nemo five could reply before he was slammed back as if hit by a truck. He didn't hear the gunfire until he was down on the ground. But by then, it didn't matter. His vest had stopped three bullets but a fourth had caught him in the neck. It didn't sever his spinal cord, but it did stun it enough that he lost the use of his arms and legs. He could only lay there and listen as his life's blood gushed out of his destroyed left jugular.

Luckily, Nemo Six had been missed by the initial burst. He immediately dropped to the sand and turned to return fire on the flashes of light forty yards away. Unfortunately, he hadn't finished zip-tying the intruder's feet and he had soon escaped in the confusion. "Contact! Contact! Six in Contact!" It was soon apparent that he was up against at least three shooters firing at him. He rolled behind the wheels of the Humvee for what little protection they could afford as he looked for a way to improve his fighting position.

At the sound of the gunfire three hundred yards away, both Anglin and the SMO dropped onto their bellies.

"Be ready," the SMO whispered. "Remember: we have friendlies out here."

Anglin barely heard him because of the rushing blood in his ears as his heart began pounding in his chest.

Moments later, they heard, "Friendly, Rhinehart," as he quickly came up from Anglin's left. "Five and Six are in contact. The immediate area is clear. You two stay here. I'm heading to help," Rhinehart said as he tossed the SMO two extra ammo clips for the Sig.

The SMO nodded. He had a pistol, but that was all. He had no other gear. His training and instincts were rusty, and he would likely be more of a liability than an asset, he concluded as he felt the cold sweat of fear trickle down his face. Fear not of being shot but of doing the wrong thing. The sound of gunfire snapped him back to that fateful night in Afghanistan so long ago. He had replayed that dreadful time over and over a thousand times in his dreams. Now the shots had him again back there, but this time, second-guessing what to do in this situation. But also like then, his ingrained training took over.

"Whoever it is, they are probably done with this area and were either sweeping that way or are on their way out. They possibly came in from the ocean only a hundred yards or so from where the shooting is occurring. It's unlikely that they came in from the lagoon," the SMO whispered. "Unless…"

"Unless what," Anglin demanded. "Unless they had a submersible capability similar to ours. Then the lagoon makes perfect sense. Shit, move slowly but quickly behind the dozer's blade."

Anglin did as he was told, and they both scanned out a side of the big machine.

"Now stay sharp and very still. Whoever it is may be headed back this way. And they likely have night vision goggles, and we don't. Movement is the quickest thing to catch the human eye."

After what seemed like an eternity but had only been two minutes, the gunfire ceased. It was eerily quiet compared to before. Now it was only the distant hum of generators running. This oppressive lull allowed his self-doubt to rare up again. Maybe they had time to run to the main compound, completely out of danger. *Staying here could be a death trap. But without knowing exactly where they were, get up and run straight into them*, he thought. *Better to lay low and pray they slip by quietly.*

After a minute, the SMO thought he saw movement against the background of the distant lights. A moment later, he could make out multiple shapes moving quickly. They were not running but still moving fast.

"I've got movement headed our way," the SMO relayed to Anglin. "Now listen, we are not going to engage these guys. We are way outgunned. Just let them pass by quietly and pray they don't see us."

"Okay," was all Anglin could manage from his dry throat as his fight-or-flight response was in overdrive.

Just then a slow but steady, pop, pop, pop started ringing out. The SMO was sure that he saw one or two figures drop before he had heard the sounds. Then almost immediately, a cacophony of automatic gunfire erupted, directed to the south. The muzzle flashes lit up the battle scene, and the SMO counted eight to nine figures firing in one direction. That was too many to be our SEAL Team, he knew. Gotta be bad guys. He suspected that Rhinehart had opened up on them as they were trying to exfiltrate. He saw a couple more drop before the gunfire ceased. Either Rhinehart was out of ammo or he was down.

"Remember what I said," cautioned the SMO.

A minute later the SMO saw movement again. As they neared, he could see that three were being carried out by others.

"Crap, take that gun off safety and be ready." the SMO whispered as he realized what was happening. They were hiding under the biggest and nearest vehicle to the approaching intruders. And they were heading for its cover too. *We can't let them get too close or we're toast*, he thought to himself.

"They're coming right for us. If you hear me fire, you open up." He already knew that it wasn't an if but a when. He only had a pistol, which would only alert them from this far away. He needed Anglin's rifle fire to act as a real deterrent. He hoped that he could at least force them to take another route out. He couldn't let them get much closer without taking devastating return fire.

He knew he would only get two or three rounds off before they returned fire and ducked for cover. He took careful aim just above his target's head knowing that the bullet would drop to center of mass. He chose the lead target, not only because it was nearest, but also because there was one intruder carrying another almost directly behind him a few yards. His own endocrine system had been in overdrive since the beginning. But he had long since learned to work with it. He took several careful breaths with both hands supporting the grip. Waiting for his natural pause in breathing he centered his aim on the approaching targets and squeezed the trigger. He continued a steady rate of fire as his targets dove to the sand.

Before the SMO got off his fourth round, Anglin was beside him, taking aim and firing. Anglin resisted flipping to the faster three round burst mode. His accuracy had always dropped dramatically in that mode when shooting on the range. He only had one extra magazine of thirty rounds so he had decided to stick with what he was best at.

"We just want to keep them away, so don't waste ammo. Shoot when you have a clear target or at least a muzzle flash," the SMO said as a hail of bullets slammed into the dozer just above their heads.

The SMO and Anglin shifted position under the dozer and held their fire, waiting either for a clear target or for the intruders to hopefully disengage. The SMO was on the right peering out at the muzzle flashes waiting for a reasonable pistol target. Anglin, with his fear still pumping was looking left and right under the sides of the dozer. That's when he caught sight of movement to his right over the back of the doc. He subconsciously flipped the selector to burst. He raised the M4 over the SMO's back and fired two bursts at the two figures creeping up on them from their right toward the back of the dozer. Both went down immediately just twenty yards away.

Both the SMO and Anglin buried themselves down behind the dozer's track wheels for what cover they provided as the hail of gunfire dramatically increased. After thirty seconds, it suddenly stopped, and it was quiet again. They both kept their heads on a swivel but had no further incoming fire or saw any movement. Anglin noticed that both the figures he had fired at were gone.

Three minutes later, they heard a loud bang, and both were almost immediately blinded by a huge flash as the fuel bladder went up in a huge fireball that rose high into the sky.

After another long minute, they heard a call from where the intruders had been firing from minutes before. "Hold your fire. It's Lieutenant Deville. We're all clear over here."

"Thank God," Anglin said as he let his forehead drop to the sand. What he didn't see was the SMO doing the same and saying a prayer of thanks that he hadn't gotten them killed.

41 MEDEVAC

Scarborough Shoal, South China Sea

It was the beginning of dawn when the SMO was able to step outside and take a break now that all of the patients had been treated and at least stabilized. Two needed immediate surgery, and three others would need surgical wound debridement. The nearest operating room was on the *Vinson*. Lieutenant Commander Sandaal, his surgeon, would be busy for the next twenty-four hours, but he could handle it. In total, there were nine who needed care on the ship. He had been taking care of the wounded since right after the firefight. *The evacuation helicopters should be arriving within the next half hour*, he thought.

The calls for a medic began shortly after all the shooting had stopped. The yelling was coming from the construction site near where the first firefight had been. In addition to the SEALs that had initially arrived and cleared the area, they were soon joined by a dozen armed Red Horse troops from day shift. They all fanned out at the direction of the SEALs.

"Anglin, we need corpsmen. Run tell them to get over to that site and to bring stretchers," the SMO had said urgently.

When Staff Sergeant Anglin had arrived at the clinic, they were already getting organized for wounded and had decided to send two RED HORSE medics and three corpsmen, including Hospitalman Second Class Vesel, ahead on foot to the site with their go bags. In the meantime, Staff Sergeant Burnham had commandeered a Humvee to take more supplies and to transport patients back. But he had no idea where exactly to go. And that was just the piece of information that Anglin was able to provide.

Anglin had thought his crazy night was about to wind down. But he had no idea.

"Anglin, go grab that emergency A-bag I told you about and hustle back here," Burnham had said.

Doing what he was told, Anglin was off and running again. They were climbing into the Hummer as he returned. As he tossed the bag in back, Burnham said, "Now hop in and show us the way."

Anglin directed them the quickest way to the hangar two construction site. When they pulled up, they saw three wounded lying out on the sand, being given first aid. Anglin saw Commander Lloyd applying a tourniquet to an Airman's upper thigh.

As they arrived with medical supplies, the SMO directed them where to start. He had IVs started on two of them and compression bandages were applied. The third was unmoving and was facedown with an obvious wound to the head. Anglin was fairly sure he recognized the body as that of his supervisor, Technical Sergeant Nickel.

Burnham yelled out, "If you are injured and can walk come over here to my right. If you are not injured go to the Humvee and grab stretchers."

Anglin was surprised to see one of the SEALs come walking over with his bloody right arm hanging limply at his side. He still had the M4's pistol grip still firmly in his left hand.

The SMO was surprised to see Anglin again. "You not get enough yet?" he had to ask.

"Well, I'm here, and I have some EMT training. How can I help?" Anglin asked.

"That medic is gathering up the walking wounded. You can start by seeing if we've missed anyone," the SMO answered.

Anglin headed over to the trench where they had been installing the footing forms. Looking along the trench on the near side of the forms he saw no one. He had to climb up on them to check the far side. It was clear left but looking right he saw two unmoving bodies down in the shadows of the trench.

"He called out, 'Over here, two down,' getting the attention of Vesel, who came running over with his medical kit. Anglin jumped down into the shadowy trench and started assessing the first one he came to. He had no obvious injury other than a large lump on his forehead.

"I think this one wacked his head diving into the trench. We better be careful with his C-spine," Anglin told Vesel, who was now assessing the other patient.

"Call for stretchers. This one's been hit," Vesel said as he pulled out a C-collar from his kit and tossed it to Anglin. "Sounds like you know what to do with this."

"Yeah, but it's been a while," Anglin responded, catching the collar.

"No time like the present to get back into it," Vesel said.

He gently put the C-collar on, and when the stretcher bearers arrived, he directed how to get him loaded while he kept his cervical spine straight.

Moments later, Vesel was directing stretcher bearers to bring his wounded patient out, and that's when Anglin realized that it was his best friend, Senior Airman Harold Stringer, and he wasn't looking good. Anglin could see that Stringer had bloody gauze on a wound in his left abdomen. After he was set down in better light, Vesel began to further pack the three-inch gaping wound with additional bandages impregnated with a hemostatic agent. He then began applying additional direct pressure.

Looking up and seeing Anglin watching, Vesel said. "Hey, can you take over applying pressure on this wound. I packed it tight, but he is pretty messed up in there, and I want to be extra sure we stop or at least slow down as much bleeding as possible. He has lost enough blood already. I need to start an IV."

"You bet," replied Anglin as he took over pushing down hard with the palm of his right hand.

The SMO arrived and began a quick assessment of the two new patients and triaging which to transport to the clinic first.

To Anglin, he said, "Good job, but you might want to use both hands and your weight as if you were doing CPR. Just lean into it and let gravity do the work."

"Thanks. Is he going to make it, Doc?" Anglin asked with obvious worry in his voice.

"No guarantees, but if we can stop the bleeding and get some fluids in him, he has a chance. So, keep good pressure on that wound," the SMO said honestly.

Anglin had stayed at his friend's side the rest of the night. He was relieved every thirty minutes by one of the other corpsmen after his arms would go numb. But it seemed to be working. He had a good blood pressure after three liters of IV fluids. He was still unconscious but was occasionally moaning.

It had been during one of his rest breaks that one of the corpsmen Anglin was talking to noticed something.

"Is that your friend's blood there on your shirt?" the Corpsman asked, pointing to Anglin's left upper shirt sleeve.

"I suppose so," Anglin answered. "Though I have noticed over the past hour that it gets to aching more as I'm holding direct pressure."

"Here, let's take a look," the Corpsman said, directing him over to an examination light. Taking off his shirt Anglin was shocked to see dried clotted blood from a puncture wound along his left deltoid muscle.

"You've been shot, my friend," said the Corpsman to a dumbfounded Anglin.

The corpsman cleaned away the dried blood so he could see what the wound actually looked like. It was a clean through and through bullet wound. Luckily, it had only penetrated the skin, barely grazed the muscle underneath and then exited 4 centimeters beyond. The bleeding had quickly clotted.

"You probably need that properly washed out on the ship," the Corpsman said as he secured a bandage in place. "It looks fine now, but that bullet could have dragged in parts of your shirt and other debris. You don't want to get an infection."

"Good, that means I can stay with Harold," Anglin had been relieved to say. "And I can keep helping with the direct pressure." On his next break, he ran and grabbed his A-bag with his clothing and toiletries.

As he was taking in the fresh air in the growing light of dawn the SMO was approached by LTJG Deville.

"How's it going in there? How's my men?" Deville asked.

"They're both stable. But they have significant wounds, and we will have to get them to surgery to clean them out. Then evacuation to an orthopedic surgeon. Both have shattered bones and muscle damage. We have them doped up and pain free for now," the SMO replied. "I'm sorry about the man you lost. That is always tough. What was his name?"

"AT2 Albert Rosefield," Deville said solemnly. "But we all just called him "Blade", because of his fondness for knives. He had a huge collection of knives he had going back to when he was a kid back in Arkansas. He was 26 and engaged to be married next spring." After a moment's silence, he added, "If you have a minute, the commanders would like you to give them a quick medical update on their troops before you fly out."

"You bet. Where are they?" The SMO asked.

"Over in the Red Horse Command tent. I'll show you," Deville answered.

To try to get Deville's mind off of his lost Sailor, the SMO decided to change the topic, hoping to get him thinking of more pleasant things.

"So, how did you come up with the NEMO Team call sign? Are you fond of Captain Nemo from Jules Verne's Twenty Thousand Leagues Under the Sea?" The SMO asked as they were walking toward the command tent.

"No, hardly," Deville answered. "It's for that little orange and white clown fish from the Disney movie. You see, my four year old son just loves that little fish. It's all he talks about. He has Nemo toys, Nemo Posters, Nemo cup and plate, Nemo sheets, and pretty much anything else Nemo my wife can find. He's our only kid and she and her parents are spoiling him. The guys got wind of it and started calling me lieutenant Nemo. So they insisted that Nemo be my team's call sign."

"I know what you mean. My daughter used to be a Disney princess for years. She probably still is but she can't find any dresses in her size now that she is grown," the SMO answered as they entered the command tent.

One of the intelligence officers had just began briefing the four unit commanders as they entered and stood off to the side of the room.

"As best we can tell it was likely a Chinese special operations team. We don't have any proof of their nationality," said Lt Henry. "Petty officer Rogers, the only surviving SEAL that saw one up close could only say that it was an oriental face. We are not sure how many were involved but roughly ten to twelve based on debriefs. We know that several were either wounded or killed but they took their dead and wounded with them. We know this by seeing the blood stains on the ground where the engagements had occurred. There were two significant blood stains at the first sight. Six at the second but we suspect that at least two or three of these was continued bleeding from the wounded from the first engagement. The last sight by the bulldozer had two close but separate blood stains. One of them was massive with what was reported as likely brain tissue."

SSgt Anglin definitely nailed those two for sure, the SMO thought as he listened from the back of the room.

"A dozen special ops troops," chimed in Captain Rochelle, the overall operation commander. "We're lucky we didn't have more casualties."

"Sir, actually we may have just been unlucky," Lt Henry began to explain. "All indications are that they were here to sabotage and disrupt operations as much as possible. Not to directly attack our personnel. In addition to the fuel depot, various pieces of machinery, and many vehicles were damaged, and their fuel tanks contaminated.

"Then why the shooting?" Captain Rochelle asked.

We suspect that one of their guys likely got trigger happy when Rogers and Rosefield captured one of them. It was just unfortunate that the Red Horse structures team was in the line of fire when the shooting started. They then withdrew and didn't directly attack anyone else until they were fired on by petty officer Rhinehart. They then continued withdrawing again until engaged by Commander Lloyd and SSgt Anglin as they were closing in on their position. There were plenty of Red Horse and Seabee troops out working that would have been easy targets if this was a kill mission. That's the overview of what we know so far," he concluded.

"Commander Lloyd, can you give us an update on our injured?" Captain Rochelle requested.

"Yes sir," he said stepping to the front. "We have nine we need to take to the ship. Two are in serious but currently stable condition and need immediate surgery. Both are Red Horse. One was shot in the chest and has what we call a hemothorax. His lung was collapsed, and I have placed a chest tube to reinflate the lung and drain blood. He is the most immediate case and the Vinson's surgery team is prepped and ready. We know his blood type from his records, and they have already gotten volunteers to donate blood for him. The next most serious has an abdominal wound but the bleeding is controlled, and he is stable. We have three with significant extremity wounds that will need surgical intervention. This includes the two

SEALs, Rhinehart and Rogers. They will probably need multiple surgical procedures over the next few weeks. Our surgeon can do the initial wash out until we can get them to orthopedic surgeons. We have one with a concussive head injury and we need to rule out a cervical spine fracture. We have two with broken bones. One has a fractured fibula in his lower leg and the other a broken forearm. The last has a minor bullet wound but it needs to be properly washed out under sterile conditions. There were a dozen others with minor cuts and scrapes, but they have been bandaged and/or sown up and returned to duty. We expect the helicopters to arrive any minute," the SMO finished.

"Thank you commander. We are all incredibly grateful for all that you, the corpsmen and medics did for our troops," Captain Rochelle said.

"Sir, if I may suggest. Now that the area is well secured with additional patrols, it could be useful if you could have the site surveyed. Then identify and plot as many positions as possible on the survey, including all of the sabotaged equipment. You should also take blood samples for DNA analysis. It will give us a clearer picture of what happened and identify the number of their wounded," the SMO added. What he didn't say was that this scenario will be dissected and taught to special operations teams for years to come. Knowing numbers and locations would be immensely helpful in recreating the event.

"Great idea Commander. We'll get right on it," Captain Rochelle said as the roar of helicopters flew overhead. "I guess that's your ride. Keep us updated on our troops."

"Aye Aye Sir," said the SMO as he headed for the door.

* * *

Later that afternoon, the SMO was checking on the newest additions to his ICU. The surgeon had spent most of the day in the OR working on the two most critical patients, and both were now stable. The surgeon was now in the OR washing out BM2 Rhinehart's leg wound that occurred when he had engaged the intruders. The one with the chest wound was awake and in pain, and the abdominal wound patient was still unconscious from the anesthesia. Sitting at the latter's side was SSgt Anglin., still in the clothes he had worn the day before, bloodstains, dirt, and all.

"Have they taken care of you yet?" the SMO asked.

"My arm? No. They said I'll have to wait till last. It's not really bothering me much. But they have brought me two great meals for lunch and dinner. I was really getting tired of those MREs after only four days," Anglin answered.

"Well, all you really need is to have that wound irrigated, and then we can give you some preventive antibiotics. Come on. I know the surgeon usually does this, but he's busy, and I have done plenty of these in the ER, so let's go. Your friend is in good hands," he said, nodding toward Lieutenant Commander Stooksbury, who was checking and charting his current vital signs.

Anglin followed the SMO to the treatment room. The SMO put on sterile gloves while Hospitalman Second Class Llortman set up a sterile work stand with a suture kit, sterile water, and a large syringe.

While he was irrigating and exploring the wound, the SMO said, "You did good out there."

"Are you kidding? I was scared shitless," Anglin replied.

"Yeah, so was I. But you still did what you were trained to do. And you really are a good shot. You took at least two of them down."

"I don't know. I should have seen those guys coming sooner," Anglin recalled.

"You saw them when I didn't, and you reacted appropriately. Then when the shooting was over, you jumped in and helped take care of the wounded. No, you did a damn fine job. You were scared but still able to do what your training taught you. You didn't freeze up," the SMO countered.

Anglin just thought it over while the SMO continued to work in silence.

After a while, the SMO said, "I couldn't help but notice that you were upset both times you saw me. I don't think we have ever met."

Anglin said nothing for a while, and the SMO didn't press further. Anglin let out a big sigh and finally said. "It wasn't you exactly. I was mad at doctors in general."

The SMO didn't say anything, letting Anglin get it out at his own pace.

"You see, it's my wife. We've had a rough marriage, and, ah, well, I just found out that she is having an affair. I found out later that it is with a medical student, and, well, I was just pissed at all of you. Honestly, though, the guy really didn't know that she is still married. Well, maybe he did, but she told him that we were separated. It has been tearing me up inside ever since I found out. I thought I had a lid on it until I saw you, then it all came flooding back. I suppose that's why I acted the way I did and why I wasn't paying attention while I was on patrol."

"I see," the SMO replied. "I know it's rough when a relationship breaks up. No matter what the reason is. And it is only worse if you keep it bottled up. Look, we have this guy who is a great listener. You should talk to him. Hey, I had to myself, back when my marriage broke up. One minute, I was pissed, the next depressed and in tears. Then I wanted to lash out, and moments later, I was pretending it wasn't really happening and that I could patch things up. The best thing I ever did then was to talk it out. It totally helped relieve that pressure I was feeling in my chest day and night."

"Maybe," Anglin replied.

"Good, let me hook you up with this guy. Heck, he can probably see you in an hour for a quick meet and greet. Your friend will probably sleep till morning." The SMO finished the last suture. Just then Vesel walked by the treatment room. "Vesel," the SMO called.

"Yes, sir," Vesel said, stepping in.

"Vesel, will you show Sergeant Anglin to the male ward shower and then get him settled into one of the semiprivate rooms so he can be near his friend. And if you don't mind, take him under your wing tomorrow and give him a tour of the ship and how to get to the galley. I'm sure you remember how lost you were the first time you were on a carrier."

"Aye-aye, sir. I'll be happy to. He was a big help back there, so I'll take good care of him," Vesel replied.

"So, Anglin, after your appointment, you can get some sleep, you've had a long day. But first, let's get you to that shower," the SMO said.

42 ESCALATION APPROVED
Hong Kong/PLAN Air Base, China

After another long hot shower to wake up, Yao dressed and headed to the restaurant for a light breakfast. He was just finishing when his phone rang.

"Yao," he said, not using his rank.

"Lieutenant Commander Yao, this is Lieutenant Ping," she said.

"Yes, Lieutenant," Yao responded curtly to the junior officer.

"Vice Admiral Jiang requests that you meet with him in thirty minutes rather than for lunch as was scheduled," Ping said professionally, ignoring his condescending tone toward her. "May I tell the Admiral you are on your way?"

"Yes, I'll leave now," Yao answered.

"He is at the same location as before," Ping added. "You do have the address?"

"Yes, yes, I have it," Yao answered as he pulled it up in his phone's Google Map history.

"Very good. See you shortly." Ping said just before the phone line disconnected.

After a fifteen-minute drive and twenty looking for a parking spot, Yao was ushered into his uncle's office ten minutes late by Ping. She led him to a couch seat on the opposite side of the room from the Admiral's desk.

The Admiral was at his desk in his large, comfortable office chair with his back to his desk and Yao. He was on the phone talking in low but serious tones as he seemed to be peering blankly out over the city through his massive window.

Yao sat there quietly, straining to hear any part of the conversation, but could make nothing out.

After five minutes, the Admiral hung up the phone and sat there quietly for another minute, continuing to look out the window. He slowly swiveled his chair back around to his desk and noticed Yao sitting there stiffly. Admiral Jiang acknowledged his presence with a slight nod. He closed out his computer screen, stood up, walked over, and sat in a chair opposite Yao. He sat there a moment rubbing his chin and the side of his face with his left hand, obviously deep in thought.

"Greetings, Commander. I am glad you could make it earlier," Jiang finally said. "I well remember my single days and the fun weekends I had on the town," he said seemingly forgetting that Yao was a LCDR in his thirties and should be no longer chasing skirts.

Yao, on the other hand, just smiled because the comment was, of course, right on target. "Yes, Admiral, it was no problem at all. I always welcome any chance to see my uncle."

Jiang briefly allowed a hint of a smile before returning to his serious troubled face. "Well," Jiang began. "You are well aware of what the Filipinos and Americans have done at Scarborough Shoal."

"Yes, Admiral. I was heavily involved in the planning of our response. We briefed the wing Commander yesterday," Yao said.

"Yes, of course. I know the plans," Jiang said matter-of-factly with a dismissive wave of his hand.

"That is all old news. What I am about to tell you is Top Secret. At least for now, until this information is released by the outside world," Jiang said. "That is why I have decided to share it with you now. It may be widely known soon, depending on what the Americans decide to do."

Yao leaned forward in curiosity saying nothing.

"Because we were not quite ready for our major fleet demonstration, we decided to send in a special operations team to slow down their work progress," Jiang said.

Yao could not suppress an immediate smile across his face at the news that someone was finally taking definitive action against the arrogant Americans.

"They were to go in quietly and sabotage their equipment, fuel, and water supplies in the night and slip away," Jiang continued. "Instead, the inept fools got themselves involved in a firefight. So much for them being the best of the best. What idiots!" Jiang spat. "We sent in a team of twelve, and they ended up with four killed and three wounded. The only good news is that they got everyone out and did not leave any equipment behind. It was a total fiasco!' Jiang ejaculated. "Still, it may yet prove useful to achieving our ultimate goal."

"Have the Americans said anything yet?" Yao asked as his joy turned to disappointment.

"No, nothing yet. Nothing official, unofficial, but it is now being reported on several news channels. They may be formulating their response. It happened just over four to five hours ago. Regardless, we have now lost the element of surprise, not that we had much advantage either way."

"Did the Americans have any casualties, Admiral?" Yao asked.

"Yes, we believe so. From the initial after-action reports we know that at least one American was hit at the very beginning. After that they have no idea. The had a running firefight as they extricated themselves. But there were likely to be others," Jiang answered.

Yao nodded and then said, "Admiral, President Hsu will now surely agree on us taking more aggressive action. Chinese blood has now been spilled. We must continue until they are driven into the sea."

"I totally agree. I was the one that had you planning on a response to this," Admiral Jiang said. "I had no guidance from the central party or President Hsu. But they are often very deliberate, and we must be prepared once they decide. I have been pressing for more aggressive action with my boss Admiral Kao. He agreed and has been in communication with the command staff and President Hsu's staff. They are well aware of our stance and recommendations."

Yao nodded as he took it all in.

"I hear that you were instrumental in getting your Air Wing Commander to request to be armed with live missiles and bombs," Jiang noted.

"Yes, Admiral," Yao said with a slight bow.

"Excellent work, Commander. I'm glad to see that my assessment of your potential was not misplaced," Jiang added. "I like your aggressive approach. China can go far if we have the proper attitude and motivation. We have been willing to bow to the military power of others for far too long. It is now time to assume our rightful place in the world."

"Thank you, Admiral," Yao replied, not wanting to spoil the moment by saying too much. But after a brief hesitation, he asked, "Admiral, will we be changing our plans to an attack rather than an air demonstration?"

Jiang smiled before he answered. "You do cut straight to the heart of the issue, Commander. That is indeed what I am pressing hard for. We have the advantage in ships and aircraft. The Americans have limited capability in the region even though they have been slowly increasing their presence over the past several years. They only have one aircraft carrier locally, and we could blow it out of the water if we wish. They do have fighter squadrons in Okinawa, Japan, and some in the Philippines. Their Japan-based carrier is currently in port and would take several days to arrive close enough to pose a threat. Now we have the clearest advantage. We should not wait until they can marshal their forces to oppose us. I will be insisting that you be allowed to carry live weapons. We need to be prepared just in case it gets ugly. We are engaging in an international game of chicken. It has already resulted in open hostility. But we still can deny that it was our forces. Some want no live ammo to prevent the possibility of another incident like has just occurred. But if they shoot and we are unarmed, we will be sitting ducks."

"Excellent, Admiral," Yao commented. "Surely, it will be approved."

"We can only hope. I and others doubt a simple air show demonstration will work this time. This is not the weak Filipinos we are dealing with. The Americans are used to getting their way on the battlefield. They will not readily back down," Jiang opined. "Unfortunately, from what I was just told, President Hsu is unlikely to authorize a full attack. He believes that just threatening one with an air demonstration is enough. In addition to Hsu's timidity, there are some on the senior staff of both services that fear any direct action. They prefer to stick with maneuver and threats rather than actual engagement. The fools do not see that even though the special forces were idiots, they have inadvertently provided us with an excellent opportunity to act decisively. So we at least want to go in fully armed. We still have an equal number on our side pressing our cause. We may yet prevail."

Yao nodded in frustration at the thought of the American's possibly being allowed to get away with their brazen act against their territory.

"Well, you are now up to speed, Commander. You should head back to your squadron. I have issued an order for all to report to duty. You can expect to be recalled soon, so you had better get on the road," Jiang said as he stood up. He reached out to shake Yao's hand and added, "Good luck, Nephew. And happy hunting!"

"Thank you, Uncle. I will make you proud."

Yao was just stepping out of the Admiral's office when his cell phone began to ring. It was the recall order to report back to base.

By 1500, Yao was busy reviewing and updating the details of the air operation. The day before they had developed the concept of the overall operation, how many and of what type of planes would be involved. It was to be two impressive displays emphasizing tight timing and formations.

Yao pushed for carrying live weapons and he had won the support of the wing commander who had recommended it up the chain. Knowing now that his uncle, Admiral Jiang was also strongly pushing for it he worked on the recommended mix of weapons to be carried by the aircraft in his squadron. Others in the squadron were busy working on the timing of take-off. This was not as straight forward as it seemed. The air wing's aircraft would be flying over the Vinson. Aircraft from units at other bases would be flying over Scarborough Shoal. They would ultimately have to coordinate takeoff times with them so that they meet the goal of hitting both targets at the same time.

They had the Vinson's current location from the spy ship that was constantly within 10 miles of the carrier. But anticipating where it would be at their take off time was trickier. It could move vast distances in twelve to twenty four hours. And they had yet to be given a tentative time on target. Additionally they had to consider fuel requirements and their operating range. It was not a simple in and out mission. They would have to burn some fuel at a marshalling point for the aircraft to assemble for the final push toward their target. All these unknowns impacted the mix of weaponry vs number of fuel tanks they may need.

The weapons that his squadron would carry on each fighter were two PL-12 air-to-air missiles and two YJ-83 antiship missiles. The YJ-83 carries a punch with 190 kg of high explosives. Not a carrier killer but it could inflict some severe damage. But a squadron of twelve aircraft launching these missiles could do major damage and take a carrier out of commission if not outright sinking it.

At 1700, they were sitting in their seats in the squadron auditorium for a meeting.

"Attention on deck!" someone called out, causing them to all jump to attention as Commander Chen strode to the front podium.

He left them standing at attention for a long moment as he scanned each of their faces.

"Gentlemen, please be seated," Chen said. "Good news. We have just received an alert message notifying us that the mission you have been planning is a go." Chen smiled.

A cheer broke out in the room at the news.

As the cheering quickly died out, Chen added, "And, yes, we have been authorized to carry live weapons."

An even louder second round of cheering broke out.

Waving them to quiet down, Chen added in a serious tone of voice, "We are not, I repeat *not*, authorized to release those weapons unless we receive authorization from central command. Not even if you are fired upon. A command aircraft will be in the area monitoring events and keeping a channel open to them in real time. If you are attacked our leaders will be aware immediately and can authorize you to return fire in self-defense. They could also possibly command a full-scale strike on either or both targets. They have insisted that the goal of this mission is to demonstrate to the Americans of the ultimate futility of trying to defend Scarborough Shoal. They have achieved a temporary advantage, but the American's are never willing to commit long term to such ventures. Our leaders believe that this is likely just some move by the American president to gain political advantage over his opponent in the next election. But we intend to show them of the untenable path they have embarked upon. We will help them decide sooner rather than later this time around to abandon this misadventure. Any questions?"

He stood there for a full thirty seconds before he saw a single hand go up.

"Commander Chen, sir, um, so if one of us is shot down, we have to wait for approval to shoot back?" asked one of the newer junior officers.

"Yes, that is exactly what your orders are," Chen replied. "But understand that in all likelihood this will never happen. And if it were to, then we would be cleared to fire back in mere moments."

Then Commander Chen noted that all the junior officers, the majority of his squadron pilots, appeared satisfied with this answer. He also noted a hint of skepticism from the older pilots. He hoped his facial expression did not betray his own doubts. He knew that in a dogfight or when dodging surface-to-air missiles, waiting even one minute for authorization to return fire would be an eternity. And that is if they could even decide that quickly, which he seriously doubted. There were just too many strong personalities on the central committee, and few would want to take responsibility for committing to an all-out shooting war. Not when they had carefully prepared and debated the details to avoid such a possibility. The one thing the central committee was actually good at doing was endless talk with few decisions.

Yao was smiling to himself that his uncle had won the argument on them being armed. He was soon lost in daydreaming on the various scenarios that could lead to him actually firing his missiles at America's ultimate war machine, the symbol of their power and pride. If only.

43 ON A BIG BOAT

USS *Vinson*, South China Sea

Staff Sergeant Anglin woke himself up yelling, "No! Stop!" He was having another nightmare about his wife Kara making love to a stranger. As his eyes opened, he had no idea where he was. The room was dark, and he could sense a slight movement rocking back and forth. It was a full minute before he realized he was on a ship. He reached over and felt the bandage on his left arm, which was now very tender. He rolled over and checked his watch to see that it was 0435. *Oh great*, he thought, as he rolled over trying to forget the nightmare. But of course, he couldn't. It was all too real. He laid there tossing and turning for half an hour and decided to go ahead and get up.

Sitting up in frustration, he decided to take the psychologist's advice and write his wife a letter telling her how he truly felt. Lieutenant Commander Frasier had said to pour out his heart and soul, hold nothing back, and then he could tear it up if he wanted. She would never need to see it. But it was supposed to help him come to grips with his own feelings and emotions. What did he have to lose? he thought. He sat their staring at the note pad for ten minutes in mental agony before finally putting the pen to paper.

Dear Kara,

So here I am in the middle of the Ocean on a ship. But that's another story. I guess if you were ever to get this you will have long heard the crazy circumstances that got me out here on an aircraft carrier. I may decide to put this in a bottle and toss it overboard. I don't expect that you will ever see this letter. But I need to write it as if you will someday. Maybe writing it will help me purge my soul of you somehow. I don't even plan on fixing any typos, I will just write as my mind wanders. I have been obsessing about you day and night. For you are the first thing on my mind when I wake up every day and the last thing on my mind when I go to bed at night. I have tried not to, but I am constantly thinking of you and what you have done has caused an ache deep in my soul.

It is hard to believe that it has been five years since we met, and my world was forever changed. From my perspective, our time together has truly been "the best of times and the worst of times." If I had the power, I would put the first two years I spent with you into a continuous loop and let my life consist of only that. Even now with all that's now happened, I would still do it. And if I could, I would take the last two years of our marriage, and I would rip them from my memory. My heart has been shattered into hundreds of pieces. At least, it feels that way.

I have loved you deeper than I had ever thought possible. But now, no matter what, though I don't see how I could ever trust you again, I believe I will carry the love we once had with me to my grave because I believe your essence merged with my soul and the two of us will forever be intertwined. I want you to know, though I am devastated, and our time together may be over, that I will do my best to forgive you. I can't live with the anger and hate continuing to tear me apart. I need peace to move on.

Your betrayal hurts more than words can say. We have had a rough couple of years, but I had believed that we could work things out and we could get back to what we once had. But given what you have been up to, I—.

Just then reveille began blaring through the ship's 1MC speakers, ending his soul-bearing writing. The sound of the bugle shifted his thoughts back to his friend Harold, and twenty-five minutes later, he had finished with the head and was dressed and at the ICU nurse's station checking on his status.

"He did fine out of surgery last night, and he has been asleep all night," Lieutenant Commander Stooksbury told him. "He is stable and should be waking up soon. You're welcome to sit with him if you wish."

"Thanks, ma'am. I believe I will," Anglin replied.

Anglin had been sitting by his sleeping friend only ten minutes when Hospitalman Second Class Vesel stuck his head into the ICU and asked, "Hey, Anglin, you hungry?"

Anglin looked Vesel's way and nodded. "Sure, I don't think he will be waking up anytime soon," Anglin replied softly as he got up to follow Vesel.

Vessel led him across the main medical ward through the jungle of about forty bunk beds. About a dozen or so had patients on the lower bunk. No one was on the upper levels. Once outside in the main passageway Vesel led them aft toward the main enlisted mess decks. Not that Anglin had any clue where he was. It all looked the same to him as they headed aft to the chow line.

"How do you know where you are," Anglin asked? "I was lost as soon as we left medical."

Vessel chuckled. "It takes a while, but it is pretty easy once you know what to look for. I remember getting lost for weeks my first time on the carrier."

"I bet," Anglin answered as they reached the end of the chow line. There were about fifty Sailors in line ahead of them.

"See that yellow square on the bulkhead with the black numbers and letters on it," Vessel pointed. That's called a Bullseye. Every compartment has one. That first number is the deck we are on. In this case we are on the 2nd deck. The hanger bay is the main deck or 1st deck. The numbers go up as you go down in decks. For the superstructure above the main deck they are labeled O1, O2, O3 and so forth as you go higher. The second number after the deck is the frame number. The frames of the ship begin with 1 at the bow and go to well over 200 toward the stern. They represent about 6' or so per frame. The third number represents the port and starboard position of the space. Odd numbers are right of center and even are on the left. The bigger the number the further out from the centerline it is. A zero would be for a centerline compartment. The letter tells what type of space it is. For example, L is for living space."

Anglin just nodded as he studied the bullseye as Vessel continued.

"So as you are going down a passageway like this one, if the frame numbers are getting bigger you are heading aft. And you can see that the space number there is even, so we are on the port side of the ship. Just memorize the space number in medical and you can eventually find your way back there."

As they picked up their trays Vesel asked, "How's the arm?"

Anglin glanced at it and said, not too bad, downplaying the constant ache he was feeling.

"Well, after morning muster, I'll check that bandage. It is soaking through a bit."

"Thanks," Anglin said. "And maybe you could give me some Motrin or something," he added as they finally reached the serving line. "Hey, is there any way I can get in touch with my wife? She has no idea where I deployed to. But I saw that the firefight was reported on CNN International on the ship's TV last night. They mentioned Navy Seabees and Air Force RED HORSE units being involved. So the word is out about what happened, and she may be worried. I would like to call Harold's wife too if possible.

"Sure, I can set it up," Vesel answered. "We Sailors have limited access to phone lines off the ship. But the docs have unlimited access so they can call about their patients as needed. We just need to use one of their phone lines. We corpsmen do it all the time."

"Thanks again," Anglin answered gratefully.

After breakfast, Anglin had a fresh bandage and his vitamin M was slowly taking the edge off the throbbing pain as Vessel led him into the officers offices. All the docs were busy with medical appointments. All except the SMO whose office was wide open, and he was out at meetings for a while. Vesel checked with Lieutenant Commander Alverez who said it was OK to use the SMO's phone and then he explained to Anglin how to make the call off the ship.

Anglin felt a cold sweat as he nervously held the ringing phone. He had been left alone in the office for some privacy. He didn't really know where to begin. Their last contact almost a week ago had ended badly. Logically he knew their marriage was over. But emotionally he was still pinging off the walls. Talking about it with the psychologist was a help but that was just starting. What would he say to her? Would she care? Maybe she was sorry and wanting to give their marriage a fresh start.

"Hello," Kara answered in her usual happy bouncing voice.

"Kara, it's Ron," he said trying to ignore the gnawing ache in his gut.

"Oh," she said after some hesitation. The excitement in her voice evaporating. "Hi, Ron. Are you okay?" she asked without much concern in her voice. "I really didn't expect to hear from you. I thought you were at some secret location or something."

"Yeah, I'm fine. Did you hear about what happened?" he asked.

"Um, no. I haven't heard anything from the other wives, and I don't watch the news. I rarely pay attention to it, as you know. Did something big happen?" she finally asked with some slight concern in her voice.

"Yeah, we were attacked the other night. Technical Sergeant Nickel was killed, and several others were wounded, including Harold Stringer."

"Oh my God! Are you kidding me?" she blurted out. "Are you serious? How is he? His wife must be worried sick."

"He has had surgery and should pull through. I'm here with him and waiting for him to wake up."

"Oh, that is a relief," she managed to say before a long, awkward silence began.

In her long silence, Anglin could only hear the background buzzing on the phone line as he struggled with what to say next. He also noted that she didn't seem to care where "here" was. "Kara, I...um, I don't know what to say. I miss you. I miss us."

A weak "Hmmm," was all Kara managed to reply. She just left him hanging. No me too, or I'm sorry. Not even a 'Forget it, Ron. It's over.'

"What about you?" he asked.

"I suppose," she said half-heartedly. Then finally she asked with some actual interest, "Do you know when you will be back?"

"No idea, probably still several months as originally planned," he replied.

"Okay," she said with some cheerfulness she couldn't hide.

Then more awkward silence. He didn't know what to say. She didn't seem to want to talk about them.

"Do you have anything to say, Kara?" he had to ask. "About us? About our future?" He thought he heard the doorbell ring in the background.

"Now's not a good time, Ron," she said hurriedly. "I have to go."

"Is someone at the door?" he asked suspiciously, realizing for the first time that it was about 1930 in the evening there. About the time her lover would arrive after work.

"Uh, no. It was on the TV. Gotta go," she said quickly before he heard the line go dead.

He sat there stunned. She clearly didn't want to talk to him, had little concern for his welfare, and rushed off the phone when the doorbell rang. Well, that seals it, he decided as his anger rose within him again.

He took a few minutes to compose himself and then started dialing his friend Harold Stringer's wife, Carla.

An hour later, Anglin was back in the ICU at Stringer's side after checking on the others from his unit. Carla had taken the news fairly well and insisted that he tell Harold that she loved him. Anglin was still ruminating in his self-pity about the disparity between Harold's marriage and his when Stringer opened his eyes and began to look around. He was clearly confused and had no idea what was going on or where he was. He was looking around when his eyes fell on Anglin's concerned face.

"About time you woke up," Anglin said, momentarily forgetting his worries and focusing on his best friend. "I thought you were going to sleep the whole day away."

"Where are we?" Stringer asked with a dry, raspy voice. "Any water?"

"We, my friend, are on the USS *Vinson* somewhere out in the ocean," Anglin answered as he poured him some ice water from the pitcher next to his bed.

"What happened?" Stringer looked at the IV pump that was giving him fluids and a steady dose of Demerol for the pain. "What the hell happened?" he asked again as he the sipped water.

"We were attacked—by the Chinese, but we can't prove it yet," Anglin answered. "And you, my friend, were shot. You took a bullet to your abdomen."

"I remember thinking someone had hit me with a two-by-four. Then just pain, noise, and confusion. Was anyone else hit?" Stringer asked.

"Yeah, almost a dozen," Anglin answered.

"Any killed?" Stringer asked the obvious question.

Anglin nodded and looked away as he said, "Nickel and one of the Navy SEALs. Most of the seriously injured were stabilized and flown out here for surgery and further treatment. The medics and the docs took good care of you guys."

After a long pause to take it in, Stringer said groggily, "Sergeant Nickel. He was a great guy." He yawned. "I'm still pretty tired. Can you let Carla know I'm okay?"

"I already have. She is pulling for you and wanted me to tell you that she loves you," Anglin told him.

"Thanks, man, you're the best," Stringer managed to say before drifting back to sleep.

Anglin sat there a moment watching his friend sleep before picking up the pad of paper and resuming work on his letter to Kara.

After an early lunch, Vesel took Anglin up to Vultures' Row up on the O-10 level of the island overlooking the flight deck. Anglin was mesmerized by all the flight activity. They had arrived at the beginning of a launch cycle. He was totally immersed in the launch of the roaring planes as they were catapulted into the air. He stayed there until the last of the recovering planes had landed.

"That was amazing to watch, Vesel. Definitely took my mind off my problems for a while," Anglin said. "Hey, I need to get going. I have another session with LCDR Frasier, your psychologist at 1430. CDR Lloyd thinks that he can help me through some things."

"Well for what its' worth, commander Frasier has a great reputation on this ship," Vessel explained. "Ignore his looks. His gruff demeanor, bald head, and fireplug body may make him look like a 6' tall ogre, but he is actually very easygoing. And I hear he is a great listener."

As they headed down, Vesel gave Anglin a tour of the hanger bay packed with aircraft.

"What are those?" Anglin asked, pointing to the trunk-size white boxes with bright-red crosses painted on them. "I've seen them all over the ship."

"Those are our mass-casualty boxes," Vesel explained. "If the ship is damaged, we have these boxes strategically located around the ship. So no matter what happens or where we are hit, we should have some first aid equipment nearby. We also have five Battle Dressing Stations around the ship that are mini-clinics.

"Impressive," Anglin commented. "Has a carrier had to use these in recent history?"

"Hmmm, my history may be a bit fuzzy, but I believe that no carriers that I know of have had combat damage since WWII," Vessel answered. "Though, during the Vietnam War there was a bomb accident on the Forrestal that killed well over a hundred. Bombs exploded and the fires took over eight hours to contain. What isn't as widely known is that the medical department was busy that day with over one hundred sixty injured. The Vinson's medical department has only a maximum of fifty beds."

"That sounds like a pretty rough time they had," Anglin noted.

"Yeah, I bet it was, Vessel replied as he led them into main medical. "Since then the Navy has had every Sailor trained in shipboard firefighting. And they almost always show a video of the Forrestal fire. They make sure everyone is well aware of how bad it can be. Since then the Navy has had several shipboard fires but their crews were able to get them under control. There was a pretty big fire on the carrier George Washington a few years ago that almost got out of control."

"With all this metal everywhere you wouldn't think there is much around that can burn. Well anyway, thanks for the tour. Watching the planes take off and land was great. I think I'll go check on my friend before my appointment."

"Anytime," Vesel said as he returned to his office.

44 CALM BEFORE THE STORM
USS *Vinson*, South China Sea

"CDR Lloyd was up at reveille, grabbed a coffee in the wardroom and headed to the ICU to check on the patients. He had just reviewed the charts and gotten an update from the overnight crew when his brick barked to life.

"Ninety nine, everyone listen up, the CO's morning meeting has been changed to 0930," said Commander Thomas, the big XO.

All the other HODs began acknowledging and the SMO waited for his opening while checking his watch and noting that the meeting was being delayed an hour and a half. Finally he got to say, "SMO copy."

The chatter on the brick had just died down when he heard. "SMO, Captain. Report to the bridge."

"Aye, Aye Captain," the SMO answered. "On my way."

Up on the bridge, he gave the CO a more detailed account of what had happened the day before on Scarborough Shoal. He had only given the briefest of reports the day before. After a fifteen minute discussion the SMO had to excuse himself because he had been requested to brief the Admiral and his staff in twenty minutes on the same thing.

As the SMO neared Jeanna's office in Admiral country, he could hear voices behind the closed door, so he headed on into the conference room to the right. He had hoped for a minute to chat with her since he hadn't had the chance since leaving for Scarborough Shoal.

He was headed for his usual seat in the second row of chairs behind the Chief of Staff when the Operations Officer, Captain "Speedtrap" Ball, waved him over to the conference table.

"SMO, sit here," Speedtrap said, pointing to a chair next to him. "Just a limited group today. One hell of a week you've been having."

"You can say that again," the SMO replied.

"Well, you can tell us all about it in a few when the Admiral and the others get here," Speedtrap added as several other key staff members arrived. "Glad you are okay."

Master Chief Goodpine stood to call the room to attention when the Admiral waved him down.

"As you were," the Admiral said as he got into his seat.

"Welcome back, SMO" Rear Admiral LaSalle said as he entered the briefing room with Jenna right behind him. Well, SMO a lot has happened in the three days since you last briefed us."

"Yes, sir," the SMO agreed.

"SMO, I don't know whether to consider you lucky or unlucky," the Admiral went on. "You have been in a knife fight, a dogfight, and now a gunfight! I think we will keep you on the ship for a while to give you a break."

"Thanks, Admiral, it has been crazy," the SMO said.

"So, SMO, we have reviewed the official report of what happened out there. Tell us how you saw it," the Admiral requested.

Over the next fifteen, minutes he retold the events from his perspective, starting with being on patrol with Bosun's Mate Second Class Rhinehart through to the evacuation of the patients to the ship.

The Admiral and his staff sat in rapt attention through it all.

"Hell of a story, SMO," the Admiral said, shaking his head. "So, why do you think the shooting started?"

"Sir, I agree with the assessment that it was just plain bad luck and someone not having proper discipline," the SMO answered. "I don't think they had intended to do much more than get some good reconnaissance and do some minor sabotage that could possibly be passed off as accidents or mechanical equipment failures. Just enough little things to slow down the building progress. From my perspective, the firefight was a bit of an accident. The Chinese team was probably almost finished and were about to be on their way out when they were discovered. I think someone got trigger happy when one of their guys was apprehended. I do think they had clear orders to not get caught. A captured Chinese Special OPS soldier would be hard to deny. As it is, even though it got very ugly and likely resulted in fatalities on both sides, they can deny all day that it wasn't them. And they have enough allies in the world in their back pocket to back up their denial at the UN. So, no body, no proof."

The Admiral nodded thoughtfully and then asked, "Speaking of that, how was the construction going?"

"I'm no engineer, but pretty well from what I can tell," the SMO surmised. "I sat in on one of their shift change briefings, and they appeared to be almost a day and a half ahead of their schedule."

"Really? This early on," asked the logistics officer, Commander Grant, sarcastically. "Any reason why?"

"That's what I heard. They are working 24-7 out there. But it appears that there has developed a bit of a competition between the Navy Seabees and the Air Force RED HORSE units. And not only that, but within each unit, the day and night crews are trying to outdo each other," the SMO explained.

"Nothing like a little interservice rivalry and unit pride to get them motivated," commented Captain Mike Deville from Plans.

"Glad to hear it is progressing well. Hopefully, this incident won't delay them much," the Admiral said. "It's unlikely they will try that again."

"That's true admiral," added Commander Monroe the intelligence officer. And to make sure, Filipino troops are already arriving on the island early to provide a more robust security presence. They will be providing a heavy patrol ashore, and they are also doubling the patrol boats in the lagoon and outside the reefs. But that doesn't mean that the Chinese are giving up. We need to be prepared in case they try some other stunt."

"George, what's the latest from Seventh Fleet?" the Admiral asked his communications officer.

"Sir, as you know we have been placed on heightened alert. But we are still officially at DEFCON 3," said Commander George Grayson, the Admiral's head of communications. "I have heard through the grapevine that the president is being advised by the Joint Chiefs of Staff to go to DEFCON 2 in the Seventh Fleet AOR."

"Are they sending us additional assets?" the Admiral asked of the group.

"Sir, the cruiser USS *Antietam* and destroyer USS *Mustin*, are getting underway from Yokosuka, Japan, and headed our way," began Commander Hill, Resources and Assessment. "The USS *Ronald Reagan* is delayed undergoing maintenance and system upgrades. The shipyard is now working 24-7 to get it completed. The USS *Nimitz* has been on their last phase of workups off the coast of San Diego and is being diverted our direction early. But it will take them ten days to get here."

"So, things are heating up, and it looks like we will be the only carrier on station for a while," the Admiral said. "Speedtrap, let's keep our normal routine flight ops the next several days. I have ordered the CAG to have four F-35s on Alert Five for the next forty-eight hours. I want to be ready for any surprises. We will also be doing an unscheduled General Quarters drill this evening. I don't want to wait until our scheduled weekly drill this Thursday. SMO, thanks again for the brief. And I am sorry for putting you in danger, but all in all, you were right where you needed to be. We could have lost more troops if you hadn't been there. That is all for now." The Admiral stood up to leave.

They all rose to attention as he departed the room, and then they all began to follow him out.

Jenna, who had remained silent during the whole meeting, lingered as the others left. She caught Derek's attention as he finished chatting with Master Chief Goodpine.

Once he was looking at her, she nodded for him to follow her as she headed to her office. Once in her office behind closed doors, she just stood there with a pensive look on her face.

"Damn, Derek. You really had me worried when we heard that there was an attack on the base. We only heard that there were casualties. At first, I thought, well, he is there where he can help take care of the wounded. Then I got to thinking how you tend to end up in the middle of everything, and I got really scared for your safety. And apparently for good reason."

"Yeah, it got pretty hairy there for a while," Derek said. "The Air Force Sergeant with me at the time save our asses. He took out two guys sneaking up on us. He did pretty well for a carpenter never trained for hard combat." As he was talking he continued to ease closer to her and reached out for her hand as he finished. He gently squeezed it and said, I was busy out there, but I did find myself thinking of you quite a bit."

"Oh really. Do tell," she said, playfully squeezing back. "How so?"

"Well, while on patrol with Rhinehart, we kept hearing the loud croaking of frogs. Anyway, we came on more than one couple, um, that were being very froggy. They were really getting it on, and, well, I couldn't help but be jealous of them and wishing I was with you again."

She leaned in to him and said, "Well, I've never been compared to a frog before, but I'm game if you are." She continued forward until their lips touched into a soft kiss, and Derek wrapped his arms around her.

After second longer kiss, they gently pulled away.

"Wow!" Derek said a bit breathlessly. "I am definitely feeling froggy now!"

She pushed him away playfully. "Well, not now Kermit," she said. "I have work to do."

"Yeah, me too," he agreed. "I have to get to a morning meeting that starts soon. Maybe later?"

"How about 1430?" she asked. "We can have some time before I go for my afternoon workout in the gym."

"Sounds great. See you then," he answered with a big grin.

At 0930, the SMO was just in time for the Captain's morning update meeting. The talk was of the events at Scarborough Shoal, and everyone, of course, wanted to hear his story. After the intel update, the Captain asked him to tell what had happened. All the department heads were anxious to hear his part in it. He told pretty much the same story he had earlier given the Admiral.

The Captain then told everyone of the flight operations plan and their heightened alert status. He explained the planned GQ drill later at 1900. He wanted to make sure that each and every department was passed the word that he expected them to be on top of their game. He also wanted to know of any issues that would affect their combat capability. Each department head in turn gave a quick status of their department and any issues they were having. The SMO reported on his wounded patients and that they were ready for anything.

After the meeting, the SMO headed to wardroom three for lunch. It took him a while to get there because the word was out on him, and half the people he met in the P-way wanted to stop and chat to hear his story. When he finally got there they were serving Mexican and he grabbed a burrito, tamale, and plenty of rice.

He spotted an open seat at a table with the MAO, LCDR Alverez and LCDR Frasier the psychologist.

"Mind if I join you," asked the SMO. One reason he picked them was that they already had heard his story and he didn't want to have to tell it again during lunch. The other reason was he wanted to hear what LCDR Frasier thought of SSgt Anglin so far.

"Not at all, SMO," the MAO answered for the both of them. "Please do."

"You're looking well for someone recently shot at," Frasier said. "Did you sleep well?"

"I did thanks. Like a baby," the SMO answered honestly. "So, what do you think of our Air Force sergeant? And thanks for seeing him as such a short notice."

"No problem SMO. Just another day at the office," Frasier answered. "Well it's the typical relationship gone bad scenario we see all the time out here. She appears to have really done a number on him. From what I have learned so far their marriage had been on the rocks for years, but he was just used to it. He just found out that she is sleeping around. What is unique in this case is he knows that it is a medical student. Hence his initial animosity toward you that you noted. Anyway, he is at least talking about it and that is a good start. He will be on the emotional roller coaster for a while, but we can help him through it. I can find a colleague at his home base to continue counseling him. He is actually my second appointment after lunch."

"Sounds good. Do what you can until he heads back to his unit in a few days. I think they will let him stay here with is buddy until he is ready to be air evac'd back stateside."

Back in his office after lunch, Lieutenant Commander Alverez stuck her head in and asked, "So really, how are you holding up?"

"I'm fine. Don't worry about me," the SMO replied. I've seen too much blood and guts over the years to have this faze me much. Both on the battlefield and in the ER. I am however getting tired of everyone wanting to hear about what happened."

"You can't really blame them, SMO," Alverez answered. "You were already highly respected as the head doc and your active SEAL background. But now you are using your SEAL skills more than being a doc. Everyone is talking about you."

"I guess that is to be expected," the SMO answered. "It's just that I still have a lot to focus on and the constant discussions in the passageways is slowing me down. It took me thirty minutes to get here from the wardroom." He tried to change the subject. "Now, to more pertinent matters, how do you think the Jags will do against the New Orleans Saints this week? We have a good shot at beating them. The Saints just don't have a powerhouse offense any more since Drew Brees retired."

Ignoring the growing pile of charts, he instead decided to catch up backlog of emails over the next few hours—ship business and issues, assignment requests for Sailors with various chronic conditions, and some from friends. He hit send on the latest email response and leaned back to stretch when he noted the time on his wall clock: 1405. A big grin crossed his face as he thought of seeing Jenna. He had just enough time to get an update on his ICU patients and get up to her office by 1430.

On his way up, the angst he was carrying about his ex-wife Rachel bored back into his consciousness again. He was now envisioning his future with Jenna, but he couldn't yet shake the recurring guilt he felt at the thought that he was letting down his kids and Rachel.

When he reached her office, he stood their admiring Jenna as she was turned away staring at her computer screen. He didn't want to interrupt anything important, and he was definitely enjoying the view. He gave her thirty seconds before he knocked lightly on her door frame.

"You still busy? I can come back later," he said, hoping the answer was no.

"Not really. I'm pretty caught up and was just killing time," she said with a smile and to his obvious relief. "Have a seat, Derek."

"Door open or closed," he asked.

"Closed is fine," she said nonchalantly. "If they need me, they can knock."

He sat down across from her and relaxed. "Anything new on the Chinese front?"

"The president has issued a formal complaint to China and with the UN," she started. "They, of course, have denied it but have otherwise been pretty quiet. Their lap dog supporters in the UN are demanding that the president provide proof. Which we, of course, don't have, other than Chinese-made brass from their ammo. Which isn't really proof."

"None of that is surprising," Derek answered. "Anything else?"

"Several of their ships that sortied before we began operations at the shoal have been loitering within forty to fifty miles out."

They sat there quietly a moment looking into each other's eyes.

"You are looking wonderful," Derek said.

"Mm," she replied with a coquettish smile. "And you, my dear, are looking vigorous! In spite of the week you have had."

"So," he stumbled out. "It looks like Dubai is our next scheduled port."

"You anxious to see the desert?" she asked playfully.

"Seeing the desert isn't what comes to mind," he answered.

"Do tell," she said.

"I know this great little restaurant downtown," he began.

She waved him off. "As I recall you promised me a nice dinner in Hong Kong that I never got."

"Not my fault," he said defensively. "At least, we got to have dessert." He gave her a big grin.

"Several times, as I remember it," she said, leaning forward and reaching both hands across her desk to his.

"Well, that particular dessert is still on the menu if you like," he answered gently taking her hands in his.

"And I may want my sweets before we go out for the main meal," she answered, feeling the thrill of his touch.

"Your wish is my command, my dear," he whispered.

She just looked back and him and nodded her head slowly and deliberately. "I think we both like how this is going," she said.

"I most cert—," he began as Rachel's smiling face, and then his kids, intruded on the moment. He let go of her hands and sat back in his chair with a trouble look on his face.

"What?" Jenna said, alarmed at his sudden change of mood. "What is it, Derek?"

He sat there in silence for an uncomfortably long time before speaking. "Jenna, before this goes any further, there is something I need to tell you."

"Oh," she said, sitting back and distancing herself while she looked intently into his anxious face.

"Jenna," he began slowly, "it's just that, well, um, well, Rachel and I started seeing each other again a few months before we deployed. We were taking it slow, but she has made it clear she wants to get back together. I thought I wanted it too until you showed up."

"Seeing how?" she asked, cutting to the chase. She could tell by how he began to squirm what the answer truly was.

He dodged the answer and continued. "I thought that for us and the kids that it would be best all around. Now I am not so sure. The best Rachel and I ever had pales in comparison to what we have. But..."

"But," Jenna said answering for him. "But you are feeling obligated to do what is right for your family. Yeah, I know. I've heard it before," she added coldly.

"That's true, Jenna, but this time I..."

Gong, Gong, Ggong, Ggong blared the alarm from the 1MC speaker in her office before he could finish his explanation.

"General Quarters! General Quarters! All hands, man your battle stations."

Derek looked quizzical and said over the alarm announcement, "The drill isn't supposed to be until 1900."

"Set condition Zebra," the 1MC voice continued.

"I guess he wants to keep the crew on their toes," Jenna said over the announcement as they both stood up, until they heard, "This is *not* a drill!" said the 1MC voice emphatically.

The alarm was sounding again as surprise and worry crossed each of their faces.

Derek stepped hurriedly toward the door and paused. He turned back toward Jenna, reached out, and gave her hand a quick squeeze, and said, "We'll have to finish this later. Stay safe." There was clear concern for her in his eyes before he turned and bolted out the door.

He heard her say, "You too," with a choked voice as he rounded the corner heading to the nearest ladder leading down to medical. He then realized that he had seen tears in Jenna's eyes.

45 AIR STRIKE

South China Sea

Lieutenant Commander Yao was finally heading out to his jet, but he was royally pissed. He had awoken that morning happy and thrilled at the day's prospects. The massive air demonstration against the American carrier and Scarborough Shoal was all planned out to the last detail was falling apart.

The day turned sour soon after arriving at the squadron that morning. Yao had noticed LT Suyong the intel officer keeping an eye on him. And on several occasions Yao thought he had seen a smug smile cross his face. It was definitely not the cowed look he usually elicited from the junior officer. Suyong surely knew something was up and it didn't bode well for him. Yao had an ever increasing sense that the hammer was about to drop and fall squarely on him. If the truth about his fight with the American's became widely known he could become a laughing stock and worse, be reassigned to a non-flying job. He had seen it happen to others. In fact he had orchestrated it himself on one occasion. Now '*he*' seemed to be in the crosshairs. Maybe Yao could find some way to discredit Suyong, he thought for a moment. For now it was to everyone's benefit to believe the original story. No one wants to upset the apple cart before such an important mission. Besides, maybe his wingman was right. He could try and take a less condescending approach to Suyong and others.

With Yao's push and that of others in key places like his uncle, they were going in fully armed. He was hoping the stupid Americans would blunder in their response and give the provocation to turn the *Vinson* into a huge smoking hole in the water.

But obviously someone higher up the food chain had similar thoughts. Yet that was not the worst of it. The massive low level fly over of the carrier at five hundred feet was now changed to two thousand feet. This would send their intended message without risking a miscalculation on the American's part, so they had been told. There was even talk of disarming all the aircraft. But this was rejected only because there was not enough time to download all the weapons without throwing off their scheduled takeoff times.

Well, thank the ancestors for small favors, he thought.

As he approached his assigned aircraft, he recognized the female crew chief and broke into a big grin as he recalled her coveralls being ripped open exposing her. He had no doubt that she was now wearing both a regulation T-shirt and bra. He found himself wishing he could find out for sure as she snapped to attention and saluted as he approached.

"Good morning, Commander," said the young Airman, holding her salute and waiting for his response.

He continued his approach and leered at her. He carefully appraised her from head to toe, remembering what lay concealed beneath that work uniform.

After what was an uncomfortably long time for the crew chief who was well aware of his leering eyes, he finally gave her a lazy salute in return.

"Let us hope so," Yao said, handing her his helmet bag to hold as he turned to begin his preflight walk-around inspection.

The crew chief followed him at a respectful distance ready to answer any questions he may have. Most pilots want a report on the status of their plane when they arrived in case any issues had been discovered after they had reviewed the maintenance log. But the word was out on Commander Yao that one did not speak unless he asked a question, which rarely occurred.

Yao stopped briefly to smile as he gazed at the powerful YJ-83 antiship missiles and then completed his preflight.

Minutes later, the sound of dozens of jet engines begin their whine up to idle speed, including Yao's.

Yao was leading a flight of six aircraft as part of the massive sixty plane formation headed to the carrier. Twenty minutes later all were airborne. They had completed a loose rendezvous west of the base and were now heading east out over the Taiwan Strait. As they crossed the shoreline he used his assigned call sign as leader of the sixth flight of six aircraft to call, "Cobra Six-One, feet wet." As planned they skirted just south of Taiwanese airspace.

They surely are aware of our presence, thought Yao. Now let's see how they respond, if at all. He smiled inwardly at the surprise they would get on the return trip home.

As they got closer to the Vinson's last reported position the secure radio calls made it clear that the formation leader was having trouble identifying which radar target was the American carrier. The South China Sea is a remarkably busy maritime area with almost a hundred ships traversing the area at any given time. Soon they received a real-time intelligence update from the Chinese spy ship on the carrier's location in the busy waterway.

One hundred miles from the carrier, they were told to tighten up their formation and descend to their planned altitude of two thousand feet. At that distance, they were ten minutes out.

"Incoming contacts," a voice from one of the lead aircraft called out.

"How many?" asked another that Yao recognized as the formation leader, Cobra One-One.

"Stand by," the first voice said. "I count twenty-six solid contacts at eighty miles. There also appears to be some other intermittent contacts in the general area, but they appear to be migrating birds most likely."

"Cobra One-One, copy," said the formation leader. "Proceed with plan Alpha."

Yao was both excited and pleased with what he had heard. The American's were responding but were clearly outnumbered almost three to one. What could they do anyway. It was officially international airspace, though China considered it theirs, and therefore by the rules the Americans played by, they both had the right to be there. All that was likely to occur was that they would get a nice escort as they overflew the carrier. Oh, how he wished that this were a real attack mission. But he was still happy to be a part of even this timid response.

Things were about to get fun, Yao thought with a grin hidden under his oxygen mask. He welcomed the slight chance to get revenge for his less than ideal performance against the American fighter before the F-35s had shown up.

F-35s! "Lead, Cobra Six-One, those reported birds could be stealth F-35s," Yao interjected hurriedly.

"Copy Six-One," the formation leader responded.

"How many birds do you see," asked the leader.

"Twelve, and they are keeping pace with the other twenty-four contacts," came a response.

In the long silence that followed, Yao realized that their numerical advantage had dropped from almost three to one to now less than two to one. He was sure that the formation Commander and every other pilot was drawing the same conclusion. Surely, this would not stop them. They had known about the F-35s and taken that into account in their planning. But the silence of the Commander was disconcerting. Could the sudden appearance of these stealth aircraft have rattled him? Surely not.

"Intercept in three minutes," someone called out, breaking the long silence.

There was still no reply from Cobra One-One. The lead aircraft should soon be able to see the approaching aircraft.

Then it finally came. "This is Cobra One-One, switch to plan Charlie. I repeat, switch to plan Charlie."

"*Charlie!*" Yao shouted into his facemask. Not Charlie! Plan Charlie had them now approaching the carrier even higher at five thousand feet, but not directly overflying it. Charlie had them offsetting by two miles. They would just be barely visible on the carrier. This to Yao was almost worse than doing nothing. It showed weakness, not resolve. He pounded his fists on the cockpit dashboard in frustration. All that planning, all that effort. For what? A nonthreatening distant flyby. They would just be seen as inquisitive tourists, not a threatening military force. He had wanted to personally be a part of an obvious poke in the eye of the arrogant Americans. Now they were resorting to a friendly wave.

Each section leader acknowledged in turn, and reluctantly even Yao through gritted teeth.

"Talley six, twelve o'clock high."

For decades the Chinese have been intercepting intelligence gathering aircraft that were flying off the Chinese coast in international airspace. The Americans had complained for many years that these intercepts were becoming increasingly aggressive and dangerous. Rather than keep a safe distance from the large lumbering military aircraft, the Chinese had frequently flown dangerously close and on many occasions performed unexpected maneuvers. Once, they had actually collided with an American plane causing it to make an emergency landing on a Chinese island. Of course the Chinese claimed it was the fault of the American pilot. In reality, the Americans had never been aggressive or mounted a serious response in these encounters. They just flew straight and level, recording the events on video or turned to return to their base. The Americans had a history of being relatively passive. This historical behavior was part of their calculations as they formulated their plan.

Having anticipated being intercepted, their plan was to stay in their tight formations and let the Americans follow them helplessly on either side as they approached the carrier. So as planned, they held formation as they climbed back up to five thousand feet as the American fighters came into view.

The American F-18s divided into two groups with each swinging into position with ten on either side of the large Chinese formation. The F-35s split high and low as they approached. The higher section maneuvered to just above the leader's formation. The lower group of six mirrored that maneuver to come up from below. They then tightened their squeeze by the F-35s moving within thirty feet of the lead aircraft from above and below as the F-18s moved in tight from the sides, all without radio calls. In the past, the Americans were jabbering away, telling the Chinese to back off or move away. The American silence was both eerie and intimidating.

The lead formation of Cobra One-One was completely boxed in. The Chinese were completely at the mercy of the surrounding American fighters pressing ever closer to his aircraft. Instead of following his desired heading, Cobra One-One was now forced to focus on intense close formation flying to avoid hitting someone. Ever so subtly, the Americans changed their heading to the south. It was like leading a bull by the nose. The others in the Chinese formation could only follow their leader as best they could.

"This can't be happening!" Yao yelled. Within two minutes, the entire formation was heading southwest away from the carrier.

Yao was seething in frustration as he observed all this from his aft position back in the formation.

Then it came, not a call for an aggressive response. No, it was something else entirely.

"Cobra flight. This is Cobra One-One. Break formation as briefed and return to base. I repeat, return to base. Cobra One-One, out."

"No! This can't be happening!" Yao screamed in a blind rage as he pounded against the canopy with his left fist. "Doesn't any of our wing leadership have a spine?"

Along with the others, once the Americans had backed away, he and his group of six slowly dropped back from the other groups. Then each group was to fly an assigned separate path directly over Taiwan on the way back. It was to be further intimidation of the breakaway province.

Yao stopped pounding on his canopy and was reluctantly pulling up the previously entered flight path data for this important but minor part of their mission, called "Wolf Fang." Normally they had to avoid Taiwanese airspace though some incursions were sanctioned on a regular basis. Yao didn't think things could get any worse.

"Cobra flight. This is Cobra 11, Cancel Wolf Fang. I repeat, cancel Wolf Fang. Return to Base. Cobra 11 out."

"Noooooooo!" Yao yelled now in a blind rage. This cannot be happening. Chinese blood has been spilled! "The Americans need to be taught a lesson once and for all," he inadvertently said on the radio as he did a snap steep-banking turn back toward the *Vinson*. As soon as the turn was started, he flipped a switch on his control stick bringing up the antiship missile targeting on his Heads-Up Display. They were still just within missile range.

The American fighters saw him and started maneuvering to intercept him.

"Cobra Six-One, this is Cobra Six-Two. What are you doing?" called his wingman and friend, Lieutenant Junior Grade Hu, who was turning to keep pace with his section leader.

Yao did not answer. He was concentrating on the ship contacts at the last reported location for the carrier. He had three contacts there and one was clearly larger than the others and matched the radar signature of American carriers that he had studied for years. He switched on the master arm switch to the two YJ-83 antiship missiles. Within seconds, Yao heard the locked-on tone in his headset. Before the American fighters had a chance to close the distance, Yao had thumbed the missile fire switch twice. Both missiles were instantly off the rails and headed toward the *Vinson*, each with its 190-kilogram warhead. The missiles were fire and forget, needing no further input from the J-15's radar.

He took a moment to yell, "Take that, you Yankee bastards!" Again not realizing he had transmitted it to the world.

With grim satisfaction, he banked his plane toward home and kicked in his afterburner to catch up with his formation. He had put the accursed Americans in their place, hopefully at the bottom of the South China Sea. There was nothing LT Suyong or his squadron Commander could do to touch him. He would be a genuine hero now. He had the full support and confidence of his uncle, Vice Admiral Fa Jiang and others like him in the military and government.

"What have you d—," came the broken call from his wingman.

Yao turned to look back at where he expected his wingman to be a half mile back on his right. But Hu had been slow to match his lead's turn away from the *Vinson*. All Yao saw was black smoke and falling debris in a fireball. His friend, Lieutenant Junior Grade Gan Hu, had been blown out of the sky.

46 MASS CASUALTY
USS *Vinson*, South China Sea

The SMO made it into medical well before they started closing down and dogging closed all the hatches and scuttles. He went straight to main medical's central space next to the treatment room. He watched as the personnel assigned to the medical department for general quarters were filing in. It is the area where the corpsmen and officers hold morning muster each day and later becomes the patient waiting area for sick call. Getting settled at the desk with a clipboard in his hand was the phone talker. He was a non-medical Sailor assigned to the department strictly for communications using the emergency back-up sound powered phones that were wired throughout the ship. The ship's radios and telephones were more easily compromised with ship damage and this old tried and true system was still used just in case. Another group of ten non-corpsmen was sitting on the deck in the corner. They were there to be stretcher bearers. He then headed to the ward and ICU to do a quick check that preparations there were underway.

Assessing that all was well, he headed straight to the phone talker and asked, "Have all the Battle Dressing Stations reported in yet?"

"Yes, sir, the last one just reported in manned and ready," answered the phone talker.

"Good," the SMO replied with satisfaction. "Let me guess, Battle Dressing Station Four reported in last."

"Yes, sir, as always, sir," the phone talker replied.

Those guys in the aft BDS are always slow reporting in. Why? The SMO asked himself. After all, he thought, it wasn't all that far back on the starboard side aft on the second deck, the same as main medical. BDSs five and six, fore and aft up on the O-3 level, were much further away, yet they always were quick to report in.

"What is it with those guys?" the SMO said aloud to no one in particular. He was definitely going to have to have another talk with HM1 Nebo, the Independent Duty Corpsman that was in charge of that particular BDS. *They need to get their act together*, he thought as he headed to his office for his float coat and cranial. He wanted to have them handy in case he had to respond up on the flight deck.

As he reached behind his office door for his float coat and cranial hanging there, he heard the 1MC announcement that condition Zebra was reported set throughout the ship. *Hmmm, set in just under eleven minutes. Not too shabby*, he thought. His TV as usual was tuned to the PLATT channel that showed flight operations up on the flight deck. He noted that the Alert F-35s were being launched. He was watching the last plane takeoff when he heard a knock at his door.

Standing in the door was Lieutenant Commander Alverez and Senior Chief Owens with expectant looks on their faces.

"Any idea what's going on, SMO?" Alverez asked.

"Not a clue," the SMO answered. "But they just launched the alert fighters."

"Got to be the Chinese," Owens opined.

"You want get any argument from me," the SMO answered. "You guys all set?"

"Yes, sir, SMO," they both said in unison.

The SMO smiled at their simultaneous response. "Excellent, I'm going to make the rounds like I usually do. Well as much as I can without breaking Zebra. You two stay on top of things here. And keep your game face on."

"Aye-aye, sir," they again replied in unison.

The SMO headed back past the treatment room and down the short passageway that had the entrances to the lab, surgical suit, and X-ray and proceeded into the main ward. He noted that the ward currently had only thirty six bunk beds set up. Part of the ward space had been left open in order to accommodate a physical therapy section. If need be, that equipment could be set aside and the remainder of the fifty bunk beds could be set up from storage in less than an hour. Well, let's hope we don't need them he decided.

At the nurses station he inquired about the ICU patients. "Commander Stooksbury, how are our guests doing?" he asked of his ICU nurse.

"They are all stable and doing well. They are all awake, and we are keeping their pain controlled," Stooksbury answered.

"Good to hear," the SMO answered. "So if it hits the fan, they will not need too much babysitting."

While looking into the ICU, he noted Staff Sergeant Anglin heading his way. He obviously had been sitting with his friend.

"Commander Lloyd, can you please tell me what the heck is going on?" Anglin asked.

"We're at General Quarters. We are locked up tight, and everyone has manned their battle stations."

"Is it some kind of drill?" Anglin asked.

"I'm afraid not. This one is for real," the SMO answered.

"Oh shit!" Anglin said, wide eyed. "Oh, I'm sorry, sir. Please forgive my language."

"No need, Sergeant," the SMO answered. "I think that sentiment pretty well sums up what we are all feeling right about now."

"What do you want me to do sir?" Anglin asked.

"You just stay here and keep your friend company," the SMO answered.

"I don't want to just be sitting around if I can be helpful," Anglin said earnestly.

"Thanks for the offer, the SMO replied. "But I don't want you getting lost. This ship is a whole different beast to navigate when every door and hatch is shut. You can barely find your way to the head as it is."

"Sir, I really want to help if something happens," Anglin said with a hint of pleading in his voice. "I can't just watch from the sidelines."

The SMO was about to refuse outright when he recalled how useful he had been caring for the wounded on Scarborough Shoal. He had held up well and been a real asset. Though not an official medic, his medical training was far more than the average Sailor. He could be an asset. And in reality the chances of something serious actually happening were pretty remote he figured.

"Hmmm," he said as he noted Hospitalman Second Class Vesel sitting on a bunk twenty feet away chatting with two other corpsmen. "Vesel, over here." The SMO waved the Corpsman over.

"Yes, sir," Vesel said as he arrived.

"Vesel, what is your assigned GQ station?" the SMO asked.

Sir, I am assigned to the treatment room here in main medical for GQ and during a mass-casualty event.

"Perfect," said the SMO.

Turning to Anglin, he said, "I'll tell you what. You stick with Vesel here, and maybe you can help out. Vesel, you okay with this?"

"Yes, sir, not a problem," Vesel answered. "Me and the Sergeant have been getting along great."

"Excellent," the SMO said as he turned and headed towards the exit on his way to the aft BDS. He decided that now was as good a time as any to have that chat with HM1 Nebo. Besides, he wanted to keep moving. He was too keyed up to sit quietly and typically during GQs he kept on the move monitoring training events. His corpsmen were typically out teaching self-aid/buddy care using the GITMO eight basic wound scenarios, amputation, burns, electrical shock, abdominal wound, eye injury, sucking chest wound, fractured leg, and fractured jaw. He hoped they wouldn't need those skills but if they did the ship's crew should be ready.

"What exactly is your job during GQ?" Anglin asked Vesel.

"Well, my usual job is to help the provider in the treatment room with whatever they need. So we will be staying here I expect."

Copy," Anglin said, realizing he would be likely helping with injured here on the ward if it actually hits the fan.

"But stay close just in case," Vesel added. "We've never had a real GQ before."

A minute later the SMO was back on the medical ward. He noticed the quizzical looks and explained, "I was headed back to the aft BDS. But when I called Damage Control Central for clearance to momentarily open the first hatch, they refused to allow me to break Zebra. So I guess we'll all ride this one out here."

After ensuring that his department was manned and ready, he headed back to his office. He noted continued normal launch activity on the fight deck. There was little he could do at the moment so to distract himself he picked up a chart from the stack on his exam table and began reviewing a flight physical. He had allowed himself to calm down a bit and was signing off the physical exam when the 1MC again crackled to life.

"Missiles inbound! Starboard side! Brace for impact!" the 1MC voice said excitedly.

The SMO froze for a moment and immediately felt a cold sweat breaking out. This was an experience he had never had before. Sitting there, he felt helpless. In all his previous combat situations, he had been where he could see his attacker and fight back. Here in his office, he could do neither.

From outside, he heard someone yell, "Oh my God! Jesus help us."

He sat there for what seemed like hours but was only about thirty seconds. They all sat there in mostly silence, and he kept his eyes glued to the TV and the view of the flight deck. All the while his mind was racing. *Surely, if there were missiles headed to us, we could shoot them down.* He was well aware of the ship's defensive systems. These included missiles, electronic countermeasures, and Close In Weapon System, or CIWS. The CIWS was the last-ditch weapon that sported a multibarreled Gatling gun that could essentially put up a wall of twenty-millimeter lead within a mile of the ship for any missile to fly through.

And then he heard the distant and faint but unmistakable sound. *Burrrrrrrrrrrrp-burrrrrrrrrrrrp* was reverberating through the ship. The CIWS was firing. *Oh crap*, he thought. *Burrrrrrrrrrrrp-burrrrrrrrrrrrp.*

After several seconds, he began to let out the breath he had been holding. They must have got them he concluded. Then a loud clang and shudder jolted the ship, followed almost immediately by a second, more distant boom. With the jolt, the SMO in his wheeled desk chair slammed sideways into his desk. His mind consciously registered two hits. Where? He hadn't seen anything on the TV that was focused on a launching F/A-18F.

The 1MC again blared, "Missile hits starboard side, make damage reports to DC central."

The SMO leaped out of his chair and raced out of his office. Seeing no obvious damage in his department, he went straight to the phone talker.

"Have each Battle Dressing Station report their status," the SMO demanded.

All but one replied immediately. After repeated calls, the phone talker said, "Sir, there's no response from Battle Dressing Station Four back aft, nothing."

The SMO nodded grimly and said, "Keep trying."

The SMO switched his radio to scan all channels and picked up the calls for the damage control repair lockers three and seven B to activate. The ship has Sailors assigned to ten repair lockers to fight fires and deal with any battle damage. Hearing which lockers were activating gave him the general location of the missile hits. Repair locker three covered the aft section of the ship from the second deck and below, where Battle Dressing Station Four is located. Seven-B was responsible for the O-3 level and above, including the ship's island superstructure.

There had to be injured Sailors out there. His mind mapped out where they would likely be responding to. Two hits on the starboard side, one aft closer to the waterline, and one up on or near the flight deck. The fact that the flight deck Battle Dressing Station was intact told him something. It was strategically located on the first level of the island on the starboard side.

Commander Derek Lloyd was a man of action and standing there and waiting, even for a few minutes was infuriating to him. His thoughts were racing on what he needed to do. But having taken hits, the CO would be even more reluctant to break Zebra he realized. Were more missiles inbound? The SMO switched to the command radio frequency and called. "Medical standing by to respond."

The XO replied, "Copy, SMO. Stand by."

After the call, the SMO had an idea. "With me, Senior Chief," the SMO said to Senior Chief Owens who was keeping close by. Knowing the CO had his hands full at the moment he decided to make further preparations.

The SMO headed back to the medical ward and was pleased to see that the initial response team was standing there with their gear and a Reeve sleeve stretcher ready to go.

"We're on standby, guys," the SMO said to everyone standing there with expectant looks on their faces. "Senior, I want a second response team. We took hits on or near the flight deck and back aft. As soon as we are cleared to respond, I want to send one to each location. Primary team aft, and secondary up. And make sure each team has a radio and is tuned to the medical channel." He then turned and headed back to see if BDS four had reported in yet.

"Aye-aye, sir," Owens answered. He looked around and started calling out names.

"Initial response team, over here," he called. "Llortman, Vesel, Trout, Long, front and center, *now*!"

They all hustled up to the senor chief who was standing by the ward nurse's station.

"As the SMO just said, the original primary team is heading aft. You new guys, you're now the new secondary team and will be heading up to the O-3 level. Get your gear and be ready. Vesel, you are in charge. It's going to be crazy, so keep your calls short but informative. Okay, guys, time to get your game face on. We have no idea what you may come across out there so be ready."

Anglin was there standing off to the side having followed Vesel to the ward at a distance and had been listening in. "So, what are you doing now?" Anglin asked Vesel.

"Now I'm leading an initial response team," Vesel answered.

"Initial response team," Anglin repeated inquisitively.

"Yeah, we're going to be heading out to take care of any injured once we are cleared to go. The initial response team of four are the first to head out to the scene."

"Oh," Anglin said, nodding his head. "So much for staying here on the ward." Anglin had a bemused look on his face.

"That's right. We can really use an extra hand today. We can use some help lugging the response bags. But you better keep up."

"You got it, mate," Anglin replied, wondering what he had gotten himself into.

Back in the waiting room, the SMO again asked, "Heard anything from the aft Battle Dressing Station?" A shake of the phone talker's no was all the response he needed.

"SMO, the flight deck Battle Dressing Station reports that they have five casualties, one serious," said the phone talker

The SMO picked up the desk phone and called the flight deck Battle Dressing Station.

"Battle Dressing Station Two, Benson," said Hospitalman Second Class Benson.

"Benson, SMO, what do you have?" asked the SMO.

"We have four wounded, three with burns and cuts, and the fourth is unconscious but breathing with a nasty laceration to his head. We have started an IV on him of normal saline.

"Okay copy, you are doing fine," the SMO answered reassuringly. "Keep an eye on his vitals. We'll let you know when we will be able to get them to main medical."

"SMO," Benson said. "There are probably many more injured. They said they heard lots of screams and hollering for help on the other side of the smoke and fire."

"Copy," the SMO said grimly, then added, "Benson, did they say where they were?"

"They were in a maintenance space just forward of the number two elevator along the starboard catwalk."

"Got it, thanks. SMO, out."

"Commander," called the phone talker.

"Yes, what do you have?" the SMO said turning to him.

"Sir, Battle Dressing Station Five is reporting two walking wounded with minor injuries. One has second-degree burns, and the other has minor puncture wounds."

"Thanks," the SMO answered. He stood there pondering a minute putting it all together. Battle Dressing Station Five is up near the bow on the port side on the O-3 level. Possibly only slightly farther away than the flight deck Battle Dressing Station, but on the opposite side of the ship. Makes sense that injured up there would go there as well.

"Well, this may very well turn into a mass-casualty situation," the SMO began addressing the anxious faces that had been watching him. "We won't know until we get on the scene. You can bet that it is going to be chaotic out there. But you all know what to do. I have absolute confidence in each and every one of you."

Turning to his surgeon, Lieutenant Commander Sandaal, the SMO said, "Kris, I hope you got a good night's sleep and have your knives sharp. Your skills will surely be needed."

"Aye-aye, SMO," said Sandaal as he turned to his surgery techs to go and prep the OR.

"SMO, XO," called the big XO on the command channel.

"SMO, standing by," Lloyd replied.

"Get ready to respond, the announcement is about to be made," the XO explained. "We have two locations that have been hit. Down on the third deck starboard aft and up on the O-3 level just forward of the number two elevator. We have reports of numerous injured at both."

"Aye-aye, sir. We're ready to go, sir," the SMO responded as the 1MC crackled to life.

Ding! Ding! Ding! Ding! Ding! began the bell from the 1MC.

"Response teams, this is it," the SMO yelled out. Then he turned to Owens. "Senior, you go with the primary team heading aft."

Aye-aye, SMO," Owens replied.

"Medical emergency! Medical emergency," continued the 1MC announcement.

But the SMO was no longer paying attention. "Secondary team, with me. We're heading up to the O-3 level. Last man through dog the hatch," the SMO said.

The SMO was almost running up the Admiral's ladder well. After several GQ drills the SMO had found that this particular ladder well, usually reserved only for the Admiral and his staff and other senior officers to be the quickest way to move up and down during a GQ. It always had less foot traffic and it led straight up into the island and up to the O-10 level if he need to go up that high.

On their way up the SMO heard DC central activate repair lockers five and seven F. Both were responsible for areas adjacent to and just forward of the already activated repair lockers. Five on the second deck and seven F on the flight deck. The fires and damage may be greater than initially reported, spreading, or the other teams needed help, the SMO decided.

Upon reaching the O-3 level, he met the XO heading the same direction.

Without slowing down, the SMO asked, "XO, what do we have?"

"We're going to need you today SMO," the XO began. "I just came down from the flight deck. The hit just forward of the number two elevator appears to have blasted one of our fueling stations, and there is a raging fire. I counted five wounded down in that area. DC central is shutting off all the fuel lines to that part of the ship but there was still a hell of a lot of fuel already in the lines."

The SMO nodded grimly.

"I'm coming down to see how the fire fight is going down here," the XO continued. "Most to the damage is below the flight deck."

As they entered the main passageway, they could see and smell smoke coming from further forward. They could see Sailors in full firefighting ensemble just ahead of them heading into the smoke. Emerging from the billowing black smoke came two firefighters in their full firefighting gear dragging out a body. They could see that it was a female wearing the partially burned and torn purple flight deck jersey worn by aviation fuels personnel. They were commonly called 'Grapes' on the ship. She was probably in or near where the missile hit. Beyond them they could see black smoke and flames further up the P-way. The fire fighters ahead of them continued on forward to relieve the fire team that was currently manning the hose. The XO, SMO and response team knew they could go no further without some sort of respirator.

The approaching firemen spotted the SMO in his white float coat sporting a big red cross and brought the unconscious Sailor to them. One pulled off his mask and said breathlessly, "This is the only one we could get to."

Corpsmen Vesel and Trout immediately began to assess the injured Sailor.

"The only one," the SMO asked. "Yes, we saw several down in the space on the other side of the flames, but there is no way to reach them until we get the fire under control. Sir, I honestly don't think it will matter."

"How far does the damage go, Sailor?" the XO asked as he watched the SMO begin to assist with the patient.

"It's on both sides of the starboard passageway," the firefighter answered. "It blew right through into the center of the ship, and I'm pretty sure it penetrated much further."

"SMO, I'm not getting a pulse," Trout said excitedly.

The SMO immediately for the carotid pulse on her neck, as he said, "Stethoscope," to a wide-eyed HM Long. He couldn't detect a pulse or hear a heartbeat, and her pupils were fixed and dilated. He shook his head and said, "I'm afraid she's gone." Turning to the firefighters, he asked. "Can you get her up to the flight deck?"

"Yes, sir," the senior firefighter said grimly. "Where exactly?"

"I'll show you," the SMO answered. "Follow me."

The SMO knew he needed to get a handle on what was happening up on the flight deck and the Battle Dressing Station there. To Vesel, he said, "Swing around to the port side and come back down from up forward. There may be others injured on the other side of these flames. And keep me posted." He waved the brick in his left hand at them."

"Aye-aye, sir," Vesel said.

It wasn't until he was heading back past his response team that he noticed SSgt Anglin standing there with a response bag in his hands. He stopped dead in his tracks as his jaw flew open in astonishment. He was about to say something when he suddenly recalled what he had said earlier. He turned back and saw Vesel there about to head down a cross passageway to the port side of the ship leading Llortman, Long, and Trout.

Shaking his head side to side, he said, "Damn, Anglin, hell of a time we keep having! Thanks for the help. Now you better get a move on." He nodded to the team rounding a corner. "And don't get lost."

"Yes, sir," Anglin said, turning back with a determined half smile on his face as he raced off after the others.

When the SMO, followed by the firemen with the Sailor's body, reached the catwalk, he directed them to take her to the aft part of the flight deck island.

Outside the flight deck Battle Dressing Station the SMO saw six Sailors sitting on the deck near the hatch. A Corpsman was tending to them. The SMO gently touched the shoulder of the Corpsman who had his back to him at the moment to get her attention.

"Just a minute," she snapped. "Can't you see I'm bandaging this guy!"

The SMO waited the few seconds it took for her to turn around.

"Oh, sorry, SMO, I thought you were—"

"Not to worry," the SMO said, cutting her off. "What do you have?"

"Sir, we have two severely injured inside they are working on. We moved the walking wounded out here to make room. It gets tight in there really quick."

"How many?" the SMO asked.

"So far I've treated nine."

"Keep up the good work," the SMO said as he undogged the Battle Dressing Station hatch. Inside, he could see at once that they were really busy. At that moment, Lieutenant Olson, one of the Air Wing's two flight surgeons, was packing quick clot impregnated gauze deep into an unconscious Sailor's open abdominal wound.

Glancing up at the SMO, he said, "I can't find the source of bleeding, but I believe I about have it stopped with this third package of gauze. He was in shock, but we have two large-bore IVs going, and his vitals are improving."

"Great work," the SMO said, seeing that they were doing what was needed.

Before he could take another step the brick crackled.

"SMO, Senior," said Owens.

"Go, Senior," the SMO answered.

"SMO, we have seven severely injured here, but they are still bringing them out," Owens relayed. "At least, on this side of the flames. SMO it appears to have hit the starboard side of the number two MMR, but we have fire up on the second deck as well."

"Copy seven," the SMO answered. MMR the SMO knew stood for Main Machinery room. Plenty of vital equipment in that room along with lots of Sailors that could be injured he was calculating.

"And, SMO, we are just forward of the aft Battle Dressing Station," Owens said as he paused with some hesitation. "It appears that area is engulfed in flames."

The SMO took in a deep breath, imagining the face of Hospitalman First Class Nebo and his team. "Have you seen any of our corpsmen?"

"Not yet," Owens answered.

"SMO, copy," was all he could say as he continued forward.

Once clear of aircraft he could see flames along the starboard catwalk. There appeared to be no holes in the flight deck itself, which is several inches of steel plate. So the brunt of the blast must have blown inward. Farther forward he saw a group of injured Sailors down on the deck.

He had already realized it earlier, but this did indeed meet the criteria for a mass-casualty event. This was any time there are more inured than the initial response teams can handle and will require an all hands on deck effort. He just wanted to estimate the numbers on the flight deck before making the call. Under normal operations, only three people on the *Vinson* can declare a mass-casualty situation, the CO, the Air Boss who controls the flight deck, and the SMO. But during General Quarters only the CO can make that ultimate call.

But first he had to decide where to have everyone respond to. It had been so cut and dried in all the drills. They always had simulated wounded on the flight deck and others injured in or near the hanger bay. The mass casualty teams were trained to respond to the hanger bay and that was where they would naturally go unless told otherwise. The simulated injured were taken down an aircraft elevator and just out from that elevator the triage area would be established. Near there the other treatment stations, Immediate, Delayed, Minimal, and Expectant would be set up depending on space available in a hangar bay usually full of tightly packed aircraft. But now, in reality, he had two major sources of wounded separated far apart from each other on a 1,100 foot long ship, 1/5th of a statute mile. It hardly made sense to have those being gathered down on the second deck to be brought up a deck to the hanger bay, triaged and initial stabilization treatment began, to ultimately be taken back down to the second deck where main medical was located. Ideally he would set up triage on a mess deck near the source of the injured from decks below there. But then it would be much more difficult to quickly get those from the flight deck down to the triage area. '*Damn*,' he thought. In the simulations the injured were always much more conveniently located in similar locations even if from multiple decks. Could he split his teams in half and send smaller groups to two locations? *'Kill two birds with one stone'*, he thought as he cursed himself for using such and inappropriate cliché. In the end it was raw numbers and another cliché that came to mind. He just didn't have enough corpsmen and providers to split them up. He had only one provider and three corpsmen per station. Others had key jobs as the patients flowed on from triage and ultimately down on the ward. He would have to rely on another old cliché, *'Train as you'll fight'* and *'Fight as you train.'* The injured from below will just have to be brought up to the triage area in the hanger bay as best that they can.

He did a rough number crunch in his head and then keyed his radio mike on the command channel.

"Captain, SMO," he began. "We have at least twenty injured on the flight deck and many more down on the second deck. I'm requesting that you initiate a Mass Casualty response to hanger bay two."

If he agreed, the CO would have the Officer of the Deck make a ship-wide announcement. This would alert both the medical and dental departments to respond along with the designated trained stretcher bearers. Without that announcement, only the medical response team could leave their assigned GQ stations.

"Copy, SMO, Mass Casualty," the CO replied. "Stand by."

The SMO, of course, didn't just stand there. He continued on toward the wounded on the deck ahead.

47 DIRECT PRESSURE

USS *Vinson*, South China Sea

As the SMO headed to the flight deck with the firefighters, Hospitalman Second Class Vesel called out, "This way." He led them to the other side of the ship. Once on the port side, they headed forward to get around to the other side of the fire.

Staff Sergeant Anglin was trailing behind the others when a door to his right opened up and he heard heavy coughing. He looked in toward the center of the ship and saw a blackened, soot-covered face with wide white eyes staring back at him.

"Corpsman. We need a Corpsman in here. Please, hurry," the Sailor said, coughing heavily between words.

Anglin pursed his lips and let out a shrill whistle to get the attention of the others. "Over here! They need help in here," he said pointing into the room. Following the Sailor in, Anglin could see damaged, blown-out walls laying over like twisted mangled dominoes. The once pristine gray was now charred and blackened with smoke. Luckily, he noted that firefighters were putting out the remnants of fires in this area. Anglin realized that he was facing the starboard side, the side the missile had hit. He could make out what remained of a conference room and closer to where he stood what had been a wall and the remnants of a large office.

Anglin immediately heard the moans and calls for help from the injured. Hospitalman Long and Hospitalman Third Class Trout were each soon assessing a patient. Vesel and Hospitalman Second Class Llortman had gone through a door into the room beyond.

"Anglin, over here," Vesel called out, waving him over.

Anglin was unsure of what kind of place he had stepped into. It was eerily hazy and smoky and a complete jumbled mess. The starboard wall of the twenty foot by fifteen foot room was blown in knocking the desks and equipment into a jumbled pile in the center of the room. Computers and monitors were strewn on the deck. The two remaining walls were covered in large screen TV monitors, but the screens were blank. The room appeared to be some kind of command center of sorts Anglin guessed. All this took only a moment for him to take in.

"Here, I need you to give me a hand," Vesel said, pointing to a pair of legs jutting out from under a pile of debris of desks, tables, computers, busted TVs, and pieces of what had been a wall.

"What do you need me to do?" Anglin asked as he set the response bag down.

"Help me get this table off of him," Vesel replied.

It took a few minutes, but they were soon able to get most of the fallen debris off of him. But they soon realized that the him was a her.

She was lying there with a grimace on her face, indicating obvious pain, but otherwise silent. Blood was oozing out of a laceration to the top of her head. There was a small pool of blood on the deck under it. They both could see that part of the crushed in bulkhead was still pinning her left shoulder to the deck.

"Glad you guys could make it," she said through gritted teeth.

Vesel began to check the pulse on her right wrist.

"Are you hurting anywhere?" Vesel asked.

"You're kidding, right?" she answered. "I feel like someone hit me on the head with a sledgehammer, and my shoulder is throbbing."

"Yes, ma'am. You took a pretty good whack on your head. We will get you bandaged up in just a minute," Vesel said. "I'm going to bandage this small cut you have on your head. Do you remember losing any track of time, or have you been conscious the whole time?"

"I'm pretty sure I've been awake for what seems like hours," she answered. "I just couldn't move, and I was feeling the wetness at the back of my head."

"Because of where the cut is, this gauze will be covering part of your face, so don't be worried," Vesel added.

"You do whatever you have to do," she said. "And thanks."

"Let me know if you are hurting anywhere else," he added as he finished the head bandage.

"Well, I can't feel my left arm. It's totally numb," she added.

"We'll get a look at it when we get this piece of metal off you," Vesel answered. "Anglin, you get on that side and help me lift if off her." Then he turned to Llortman. "Joe, you slide her out after we lift this up. We should just be able to lift it enough to get her out from under it."

"Just a sec," Llortman answered.

Anglin nodded and positioned himself on one side of the fallen wall while Vesel got to the other side as Llortman joined them.

"Lift slowly on three," Vesel directed. "One, two, three."

They both strained upward, pulling on the edges of the fallen bulkhead. They moved it only four inches, but it was enough.

"Pull her out," Vesel said through gritted teeth from the strain.

Llortman slid her out from under the bulkhead over into a clear area of the floor.

"She's clear," Llortman called out.

Vesel nodded to Anglin, they both let go, and the bulkhead dropped to the deck with a loud clang.

As soon as the bulkhead had been lifted off of her shoulder and upper arm, a pulsing spurt of blood began pouring out of a jagged laceration of her inner arm. The weight of the bulkhead had kept the cut artery clamped closed. The wound was to her left upper inner arm. Now that the weight was gone, there was nothing to hold back the bleeding. The heavy metal pushing her artery closed had actually kept her alive.

"Oh crap!" Anglin said, seeing it before Vesel. Llortman had already seen it and was digging out a pressure bandage. If they didn't get is stopped quickly, she could bleed out in minutes. Llortman handed the bandage to Vesel, who took it and pressed it firmly down on the gushing wound immediately staunching the flow.

"Anglin, take over holding pressure on this while I get a tourniquet," Vesel directed.

"You got it," Anglin said as he took over.

"What is it? Am I bleeding," asked the wounded Sailor.

"Yes, ma'am," Anglin answered her. "But we have it under control. We're going to get you taken care of."

After multiple attempts to position the tourniquet, they couldn't stop the bleeding. "Damn, put the direct pressure back on," said Vesel. "That laceration is just too high up to get the tourniquet around it effectively."

Anglin complied immediately. They were both gratified to see that the bleeding stopped completely this time, but the current dressing was becoming blood soaked.

"Here, place this bandage on top of that one and keep the pressure on," Vesel directed handing Anglin a fresh dressing. "Someone is going to have to hold that pressure until we can get her to a doc that can stop it."

"No problem. I've got it," Anglin said confidently.

Vesel did a quick head-to-toe survey of her and saw no other obvious injuries.

"Okay, I'm going to check for more injured in this area," Vesel said to Anglin.

"How are you feeling? Are you still with me?" Anglin asked, noting that her uncovered eye was closed.

"You mean other than feeling like I was hit by a truck and my arm almost torn off?" she asked with a twist to her face. "Other than that I feel just peachy. I do feel a bit lightheaded."

"Okay, ma'am, we've got the bleeding under control," Anglin said reassuringly. "I'm going to be right here with you until we get you patched up downstairs."

"Thanks," she answered as she closed her eyes again.

Anglin continued holding the pressure as Vesel and the others tended to the other injured they found in the area.

Five minutes later, Vesel was back at his side. "How is she doing?" he asked.

"She's resting quietly. I've kept the pressure on," Anglin added.

"Good job," Vesel said. "I'm going to get an IV started before we start moving her. As he was getting the IV tubing and fluid he called out; "Llortman!"

"Here," Llortman called back from the adjacent room.

"Llortman, check in with medical and tell them what we have here," Vesel instructed. Then he addressed the other corpsmen. "Trout, you get stretcher bearers and stretchers. Long, you head forward where we were headed and check for more wounded." They both nodded and headed out. Vessel started examining her right arm to decide the best vein to get the IV line going in.

"Vesel," Llortman called several minutes later. "A mass casualty has just been announced. We need to get going to that ASAP. But the senior chief cut in and told us to finish up here and then move these patients before heading to our stations. He said to work fast."

"Got it," Vesel answered without looking up from what he was doing.

"Vesel," Anglin said, trying to get his attention. "Just how are we going to get these folks down all those steep ladders without dumping them?"

"We don't have to," Vesel answered. "We just have to get them up just one ladder. It's much easier that way. We will get them all up to the flight deck, and then they can ride an aircraft elevator down.

"Oh," was all Anglin could say, trying to imagine just going up one ladder with his patient. Of course, he was totally lost and had no idea where he was on the ship.

"You know," Vessel said as he continued working to get the IV going. "It's pretty funny that I ended up being a corpsman. I used to faint at the site of blood. I once wacked my head playing in the back yard with a friend when I was a senior in high school. It started bleeding and I reached up to touch it and my hand came back bloody. I felt queasy and the next thing I knew my mom was leaning over me with a dishtowel to my head. Then later after I had enlisted and was waiting to go to boot camp my friend cut his arm playing with a knife. Same thing, and I hit the floor. But eventually I got used to it. Especially after a tour with the Marines at Camp Pendleton." As he finished talking he was ensuring that the IV was flowing well and then he properly secured the line in place with plenty of tape. "We don't want that coming loose as we are transporting."

On cue, Trout arrived with a dozen stretcher bearers. "I had to use my pissed-mom voice, but I rounded these guys up."

"Great, let's get them loaded up and moving. We have an official mass casualty to respond to," Vesel answered.

A minute later, Long returned.

"No other patients where we were headed. They had several, but they have already been taken either to the forward aux Battle Dressing Station or up to the flight deck," Long reported.

"All right," Vesel said. "Let's get moving." Then looking at Anglin, "You good?"

In the next few minutes, the patients were carried out on the port catwalk on the way to the flight deck. Looking down through the grate he could see the ocean waves sixty feet below them. Once on the cat walk he could see that there were only two short half ladders leading up to the open flight deck. Out on the catwalk he had plenty of room to stay beside her. This was definitely better than the narrow steep single file ladders they would have had to take otherwise. Anglin stayed at his patient's side the whole way, keeping a tight grip on the bandage compressing the torn artery.

As they arrived, Vesel found out they had already made one elevator run, and it would be back up in a few minutes to get the latest arrivals. "We have to get to our mass-casualty stations now," Vesel said. "Anglin, are you good staying with her? Someone has to hold that pressure."

"Absolutely," Anglin said without hesitation.

"Great," Vesel said as he and the others headed down to the hanger bay.

With bells ringing in the distance the aircraft elevator rose into position.

"Well, ma'am," Anglin said to his patient. "It's just me and you now. And it looks like we're about to take one hell of an elevator ride."

48 BLOOD & GUTS

USS *Vinson*, South China Sea

The SMO continued forward toward the injured Sailors on the deck. As he got closer, he was pleased to see that most were being tended to by their fellow Sailors. The self-aid buddy care that had been drilled into them by his corpsmen was working. The GITMO 8 gods must be smiling down at this moment, he thought.

As he neared, what he saw brought a grim set to his jaw. Several were screaming in pain. He saw most were covered in black soot. There were several with third-degree burns, recognizable even from a distance. One was missing his right arm, with an applied tourniquet to stop the bleeding. Two were just sitting there rocking back and forth, moaning, with no obvious injuries. Four were lying there quietly, either unconscious or, God forbid, dead.

The SMO had to fight his years of Emergency Medical training and his natural inclination to jump in and start evaluating and treating what were obviously severely injured Sailors. But as SMO, his job was to make sure all of them were treated in the most efficient way possible. And to do that, he had to keep moving, keep the big picture, and deal with glitches and problems that always arose in these situations. He doubted that he would have the usual problem of the non-medical support Sailors not showing up. At least if they weren't among the injured. During drills almost a third of the assigned stretcher bearers and security personnel were no-shows.

After what seemed like an eternity, the SMO heard the mass-casualty announcement being made. Seeing that everyone was getting some form of medical attention, he turned on his heels and headed to find out which aircraft elevator he could use to transport the wounded. He met the arriving flight deck Battle Dressing Station corpsmen with their gear and Flight Surgeon headed to the wounded.

With the info he needed, the SMO scanned the flight deck again before heading down to the hanger bay. He was pleased to note that the flames were now extinguished on catwalk. The firefighters appeared to be getting the upper hand.

"Lieutenant Junior Grade Belah, SMO, we will be using EL Two," he called, using his radio.

Copy SMO, EL Two," repeated Belah, his designated triage officer. "We'll be setting up."

That last response made the SMO smile. Belah, his Physician's Assistant, was a true gem. He had spent two combat deployments with the Marines in Iraq. He had been there and done that and had the Purple Heart to prove it.

Historically on many carriers the triage officer was the senior dental officer, or DENTO. The SMO's counterpart in the dental department that had many dental trained corpsmen. In this situation they all worked under the SMO. But in several drills the SMO could see that the DENTO was awfully slow and totally out of his element. In several instances he totally triaged patients to the wrong group. So the SMO had 'Promoted' him out of the triage job and given it to his PA, who proved to be a natural. He did the job in less than have the time of the struggling DENTO. The DENTO was now in overall charge of patient movement, from triage to the care stations and from there down to the second deck for further treatment and reevaluation.

When the SMO arrived at the triage station in hanger bay two set up next to the elevator, he saw Belah and his corpsmen were busy checking and tagging the patients. He was pleased to see that Belah had his area marked out. Next to Belah was Lieutenant Commander Sandaal, the general surgeon. He caught the SMO's eye as he approached and gave him a curt nod of acknowledgment. He was triaging alongside Belah until he identified the two most urgent surgical cases. They would then be rapidly transported down to sick bay. One would go directly into the surgical suite that was being prepped by the surgical techs. The other would be in the treatment room next door and other life sustaining measures taken until the first surgical case was finished. The SMO had complete confidence in his surgeon's judgement.

Working around the aircraft, the treatment teams were setting up their stations. Each team had already opened up their response foot lockers and were unpacking their gear. They were in the process of donning the colored vests that helped identify them and their station. Red vests for Immediate, yellow for Delayed, green for Minimal, and black for Expectant.

Off to the side of the Triage location the SMO was pleased to see LTJG Burger, the Physical Therapist standing there holding a chicken wire encased Stokes liter high overhead. He and his one assigned corpsmen were there in their white vests to lead the Primary Stretcher Bearer Team. The upright stretcher was to identify the rally point for all the arriving non-medical stretcher bearers in the crowded and chaotic hanger bay. They are to organize teams and then coordinate dispatching them as needed to the triage and treatment team areas as patients are ready to be moved. Once enough arrive on scene in the hangar bay Burger will have twenty or so report to the Secondary Stretcher Bearer Team Chief down on the mess decks where a patient receiving station was being set up. This will ensure that enough stretcher bearers are on hand at the secondary triage location to receive patients as they arrive three to four at a time on the smaller weapons elevators.

Seeing that patient triage was well underway and that the other stations were almost ready to receive patients, he started looking for the Senior Dental Officer, his patient flow coordinator. His assistant, Senior Chief Owens, was there in his orange vest, but no Dental Officer.

"Senior, where's the Dental Officer," the SMO asked his senior enlisted.

"No idea, SMO. But he called to say that he was on his way a couple of minutes ago," Owens answered.

"Any word on the aft Battle Dressing Station," the SMO asked.

"No, nothing," Owens answered grimly. "It's not looking good. Two haven't shown up here to their stations. Both the delayed and minimal teams are short a Corpsman."

The SMO nodded. "Let me know if you hear anything," the SMO said as he noticed someone running his direction and ducking under the wing of an F-18 while pulling on an orange vest.

"Sorry, SMO," the Senior Dental Officer said breathlessly. "I couldn't find my damned vest. It was stuffed in the bottom drawer of my file cabinet and covered by some loose paperwork. I've been frantically looking for it the past ten minutes."

"Not to worry," the SMO answered calmly to reassure the sensitive and obviously nervous Senior Dental Officer. "You're here now. The teams appear to be about set up, and we have a steady stream of stretcher bearers arriving."

"Okay, good," the Dental Officer said, looking around, trying to get his bearings as to where everyone was setting up.

"Remember, John, this is going to go just like we have practiced the past three times," the SMO said reassuringly while placing a hand on his left shoulder. "It will be chaotic, but we've trained hard to deal with it. You keep roving from station to station and be visible to everyone. You are to keep the patients moving and to help identify and resolve any bottlenecks. You can do this."

The Senior Dental Officer stared back wide eyed and nodded yes.

"Okay, good man," the SMO added. "I'm only a radio call away if you have a question." What he was thinking was, *Call when you get in over your head, which would probably take about five minutes, given how he did on the last mass-casualty drill three weeks ago. You come to the fight as you are, not how you want to be,* he thought as he heard, "SMO!" being called. Thank goodness Senior Chief Owens was there to back him up. Which is why he had placed Owens in that job in the first place.

A chief was rapidly approaching him. The SMO recognized him as from the weapons department. They own and operate the weapons elevators they would need to use to transport the litter patients from the hanger bay down to the second deck.

"SMO, we have both lower stage three and upper-stage-two weapons elevators today," the chief said with some unaccustomed excitement in his voice. "Both are manned and ready, sir."

"Excellent," the SMO said. "You'll have plenty of business soon. Thanks. Go let the Senior Dental Officer and Senior Chief Owens know."

"Aye-aye, sir," the weapons chief replied as he turned toward the two in the orange vests.

This was particularly good news. Both go directly from the hangar bay down to the second deck just aft of the medical department.

Just then, the loud ringing of the aircraft elevator's warning bell sounded. *Here more come*, he thought.

The SMO took one glance at the now rapidly descending elevator loaded with wounded, and then double-checked his personnel ready at their stations. They were ready. *Good*, he thought as he turned to head down to the second deck and check preparations there.

The SMO stepped onto a mess deck below set up with several treatment stations in the now wide open floor space. After the patients are triaged and then provided initial treatment up on the hanger bay, they will be transported down here. The arriving patients from above would be reassessed and cared for by Dr. Searcy's team until beds were available to move them to a treatment room if more lifesaving care was needed, or directly to the medical ward for admission and treatment there.

Any walking wounded that arrived at this station would be sent for treatment in BDS three which was further forward on the same deck. The minimally injured were often the ones being most demanding and in the way. So the SMO had decided in an earlier drill that a distant BDS was the ideal location to treat the walking wounded with minor injuries. Normally it would be shut down to support the mass casualty. But they found a way to man it. The treatment would have occurred somewhere, by someone, so they just rearranged things a bit. It had worked great on their last drill. Thus they were able to keep the volume of patients on the mess deck more manageable, and let the medics here focus on the more seriously injured.

"You all set, Lieutenant?" the SMO asked as he approached her.

"Yes, sir," Searcy answered energetically. "Any idea what we can expect?"

"Great, we will have lots of business today," the SMO said.

"We have over twenty that I know of so far," the SMO replied. "But I fear there will be many more. Expect pretty much everything, lots of burns, blast injuries, amputations, and at least one evisceration. And Lieutenant Commander Frasier is really going to have his hands full after this one with psych cases, I'm afraid," the SMO added.

"Like I said, SMO, we're ready to go," Searcy said seriously.

As the SMO turned to head to the medical department, Searcy asked, "SMO, we still need some stretcher bearers down here."

"I know, they were still arriving up there as I came down," the SMO said as he turned back to answer. "JG Burger has his act together and will send you some soon. If not call the DENTO on your brick to remind them."

"Aye aye sir," Searcy said to his now retreating back.

Just thirty feet down the passageway, the SMO entered the open door into what usually was the aviation physical exam section. Now it was transformed into a secondary urgent treatment room to augment the usual one next to the OR. The corpsmen there were ready for their first patient to be sent to them by Searcy. Crossing into the patient waiting area, he saw the primary treatment room was similarly manned and ready. Corpsmen were standing by ready to receive patients as they arrived. Except there was no physician there to treat them! The other Flight Surgeon was supposed to be there ready to go.

"Where's Lieutenant McCluer?" the SMO barked out in frustration. Standing there in his place was Lieutenant Okamyra, a junior dentist, supposedly there to take care of the more seriously injured patients.

"SMO," began Okamyra, "sir, this was part of the changes after you moved Belah from the minimal team to triage officer. Lieutenant Commander Stooksbury reassigned doctor McCluer from the treatment room here up to the hanger bay to replace Belah on the minimal team and moved me here. I asked if putting a dentist here was the best choice."

"Seriously," the SMO answered.

"I thought that you had approved the change," Okamyra answered.

"Go take his place and send him back down here," the SMO said to Okamyra. "Let's get you to a station where you are better suited." The SMO thought to himself; *There is always something that goes wrong. Well, that is why I keep moving around. So I can identify and correct problems on the fly.*

"Okay, now we'll be set," the SMO said to the treatment room team. "I'll have to have a talk with Stooksbury later he thought as he resumed his inspection of the preparations."

Next door to the treatment room, he looked through the window into the operating room. The two surgical techs were in their OR scrubs and had the surgical trays set up waiting on the first patient. He tapped on the window and gave the techs a thumbs-up.

On the main ward, the few remaining corpsmen were very busy setting up additional bunk beds. The ICU patients that were recovering well from surgery had been moved into the semi-private rooms at either corner of the ward in anticipation of new more serious cases. For the first time since he joined the crew of the *Vinson*, they were going to have a complete fifty-bed ward. Something he was sure hadn't happened on the *Vinson* since *it* had responded to the Haiti earthquake back in January 2010.

Passing back through the patient waiting area, he met the quickly arriving surgeon.

"SMO, the first two are on their way down. And I saw at least four with serious blood loss," Sandaal said, looking him directly in the eye.

"So they will need more than just IV fluids to tank them up," the SMO replied.

"Indeed," was all he said.

"I'll call the CO and request to activate the walking blood bank," said the SMO. The Navy has relied on its crewmembers as a source of whole blood when needed, hence the term "Walking Blood Bank." These volunteers were from departments throughout the ship, so activating the walking blood bank would pull them from whatever critical duties they may be doing at the time. A potential problem during a real General Quarters. That was why the captain had to assess the overall situation and make the call and assume the risk. He has to weigh saving lives vs defending and saving the ship and its crew.

"Excellent," he said, "We need O negative, A positive, and B negative to start." He turned to change into surgical scrubs.

Before calling the Captain, he checked in with Owens on the medical channel.

"Senior, give me a count," the SMO requested.

"Standby, SMO," Owens answered. "Okay, we currently have two on the way to surgery, five immediates, seven delayed, thirteen minimal, and ten expectant, of which five are clearly deceased. And, SMO, there are still almost a dozen in the triage area we haven't processed yet, and we have been told to expect another EL Two run soon.

"Copy all. Keep me posted. SMO, out." Forty-nine in the pipeline so far, he quickly calculated. And more on the way. The SMO had to wait for a break in the chatter on the now jammed command channel to make his call.

"Captain, SMO," he said into his brick.

"SMO, stand by," the CO replied immediately.

All other conversations on the channel silenced after hearing the SMO make that call. They all had Sailors injured or at risk, and the SMO was not known to jam the radio with unimportant calls. They would wait until the CO and SMO were finished.

"SMO, go," the CO said after less than thirty seconds of silence. He had clearly been busy with something else at the moment.

"Captain, I have an update," the SMO began. "We currently have a total of forty-nine injured with more arriving. Two are headed to surgery now. Captain, I recommend that we activate the walking blood bank."

"Copy, SMO. Request approved. Wedge, out," the CO said ending the call.

Back up in the hanger bay, he took a moment to observe the chaos. There were wounded patients screaming in pain and begging for help. Some wounded were dazed and wandering around, but being corralled by the security teams. Corpsmen were treating the wounded, stretcher bearers were transporting the patients, and the radio calls continued unabated either demanding or relaying info. It was chaos all right but an organized chaos. Once Belah identified the immediate (red tag) patients, they were transported to the immediate station and stabilizing treatments were started. Open airways were established, bleeding controlled, IVs started, and splints applied if necessary. Once they were stable enough to move, they were taken by litter to one of the two weapons elevators being used for transport to the second triage and treatment station on the mess deck.

The SMO noticed the Big XO standing by the nose of an F/A-18 taking a moment to watch all the activity. The SMO made a beeline to him and gave him a quick update. Reassured that the medical end of things was under control the XO headed back to deal with the damage to the ship, his most immediate priority.

Just over an hour later almost all the patients on the hanger bay had been processed and sent down to the second deck. All except for the obvious deceased. They would soon be moved to one of the SUPPO's larger refrigerators near one of the sculleries. The fires were reported to be out but some of the spaces were still too hot to enter. It was unlikely anyone survived in those burned out areas. There was now only a trickle of patients arriving. Mostly the walking wounded. They had fairly minor wounds that they had ignored while fighting the fires and performing other critical duties. Most were sent down to BDS three and treated on the spot, then returned to duty with instructions to get it rechecked the next day.

As per their plan, most of the personnel from the red, yellow, green, and black teams had been relocated below to where the patients now were. Some to the mess deck and many others onto the rapidly filling medical ward. Only a single composite team remained on the hanger bay to catch stragglers.

The SMO continued his roving around, dealing with the major and minor glitches that always occurred. He kept giving updates to the CO about every ten minutes. He stayed focused on the big picture of seeing that the patients were being tended to and moving further up the chain of care. Occasionally he would notice a face he recognized among the wounded. One was a Sailor he saw regularly in one of the ready rooms and another was one he chatted with on the fantail of the ship while they watched the sunset after a workout in the gym. But he rarely had the time to notice if he recognized any of the injured. Finally, it was clear to everyone that most of the patients had at least arrived at the triage area. All of the immediates had been transported below to the secondary collection point. The surgeon was on his second surgery case, and he was getting all the blood he needed.

Seeing that the rush in the hanger bay was winding down, the SMO called the CO with the latest count.

"Thanks, SMO," the CO said.

"Captain, almost all the patients have arrived and been sent to the second deck. Things are pretty well under control. I request to shift modes and help treat some of these patients. My team is working hard, and my skills now need to be in the treatment room. The Senior Dental Officer can keep you up to date on the latest patient count.

"Approved. Check in later. I won't call you unnecessarily," the CO said.

"Aye-aye, sir, SMO out."

As they were getting the next group of patients ready to go down the upper-stage-two elevator, he took time to check some of them to assess their wounds and the treatment they had received. He felt a momentary surge of pride as he saw that all of these were properly taken care of.

Back down on the mess deck, the SMO spotted Searcy on her knees assessing a patient with her stethoscope. He couldn't help but see how disheveled and haggard she looked. Her typically tightly wrapped hair bun was undone and now hanging in a braided ponytail. Clearly out of regulation. But who the hell cared? Not him or any of the patients she was treating.

"Lieutenant, how is it going?" the SMO asked her when he was closer and she was finished listening to the patient's chest.

"Busy, SMO, but we are cranking through them," Searcy replied. "We burned through the IV fluids, tubing, and bandages in our response lockers pretty quick. We had to send for more from storage. We have plenty now."

"Good. I want you to know that you guys are doing great," the SMO said honestly. "The good news is that the flow of wounded has really slackened up there. I'm sure there will be a few seriously injured yet to be found and transported, but there are mostly Delayed and Minimals up there now.

"That is welcome news," Searcy said with a tired smile. "But we still have all these waiting to be sent back for treatment or surgery. Over half were not too critical, and we were able to send them directly to a bed on the ward after some basic treatment. The issue is we have over a dozen who will need surgery. Surgery and emergency care is our bottleneck. As you can see we still have quite a few immediates out here."

"Well, I'm here to help," the SMO added. "I'm going to be taking over in the secondary treatment room. Maybe we can up the pace a bit."

"Oh, thank goodness, SMO," Searcy said with obvious relief in her voice. "We really need your expertise."

"Hang in there. It's going to be a long day, but we'll get through it," the SMO answered. But that triggered a thought. Currently everyone was on duty, including the four ward corpsmen that were normally on night shift. They normally wouldn't be awake for another two hours. It was sure to be a longer night than usual for them, but likely an even longer day for the majority that worked the day shift. With the major rush now under control, he needed to think about tomorrow. He was going to need some rested corpsmen to man the ward tomorrow. He realized he better deal with this now before he got caught up treating patients.

"Senior Chief Owens, SMO," he said into his brick on the medical frequency.

"Go, SMO," Owens answered.

"Senior, I want five identified for ward duty tomorrow morning," the SMO said as he was heading down the port P-way to the newly created treatment room. "Break them away at 1930 so they can get some chow, shower, and hit the rack. Get the names to JG Belah and tell him I want them to each have a script for thirty milligrams of temazepam. They are going to need something to help get to sleep quickly after all this. I want them fresh and ready to go tomorrow." The rest of us will be dragging our asses, he didn't say.

"Copy SMO. Cut five loose at 1930 for ward duty tomorrow," Owens repeated back. "Belah to get scripts for temazepam for each."

"You got it. SMO out," he answered entering the secondary treatment room.

He clipped the brick onto his belt, grabbed a pair of vinyl gloves, and went to work.

The SMO quickly evaluated and treated two immediate patients. The first had burns involving his upper torso, neck, and face. Seeing black soot in his mouth, the SMO decided to intubate him before the swelling worsened and cut off his airway. There were two large-bore IVs going, and Dr. Searcy had already gotten well on the way to meeting the Parkland formula for replacing the fluids lost due to the extent of his burns. They then bandaged him up after first applying Silvadene cream to the burns.

The second had a puncture wound to the right-front upper-chest wall. Someone had already applied an occlusive dressing and performed a needle decompression for what is commonly called a sucking chest wound. Hearing no breath sounds on his right side the SMO next inserted a chest tube and connected it to a suction device to help reinflate the collapsed lung.

His second patient was headed to the ward, and he was getting a fresh set of gloves when his third patient was brought in. He began assessing her injuries as she was carried in. She apparently had a head wound because of the large pressure dressing wrapped tightly around her head and partially covering the right side of her face. She was turned away from him, and that wound appeared to be under control for the moment. Her clothes were partially torn and heavily singed and were black with smoke, but there were no obvious burns. The major concern appeared to be a significant cut to her left upper inner arm. Right next to her armpit. This was because of the large pressure bandage that was almost completely soaked in blood and was being held tightly in place by Anglin!

"What the hell!" came out of the surprised SMO at seeing Anglin.

"Just doing what I can, Commander," Anglin replied with an engaging smile.

"Ok," the SMO replied, stretching out the vowel. "We can definitely use all the help we can get. Thanks for pitching in."

"We came across her right after leaving you upstairs, somewhere," Anglin began to explain. "She had this arterial bleed, and it was too high up to effectively control with a tourniquet. Vesel tried. It just kept slipping down and wasn't stopping the bleeding that was really spurting. He slapped a couple of thick gauze bandages on it and had me hold pressure on it while they tended to other injured Sailors. I've been with her ever since."

"Okay, we need to see if we can find that bleeder and clamp it off," said the SMO before calling out to the Corpsman. "Scissors. Anglin, I can use your assistance a bit longer. I'll need you to clamp down as hard as you can while I try to find the end of that artery. You okay with that?"

"Yes, sir, I sure can," answered Anglin. "I'm going to see this one through."

The SMO nodded in acknowledgment as he took the scissors from the Corpsman.

"And get a clean sheet to cover this patient when I am done," the SMO added as he began to cut off the rest of his patient's shirt so he could have even better access to the area and to make sure that whatever had injured her arm hadn't also punctured her lung, as was a frequent occurrence. The shirt was cut away in seconds, and then he immediately cut through the straps and main body of her bra to get a good look at the entire area anywhere near that wound.

Then the patient that the SMO had thought was unconscious turned and looked at him with her one uncovered eye and a half-exposed smile and said, "So, SMO, do you undress all your women on the first date?"

The SMO stared at her speechless. That voice. It was Jenna! His Jenna! He totally dropped out of doctor mode for a moment and said, "Jenna? Oh damn. Hang in there, babe." Then he regained his composure and shifted back into professional doctor mode. He finished checking her chest, side, and back and was relieved that there were no other injuries. He covered her with the sheet and focused back on her arm.

"Jenna, we have to clamp off this bleeding. This might be a bit uncomfortable," the SMO explained as he reached for a hemostat.

"It's already uncomfortable. Do what you have to do," Jenna replied stoically.

"Okay, let's do it," the SMO said as he nodded for Anglin to clamp down.

There was a weak pulsing flow of blood from the wound still obscuring what he could see. He couldn't wipe it away fast enough.

"More pressure," he said to Anglin, who clamped down as hard as he could.

Finally, the blood flow slowed to a trickle, and he was able to see. He worked the tip of the hemostat around, and there it was! The brachial artery. It was severely nicked but not completely cut in two. Within seconds, he had the bleeding stopped.

"Got it!" he said with satisfaction. "You can let go, Anglin."

Anglin let go and slumped. His hand had been cramping with the pressure he had been applying. His face was beet red and covered in sweat from the prolonged exertion.

"Great job, Anglin. I couldn't have done it without you," the SMO added. "Now go take a break and get yourself something to drink."

"Jenna, how do you feel?" the SMO asked softly.

"Better, now that you're done digging around in my arm with that butter knife," she answered.

"It was just a small clamp," he explained as he checked her finger nails for good blood flow.

"It didn't feel small," she replied.

He pinched the tips of her fingers relieved to see that she wasn't wearing fingernail polish. The nail beds blanched white and immediately returned to a rosy pink. One of the main arteries to her arm was clamped off yet her blood flow appeared completely normal. The body's redundancies never ceased to amaze him. Good capillary refill thank goodness.

"Okay Jenna, we have that bleeding stopped. Let's take a look at that head of yours," the SMO said as he carefully removed the bandage. He uncovered a three-inch scalp laceration that had clotted and stopped bleeding.

"That's going to need stitches, but it can wait a bit," he said as he applied a fresh bandage.

"Well, fine, but I want my Minnie Mouse Band-Aid on it when you are done. I want something to show to the boss to prove I haven't been goofing off," she said jokingly.

Her sense of humor and her recognizing him was a good sign. "Were you unconscious?" he asked as he replaced the bandage and resumed examining the rest of her after cutting away her trousers."

"No, I don't think so. But how would I know for sure?" she asked jokingly. "You really take checking a lady out seriously." She watched as he continued a very thorough exam looking for other injuries. "We were in the Admiral's combat center when the blast hit. I was pinned under some debris and couldn't move. I remember lying there for what seemed like forever, hearing the moans and cries for help. I later learned that one of those calling for help was me."

"Well, I'm pretty sure you have at least a concussion," he said. "When things slow down around here, we will get an X-ray of your head. I don't see any other obvious injuries, but you are pretty bruised up from getting slammed around."

He then did a quick neurological and mini mental status exam on her that were both normal.

"Jenna, I have to send you to the ward for now," the SMO explained. "My surgeon will need to look at that arm later, but you are okay for now. We still have plenty of patients out there."

Jenna just nodded gravely and then said, "Take care of our Sailors, Derek. I'll be fine," she said as four litter carriers came in to take her away.

The SMO reached down and gave her left hand a gentle squeeze as he met her eyes and gave her a caring look. "I'll check on you later," he said as she was lifted off the treatment table.

The SMO pulled off his exam gloves and tossed them into the red biological-waste can as he watched her being carried out the door into main medical. He turned and reached for a new pair of exam gloves just as the next patient was being carried in from the passageway.

49 DEFCON TWO

Washington, DC, White House Situation Room

It had been just over an hour since the initial flash message traffic had arrived. President DeSiard was down in the situation room in the West Wing of the White house staring at the screen at the end of the table. Looking back at him via video teleconference was the US Indo-Pacific Commander, Admiral Vince Crenshaw. On either side of him was most of his national security team that could be assembled on short notice. On a corner of the screen was a smaller shot of Vice President Blake, who had just taken off in Air Force Two returning from a trip to Poland.

"So, Admiral, what is the latest on the *Vinson*? Just how bad is it, Vince?" asked the president.

"It's pretty bad, Mr. President," Admiral Crenshaw began. "The ship isn't in danger of sinking and is still operational. But they have taken numerous casualties and are operating on only one reactor. A main machinery room was hit requiring one of the two reactors to be shut down."

"Do we have a casualty list yet of the killed and wounded?" asked Secretary of Defense Winston.

"Not a complete list yet. There are twenty missing, and the medical department reports treating sixty-two wounded and eleven deceased. And, sir, we still haven't heard the status of Admiral LaSalle. His Operations Officer, Captain Ball, has been sending us reports and appears to be the senior acting officer from Admiral LaSalle's staff. It appears that one of the missiles had an almost direct hit on the Admiral's command spaces. No one has heard from the Admiral as of yet. We can only assume at this point that he is a casualty."

"Are we certain that it was the Chinese who fired those missiles?" asked Winston.

"Absolutely, Mr. Secretary," answered Admiral Crenshaw. "Our planes had intercepted one of the two air armadas that they had launched. They had been successful in turning them away, and it appeared that they were heading for home. A few minutes after that, one of the trailing aircraft turned back toward the ship and fired the two missiles before our aircraft could close on him. The shooter got by running back to the safety of the others. However, his wingman who had not yet launched his missiles was taken out before he could fire."

"Mr. President," began General Finan, the Chairman of the Joint Chiefs. "This is the second attack on our forces by the Chinese. And this time there is no doubt about who is responsible. I recommend that we go to DEFCON 1."

"General, DEFCON 1 puts us on a full war footing," President DeSiard answered.

"Yes, sir," General Finan answered. "It will send the message that we are not fooling around and ready to take them on with a total response."

"I agree," chimed in the vice president. "We can't be seen as looking weak on this one. The world is watching."

"We have recently fought long wars in Iraq and Afghanistan and were never at DEFCON 1," responded the president. "Going to DEFCON 1 isn't sending the message we are ready for war. It says that we consider ourselves to be at war. They may decide that further conflict is inevitable and really come at us full bore. Our goal is to prevent further escalation. Not send the signal that it already has.

"Mr. President, if I may," started Lee Huff, the Secretary of State. "From what I have seen thus far, it does not look like a planned all-out attack. If it had been, wouldn't more than two planes have turned to fire at the *Vinson*? Only one plane out of sixty actually shot its missiles. We don't know if his wingman was going to shoot as well. He could have just been staying with him as a wingman is supposed to do."

"I don't buy it," said the vice president. "They are playing some kind of game of deniability. This is the second, no third, attack on our forces if you count what happened in Hong Kong. It was open season on our Sailors, then the attack on our troops on Scarborough Shoal. Now this. They will claim it was some rogue pilot that they will punish. All this while they gauge our response. Or lack of one. Meanwhile, we have a carrier severely damaged and numerous American lives lost. The American people will demand a response in kind."

The president continued to sit there and let the discussion play out. He listened and considered the history going back over the past decade. The Chinese have continued to boost their military capability, particularly in the Navy. They have aggressively claimed sovereignty over essentially the whole of the South China Sea. They have been ratcheting things up for years. Maybe they view themselves as ready to take us on head-to-head.

"Or it could be just that, a rogue pilot shooting at us," Secretary Huff answered. "Let's acknowledge that the Chinese may have gotten wind of our plans on Scarborough Shoal. But it was too late for them to block what we had going. They may have told the Triads that our Sailors were fair game this last port visit. And it makes sense that they would send in a reconnaissance team to see what we are up to. The firefight was probably accidental given that they were heavily outnumbered. That pilot could very well have been a hothead. Remember the unhinged general in the movie *Dr. Strangelove*.

"That was pure fiction," countered General Finan.

"Yes it was, but that general's personality and attitude was a brutally true depiction of those held by plenty of officers in the military at the time," Secretary Huff answered. "My point is that every military can have rogue hot heads not in sync with their leadership. And if that is the case in this situation, are we ready to go to a full-up shooting war over it?"

"Admiral Crenshaw, what happened with the Chinese formation that flew over Scarborough Shoal?" asked President DeSiard.

"Sir, they flew over in two waves of about thirty-six planes at two thousand feet," answered the Admiral. "They appeared fully armed. After that, they flew back toward the mainland."

"So, just a simple overflight to send us a message," the president surmised aloud.

"Sir, if I may," added Admiral Crenshaw. "The after-action reports note that when our aircraft gained initial radar contact with the Chinese formation, they were also at two thousand feet. They then climbed to five thousand feet just before being intercepted."

"Sounds like the aggressive response from our jets caused them to alter their plans on the fly," said Secretary Huff. "The point is, as I see it, I think they were just trying to send a message that they could easily reach out and attack us. They are pressuring us so that we will abandon the buildup of Scarborough Shoal. I don't believe that they actually intended to attack us. At least, not yet."

"That's all well and good, but in the end, we were attacked, more than once," added the vice president. "Those are acts of war, and we should respond in kind."

"Gentlemen," began the president. "You all have valid points. For now, I am considering our shooting down of their aircraft as an adequate initial first response. Admiral, what additional assets do we have in the region?"

Sir, the USS *Ronald Reagan* battle group is putting to sea early and will be on station in less than seventy-two hours," said Admiral Crenshaw. "The USS *Nimitz* battle group is headed there but at least a week away. Current projection is they can be on station in seven and one half days. The limiting factor is the escort ships. They have to be refueled by the *Nimitz* and must go slower for max range. Alone at max speed the *Nimitz* could be there in half that time or less. It doesn't have to worry about fuel. We also have Virginia class and Los Angles class submarines operating in the South China Sea. In Japan, we have our Air Force and Marine bases in Okinawa and an F-16 base in northern Japan. We also have our bases in South Korea."

"Admiral, this is your backyard. What do you recommend?" asked the president.

"Sir, I say cut the escorts loose and have the Nimitz buster across the Pacific. I will have them met by some of the Regan's cruisers as they arrive on station. Also I recommend putting all the bases on alert and we should deploy the F-16s in northern Japan to Okinawa within reach of the South China Sea. I would also request moving the F-22s in Alaska to Okinawa. And we will need to mobilize additional tankers. They are going to need lots of gas in the sky.

"Anything else?" asked the president.

"Yes sir. The Chinese now have a significant submarine threat. I want more submarines and as many of the Navy's P-8 Poseidon submarine hunters we can get. If it gets into a shooting war, the submarine threat they have cannot be underestimated."

"Okay then. General Finan, take us to DEFCON 2," the president ordered. "Admiral Crenshaw, let's make it happen, your request is approved. Let's get them moving."

"Yes, sir," they both answered in unison.

"Secretary Huff, you get your ass up to the United Nations and raise holy hell," said President DeSiard. "We need international condemnation on this one. But first I want someone banging on the Chinese ambassador's door. I want him on the carpet of the Oval Office at 0700. He has some explaining to do."

"Yes, sir," answered Secretary Huff.

Turning to his press secretary who was sitting in the corner behind him where she was taking notes, he said, "Frankie, has this hit the news wires yet?"

No, sir, not the attack on the *Vinson*, which is still only within official government channels," said Press Secretary Frankie DeNagle. "The Philippine press did have a reporter and TV crew on a boat off the Scarborough Shoal when the flyover occurred. It has been on the local Manila news so far. I heard that CNN International will be running with it at the top of the next hour."

"Okay, we can't let news of this get out ahead of us. Let's arrange a press conference later this morning. I need to address the nation on this one. Let's shoot for ten. That way the West Coast folks will be out of bed."

"Does anyone else have anything to add?" the president asked all in the room.

"Sir, the situation is looking quite bad, but we need to step back a moment and see what opportunities we have here," said the president's Chief of Staff, Lester Smith who was speaking up for the first time. "We can't let a crisis go to waste. It has become a bit of a cliché since the Obama administration, but it is still true, and we may have a real opportunity here if we play our cards right."

"Such as?" President DeSiard asked.

"Such as, what has been the biggest problem in that region?" Smith asked. Then he answered his own question. "It's China's bullying of its neighbors and its military buildup of the shoals in the South China Sea. The very thing we are assisting the Philippines in doing to counter them."

"Go on," said the president.

"Well, this unprovoked attack on our carrier will likely be universally condemned by most nations," Smith continued. "Hell, even the Russians won't be able to justify standing by them on this one. So, if we can turn them into an international pariah, even temporarily, we may have the clout to get them to back down. Maybe even to abandon their unauthorized military bases in the area. Remember that back in 2012 they were protesting long and loud that the build-up of the artificial islands would never be used for military purposes. Then once built they were fortified and became forward operating bases for their fighters. And to protect their fighters they justified heavy surface-to-air batteries. Which we all know is really to be able sometime in the future to threaten both military and civilian aircraft and ships in the area they don't want there. This may be the chance to get them to back down. They are sure to lose the support of some of their regional friends on this one."

"Intriguing possibilities. Lee, get your people working on this as well," the president said to his Secretary of State as he stood up. "If we can avoid all-out war maybe we can also gain some ground in the area. "Let's plan to reconvene here at eight thirty for any updates."

They all stood up as he did and watched as he turned and headed out the door. They heard him say passing into the other room, "I need another cup of coffee."

50 AFTERMATH

USS *Vinson*, South China Sea

The SMO was up at 0600 to the sound of reveille on the 1MC speaker in his stateroom. Having finally hit the rack after 0200, he tried to ignore it and rolled over until his eyes snapped open as he remembered the previous day's events. He flung off his sheets and hopped up. Though still tired, the situation had him fully awake. He did a quick check of his stateroom computer for any critical email messages that could have arrived overnight. There were a few personal ones and a dozen official ones asking for updates on the situation. Seeing none that needed an immediate response, he turned around and stared at his tired unshaven face in the sink mirror. He rubbed his face feeling the rough stubble, sighed deeply, and reached for the shaving cream.

Fifteen minutes later, he was in wardroom three for breakfast where they only had cold sandwiches and cereal. He took a ham sandwich and grabbed a paper cup of hot coffee.

As he sat eating quickly, he began organizing his thoughts on what had to be done today. First up would be getting the most critically injured patients transferred for further care. He had several that needed to be at a burn center and others that would require follow-on surgeries.

This brought him back to Jenna. She had been sleeping soundly on the ward at 0130 this morning after the surgeon had done what he could cleaning out her wound. But it was clear that she needed to get to a vascular surgeon soon. He sighed and shook his head trying to focus back on the big picture.

Back in the medical department, he was glad to see a tired but busy Lieutenant Commander Alverez working in her office.

"Morning, Marty. We have a busy day ahead," the SMO said.

"Morning, SMO. It sure is," she answered. "I've already been on the phone with Kadena again this morning. They say that they are ready to receive patients as soon as we can fly them there, and we have a C-2 aboard ready to launch."

"Good to hear," the SMO answered. "While you're at it, you better call the PACAF Validating Flight Surgeon and give them a heads-up that we will need transport for our burn patients to Brooke Army Medical Center in San Antonio. Then get them entered into the TRANSCOM/JPMRC air evacuation system. We want to avoid any delays if possible and the Pacific is a huge ocean to cross.

"You got it, SMO," Alverez replied.

"I'm going to head back and check with the docs to sort out how many patients we need to ship out and the transport priority," the SMO said. "Marty, as you get the names have your assistant start cutting their MEDEVAC orders for them. And remind the Training Officer that they will *all* be funded! There had better not be his usual BS this time."

"Yes, sir," she replied with a smile. "Oh, SMO, don't forget that the CO's update meeting is at 0715 this morning. You have twenty-five minutes."

"Thanks for the reminder," he answered. "You are always keeping me out of trouble."

"That's what I do," she answered as she started looking up the phone number to the Validating Flight Surgeon in Hawaii.

The SMO found all his providers huddled at the nurses' station on the ward. They were reviewing the charts of the more critical patients.

"Good morning, everyone," he said to them all as he joined them. He took a moment to look into their tired but determined faces. "I know that we are all caught up in the middle of this, but I want to tell you all to stop and think for a moment what a fantastic job you and our corpsmen did yesterday. You undoubtedly saved many lives." He let them all reflect on that for a moment. "Now what I need from you is the MEDEVAC priority of these patients. We have a C-2 on standby waiting for the first load. As soon as you get that determined, get it to the Admin Officer so she can get them into the system."

After getting a quick rundown on all the patients and had it all written in his pocket notebook, he took a moment to check on Jenna.

She was on a bottom bunk on the port side of the ward. He was surprised and pleased to see that she was awake.

"Good morning, Captain," he said taking a knee beside her. "How are you feeling this morning?"

"Other than this pounding headache, and half-torn-off arm, I'm just fine," she managed with a pained smile.

"Did you sleep okay?" he asked.

"Well enough, I suppose," she answered. "The pain meds helped but they are wearing off. But this isn't the quietest place to sleep with all the understandable moaning and calls for help or pain meds."

"I'll make sure they stay on top of your pain control," he said reaching over to hold her hand. "We're going to have to get you to a vascular surgeon to patch up that artery properly. Our surgeon can only do so much out here."

"I understand," she answered. "How's the Admiral and the rest of the staff doing? Our spaces took a pretty direct hit."

"Jenna, I'm afraid I have some bad news," the SMO began. "Late last night after the fires in that area were out and the spaces cooled enough to enter, they found the Admiral's body and three others."

Jenna sucked in a breath and asked, "Who else?"

"Captain Deville, Captain Colfax, and Master Chief Goodpine," he answered straightforwardly.

"Oh, not Mike Deville too," she said. "We were just talking yesterday about his oldest daughter's wedding plans for next spring. He was all excited to be able to walk her down the aisle. He was so proud of her graduating from LSU, and he actually liked his future son-in-law."

The SMO squeezed her hand tighter in support while letting her process the news a bit longer in silence. He saw the tears start streaming down her cheeks.

"I'm so sorry, Jenna," the SMO said softly. "They were all good people."

She looked toward him, wiping at the tears from her cheeks with her right hand and nodded. He bent closer to her and gave her a hug and said, "Jenna, I am so grateful you survived. I can't bear the thought of losing you so soon. Not now. What I hadn't been able to tell you before the attack was that I see my future with you. The problem I was having was trying to figure out how to break the news to my ex that now it really is over for good."

"What about your kids?" Jenna asked tentatively.

"One will soon be focused on starting college, and the other will be a sophomore in high school next year. They are both doing great and have adjusted to the divorce. They will be chasing their own dreams. And I will always be there for them. I'm planning quite a future with you, so you better be around for it," Derek said, looking at the tears now washing down Jenna's happy face.

She hugged him back with her good arm and nodded. "Me too, Derek. Me too," she managed between sniffles.

Not caring who may have been looking, he gave her a soft kiss on her lips and said, "I have to get to the CO's morning meeting. I'll check on you later, but you can expect to be flown out today or tomorrow."

She nodded, and as he was about to stand up she pulled him back for another kiss and embrace. Then whispering into his ear, she said, "I love you, Derek. I think I always have."

He pulled back and looked into her intent eyes and said, "I love you too, Jenna, and I have no intention of letting you get away. Not this time."

Ten minutes later, the SMO was up in the CO's in-port cabin for the morning meeting. Though there had been many updates on the radio and small side meetings with various department heads since the attack, this was the first time they were all together again. It was likely to be a long meeting.

The SMO and other department heads were in their seats discussing events, and he was fielding questions about specific Sailors they were worried about when the CO came in from his side office.

"Everyone, take your seats. Okay, I have a few updates for you before we get started. First, I was just on a call with the Seventh Fleet Commander. Given that I am the senior ranking line officer, I am now the acting Battle Group Commander, until a replacement for Admiral LaSalle arrives. The *Reagan* Battle Group will be on station in thirty-six hours, and we will fall under their overall command when they arrive. Until then we will be flying patrols over Scarborough Shoal and have an alert thirty force on deck. We will have Air Force AWACS and our E-2C early warning aircraft overhead 24-7. I have a good idea of the condition of the ship. But now is the time for you to fill in any details we may have brushed over yesterday. RO, you're up first with your equipment casualty report."

"Yes sir," began Captain Hoffman the Reactor Officer. "For those that don't already know, one of the missiles hit the upper level of our number two main machinery room. There was significant damage primarily to the steam piping. Not knowing the extent of the damage the lead officer in the control room initiated a SCRAM of the number two reactor and it is still off line. We have lost propulsion from props two and three. There is moderate damage to the number three main engine and its reduction gear. We also had damage to the number two ship service turbine generator, but we have brought our backup generators on line, so our electrical output is not significantly affected. Also, our number three and four distilling units are offline for the time being. Our number one reactor plant is fully operational and able to provide enough steam for our catapults. But that means limited steam for the galley, laundry, or water heaters for the foreseeable future."

"Copy, RO," said the Captain. "OK, as of now with limited fresh water, no showers until further notice. They would be cold anyway. XO come up with a shower rotation so they can get clean every few days if we have the water to spare."

"RO, any chance we can make repairs and get the number two reactor back on line?" asked the CO.

"The Chief Engineer and his crew has already gotten a soft patch in place where the missile entered," the RO answered. "Our teams are working together to begin cutting out and repairing the damaged steam pipe sections. Luckily, the electrical damage was not that bad and can be repaired in the next twelve hours. The piping may take a bit longer. So barring any unforeseen events we may be able to bring the number two reactor back on line in thirty six hours. It and its coolant pump remained intact in their own compartment. We should be able to get the number two prop back operational and the generator and distilling units back on line. The number three main engine and reduction gear will have to wait for shipyard repair."

"So some good news then," the CO answered. "CSO, what happened yesterday. Why didn't our defenses stop those missiles," he asked of his Combat Systems Officer.

"Sir, as best we can tell, those missiles have been upgraded and were near hypersonic," the CSO answered. "As it was, from visual reports it appears that our CIWS did get a piece of each of them. Both were headed for the ship's waterline for maximum damage. Both appear to have been hit and deflected up. The one hitting the number two MMR hit up at the top of the 3rd deck level. The other one hit at the O-3 level. Eight feet higher and it would have missed all together."

"Damn bad luck," the CO said grimly as he motioned for the next HOD to provide his update as they went around the room.

Each department head reported the effects, if any, of the damage to the ship on their operations. Everyone was pleased to hear from the Air Boss that other than losing a refueling station that they can resume normal flight operations. Then it came the SMO's turn to report.

"Captain, as of this morning, we have processed a total of eighty-six casualties," the SMO began. "Of those twenty-six are deceased, including Admiral LaSalle, and three of his staff as most of you have already heard. The other deceased appear to be eight fuels personnel from the O-3 level, nine from the number two MMR and four of my corpsmen and a phone talker from the Aft Battle Dressing Station. That station was just above the blast area, and it took out that small compartment and my Sailors. Our next priority is getting seventeen severely wounded evacuated off the ship. We are already in contact with the medical center at Kadena, and they are ready to receive all we need to send. The Air Force has been notified and will be flying most back stateside after follow-on treatment at Kadena. And lastly, I have canceled scheduled routine medical appointments for the next two days. We will continue to see sick call."

After all the department heads had finished with their updates, the SMO headed back down to his office. He had a ton of medevac paperwork waiting to review and sign and then emails from the Seventh Fleet Surgeon to answer.

As he entered the medical department, he spotted Staff Sergeant Anglin sitting in a chair next to his friend who was on a lower bunk. He decided to go say hi.

"Good morning, Sergeant Anglin," the SMO said. "How are you and your friend doing today?"

"I'm fine, sir," Anglin answered. "I slept dead to the world. I got moved down to the enlisted bunkroom last night. I have to tell you that your snoring Sailors are far worse than any in the Air Force."

"I bet," the SMO answered. "Airman Stringer, how are you feeling today?"

"Much better, Commander," answered Stringer. "I'm just really sore from having my gut torn open. But the surgeon says I'll live."

"Well, Stringer, you will probably be flying off to Kadena Air Base later today with some other patients," the SMO explained. "You will probably be going on the third C-2 flight later today."

"Yes, sir, that's what I heard," Stringer answered.

"What about you, Anglin? Any news on when you head back?" the SMO asked.

"Actually, sir, this afternoon. Commander Alverez told me that my unit was asking when they can get me and the others back," Anglin began. "She has been in daily contact with them providing updates since we arrived. She made some calls, and it looks like two of us are to fly back on a helo later today. She said that they will be patrolling not far from there and can easily drop us off. We are supposed to be at some place called the ATO shack at 1300."

"Well, make sure you get someone to show you how to get to the transport shack. I see why they want to get you back. You must be a superb carpenter because you have been one hell of a medic," the SMO said. "I hate to see you go."

"Thank you, sir, but I didn't really do all that much," Anglin replied.

"Sure you did. I saw how you pitched in back on Scarborough and then again here on the ship. You have a real aptitude for it," the SMO insisted. "You didn't flinch once. You just jumped right in to help."

"I just did what little I could," Anglin answered.

"Well, it was far more than the average guy," the SMO said, reaching out to shake his hand.

Anglin stood to return the handshake.

"I want to thank you personally for what you did yesterday," the SMO said with his voice breaking. "You saved someone that means a lot to me. I really owe you one."

"Well, thank you for letting me help. You didn't have to. And besides, you helped save my best friend's life," Anglin answered. "So that makes us even, the way I see it."

"Well, if you ever get tired of swinging hammers, you might want to consider med school. You'd be great," the SMO added. "And I will write you one hell of a recommendation letter if you do. Well, I have paperwork calling my name. Good luck and have a safe flight back."

After the SMO had left, Anglin sat back down and turned to his friend. "Harold, couldn't you just see me as a doc in scrubs?" he said jokingly.

"Yes, I can, my friend," Stringer said seriously. "You and Kara are splitting up, and you need a big goal to focus on right now. And think about it: you becoming a doc can be your private revenge on her after the guy she is playing with dumps her."

"I'm too old to start all that," he mused aloud. "I would have to go to college and would be at least thirty starting medical school, even if I was able to get in."

"Well, my friend, in ten years, you could be a Master Sergeant shop supervisor, or you could be a doctor," Stringer said. "Those ten years will roll by fast. The choice is up to you."

"Hm, I am up for reenlistment next summer, and I do have college paid for with the GI Bill," he said as he began to consider his future options.

Entering the medical office spaces, the SMO went straight to Alverez's office.

"Marty, tomorrow, before we slip back into some form of routine, I want everyone to write a detailed account of what they did yesterday. I need everyone's perspective for the after-action report. This event will surely be studied for years and picked apart for what we did and didn't do right."

"You got it, SMO," Alverez answered. "SMO, how is Captain Tullos doing? If you don't mind my asking."

"She may need a graft, but as long as they can operate soon enough, she should have a full recovery. She has no evidence of nerve damage. She could be back on the job in a month or so. Maybe less."

"That's good news," she said. "For both of you." The SMO noted the twinkle in Alverez's eye.

The next hours were a flurry of activity in the medical offices. Evacuation paperwork was generated on each patient, reviewed, corrections made and reprinted. All had funded orders with no pushback. By 1000 the SMO was up on the flight deck supervising the loading of the five most critical patients. Three with severe burns and two with trauma needing further surgery. With them he sent LCDR Stooksbury, his critical care nurse, two senior corpsmen and the nurse anesthetist, LCDR Duckworth. Having intubated hundreds during surgery Duckworth was the best to deal with any airway issues in flight. After handing off the patients they would return with the COD back to the ship. The SMO made sure they were properly positioned and secured in the plane to handle the stresses of the catapult shot, the most critical part of the whole flight. Twenty five minutes later as he stood just outside flight deck control he watched the COD launch from cat one. Then he headed back down for more paperwork to review on the next patients to fly out. He was just opening up the hatch into the island when the radio glued to his left hand crackled to life.

"Ninety-nine, meeting in the CO's in-port cabin in fifteen minutes," came the voice of the big XO announcing the meeting to all department heads on the command radio channel.

The SMO was the first to arrive. And he was surprised to see the CO's steward placing platters of freshly baked chocolate chip cookies on the main table. This had been done once before two months ago. The wonderful smell brought back memories of pleasanter times. He palmed two and headed to his seat under one of the two port holes. They were still warm and soft. Just like he loved. He ate them slowly savoring every bite as the others started filing in. They were all as pleased as he was at the pleasant savory surprise.

Once everyone was in place, the CO began.

"Ladies and gentlemen," Captain Whitehall began, "I trust you all enjoyed the cookies. We have some interesting news on the overall situation. Secretary of State Lee Huff was at the UN yesterday, loudly making the case against the unprovoked attack on us. First, he met with the UN Security Council and demanded a resolution condemning the attack. Of course, China vetoed the measure but all other members except Russia approved the measure. But Russia did abstain from voting. Then, addressing an emergency session of the general assembly, he insisted that the malicious act of war required universal condemnation and be backed up with economic sanctions. The shock of the attack and its implications for an unrestricted war in the region shocked them into action. All but nineteen countries supported the measure he put forth. Their access to oil is now limited to only Iran and Russia. But they provide only two-thirds of what they need. And imports from China are being canceled across the globe or are having tariffs imposed on them. They are being hit where it hurts. Along with these, they have placed demands upon the Chinese government to be agreed to and acted upon before the sanctions will be lifted. These include paying for the repairs to our ship and compensation to the families of those killed and injured. They are to acknowledge Philippine sovereignty over Scarborough Shoal. They must remove all military troops and equipment from the artificial reefs that they built up over the last decade. Only nonmilitary use will be allowed, but they do get to keep them. Also they are to allow access to the fishing grounds in that area to all countries bordering the South China Sea. They must allow Hong Kong to resume self-determination as agreed to previously. No more disqualifying the candidates they don't have in their pocket. They must also address the documented human rights violations against the Uighurs and Tibetans. And finally, they must acknowledge Taiwan's independence. If they meet those demands which must be verified by a UN commission, the sanctions will be lifted incrementally starting six months after all conditions have been met. So no matter what, they will take an economic hit."

Everyone sat there, quietly taking it all in. Then he continued. "In the past, they had more allies, and they would generally take on one country at a time. They have been expert at dividing and conquering in the past. But this act is one that even their most ardent supporters can't ignore. They generally want to be on friendly trading terms with both the US and China. A conflict between us would be detrimental to everyone."

"Will they agree to any of this?" the XO asked what was on everyone's mind. "They are proud and used to dictating the terms, especially here in their back yard."

"They already have, XO," the CO said matter-of-factly.

"Really?" the XO said skeptically. "The news reports have them still denying that they did anything, and they are accusing us of having an accident that we are conveniently blaming on them."

"Yes, yes. That is all for their domestic consumption," the CO explained. "They know that we have them dead to rights, and we can prove our case.

They are trying to save face at home. Privately, they have approached the White House and have agreed to the terms. These sanctions could put them into a recession for years and could lead to protests in the streets like in 1989. They don't want to risk it. So they have quietly agreed. In a month or so they will be announcing a new cost-saving initiative or some other grand program that will be giving us what we demand but not appear so to the Chinese general public."

"So," the CO continued, "we will be staying on station here doing normal flight ops until both the *Reagan* and the *Nimitz* are on station. Then we are to head back to San Diego for repairs. Once things have calmed down here the *Nimitz* and our escort ships will resume our deployment schedule to the Middle East. There will also be a Tiger Team flying aboard in the next couple of days to assess the damage and plan for the needed repairs. Are there any further questions?" He heard none. "I wanted you all to hear the latest news. That is all. You are dismissed."

As they were heading out, the Gun Boss asked, "SMO, how long do you think they will honor this agreement?"

"Who knows, probably just long enough for the sanctions to be fully turned off, and their economic engine is back roaring again," the SMO guessed. "But since President DeSiard is soon entering the last year of his second term, achieving this beyond his time in office assumes our next president will have the gonads to keep the pressure on. As I see it, the leading candidates from both parties have a history of cuddling up to the Chinese. So who knows?"

Two hours later, he was back up on the flight deck watching the second C-2 be loaded with patients. This group of six included Jenna. He made sure they were all strapped down and took a moment to double-check Jenna.

"How are you feeling?" the SMO asked her.

"Okay. My headache is better, and the arm is now just a dull throb," she answered. "You have got to love Demerol."

"Yeah, but don't get too used to that stuff," he added.

"Well, Derek, here we are on a C-2 together again," she said thinking back. "Reminds me of our first meeting."

"A little different, but yeah. I still remember that day," he said. "You will be back with us in no time."

Jenna smiled and nodded.

"I hope so. But who knows?" she said. "The new Admiral may want a new Chief of Staff."

"Jenna, it doesn't matter. Wherever you end up, I will be turning up like a bad penny. The way I see it, we still have unfinished business to attend to," he said, flashing her a smile.

"Well, I have to admit that you did leave something running," she said with a flash of her white teeth.

"I'll make sure we have some uninterrupted time alone. You can bet on that," he replied. "I'll even bring takeout. How about Chinese?"

Jenna wacked his shoulder with her good right arm at the suggestion, then said, "Hell no, Italian. In a nice quiet restaurant. You still owe me a proper dinner.

"So," Derck began. "No being chased, no knife fights, no gunfights, no dogfights, or burning ships? Sounds positively boring."

"Oh it won't be," Jenna said with a huge impish grin. "It most *definitely* won't be, my dear Kermit!"

Epilogue

Six Months Later

Shache, Western China

Lieutenant Junior Grade Yao was starting an early preflight of his medium sized forty-plus-year-old Y-7 turboprop cargo plane. It was a Chinese knockoff of a Russian AN-24. He hated this aircraft and did not trust it. He had developed the habit of arriving early to do an extra thorough inspection of his assigned aircraft. Today he was there ahead of his mechanics. At least, he was still flying. After "The Incident", things had not gone at all as he had hoped. He did not expect that what he had set in motion could be undone, but it was. China was primed to step up front and center on the world's stage. He had opened the door, but they refused to walk through. Well, maybe in the next decade or so after the current leadership has been replaced. He hoped to be returning to a prominent position when that time came.

He had been grounded immediately and debriefed harshly for two months at an unpleasant secure location. He later met a board of inquiry where, surprisingly, they allowed him to keep his wings, though he was demoted two ranks from an O-4 to an O-2. He was eventually assigned to fly these ancient Navy cargo planes. He was assigned to a remote base in western China and had spent many hours flying over the Gobi Desert with his idiot of a copilot who had failed to qualify as a single-seat fighter pilot. In the "Beast" as he thought of it, they transported cargo and personnel.

Today, he was to be transporting what he had been told were Uighur dissidents and Tibetan separatists. These were the most stubborn that had so far been resistant to all efforts at reeducation. He was told they were being taken for a "Special" program located in Kashi.

As he rounded the tail, he saw two mechanics carrying toolboxes walking up to his plane, one male and the other female. They both saluted, and one said, "Lieutenant, we will be getting you launched today."

"Fine," he said, about to move on, ignoring them. He took only a half-step and did a double-take as he recognized the female.

"Weren't you a crew chief on my J-15?" Yao asked in open astonishment at her face and figure as he recalled with a smile the dirty prank he had played on her. "What are you doing here? Did you screw up too?"

"Sir, I was transferred here last week. I am surprised as you at being sent here for what they called a special assignment," she answered honestly.

"Yeah, special. You've been dumped here in the desert with me to enjoy the roaches, bad food, and no entertainment. It's special all right," Yao sneered.

"We have just a few things to check to make sure it is properly configured for passengers," said the other mechanic.

"Go ahead, but stay out of my way until I am ready for you," Yao said going back to his preflight.

They popped open the entrance hatch and disappeared inside.

Forty-five minutes later the passengers were properly seated and guarded in the cabin. All were quiet and subdued.

The engines were started, and his hungover deadbeat copilot was reading off the takeoff checklist as he called for the chocks to be pulled. He revved up the engines and was directed forward by the female crew chief and then signaled when it was time to turn onto the taxiway. As usual, the crew chief gave him a crisp salute as he began his turn. He had long ago got in the habit of ignoring these salutes and now never returned them. But because it was the pretty female, he did sneak one last glance at her as he made the turn. His jaw dropped open as he saw her crisp salute drop, and she grinned while blatantly flipping him the bird.

If he were not on such a tight schedule, he would have returned and dealt with her insubordination then and there. Well, he would deal with her when he returned this evening, he decided. He would ruin her. He would make her life even more miserable than being assigned to this hellhole.

An hour later, they were at cruising altitude out over a barren wasteland. As usual he was cursing because the "Beast" was a bitch to trim, and the autopilot was not working as usual. It would rarely fly straight and level, requiring constant exhausting control inputs to hold heading and altitude. He and his copilot had to take turns manually flying. Yao had just taken control of the aircraft again when from the rear of the airplane they heard a sharp *'Bang'* followed almost immediately by a second. He and his copilot looked at each other, then at the emergency light panel. No warning lights were flashing. Nothing. They both looked to the rear to see what may have happened. All they saw were the bewildered faces of the passengers and their guards.

"Go check it out," Yao said to the copilot.

As he turned back to his flying he saw the slight shift off heading that he was constantly having to correct. He nudged the yoke, but it was completely slack. Nothing. It was as if it was not connected at all to the control cables. He quickly turned it left and right then pushed and pulled it. Nothing, it was completely loose. In desperation he pushed on the rudder pedals with the same result. A cold sweat broke out on his face, as the copilot rushed back into the cockpit.

"All the control cables snapped and are hanging down," shouted the panicking copilot as he climbed into his seat. "What do we do? How can we control the plane?"

"How indeed," answered Yao as a cold realization dawned on him.

The copilot started calling on his radio for help until he realized that it too was now inoperative.

They both watched helplessly as the plane gradually drifted into a slow banking turn that soon became a tight nose down spiral.

As the screams of his copilot and passengers reverberated throughout the aircraft, Yao just focused in terror at the rapidly approaching ground through his windscreen. His last conscious thought was of the female crew chief flipping him off with a huge smile. What he did not know was that she too had an uncle.

Col Boyd before F-18F Super Hornet Flight on the USS *Carl Vinson*

ABOUT THE AUTHOR

James "Shotgun" Boyd, MD, is a retired Air Force Colonel. He began his forty-one years of military service as an enlisted aircraft crew chief on T-39A Sabreliners. After his first assignment he switched to the reserves and became a RED HORSE carpenter allowing him to start college. After graduation, he joined the Navy and completed Aviation Officer Candidate School and entered the officer ranks. He flew in the Navy as a carrier based S-3B Viking Naval Flight Officer/Instructor for six years. Pursuing his interest in medicine, he switched back to the Air Force and graduated from the Uniformed Services University of the Health Sciences. He became a Flight Surgeon and specialized in Aerospace Medicine allowing him to keep his medical career oriented around his love to fly, logging time in forty two different aircraft types in the Navy, Air Force, Army, Marines, and Coast Guard. From 2011 to 2013, Colonel Boyd made Air Force and Navy history by serving as the only Air Force physician to lead a Navy carrier's medical department on the USS *Carl Vinson* (*CVN 70*) as the Senior Medical Officer. Following retirement, he and his family settled in Titusville, Florida, where he continues his medical career as a civilian. He keeps his head in the clouds by maintaining and flying his Experimental *Cozy III* as often as he can.

Made in the USA
Middletown, DE
01 October 2022